Babylon Laid Waste

A Journey in the Twilight of the Idols

Novels by

Brigitte Goldstein

Princess of the Blood

A Tapestry of Love and War in 16th-Century France

Court of Miracles

A Human Comedy of 17th-Century France

Dina's Lost Tribe

A Medieval Romance

Death of a Diva

From Berlin to Broadway

Babylon Laid Waste

A Journey in the Twilight of the Idols

An Artemisia Safran Novel

Brigitte Goldstein

Pierredor Books

New Brunswick, New Jersey

ISBN: 978-1-64438-769-6

Published by BookLocker.com, Inc., St. Petersburg, Florida.

Printed on acid-free paper.

BookLocker.com, Inc.
2019

First Edition

Library of Congress Cataloging in Publication Data
Goldstein, Brigitte
Babylon Laid Waste: My Journey in the Twilight of the Idols by Brigitte Goldstein
FICTION: Historical | World War II | Action & Adventure
Library of Congress Control Number: 2019906804

Table of Contents

"The World is my perception."

Schopenhauer

"I shall send foreigners to Babylon to winnow her and to devastate her land."

Jeremiah 51:2

Prologue

Captivity

November 1946

Steinheim, Germany

US Army prison for female Nazi war criminals

Before I saw him, I heard his laughter. Before I gazed into his sparkling dark eyes, his laughter pierced the depth of my soul. Before his cackling made me sit up on my haunches, my knees went to pulp. He was still laughing when he knocked over the bucket next to me with a cavalier kick, engulfing me in a puddle of grimy suds.

The toil of scrubbing latrine floors, the taunts from the hyenas whose quarters I was condemned to share, the loss of hope for rescue or escape had numbed my senses and turned my heart into an insentient lump of stone. One more humiliation from a stranger who seemed to find sport in teasing me mattered none. What could it do to me? I would pull the carapace of indifference I had fashioned for myself since being tossed into this hell, a bit tighter around me. Nothing, but nothing, would or could touch me, so I was telling myself a hundred times a day. I was immune to all gibes and sneers. Yet, my eyes must have betrayed me. Maybe I was not able to hide the flickering despair that was consuming my soul as well as I thought. At least not from this man who had appeared out of nowhere and was now standing over me arms akimbo and laughing.

"Maybe a toothbrush would help you do a better job, *gnädige Frau.*" He spoke the words "gracious lady"—an old-fashioned way of greeting a woman in polite society—in Austrian-inflected German with a gallant bow. Missing was the furtive kiss blown on the lady's gloved hand.

What an absurd thing to say! I lifted my puzzled gaze at him from my crouched position, and for a brief second our eyes came to rest in each other's. His laughter extinguished like a shooting star. An awkward silence replaced the scornful mockery. The surrounding noises receded from the space between us. Only he and I existed. I, in suppliant, almost prostrate pose, at his feet. His head tilted, one eyebrow raised, his hands to his sides, his squinting dark eyes peering down on me from an august height. His lips parted slightly as if he were about to say something. Then, he shrugged and abruptly pivoted away with long, unhurried, ponderous strides, leaving me on my knees engulfed in a welter of grimy suds.

From then on, whenever I marched out with the cleaning detail from the adjacent prison for female Nazi criminals, his unmistakable laughter resounded in the alleys between the rows of barracks. I began to listen for it. On occasion when it wasn't there, whenever it failed to reach my ears, dread began to claw at my heart and stomach that he may have been a phantom, a figment of my feverish imagination.

The sound of his laughter had become a comfort to my wounded soul. Even at night, it reverberated in my fitful sleep. It warmed me when I lay awake on the hard bunk, shivering in the cold. I knew it was absurd to pin my hopes on a fleeting moment of recognition. But absurdity defined this entire universe ruled over by an insatiable beast that ate away at my sanity.

My hopes—hopes for what? —seemed somehow justified by the fact that he was always somewhere within view of the corners of eyes when I entered the other camp. His probing gaze seemed to follow me where I happened to be. From the corner of my eyes, I perceived his scrutinizing look even when he was standing around the yard with his comrades engaged in animated talk. I recognized my father's Eastern European cadences. He would turn his head periodically, peering in my direction as if to assure himself, and me perhaps, that we were still connected. He even approached me several times but was barred by the rifle of an MP guard. Interacting with the prisoners was strictly prohibited. Maybe they feared reprisals from the DP people against the German detainees. I would gladly lend a hand in any such action had it not been for Berlin, the goal of my journey, my looming, now seemingly unattainable, castle on the hill.

Then one day, happenstance had it that I was alone in the latrine, scrubbing the floor as usual. Couched down on my knees, I perceived a figure cast its shadow over me.

"Don't you think a toothbrush could do a better job?" For some unfathomable reason, he repeated the same absurd question. This time I noted his tone was very serious. He wasn't laughing. No mocking.

"What do you want from me?" I asked in despair.

"I want to know who you are and why you are here?" His hands reached out to help me off the floor. Shunning his gesture, I raised myself in front of him, looking up at his serious mien. He was half a head taller than I, slender rather than thin, even athletic. Most arresting were those dark eyes that seemed to have the power of delving into a person's soul.

"I am a prisoner of the United States military occupation forces," I stated the obvious.

"I can see that. But why?" he pressed on. "What have you done to deserve this? You are not one of them." He jerked his head disdainfully in the direction of the Nazi women's prison camp.

Then he added, very softly, almost in a whisper, "You are *unsere Leut*." One of us.

"What do you mean?"

I knew very well what he meant. I remembered the old saying I had heard so often growing up that a Jew could always recognize another Jew. Only Major Zweig seemed to have had no inkling. Or did he? Maybe I didn't fool him either. But why did he condemn me to this hellish place? Was he using me for a different purpose? I remembered him saying to his sergeant—did he know I understood what he was saying? – that my papers were forged and that I may have something to do with the people smuggling ring operating out of Amsterdam. Was he putting me on hold, in a holding cell, so to speak, until he could get to what was behind my presence? Was he hoping I would lead him to bigger fish? That would be a mean trick to play on a fellow Jew.

It also was a mean trick for me to play, impersonating a German. But I had a good reason. Looked at from this angle, so did Zweig. Maybe his mission of ferreting out war criminals from among the general German population was more important than my desire to rescue an old woman, who may or may not be my grandmother, who most likely had been through an ordeal so horrifying it made her lose her memory and her mind. Neither she nor I mattered in the broader scheme of things. Broader schemes or a higher order aside, to find my grandmother was the purpose of this journey. I had overcome many obstacles along the way until I ran afoul of Major Zweig.

Since the Major had disappeared or was unreachable, I was left to an uncertain fate. Maybe this man who seemed to take such obvious interest in me could help me out of this mess. I wondered what it was about me that would make him think I was not one of the female Nazis? I had never considered myself to "look" particularly Jewish with my dishwater blondish hair and blue eyes. Never even gave it much thought. But I guess it was plain to the penetrating eyes of this man with the mocking laughter who I was and where I came from. Or was it something else, something beyond outward appearances? Something more intrinsic, the baggage of history we all carry around with us, the ankle chain that ties us all together?

"Kafka," he said, extending a hand with a bright smile. Bewildered by this sudden introduction, I left his hand hanging in mid-air. "František Kafka from Prague. But you can call me Franz." He dropped his hand but kept on smiling as if to say: "Get it?"

"Safran, Artemisia Safran from New York" was at the tip of my tongue, but when I opened my mouth what came out was "Beate Hauser from Berlin." Both of his eyebrows now lifted upward, furrowing his brow with a skeptical grin.

"You are right about one thing," I managed to say, trying to keep my trembling knees from buckling, "I'm not one of them. I was never a camp guard. I never saw the inside of a camp nor what went on there. Then they all say that, don't they?"

What set my mind in uproar was the coincidence of his name, if this was indeed his name. Somehow, I suspected that his Kafka was as fake as my Hauser. Whatever reaction he was trying to get from me, I thought it better not to take the bait and play dumb. A German woman with minimal education would not get this allusion to a Jewish writer. I kept what I hoped was a blank face.

How long we stood there facing each other, I don't remember. We had reached an impasse. A wall had risen between us, which I, for my part, knew not how to breach. As much as my heart nudged me on, I was not willing to do something on impulse. My greatest fear was that my knees would buckle, and I would collapse again at his feet.

I was saved from further embarrassment by an approaching MP guard.

"Sir," he said, politely by firmly. "No communicating with the prisoners."

Without an apology to the guard or a nod toward me, the man who called himself Kafka shrugged and walked away with long, ponderous strides, his laughter echoing in the hollow canyon separating the two camps.

My eyes were still pinned on the receding figure when a nudge in my back brought me down to the ground of reality. The soldier steered me back to the vipers' nest at rifle point. Like a common criminal, I thought. When we reached the dividing barbed-wire fence, he stopped for a moment. He flicked his burning cigarette to the ground and stamped on it with a grinding motion of his foot. Any glimmer of hope of ever finding a way out was crushed out.

How on earth did I ever end up in such a living hell?

Part One

Fortress Babylon

"It was the month of November somber,
The days grew bleak and bleaker,
The wind tore the leaves off all trees,
That's when I journeyed to Germany yonder."
(Heinrich Heine, from "*Deutschland, Ein Wintermärchen*")
[translation by the author]

Chapter 1

A Letter from Berlin

The letter caused quite a stir. My mother dismissed it outright. My father, as was his way, scratched his head and shrugged. I was not so sure what to make of it but was willing to consider its authenticity. It bore my New York address. The postmark was dated Berlin, August 19, 1946. The precise meaning of its contents was not entirely clear, yet it raised hope against all hope my grandmother might still be alive and under care at a Jewish hospice in Berlin.

Since war's end in May the year before, the émigrés community—among them me and my parents—had gradually been forced to come to terms with the daily bulletins of the horrors which exceeded our worst fears and intimations. We had been spared, but could we count ourselves lucky? Numbed by the enormity of the Nazi crimes being revealed daily in news reports from Europe about the murder of millions, most of us despaired of ever finding any of loved ones who had stayed behind alive.

Many of the émigrés saw no point in a search beyond supplying names to the agencies entrusted with the task of finding survivors. Their efforts were directed toward growing permanent roots in the New World. My parents, the musical team of Paul and Tillie Safran, set up a cabaret-style haunt in Greenwich Village, complete with dimmed lighting and sawdust-strewn floors. Like the establishment they once owned on Friedrichstrasse in Berlin, *Der Taubenschlag,* this replica, now called *The Dovecote,* featured my mother in nightly performances of the songs my father composed for her.

After various fruitless attempts to break into show business in Hollywood, they found a small measure of recognition within the circle of émigré friends and a few American devotees of her smoky genre.

Upon graduating from college, I had found my vocation as a writer. The publication of my account of the investigation into the murder of a beloved actress and the trial that followed had gained me a short-lived notoriety. We seemed to have finally settled into our lives in America. No longer refugees, but grateful citizens of the country that had granted us entry when it had still been possible.

Yet, under the daily flow of what took on the appearance of a normal life ran a current of despondency, rarely acknowledged, but always present. And just then, a glimmer of hope broke through the cloud that oppressed our lives. The letter was addressed directly to me, written on lined, grayish school notebook paper and dispatched from a Jewish hospice in Berlin.

A Jewish hospice in Berlin? Doubtful, declared my mother. Hard to believe. Must be a hoax. What kind of a hoax? For what purpose?

The signature on the letter was from a Roman Davidovich. Odd name, no title nor position. It stated that among their patients, survivors from various camps, was a woman, estimated to be in her eighties— not many of such advanced age. She was in failing physical health and suffered from dementia. She is unable to speak, the letter stated, and seems to have no memory of her name, where she was from, nothing about the time she spent in Theresienstadt.

Among her sparse personal effects was a tattered envelope. When the nurse picked it up, the woman became very agitated, seized the piece of papers and clutched it to her heart. It took much coaxing from the nurse to gain a look. What it revealed was an empty envelope addressed to Gertrud Wertheim in Schöneberg Berlin. The letter came from New York with the return address of one Artemisia Safran to whom he was now turning. Due to the patient's advanced age and deteriorating mental and physical health, it was essential to establish her identity so that appropriate steps could be taken in case of her demise.

A money-making scheme, she concluded. Who knows if there even is a Jewish hospital or hospice after all the destruction?

Why shouldn't there be survivors in need? I countered.

No doubt the Allies will make sure that such people received the necessary medical care, my mother added. She refused to give the matter any further thought, preferring to put her head in the sand.

The notion of Allied help was given the shaft by Mr. Davidovich's reply to my letter to him in which I had expressed my regret about our limited ability to be of assistance due to the geopolitical realities brought on by the war.

The Russian military command in charge the part of Berlin where the hospital was located, Mr. Davidovich explained, had no interest in allocating resources for helping victims of Nazi persecution. The Russians were eager to push as many displaced persons as possible into the American occupation zone. Unfortunately, most of the severely ill, among them several older people, were not likely to survive such a difficult, arduous transfer.

"You see," said my mother.

"See what?"

"He's looking for money."

"Of course, he is looking for money! Have you no concern for your mother?" My voice reached a hysterical pitch.

"Even if she isn't my Omi, this woman, whoever she is, went through an unimaginable ordeal, enough to have her memory wiped out. Besides, how would she have gotten this envelope? Whoever she is, she must have had at least some contact with my grandmother."

"Maybe if we go there, we can find out something about what happened," I suggested.

"Now, who is being melodramatic? The man says she's demented. She doesn't remember anything. I don't see what good it would do for us, or her, to go there."

Demented or not, if there was the slightest chance that this woman was indeed my grandmother, I would not leave her to die alone in Berlin. She was the woman who had plucked me off the sawdust dance floor at my parent's cabaret when I was a mere toddler and raised me at the Wertheim villa in affluent Charlottenburg. My fondest, and even some not so fond, childhood memories were associated with my Omi and Opa. My Omi tucked me in at night, she sang me lullabies and read me stories while my mother warbled away a smoke-filled cabaret. My grandmother taught me proper manners and passed on to me a sense of what was just and right. She taught me what it meant to be Jewish.

"Then, I shall go alone! My mind was made up. I was going to Berlin!"

"Paul!" my mother shrieked, "put some sense into this girl's head!"

"She's not a girl," he replied. Turning to me, he inquired calmly how I planned to get around the travel restrictions.

"I have an American passport," I replied proudly.

"That's exactly the problem. The hospital is in the Russian zone. No love between Russians and Americans, he explained. The war-time alliance was quickly unraveling at the seams. As an American, you would not be safe in the unlikely event you were to get to the East."

We had become American citizens right after war's end. We were no longer stateless wanderers. I had rejoiced in what was, for me, an overwrought way of patriotic fervor. Holding that piece of paper in my hands filled me with pride and confidence the whole wide world was now open to me.

As I was to learn, much of the world perhaps, but not Germany. The defeated German Reich under the rule of the Allied command was sealed off from the outside world. No civilian travel permitted in or out.

I am not one to give up so easily. There had to be a way. Inquiries with anyone who had any connection to Europe, mostly returning GIs, led to the discovery of the existence of a people smuggling ring operating out of Amsterdam. My American passport would get me as far as the Dutch city. From there, I would have to enter Germany illegally with false papers and an assumed identity. In other words, I would have to become German.

"Do you really want to do that?" My mother was on the verge of what was her way of facing a crisis: a nervous breakdown.

Yes, I did, I concluded after some consideration. I was fluent in German, which we spoke at home. Many cultural aspects and customs were also familiar to me. I was sure I could easily pass myself off as German.

If the illegal way was the only way to get to Berlin, then that's how it had to be. The only real obstacle: I would need a thousand dollars in cash to pay the smugglers and their accomplices.

"That settles it," my mother said relieved when she heard of what was for us an extraordinary sum of money. Where would I find that kind of money? My father shrugged. He had no idea.

But where there's a will, there's a way. I knew someone who knew someone. My friend Viktor Erdos, the wistful violinist, was only too happy to approach his lover, the Hollywood studio mogul Alexander Levary. Both felt in my debt, as they had assured me many times, for my role in the Stella Berger murder trial, which got Viktor released from death row in Sing-Sing prison. The money was duly delivered to me in a leather briefcase in clean, crisp one-hundred-dollar bills with a little extra for my expenses.

Viktor saw me off at the Holland-America Line dock on 42nd Street.

"I'd love to go with you," he said, holding my hand in his for a long while.

I assured him I would be all right, bravely swallowing the doubts and apprehensions that began to gnaw at my stomach.

Good luck then and come back safely. He breathed a kiss on each of my cheeks and turned away abruptly without waiting to watch me mount the gangplank with unsteady gait to the ocean liner that was to take me to Rotterdam from where I would have to get a train to Amsterdam.

Chapter 2

Shabbat in Amsterdam

The ocean crossing marked the beginning of my gastrointestinal problems. Tossed about by stormy North Atlantic winds, I stayed curled up on the cot in the tight little cabin. The mere thought of food made me queasy. My mind wandered back to the only other time I had crossed this ocean. It was ten years before when I was fifteen years old. We sailed in the opposite direction then, from Europe to America, away from the looming Nazi threat. I remember standing on deck, bubbling over with a teenager's excitement, my eyes fixed on the horizon, steadily on the look-out for the New York skyline pictures in books and magazines over which I had poured in anticipation of our arrival. That was ten years ago! The tragic events which have occurred in the interim still weighed on all of us like an indigestible lump of incomprehension.

I disembarked in Rotterdam and went on to Amsterdam by train. My American passport gained me entry after a few questions from a customs officer as to the purpose of my trip. I was visiting relatives, I told him, I hadn't seen since before the war. I even had an address to show him, which the man in New York gave me.

Unlike Rotterdam, which still bore the scars of heavy wartime bombardments, Amsterdam had remained unscathed and showed few traces of war. The walk along picturesque streets lining the canals was rather pleasant. A sense of excitement rushed through me. I was in Europe, in one of the quaintest, most famed cities. For a moment, I forgot why I was there. Then I reminded myself that I was not a tourist. It was getting late. I had to find the place I had been directed to go to before nightfall. I did not dare ask anybody for directions for fear the people whose help I depended on would come to the attention of the police. After some time of meandering aimlessly, an eerie sense of dread made my bowels churn.

At my wit's end, I finally got up my nerve and approached a passer-by in the hope he would understand English. He gave me what I thought was a suspicious look, but then very politely and patiently explained how to get to the place I was looking for. The trail he described to me led into a maze of narrow, dimly lit streets becoming ever more forbidding in the gathering dark. I stopped at a corner to read a battered street sign. I strained to make out the faded letters forming the word "Jodenbreestraat." Strange, I thought. Though my Dutch was minimal to non-existent, I realized I had arrived in what was formerly the ancient Jewish quarter. At last, I found the street and the building. A sign on the shuttered storefront read "Bric-à-Brac." No name of the proprietor.

My heart beating, I rang the bell at a side door. No answer. I rang gain several times. No was light shining from the inside through the small milk-glass window in the door. Maybe I had the wrong address. Worse yet, maybe I had been sent to the wrong address. What did I know about my New York contact who had retained a hefty commission for himself? A sinking feeling overcame me that I may have fallen for a scam.

Not knowing where to turn, I lowered my weary body onto the sill of the shuttered store window. An irresistible yearning for sleep engulfed my body. I had enough money for a hotel where I could find something to eat and a bed. I had passed several such places along the way and would have to retrace my steps. I could come back to this place in the morning when I would be rested and refreshed. But my bodily needs were overridden by my mind's will not to give up. This had to be the place.

Hugging my knees against my face to fend off the damp chill of the wind blowing from the waterways weaving through this city, I persisted in a crouched position. I must have nodded off for I was startled by a gentle pull on my sleeve and a thin voice asking in Yiddish: "Do you wish for a Shabbos meal?"

Before me in the dusk stood a little man with a grizzled beard and a black hat who was fumbling to open the door. He was apparently returning home from synagogue services. I had paid no attention to what day of the week it was. Besides, I had no idea that the man I was to contact in Amsterdam was a Jew. I did not know his name or anything else about him.

"I've come from America," I replied. "I was told to come to this address. Maybe it was a mistake."

"No, no. I mean yes, yes, of course. We were expecting you," he said in broken English. Then he added in Eastern European-inflected German: "If you don't mind. German is better."

"But, please come in. You shouldn't be out here. You might catch cold."

"I had no choice," I said defensively. Was his concern for my health or that someone might see me? "Nobody answered when I rang the bell."

"My wife doesn't answer the door on the Shabbos," he explained. The door finally opened. He stepped aside and bade me enter with a quick wave of the hand. I had the distinct impression he was anxious to get me out of the street and out of sight. I followed him down a long, dimly lit corridor to the back of the house. As we advanced, my nose caught a whiff of baked bread, simmered meat, and roast chicken. The aroma evoked childhood memories of Friday evening dinners at my grandparents' villa in Charlottenburg.

The woman who was setting the table was not much older than I, in my estimate at most thirty. She was much taller than the man, and I presumed at first, she was his daughter. My assumption was corrected when he introduced her as his wife. She apologized for not answering the door. They had been expecting me a few days' hence. But, she assured me, she was happy I was here and could spend the Sabbath with them. I was more than welcome. Her German was clearer than her husband's though it too had a foreign ring.

After I had washed up and deposited my suitcase in the small chamber used mainly for storage where I would spend the night, I took a seat at the table. A pair of candles cast a subdued glow over the traditional fare festively laid out. The man chanted the blessings over the wine and bread. Images of my grandfather presiding over Friday evening dinners and pronouncing the same words rose from the well of my childhood memories. This meal was not as lavish as the ones we had at the villa in Charlottenburg; the mood while festive, not as exuberant as our family gatherings. Times were different; life had changed. If not for me, these two people would have been alone. There seemed to be no other family. Provisions were sparse and rationed. It was a wonder that these quiet, unassuming people could provide as much as they did.

Gratitude toward this odd couple warmed my heart. How could I repay them for their kindness? Who were these people? Where did they come from? Where did they spend the war years? Perhaps the camps we'd heard much about. I wanted to ask them about their lives. But I held back, afraid to touch on what might be still sore wounds. Then I remembered the contents of my suitcase. When would be a good time to get around to the business I had come for? Surely not before sundown of the next day. That much I knew.

I whiled away most of the next day, curled up asleep on the narrow, slumping couch in the windowless backroom. My slumber was haunted by dreams of horrors I had not experienced myself. I only knew about them from hearsay. They were real nonetheless in my writer's imagination. Had I been there, what would have been my fate? There was no doubt what it would have been. I thought of my grandmother, who had stayed behind in Berlin. I thought of the suffering she must have endured, and my mind was set on one goal only: I had to get to Berlin. Even if her mind is mired in darkness, if there is the faintest breath in her, I would be with her. She had raised me since the day she had appeared at my parents' night club brandishing her umbrella. She had scooped me off that legendary saw-dust strewn floor and carried me off to the Wertheim villa in the upper-class district of Charlottenburg. I have no direct memory of this incident, but I heard the story repeated many times while growing up. What I do remember and will never forget is the care and love my grandparents showered on me. What I do remember are the lessons my grandmother instilled in me about the manners of a proper lady and what it meant to be a Jew.

As soon as he had said the Havdalah prayers marking the end of Shabbat, the little man wasted no time getting down to business. I handed him the stack of hundred-dollar bills which he counted studiously, periodically moistening his fingers on a wet sponge, and set them up in neat piles as if he were readying for a poker game. His wife meanwhile pulled me aside to give my appearance a work-over.

"Those cheeks are too rosy, too American." She shook her head and made a clicking sound with her tongue. "We can't do much about that, but you do need different clothes. Too American."

Everything about me seemed to be too American.

"What does a nice Jewish American girl want in this cursed country?" she asked while she brushed my hair straight back and gathered it into a tight bun at the nape of my neck.

I told her about my grandmother and the urgency for me to get to Berlin on time.

"My greatest fear is that she might die," I said.

At first, she scrunched up her face puzzled. I thought I could see the wheels turning in her head as if she were trying to grasp what she had heard. Then her perplexed expression gave way to a bright smile of sudden recognition.

"Most people who come through here don't have such noble motives," she confessed. "No young women. Shady characters, smugglers, black marketeers, types of that sort, commonly."

"Are you sure you want to do this?" The man paused in his counting. "You can still back out, you know. It's a dangerous undertaking. If they catch you, who knows what they'll do to you."

Who would catch me? I thought. The Nazis are gone. It was hard for me to read his motive. Was his concern for me, my well-being and safety, or did he see me as a liability for his business? The clandestine chain of illegal activity, which no doubt took painstaking scheming to set up after the war, could easily be compromised if one link were to break. The continued success of the operation depended on the discretion and ruthlessness of its clientele. Not the least, a certain cunning for evading and duping the authorities. Did he fear I didn't have the mettle to hold up under interrogation should I fall into the hands of the military police? Even I wasn't sure of myself on that account. Would I become a snitch? I preferred not to think about it. All I knew was, I had made up my mind and would do anything to achieve my goal to get to Berlin

The money was stacked neatly on the table before him. What was it to him what became of me?

"You're short." His tone was suddenly gruff.

"I don't understand," I replied all flustered. I wasn't as tall as his wife, but not as short as he.

He pointed to the money. One pile was lower than the others.

"Oh, that's what you mean," I shrugged. "Your agent in New York took a cut."

"A hefty cut," he grunted. "How much did you have?"

"A thousand."

"He was supposed to get ten percent. What we have here is 750."

"Sorry, I don't know anything about this - I wasn't told about the financial arrangement."

I guess it's true; there's no honor among thieves, I thought. But looking at him and his wife, I was convinced they weren't a pair of hardened crooks; just people trying to make a living in hard times, I concluded.

"This is barely enough to cover our costs," he said. He stuck his hands in his pockets and with a sour mien added: "You'd better take your money and go home. I'll keep a hundred for expenses incurred. This is no business for amateurs. Go back to New York, to your life, and be glad you got out of Europe on time."

I was close to tears, and then unexpected happened. Ignoring her husband's moaning, the wife continued to work on my transformation. She rolled her eyes and took me into the back room where she helped me exchange my American wardrobe with some dowdy European rags. At last, she produced a battered little cardboard suitcase with a few extra pieces of clothing and underwear. She made me slip into a threadbare coat and helped me strap a canvas rucksack with provisions on my back.

"Everybody in Europe and Germany walks around with a rucksack."

"Am I talking to a wall?" Speaking in Yiddish, the little man abandoned his soft tone and raised his voice several decibels.

"She has a grandmother in Berlin who is waiting for her!" the wife too raised her voice several decibels

"She may have a grandmother in Berlin," he corrected. "Or she may not have a grandmother in Berlin.

"You should be ashamed of yourself," she said, pointing at the money. "You shouldn't charge her anything. A Jewish girl who is risking everything to find her grandmother, who may have survived. You should know better. And besides, you make enough helping all kinds of riffraff across the border.

Why shouldn't we help a girl with a pure motive and a pure heart?"

"She's young. This is a tough business. She could break."

"She's tougher than you think."

"She was already been swindled out of several hundred by the ganov in New York."

"No, you are the one who has been swindled out of the money, and that's what bothers you."

"There's also the arrangement, remember!" she added with a piercing look. Whatever that meant, I didn't linger over.

In the end, the wife won out. He returned to his oak desk and reached into the top drawer from which he extracted an elongated ledger with a thick, frayed cardboard binding. He flipped through its pages, attentively skimming the columns which looked to me from where I was standing like lists of names and addresses and numbers, possibly birth dates, drawn in meticulous penmanship. His finger finally landed on one such entry. He nodded. From the desk drawers, he pulled out some form. He dipped a writing pen into a glass inkwell and entered with meticulous strokes the information he gleaned from the ledger.

He then dried the ink carefully pressing down a rocking blotter with both hands. He finished by applying a seal with a wax stamp. From the meticulousness with which he applied himself to the task, I gathered he might have been a bookkeeper or a calligrapher in his former life. Or more likely a Torah scribe.

He rose and, paper in his hand, faced me with a serious look.

"From now on your name is Beate Hauser," he intoned solemnly boring his bloodshot eyes into mine as if he wanted to hypnotize me. "You will forget Artemisia Safran. You will forget everything about her and her life. You must memorize everything about Beate Hauser. You must become Beate Hauser. Your life depends on it.

"You are a Catholic woman. You were born in the town of Glogau in Silesia, on May 16, 1922. That's a few years younger than your actual age, but you can pass. Your family moved to Berlin when you were a child. . ."

And on and on he went. Did he make this up? Was there such a woman whose life statistics were now being drilled into me? Was I to assume the identity of a dead woman? How and where did she die? Where did he get this information?

"The less you know about that part, the better," he fended off my questions.

I felt like a snake sloughing off her old skin and slowly growing a new one. Only in the case of the snake, the new skin comes out of her own body and is still an integral part of her. I, on the other hand, was expected to slough off my very self and slip on the skin of a stranger, presumably deceased, without being allowed any knowledge of the circumstances of her demise, or her life, for that matter. Did she die in an air-raid? Was she a rabid Nazi or just a camp follower? Was she in the resistance? Was she shot under fire or executed? It doesn't matter, he told me. Did she even exist? She is alive through you.

It was long past midnight when I sank into the troughs of the broken-down couch mumbling: "I am Beate Hauser! My name is Beate Hauser."

At the break of dawn on Sunday morning, two men came to the door. Their faces were invisible under the rims of their black hats pulled over their eyes. They were part of an escort chain that would accompany me to the border.

A teary farewell. The wife pressed me to her flat bosom and whispered something in my ear in Hebrew, which I presumed was a blessing for the wayfarer. The little man with the kippah and the grizzled beard waved goodbye. I was sure I saw a tear well up in his eyes as well. Would I ever see them again? Would I ever learn the story of this odd couple? My writer's curiosity was aroused, but it was time to move on.

"I put a few slices of buttered bread and a canteen with water in the rucksack. It will tide you over till Frankfurt," she said.

I thanked her again but didn't think I would be able to get a single bite down my parched throat.

Chapter 3

Veils of Deceptions

Outfitted in wartime European basic drab, simple grayish wool suit, a threadbare overcoat of like color, a black peasant scarf wound around my head, I went on my way. The ankle-high lace leather shoes were a size too small and pinched my toes. The wool socks scratched my skin. It's all part of the transformation, I told myself. With a deep breath, I strapped on the rucksack and seized the suitcase with a firm grip.

The men steered me toward a black limousine waiting for us a short walk away. The dented, rusted vehicle of indeterminate vintage took off with a howl for the first leg of my journey. I was passed along a chain of several handlers until we reached an isolated, apparently unguarded, field across the river from the German border.

My first stop was the town of Wesel on the opposite side of the Rhine. I walked alone across one of the few bridges still intact. With every step I came closer to Germany, my heart felt as if it was going to burst. At several points, I ducked a British army patrol. I felt for the papers inside my coat pocket. Would they, and I, for that matter, hold up under the scrutiny of a patrol? Fortunately, it didn't come to that then. By some miracle, I reached the German side and got to the train station without incident.

The arrival time of the train to Duisburg was uncertain, the ticket master told me.

"Even Mussolini could make the trains run on time," he made a vague attempt at humor. "Here in Germany, nowadays, schedules, like everything else, are kaput or approximate at best."

I thanked him with a smile and walked out to the platform, not wanting to get into a discussion, either political or personal.

I stationed myself on a bench in the corner; my gaze turned away from other waiting passengers. No eye-contact. Nevertheless, I felt the probing eyes follow me. A man on crutches sidled up to me.

"Would you perhaps have a cigarette?"

I shook my head and averted my eyes.

"You from around here?" he insisted.

"Just passing through."

"Lots of vagrants, riffraff roaming the country these days."

When I did not answer, he said suddenly: "You're not one of those smugglers from across the border, are you? Wouldn't be surprised if those Jews used women now."

My heart dropped. "What's there to smuggle?" I managed to say, trying to sound cynical.

Luckily the train sputtered into the station just then. I took the opportunity to quickly duck away. The next stop was Duisburg, a much larger city where getting lost in the crowd on the platform was easier. From there I changed trains to the long-distance train to Frankfurt. With some luck and a good push of the elbow, I garnered a seat by the window in one of the overcrowded compartments. I kept my gaze turned toward the window and the scenery outside. For the first time since I had crossed the border into enemy territory, I was finally able to gather my thoughts. What was I doing here? What was I doing riding on the Reichsbahn, the rail network on which Jews had been transported to their death? Who among the passengers on this train may have been complicit in the crime? How separate the bystanders from the perpetrators? I realized this journey might be testing my mental fortitude to the breaking point. The questions tormenting my mind wouldn't go away.

The man in Amsterdam had good reason to dissuade me. The strain of being on German soil could be too much, he said. Back then, I tried to make light of it. Why shouldn't I be able to transform myself into a German woman? I was fluent in the language, was by and large acquainted with the customs of this land. The culture was still familiar from my early upbringing. What I failed to consider was something else, something much more incisive than the passage of time. Overwhelmed by the desire to reach my goal, I did not consider the impact recent history would have on me. The events of the past years, events that had profoundly affected my people, destroyed Jewish life in Europe. Though keenly aware always, I thought I could keep my emotions under wraps to succeed in reaching the goal of this journey.

You must become Beate Hauser, or you will fail, I still heard him say. Whoever this Beate Hauser was, she was supposedly born in Silesia in 1922 and grew up in Berlin. She was just old enough to have been a member of the Bund of German Girls and then, during the war, the Work Service somewhere on a farm. The details I would have to make up as I went along.

The train moved parallel to the edge of the Rhine River. Outside the grimy window, in the waning hours of the day, a leaden sky, clouds balled like fists, cast a pallid gleam over the fleeting landscapes and cityscapes mirrored in the murky waters of the river. The gloomy scenery was glazed with the soot spewing from the locomotive. I avoided looking at the faces of the people around me. I tried to block out their incessant chatter, the tales of woe and personal misfortune, in a language I once loved but which had become odious to me, all in knowing that I had to revive it once again. I had to speak my native tongue fluently again without a trace of foreignness, forget, even deny, any knowledge of my new language, English, if I was to succeed in my mission.

Mission? What mission? More like a wild goose chase! Taking account of my situation, I didn't know whether to congratulate myself for having made it into Fortress Germany or cry for having made a foolish mistake. Perhaps it was all a dream, a nightmare from which I would soon wake up in bed in my Village apartment. But I was fully conscious of my surroundings. They bore little resemblance to New York. For a moment, I entertained the thought of still getting off the train at the next stop and making my way back to the Dutch border. Somehow. Impossible. There was no way back now. The die was cast. My heart felt like a lump of ice. Desperately, my thoughts clung to the woman in Berlin. Whoever she was.

Chapter 4

Pension Maibach

The first leg of my journey got me as far as Frankfurt am Main. From there, I would take the train to Berlin, which had to cross from the American into the Russian zone. Since two of the victors of the war were increasingly at loggerheads, the connection was rather tenuous. No fixed schedule. It could be days, I am told, between departures. The Russians often held up transports coming from the West at the border, leaving passengers stranded without provisions. Sanitary facilities at those checkpoints were said to be less than adequate.

Once a train was ready to steam off, and passengers were packed in, the Americans for their part often held up its departure with fishing expeditions for Nazis and Soviet spies. Searches of luggage and persons often caused more delays.

I learned all this during my stay at a safe house in Frankfurt. My instructions were to go to Pension Maibach on Freiherr vom Stein Strasse in the West End of the city. I could pass the time there undetected while waiting for the train to Berlin.

As I stepped out into the plaza fronting the train station on a dusky late afternoon, a brisk November air blew down from Kaiser Strasse, cutting an unhindered path through hollowed out windows of ghostly buildings. A faint memory of a previous visit to this city rose in my mind. I was a child of about eleven or twelve, old enough to remember stepping out from the train station. The same street then projected the opulence of an earlier period. I was in the company of my grandparents, Max and Clara Wertheim, on a visit to the family of my grandfather's brother, the banker Siegfried Wertheim. He had two sons and a daughter and grandchildren of about my age. I vividly recalled a game of hide-and-go-seek with these cousins in the beautifully kept garden behind their villa. Their residence was in the West End, the prosperous Jewish section of town, the very part toward which I was now directing my steps. I never saw my cousins again. Soon after that, my parents took me away from my grandparents on a meandering trek across the Continent, which eventually took us to America. Nothing of that family's fate was known to me. Did they get out in time? Whereto? America, South America, Palestine? Maybe the younger ones did? But what about the older people, people like my grandmother? Were they persuaded to leave the place where they had spent a lifetime following generations before them?

I remembered my grandfather telling me about Frankfurt's illustrious Jewish past. More than Berlin, the city had been a flourishing center of Jewish learning and commerce. It was the birthplace of many famous Jews, most prominent the Rothschild family who made commercial history in the nineteenth century.

As I made my way through the field of rubble to which this city lay waste, I felt the weight of history, of Jewish history on my shoulders and mind. How could I transform myself into this German woman named Beate Hauser when all those memories persisted on rising to the surface of my mind, refusing to be kept submerged on the bottom of the pool of my memory like a sunken ship?

An older man in a tattered railway worker's uniform showed himself polite and friendly, only too willing to help a lost young woman find her way. The way he waved his hands about to describe how to find the street I was looking for aroused a sense of unease and made me want to get away. I thanked him and started to go. His erstwhile kindly demeanor suddenly changed to a peering squint. He looked me over with unabashed curiosity.

"What do you want there?" he asked suspicion lurking in his eyes.

"My aunt's place," I said, deeming it prudent not to mention Pension Maibach.

"Well, good luck to you," he said with a sneer. "I hope you find your aunt. Not much left when the Amis were done bombing us. They didn't even care about those Jews. They aren't the only ones who suffered."

Why was he telling me this? I didn't ask what he meant. My stomach began to twist into knots. I tried to get away as quickly as possible before he could launch into a self-pitying tirade. Here I was on German soil for five minutes, and I already heard echoes of the old canard: The Jews are our misfortune.

"I'd better get going before dark," I mumbled and turned away.

"Yes, you'd better," he said. "Lots of unsavory types about these days. Not like the old days when criminals were kept under lock and latch."

Is that so? I was in no mood to hear his definition of "unsavory types."

The best way, and maybe the only way, to get to my destination was on foot. More than a year since the end of the war and public transportation was still sporadic or non-existent.

The cold November wind chilled my bones and burned my face. My hands, gloveless and stiff, clutched the little cardboard suitcase like claws of clay. A bleak landscape of rubble and ashes took me in. I wandered past rows and rows of buildings whose innards were gouged out. I stubbed my toes on broken glass and debris strewn over sidewalks and along curbs; the irony of it all did not elude me. I was too numb in heart and spirit to even muster any sense of serves-you-right.

As I navigated through a maze of rubble-strewn streets, I finally arrived somehow at my destination. Turning into Freiherr vom Steinstraße, it became immediately apparent to me what had irked that man at the station and aroused his suspicion. The unexpected sight left me stunned. At the center of the street was a huge structure that was unmistakably a synagogue. The looming cupola cast a defiant shadow over the neighborhood. While the building bore marks of severe damage from arson and vandalism, the walls stood erect. Even the glass windows were intact; although any shattered ones may have been replaced already.

My calloused feet burned from the arduous walk. Weary and exhausted I walked up to the doorsteps of the house directly opposite. The number at the entrance was the one I was looking for but bore no plaque for a Pension Maibach. I was still catching my breath when the door opened. A middle-aged woman addressed me by my assumed name: Fräulein Hauser. She was expecting me, she said.

The woman climbed the stairs ahead of me one flight up. Entering the apartment was like stepping back in time to the bygone world of the turn of the century. The cozy, old-fashioned surroundings radiated a welcoming warmth and almost instantaneously dissolved the stiffness in my bones and the clot lodged in my heart. After days of what seemed like a passage through a daunting underworld, it seemed that I had arrived at the gates to paradise.

Frau Maibach relieved me of my coat and shoes. "Make yourself at home." She took me by the elbow and steered me into the drawing room toward a plush, winged armchair next to a glowing fireplace.

"I'll make us some tea. You just sit and relax," she said.

No idle small talk. No questions, no explanations. It was all so matter-of-factly. She disappeared into the kitchen. The clanking of pots was music to my ears, much like at my grandmother's house. I felt at home. All tension eased out of me. My eyes drooped, and my limbs began to sag. My mind surrendered to the lure of abandon as it trailed off into a dreamless slumber.

A gray shaft of light peering through a slit in the drawn curtains heralded the dawn. I remained stretched out motionless. My body was still unwilling to be roused. Where was I? What had happened? How long had I been asleep? Through veiled eyes, I squinted at the form of a woman tiptoeing about the room. She was setting the table. The aroma of coffee perked up my senses. Images of the past few days flashed before me. The train ride through a bleak, sunless land dotted with the ruins of gray cities that gave the appearance of being on an alien planet; chattering crowds of people jostling against me, fear of being detected, the encounter with the old man at the train station, the long walk through non-existent, dusky streets, all came into focus.

"Did you sleep well?" the woman asked. I remembered her kindness, the warmth with which she received me the night before. Why?

"I should have put you to bed. I saw you needed your sleep, so I didn't dare disturb you." Who was this fairy godmother? An angel sent from heaven?

She showed me to a room at the end of the corridor. It was small but neat and spotless—not a speck of dust on the dresser. Only the mirror showed some yellowing spots. The bed linen and cover breathed a fresh scent of lavender. I did my morning toilet and rejoined my hostess for breakfast. She had laid out an almost festive table; white embroidered tablecloth, fine china. I buttered a slice of fresh rye bread and topped it with a thin layer of prune jam. A soft-boiled egg and coffee with cream and sugar completed the fare. I wondered where in this war-torn country she garnered such delicacies.

"Most of it comes from the farm in exchange for whatever goods one has to offer," she said as if she were reading my mind. "There's nothing in the stores, and money is worthless. As for the coffee, connections!" Black market, I presumed.

She cleared the table. I was not allowed to lend a hand. When she was done, she informed me that she needed to go out for a while.

"You will be safe here," she added. "No one will bother you."

Apparently, I was the only guest at Pension Maibach.

To distract myself, I looked over the bookcases lining the walls in the parlor. They fully stocked with German and European classics. Complete sets of Goethe and Schiller, Kleist and, to my surprise, of Heinrich Heine whose works had been foremost among the books burned by the Nazis. I recognized the 1920 edition, the same one my grandparents had in their library. How many hours of my childhood had I spent engrossed in the *Book of Songs*, memorizing many of the poems and reciting them by heart! The works of Nazi banned authors, like Thomas and Heinrich Mann, Stefan Zweig, Franz Werfel, and many others, were prominently displayed next to the classics of Russian and French literature.

One volume attracted my attention. The work and author were unknown to me. I pulled it out, opened it. The title, *The Trial*, intrigued me. I started reading still standing. Right at the start, this writer struck me as more avant-garde than the others. As I read on, I sense of excitement came over me as one feels about the discovery of something new, something so utterly unlike anything familiar, like coming upon a heretofore unknown continent.

Without taking my eyes off the page, there were no paragraphs; I sank into the winged armchair in which I had spent the previous night. The fire in the hearth had died down; the smell of smoldering embers stifled the air. I was completely numb to my surroundings. Nothing existed beyond the words on the page, the sentences that pulled me irresistibly into a world so unlike any familiar reality. The scenes spinning the story evoked a sense of having been there, of having met such people, of having been in Josef K.'s place.

"Who is Franz Kafka?" I asked over an evening meal of scrambled eggs and fried potatoes Frau Maibach had prepared when she returned with a shopping net full of victuals. God only knew where she had scrounged them up.

"One of our greatest writers," she said. I wondered what she meant by "our."

"He was a Jew from Prague." She gave me a probing look. Did she think I was that German woman named Beate Hauser? Didn't the people in Amsterdam tell her anything about me? I had thought she would know who I was and why I was on this journey.

"Died young of tuberculosis in the early 20s," she added as if to let me know that he had not been a victim of the Nazis.

I told her that I had not heard of him but was intrigued. My request to be permitted to read more was gladly granted.

"By all means," she said. "More people will read his works now that the Nazis are gone." She certainly seemed well read. And judging from the books in her library, her literary taste tended toward the classics of European literature.

When we had finished eating, had washed the dishes, dried, and put them away—this time, she didn't refuse my help—I went back to reading. Frau Maibach opened the lid on the harpsichord in the corner. She sat down on the bench covered in deep red, plush velvet. She paused a moment, her hands folded in her lap as if to gather her thoughts before lifting them slowly onto the keyboard. Then with abrupt determination, she lunged into a piece from Bach's Well-Tempered Clavier. The world seemed to have been set right. I read. She played. This is how we spent most evenings.

During the day, she went out "shopping" which was probably more like bartering. I suspected there was some other matter she tended to as well judging from her long absences. When she returned at the end of the day, her brow was furrowed with stress or worry. We had a simple, quiet meal then and after clean-up, I read, while she played Bach. I was glad to see the furrows smooth out as her fingers glided caressingly over the keys.

One evening I stood by the window looking out on the looming synagogue building across the street – a group of men in black hats and long, dark overcoats filed into the side door of the building.

"It's Friday, the beginning of Shabbos," my hostess explained following my gaze. Her use of the Yiddish term for Shabbat struck me as odd coming from a German. The common usage would be Sabbath.

Who is this kind woman? I thought. Only a week before I was warmly welcomed to the Shabbat table in the house of the little man in Amsterdam and his young wife who then gave me a new identity and the address of Pension Maibach for me to rest after the first leg of my journey to Berlin. I still didn't know what a woman like Frau Maibach would have to do with a ring of people smugglers. My curiosity got the better of me. I looked around the room: no candles or other signs of Shabbat observance.

"Did you always live here?" I asked.

"More than thirty years."

"A long time," I nodded, waiting for her to go on.

"It is a very long time, and much happened in that time," she said with a sigh after a long pause.

"I've seen it all. We watched the drama unfold from this very window. We stood helplessly by when the thugs set fire to the building in November '38. Luckily the local fire squad arrived in time to put the fire out before the building was destroyed like others. It was almost like a miracle. Much of the damage you see came from Allied bombing.

"Oh, I am not belittling the Nazi terror by any means. Believe me." She placed her hand on my arm. "What I mean to say is . . . it's just how it was."

I made no reply. I was not inclined, or even in a position, to argue with this generous woman on whose kindness and good will I depended.

"You Americans have no idea what it was like," she said after another long pause. She shrugged her shoulders without elaborating further. I remained silent, but in my head, a bell went off. She did know who I was! How much more did she know? What about my mission?

We turned away from the window. She pushed me rather forcefully into the armchair that had become mine. She placed herself in a chair opposite. A stern look appeared on her face. Like the principal calling a third grader on the carpet. Would I be raked over the coals?

"My father was a goy," she began. No beating around the bush here. It didn't take much for me to put two and two together. If her father was a goy, her mother must have been (or is?) Jewish; ergo, she was, in the Nazi lexicon, a "Halbjüdin" a member of the tribe. The weight of unease lifted from my heart like a lark ascending into a blue sky.

Frau Maibach kept her gaze fixed on a small reproduction of Rembrandt's painting of the prophet Jeremiah on the wall behind me. Her tone was soft and measured, undramatic, almost a whisper devoid of emotional flurries. More like a witness testifying at a trial in a courtroom than a casual conversation with an eager listener.

She spoke at length about her father. He was a socialist and a pacifist. He was active in the peace movement and a leading labor union organizer. Karl Marx's writings were his bible. In the pristine form, he would emphasize; not the Bolshevik distortion. From his pacifist perspective, class struggle was a battle on the ground of ideas, not the kind of street fighting between gangs that became endemic in the Republic. Violence was abhorrent to him. He found it more and more difficult to find his niche on the political spectrum. The Nazis arrested him and incarcerated him at Dachau in April 1933. When he returned to his family, he was a man broken in body and spirit. He never spoke about what they had done to him in there. Despairing over the course the country was taking, he withdrew into himself. In the end, he just gave up.

She held back the tears that clouded her bright blue eyes. I didn't dare ask what it was he did.

"His ashes were strewn to the wind. He had left a note with the express wish. No permanent burial place. In some despondent way, he seemed to have thought of it as an act of rebellion. My mother still bemoans the loss and the lack of a grave site we could visit."

I waited for her to gather her thoughts.

"I know you must be wondering. Yes, my mother survived the Nazis. It was my status as Halbjüdin, by the Nuremberg laws, that spared her from being deported. Right here in this apartment, we sat out the years; terror striking our hearts with every knock on the door. Never knowing what would happen at any moment. And then came the end of the war. She survived but is alive in body only. Her mind. . . she lives in another world."

Not knowing how to respond, I said, "You needn't say more." My hand touched hers. She pulled back. Did I overstep? It was clear she didn't want my pity.

"She lives in a home. The doctor thought it best for her rather than staying within these walls; with all those memories. The room in which she lives out her days is like a cell, bare, dim. The only ornament is a youthful picture of her husband, my father.

'There he is, the one who left me,' she often says pointing at the photograph. It's all she ever says. I am not sure she knows who I am. She is still waiting for him to return, from somewhere."

She got up and went into the kitchen. I heard her putting up the tea kettle. She remained in the kitchen until the whistle indicated the water was boiling. A few minutes later, she carried in a tray with the teapot and a plate of her special biscuits I'd come to relish.

"Enough of all this," she said as she set the tray down in front of me with enough force to make the cups jingle. How could it be? It was her life. I kept my thoughts and curiosity in check for fear of pouring acid on her wounds.

Sunday morning. I had been at Pension Maibach for more than a week. Still no news about the train. I sat propped up in bed, reading Kafka's novel *The Castle*. The story of K.'s quest for admission to the castle up on the hill, in clear sight and yet unattainably far, was not unlike my quest for admission to Berlin. Would I ever get there? Would I find my grandmother alive? Was the woman in that home even my Omi? A gentle knock at the door to my room alerted me to Frau Maibach's unobtrusive presence.

"Fräulein Beate," she called out in hushed tone as if afraid she might wake me. Why did she call me by that name she knew wasn't mine? She had never asked me what my real name was, nor why I was here, in Germany, far from home. Was it a lingering mindset from the time of the Nazis when it was better not to know too much? Now she was a link in an illegal people-smuggling operation. One never knew what the consequences might be for her were she found out.

"Fräulein Beate," she repeated when I opened the door. "Please forgive the intrusion. My friends from our Esperanto group are coming over for coffee and cake this afternoon. Though I would love to introduce you to them, under the circumstances, it might be better if you stayed in your room. I hope you understand."

Of course, I understood. I was happy not to be expected to meet a group of strangers and be asked questions.

Esperanto! I vaguely remembered it had something with what my mother was either involved or interested in back in the day. A kind of made-up, international language.

"Any news about the train?" I prodded her. As comfortable and hospitable Pension Maibach was, I was eager to move on, to get to Berlin and, hopefully, to accomplish my mission and return to America where my life was now.

"I will let you know the minute I find out," she assured me.

In the afternoon, I watched from behind a crack in the door a line of mostly elderly ladies in fur coats and hats with heavy netting veiling their faces file into the apartment. Several had a fox fur, the snout biting the tail, wrapped around the neck. I noticed one young man among them but was unable to make out his features. He helped the ladies out of their coats and hung them on the rack in the foyer.

They put coats and hats on the hooks in the foyer and proceeded into the parlor closing the door behind them. The flowery design of the beveled glass door distorted the figures moving about inside. Muted chatter. Sporadic laughter.

Clattering of teacups. A convivial company - a kaffeeklatsch. I closed the door and returned to my reading.

After a few minutes, I put down the book. The image of an old woman in a Berlin hospital without memory haunted my thoughts. The woman, who once presided over similar occasions, whose elegant table, set with the finest Rosenthal china on which were served the finest cakes and tastiest petit fours with coffee and tea, was one of the most sought-after in Charlottenburg. My heart ached. Where was that train?

It was now Monday, the tenth day since I had left Amsterdam and the ninth day of my stay at Pension Maibach. My benefactress had gone out on her errands as usual. I waited anxiously for her return. I paced back and forth between my room and the parlor. I looked out the window as the hours went by. A leaden sky reflective of my dreary mood hung over the blackened dome of the synagogue. Finally, in the late afternoon, I saw her turning the corner, her gait was slowed by the weight of the victuals she carried. I tried to read her demeanor. Did she have any news? At breakfast in the morning, she had remarked on my impatience and, at the same time, had expressed her understanding.

"The train for Berlin leaves at midnight." She was short of breath, barely able to speak. I reached out to relieve her of the load she was carrying.

"Are you all right?" I asked. Her face was pale. Her eyes had dimmed. The furrows on her brow had deepened even more. A sense of guilt came over me that through my presence I had added more grief to her already difficult life.

"Nothing unusual.," she replied shaking her head. "My mother went into one of her rages. It took medication that's in short supply these days to calm her."

Her mother had lost her mind; my grandmother had lost her memory – two more victims of evil.

Frau Maibach insisted on walking me to the station. She knew how to avoid being picked up after curfew, she explained, lighting the rubble-strewn way with the dim beam of a flashlight. Another paradox. Why does the train leave at midnight if people are not allowed out in the streets after dark? It made no sense.

"Nothing makes sense in this country," she shrugged and added: "Not that anything ever did. We live in a land of paradoxes and absurdities going back a thousand years."

From my own, more recent, experiences, I could attest to paradoxes and absurdities in the country of my birth. In this case, however, the ordinances were decreed by the US military authority which ruled the defeated nation. I was grateful she took the risk and trouble to get me on the long-awaited train.

She even purchased my ticket with who knows what currency. One-way to Berlin. I would have preferred a round-trip, but that would have aroused suspicion.

Luckily, once again I was able to curl up in a window seat, a light blanket Frau Maibach had handed me as a farewell gift wrapped around my shoulders. To keep me warm on the drafty train, she said. She wished me good luck, embraced me quickly, and turned away. Alone again, utterly alone, I felt like an outcast left exposed in a barren wilderness of uncertainty. For some reason, Hagar, Abraham's concubine who had been left abandoned in the desert came to my mind.

I pulled out my little notebook and started jotting down with trembling, clammy hand some of the impressions I had gathered as I had done since I had entered this strange, forbidding land. Above all, I wanted to hold on to the thoughts and feelings this journey aroused in me. Someday, when I would be back in America, I would write it all down in a kind of travel memoir.

Chapter 5

Major Zweig, US Army

The train's departure was delayed. At first, I was unconcerned. Nothing ran on time in post-war Germany as I had already found out. The time when trains ran on schedule, when there even was a schedule, was long gone. German punctuality was a thing of the past. I huddled at the window as I had done on my previous train ride, withdrawing into my carapace to shield myself against the surrounding and waited. My thoughts were on Berlin, that castle on the hill. My heart beat higher in anticipation of seeing my grandmother again. Would she recognize me? Seeing me, I hoped beyond hope, would trigger her memory, revive her speech. We would embrace. We would talk. She would tell me about what she went through. I would promise her from now on I would protect her against the evil in the world. I would take her to America, far, far away from this cursed place and any reminders of the horrors she had been made to endure.

Steeped in thought, I was unaware of what was going on around me until I felt a hand on my shoulder. Two military policemen recognizable by their white helmets marked MP stood over me.

"Your papers, ma'am!" one of them said in English. For a moment, I felt a sense of relief to hear the familiar language. But I must have had a puzzled look on my face for he continued in broken German: "Sprechen Sie English?" Getting a hold of my bearings, I thought it the better as a German with limited education to fain ignorance.

"*Papiere*!" he bellowed.

I handed him the identity paper of Beate Hauser, explaining in German that I was on my way to Berlin to be reunited with my family. I spoke quickly to test his understanding of German. It obviously wasn't much. He waved his hand and gave the paper a thorough inspection. His gum chewing colleague meanwhile kept a close eye on me.

"Where is the 'shine'?" he said, pointing to the paper I had handed him. I had no idea what he meant by that. A back and forth of misunderstandings in two languages ensued, one he didn't know and one I pretended not to know.

"He means a *Persilschein*," a woman next to me chimed in. "You know, like the laundry detergent, a piece of paper that certifies you are clean. You can't go anywhere without it these days. It tells the Americans you weren't one of them." She chortled derisively and rolled her eyes, obviously expecting me to understand who "them" were.

"The Amis are so naïve," she added, waving her *Schein* in front of the MPs' faces. I could have wiped the gloating smirk off her face.

Here was a glitch even the little man in Amsterdam had not foreseen. No warning from Frau Maibach either. A sense of having been betrayed by the two people on whom I had come to rely made me shiver. It was hard to believe they didn't know anything about this. Frau Maibach at least must be in possession herself of such a certificate. I desperately wanted to give her the benefit of the doubt. Maybe she thought such a Schein was part of my forged ID. At any rate, this obstacle hit me like a brick wall in a dark alley.

The MPs escorted me off the train like a criminal, forcing me to pass through a gauntlet of staring German eyes whose owners I presumed were all in possession of this vaunted piece of paper, the prized *Schein,* absolving them of all guilt in the crimes committed in their name by their country. One of the MPs, instead of getting into the front seat next to the driver, sidled up to me. I was shivering in the back seat of the jeep whose flapping canvas sides provided little shelter from the biting November air. It was night, and the city was shrouded in pitch darkness. The vehicle's headlights cut a ghostly slant of light through the street as it careened toward an unknown destination.

"You'll meet the Major. I'm sure he's looking forward to this," my captor informed me, his mouth close to my ear, in his southern twang. Arkansas or Oklahoma, I surmised. I had never been in the South of the United States, but my ear had become attuned to Southern speech patterns during long hours at the movies. I must have seen "The Grapes of Wrath" half a dozen times and "Gone with the Wind" just as often if not more. But I was careful not to let on about this. My face remained unmoved. He could have been talking to a deaf person.

"The major is a Jew. A very smart guy from New York." He made this pronouncement slowly, drawing out the syllables even more than would be common. His squinting eyes searched my face for a reaction.

"Do you like Jews?" he said. "The Major most certainly doesn't like Nazis. He eats Nazis for breakfast." He made a crunching noise as if chewing on a savory piece of meat. He blinked his eyes and tilted his head and made weird faces to draw me out. After a while, he gave up. "I guess you don't understand a word of what I am saying. You just watch out. The Major speaks very good German. Fluent in fact. You won't be able to put anything past him."

The man-eating Major turned out to be a perfect gentleman of impeccable manners and dress. His uniform fit his stocky, slender figure to a tee. His trousers creased, buttons shined, his brown leather shoes polished to a brilliant shine, he was the picture of a Yecke, a German Jew.

"My apologies for the inconvenience," he stated with perfect German diction. With a gallant hand gesture, he invited me to have a seat in front of his desk. "I am most sorry, very sorry indeed for this interruption of your travel plans

"Forgive me, my dear Miss, I am forgetting my manners." He extended his hand, which I took after some hesitation: "Major Emil Zweig. . . and you are?"

"Beate Hauser. I need to get back on the train to Berlin."

"That, unfortunately, is not possible. This train has left. But there will be others."

"When? The schedule seems rather sporadic."

"Too true," he sighed. "Unfortunately, we are dealing here with the Russians who seem intent on maintaining chaotic conditions."

If he said the word "unfortunately" one more time, I was ready to strangle him. Blaming the Russians!

"Consequences of the war," he mused. "Meanwhile, let's have a little chat. As you must be aware, your papers are, unfortunately incomplete." I started to rise in my chair but then thought the better of it. It would be most unwise to arouse this man's displeasure.

"I must get to Berlin as quickly as possible," I pleaded.

"The wheels of justice turn very slowly these days."

What was that supposed to mean?

"Am I under arrest? For what offense?"

"No, no. At least not yet. It's just curious. The war has been over for a year and a half. We interrogated thousands of civilians and certified thousands, absolved them, so to speak. The military command requires each German citizen to fill out a questionnaire; a tool to ferret out the big Nazis, the top echelon, from the general population, the little Nazis and opponents of the regime. However, this *Bescheinigung,* which you don't seem to have, must be presented with the rest of the papers. My question is, why don't you have one? My colleagues from the military police and I are puzzled that you should not even have heard of it."

"I was in the British zone at the end of the war. I am just traveling through here on my way home to Berlin."

"And where were you during the war?"

"On a farm doing work service."

"This farm wasn't called Bergen-Belsen by any chance?" The pupils of his grayish/green eyes contracted, piercing me like daggers. I held his gaze even though my stomach began to churn. Maybe under that suave façade was a man-eater after all. I hadn't heard of such a place, not then.

"I don't know what you mean. It was a farm in Lower Saxony."

"What did they grow on that farm?"

"The usual things one grows on farms."

"Such as?"

I had never been on a farm in my life and searched my brain for what I had heard or seen in the movies. I was treading on unfamiliar terrain. Drawing on my movie experiences yielded very little. Most films were about New York gangsters or Hollywood dancers. Rebecca of Sunnybrook Farms hardly fit the bill.

"There were wheat fields," I ventured. "But I was mostly with the livestock."

"What kind of livestock?"

"Cows. I was mostly cleaning out the cowsheds."

"For the fatherland. You did your duty for the fatherland."

"Something like that. Everybody had to pitch in."

"For victory and for the Führer. And you are sure you weren't anywhere near Bergen-Belsen?"

"I told you. Never heard of it."

"And why should I believe you?"

By then, I was writhing in my seat. This man was an expert at putting people at ease and then coming down with a hammer gloved in velvet. It was easy to imagine how a simple farmhand would crumble and confess to anything.

"Why such a hurry to get to Berlin? Somebody waiting for you?"

"I hope so. If they are still alive."

"Who is they? Mother, father, siblings, aunts, uncles, cousins, maybe friends and neighbors?" With every point of the litany, my stomach crunched up further; bitter bile rose in my throat.

"My grandmother. I'm worried about my grandmother."

"Were you worried about the grandmothers they sent to the ovens?" His voice changed to a higher register sounding almost shrill.

"I don't know anything about that." I heard myself whimpering pitifully. What was happening to me? I permitted this man to force me into the role of a Beate Hauser. I became Beate Hauser, the simple German girl, who was cleaning out cowsheds on a farm during the war and who knew nothing of about ovens or camps. She was only fulfilling her duty to the fatherland. Close to tears, I considered confessing who I was. To tell him all about the scheme and why I had come to Germany illegally. I longed to tell him: I am one of you, I too am a Jew! In that case, I would also have to reveal the identity of the people who helped me pull off this deception. Even if he believed me, even if he were sympathetic, there was no guarantee he would permit me to go on to Berlin. He would most likely send me back to America, and I would never know about my grandmother's fate.

Just then he called in the soldier who had taunted me during the ride from the train station – Sergeant Harvey Bickers from Arkansas as he revealed.

They conferred in mumbled English, still clear enough for me to catch the gist.

"These papers are counterfeit," I heard the major say. "Question is their provenance."

"Could be from the Nazi underground or could be from that smuggling cell in Amsterdam." The blood froze in my veins.

"Either way, she might lead us to break one or the other."

"Do you think she's a big Nazi or a little Nazi?" the sergeant inquired.

"Could be one or the other, or neither. One can't tell by looking at them. But something is fishy, and I intend to find out. Meanwhile, let's send her to Steinheim until we sort this matter out."

"You mean the DP camp or the other next to it?"

"Of course, the other one. Let her bunk with those lovely ladies for a while."

"Do you think it's the right place for her? She seems like a nice girl," the sergeant demurred.

"Bickers, Bickers! You are getting weak. You're losing your nerve! Before you know it, these Fräuleins will wrap you around their fingers." The Major waved a finger of his own at him jokingly, though not so jokingly. "You may be right, but I have my reasons."

"What is going on?" I said in German.

"You will have to accept the hospitality of the United States Army for a while. Unfortunately, sorry to say, there's an irregularity in your papers that needs clarifying."

Here was that word again and punctuated with a "sorry to say "as insincere as it gets. I realized he was playing a cat-and-mouse game; and the cat had the mouse cornered. How could a Jew behave like this? I caught myself thinking. Then again, I understood perfectly well how he could behave the way he did toward a German citizen. Like me, he was a refugee from the country that had just murdered his people, possibly relatives and friends. Yet, the situation I was in, the situation I had gotten myself into made me the subject of his ire. Beate

Hauser was becoming a monkey on my back I was unable to shake off.

"Am I a prisoner? When do I get to go on to Berlin?" I raised my voice in desperation. "You can't do this to me!" I raged, knowing very well that he could do anything to me he pleased. To the victors belong not only the spoils but also absolute power.

From somewhere a clock tower struck the hour of three. The major rose from behind his desk and declared the interrogation over.

"Enough for now. It's getting late," he said, showing none of the signs of fatigue that overwhelmed my body.

"For tonight you will be a guest here," he said and indicated to his waiting flunkies to take me to a room.

At last, I was alone. Looking around through the veil of bleary eyes, I realized we were in what was once a luxury hotel that had been requisitioned by the US Army. The room was not altogether uncomfortable and still betrayed some of the former opulence in the gilded though chipped wood trim and the faded red velvet wallpaper. The matte-gold bathroom fixtures too attested to more glorious days. The water that trickled out of the faucet, however, was not of a color to inspire confidence in its cleansing propensities. There was a deep tub standing on lion feet. Nothing was further from my mind than to seek relaxation in a hot bath even though my body was grimy with sweat. The bed was bare of any linen but had a lumpy down cover. It suited me fine as I crawled under it immediately sinking into a deep, exhausted slumber. All I wanted was for the world to go away.

Sergeant Bickers met me in the lobby the next morning with a benevolent smile. He proffered me a hot cup of coffee and a doughnut. Both never tasted so good. I took small sips of the steaming dark brew, stuffing the doughnut into my mouth without regard for the good manners of my upbringing. The sergeant stayed close to me and immediately offered me a second, which I consumed with equal relish and indelicacy. After the third morsel had found its way into my stomach, I wiped my mouth on my sleeve with a satiated burp. My grandmother would be appalled at this gross violation of all prim etiquette and decorum. What a strange thing is the human mind! Rather bizarre to have such a thought pop into my head at such a time. After all that had happened, the rules of proper behavior as my grandmother understood them were certainly no longer in force.

Major Zweig did not honor me with a personal send-off. To my dismay, I had to admit. Instead, I was in the custody of Sergeant Bickers and an MP driver who transferred me from Frankfurt to a detention camp I heard them refer to as Steinheim. Maybe the Major was busy grilling real Nazis, I thought. And is gobbling them up for breakfast.

Chapter 6

Descent into Hell

The two-hour jeep ride ended in the town of Steinheim on the Main River in the wine growing region of Franconia. Flowing terraces of vineyards descended from the gentle hills to the river's edge, no doubt sun-drenched in the summertime, were visible from the other side of the river where the drab military complex was located and where the sun never seemed to shine. At least, so it seemed to me in my dim mood. I found myself thrown together with the basest Nazi riffraff, women who bragged unabashedly about the services they rendered to the fatherland as guards in various ghettos and concentration camps. The worst among them, a real beast, was a broad-boned, busty sadistic specimen named Ilse Kunz. No resemblance to the ideal woman promoted by the Nazi cult of beauty this one. Her boasting about the punishments she herself had meted out to Jewish inmates raised my hackles.

"I bet none of you can match me!" she preened, peering at me with sly, probing eyes.

"What about you? Ever been to Ravensbrück or Belsen?" she taunted me. "Those were like fresh air spas. Oh my, that stench, the screams, the mire, the blood! We were there and proud of it. We carried the burden, without complaining, to make the fatherland free of the vermin. The Amis can't take that away from us."

I said nothing, but she wouldn't let go and moved menacingly toward me.

"You must have some influential protectors that they didn't get you until now. That Jew Major won't let anyone off the hook."

The call for lights out saved her, and me, from being pummeled by my clenched fists.

My bunkmate was a timorous speck of a woman, rather young to have been a guard. Who knows what her story is? I thought. Nor did I want to know. I didn't want to listen to laments of how they suffered in the war and during the bombings.

But this wasn't the only reason why her latching on to me was an annoyance. She didn't quite fit in with the other brutes and seemed to be looking for a friend who would feel sorry for her.

"What do you think the Amis will do to us?" she whimpered.

"Probably not much. They are all talk. In the end, they'll let everybody go." I made that up to get her to calm down. "They want us to stew for a while. Like in purgatory." Where that bit of wisdom came from, I had no idea. I was becoming an expert in making things up as I went along. On the seat of my pants, if I had any.

"How long have you been here?" I asked more sympathetically than I intended.

"Just two weeks. I should have stayed on the British side. They are not as fanatic as the Amis." She referred to Americans in the slightly derogatory term "Amis"—which irritated me.

"Well, I wouldn't worry too much." I turned my back toward her to get some sleep.

"Were you in Belsen?" I heard her hushed question. That name kept coming up. The Kunz woman too said something about that place. The Major had asked me if I was in Bergen-Belsen, I presumed was a camp.

"Were you?" I probed likewise in a hush.

"I wasn't a guard. I never was a guard. I never did any of the terrible things they did." She jerked her head in the direction of the hyenas. "But I saw things. Things I can't get out of my mind. I see it all in my sleep."

I didn't encourage her, didn't prod. My heart was pounding. Did I even want to hear any details of her nightmares? Yes, and no. A clamp tightened around my chest, threatening to squeeze the air out of me. I breathed in and out quickly to hold back a wave of fear threatening to engulf me.

"They made us bury them."

"Who made you bury what?"

"The Brits. They came to the farms and the villages and rounded us up, women and girls. They marched us out to the camp. The only men around were old or foreign workers. They took us to a yard where heaps of dead bodies were piled up high. They lined us up in front of them and forced us to look at them for hours, poking us with sticks if we averted our eyes. Then they gave us shovels and told us to dig a ditch. We were digging and digging until our backs broke. A huge pit, at least two meters deep. We lifted them onto wheelbarrows, dumped them into that ditch."

"Who were they?" I asked.

"The corpses? Dead Jews. Hundreds of them."

"Are you sure they were Jews? How could you tell?"

"The Brits told us. Even those prisoners who were still alive looked like corpses. They must have starved them. Many died of typhus. I'll never forget. Still haunts me to this day. After three days, I couldn't take it anymore. My grandmother did what she could to comfort me when I got home at night.

'Just remember, as terrible as all this is, the Jews had it coming to them,' she told me.

She meant well, but it didn't make me feel any better. I had to get away. My grandmother suggested I stay with her sister in Würzburg for a while. We hadn't heard from her since the end of the war and didn't know if she had survived the fire-bombing, but I had to get away from the Brits. Maybe the Americans are better, I told myself. Now, look where it has gotten me! And all because I didn't have that silly "Schein" they always talk about. Some piece of paper showing you weren't a Nazi. I also didn't do well on that questionnaire. How could I? I didn't understand the half of it. It was all supposed to be so wonderful. Not like that at all," she sobbed.

I didn't ask how it was supposed to be.

Heavy breathing on the other side of the thin wall. The hyenas were sleeping the sleep of the unburdened. I was afraid the girl's sobs would wake them and expose her to scorn and taunts. Why should I care? Why should I show her any sympathy? Because you are Beate Hauser, one of them, I told myself exasperated.

"You'd better get some sleep," I said and turned back toward the wall. I have heard enough, more than I could bear. Neither that night nor any other did I find any rest for as long as I was imprisoned with those criminals.

In the morning, I told the MP guard that I needed to speak to Major Zweig. My mind was made up. I had to get out of his hell, out of this country before I went out of my mind. I would confess who I was. I would beg for mercy, appeal to his kindness, on my knees, if necessary. Hopefully, he would understand my reasons for having broken the law and would send me back to the United States if not to Berlin. I was willing to give all up, to declare defeat.

The MP sneered at my request. There was nobody here by that name.

"Then take me to the camp commander. I am sure he knows him. He is a high-ranking officer in Frankfurt. He sent me here. You must help me get in touch with him. I shouldn't be here. It's a matter of life and death."

"Life and death, you don't say?" he sneered. "Still don't get it, do you? We don't take orders from scum like you. We don't give a damn. You can rot in hell. Even your English won't help you."

Only then did I realize that I had inadvertently fallen into speaking English, a language I supposedly didn't know.

Chapter 7

A Recovered Memory

Someone had seen us, Kafka and me, conversing in the latrine. They must have been watching us from behind the grimy windows. Word got around fast in this shadow world. I saw it in their crooked glances. The new one consorts with the Jews, they said. A piece of paper, torn from a notebook, was left on the pillow of my cot. The penciled scribble in old German was hard to decipher. With trembling hands, I made out the writing. Bitter bile rose in my throat, and a violent tremor seized my body.

A distant memory from a holiday in the summer of 1933 came back with a vengeance. As they had done every summer for many seasons, my grandparents spent several weeks in Bad Kissingen where they took the cure. They were especially eager that year for a rest in this peaceful resort away from the turmoil in Berlin.

While they took the waters and consulted with the spa physician, I was bored like any thirteen-year-old would be. Looking for something to distract me, I wandered down from the sprawling hilltop where the hotel compound overlooked the town below. My spirit as bright and carefree as the blue summer sky dotted with tufts of white clouds, a warm breeze caressing my skin, I skipped along rows of elegant villas in the opulent style of the previous century. A peaceful afternoon stillness reigned over this part of the town.

As I approached the town center, the raucous sounds of a commotion filled the air. Soon I made out shouts and laughter coming from a crowd that ringed the fountain at the center of the market square. Maybe a group of street performers attracted their attention and garnered their approving applause. My curiosity aroused, I pushed through the wall of people for a better look. On the steps to the fountain were seated three young women, their swollen faces blue and caked with blood, their hair disheveled. SA troopers, recognizable from their brown uniforms, strutted in front of them, poking them with sticks, taunting, spewing insults at the pilloried girls. Pieces of cardboard hung from their necks. When I got close enough to read the inscription, the air escaped from my lungs.

"Ich bin am Ort das größte Schwein und laß mich nur mit Juden ein." Something to the effect "I am the greatest swine in town and carry on with Jews alone."

This scene had been my first direct encounter with the new regime that had come to power in Germany a few months before. I had a gut feeling then: the "spook" as I had heard people around me refer to Hitler and his thugs would not go away soon. The jeering, cheering bystanders brought the point home to me even then. I never told my grandparents what I saw. Perhaps I didn't want to hurt them and spoil their holiday. Then the opportunity passed. There were no more summer vacations to follow.

The summer after that one, I left Germany with my parents. We went on a long odyssey through various European countries wherever we could find a temporary home. In the winter of 1936, we landed in New York. Luckily for us, the gates to the "goldene medineh" -- my father's expression -- were still open then to stateless refuge-seekers.

My grandparents stayed in Berlin. They held to their belief in the ephemeral nature of this "aberration" as they wrote in letters to my mother. Even when Nazi thugs vandalized the prestigious Wertheim Art House on Friedrichstraße just off Unter den Linden and thrashed its treasures forcing the gallery to close its doors after forty-five years of mentoring avant-garde artistic genius, my grandparents' faith that Germany and the Germans would come to their senses in due time remained unshaken.

My grandfather mercifully died in the summer of 1935 before the Nuremberg Laws signaled more ominous events to come. My grandmother stayed the course, first in her Charlottenburg villa then in a small, crowded apartment she and my aunt had to share with a dozen other dislocated Jews at a Judenhaus in Schöneberg. Then, on Rosh Hashanah of 1942, she was deported to Theresienstadt. My aunt's fate is unknown.

Now, these same words that I had seen on a cardboard hung around the necks of three hapless women had been pinned to my cot at a prison for female concentration camps guards. The scribble bore the mark of the top hyena, Ilse Kunz, who made no bones about her love of the Führer and her hatred of Jews.

One evening, she mounted a chair and exhorted the troops with mad, hate-spewing eyes to swear their eternal allegiance to Führer, Volk, and Fatherland. She tendered her hand with a nudge toward the others to place theirs on top. Capping the conspiratorial heap, I spotted the little hand of my bunkmate, timorously placed on top of the stack of claws. Kunz flung a challenging look my way, moving her protruding chin up and down in quick succession as if to say, "how about you, are you with us?" I turned toward the door, struggling to keep the contents of my stomach from gushing over. Hisses of "Judas" rang in my ears all the way to the latrine.

I fled to my cot in the corner. Curled up in fetal position, I was only barely able to calm the spasms that convulsed every muscle in my body. Through my chattering teeth, I cursed the Nazi hags, the elusive Major Zweig, and most of all myself. What was I thinking? What hubris befell me to think I had the mettle for this journey into this inferno? What did I expect? That I could deceive the powers that be and travel unhindered straight to Berlin? And what did I expect to find once I was there? My grandmother?

Why didn't I try to find out more about the writer of that letter before rising so eagerly to the bait? In my bitterness, I turned my ire against the man in Amsterdam. He alone, I told myself somewhat irrationally, stood to benefit from the people smuggling ring operating out of his home. Maybe the letter writer, who claimed to represent a Jewish hospital in Berlin was in on it too for his cut. A Jewish hospital in Berlin? That alone should have tipped me off.

But why me? I wasn't rich. They must have read about me in the papers and my book published earlier this year about the murder at a Broadway theater of a formerly beloved star of the German stage and screen. Still, what could they possibly have thought they could gain from putting me through such pain and anguish? The thought turned in my head like a spinning wheel churning out ever more fantastic conspiracy threads.

My ire settled on the elusive Major Zweig. What was his role in all this? He seemed to have vanished. Or maybe he too existed only in my head. The MPs I questioned about him had never even heard of him. So, they said. If at least Sergeant Bickers who brought me to this cursed place could be found. He too seemed to have disappeared. No amount of rage against myself, no banging my head against the wall, no rebelling against this world brought me any relief from the cascading self-recriminations.

I held back my tears in front of the hyenas so as not to appear that their taunts affected me in any way. Alone on my cot in the corner, my face to the wall, there was no holding back. The floodgates burst open with all the full force utter despair and despondency can unlock.

As my tear ducts began to dry, I came to a sobering verdict: *Artemisia Safran is going insane, and she is going to die in this hell.* That was the bottom line of my cogitations, pure and simple.

Then one day, a flash of light, hope of a lifeline, had appeared in the darkness. In the moment of my greatest humiliation and hopelessness, this man with the mocking laughter and dark sparkling eyes materialized out the mists of the neighboring camp. He said his name was František Kafka and told me flat out: "You are not one of them; you are *unsere Leut.*" Yes, yes! I wanted to say; I am one of you, not one of those Nazi whores. In retrospect, I am not sure what held me back. Was its fear of endangering my mission, my elusive goal of reaching Berlin, that ghostly castle on an even ghostlier hill? I remained silent, guarding what I considered to be my secret. The interrogation by the Major and confinement in this prison had made me distrustful of anyone.

In the days that followed our first encounter in the latrine, Kafka seemed to be nearby wherever I was on work detail in the neighboring camp, be it scrubbing tops and pots in the kitchen or floors and toilets in latrines—the prisoners were made to perform the most degrading, back-breaking chores—his laughter followed me like a shadow. He cornered me in places where we could chat alone. I began to look for ways to get away from the pack for a few minutes before the MP guards ordered me back. I am not sure what we talked about, just idle chitchat, I guess. At one point, he hinted something about getting away from this Gehenna. He baited me with Jewish talk. I still held back.

Then one day he was gone. I had become used to his tall, lanky frame filling the doorways, his laughter resounding in the yard. Not a trace. No more. The laughter had died. Maybe this too was a figment of my overwrought imagination. Kafka? Was that his real name or had I made it up?

I had devoured the works of the writer Franz Kafka during my stay at Pension Maibach while waiting for the train to Berlin. The discovery of this Jewish writer had been like a revelation, an almost mystical experience that drew me into a world so bizarre, yet so real and palpable. What were the chances of a Jew from Prague by the same name crossing my path? He said his name was František Kafka. But you can call me "Franz" he had added with a you-know-what-I-mean wink. His words "you are not one of them; you are one of us. His phrase "you are *unsere Leut*" spun a bond of kinship between us. Then doubts began to creep in. Did these conversations take place? Me, on my knees, scrubbing the rough, concrete latrine floors; he, looking down on me with his dark, sparkling eyes so incredibly full of life. Did I make all this up? His boisterous voice, his cheerful, mocking laughter still echoing through my dreams at night rang so real. A ghost? An apparition? Was my mind that far gone?

Through the thicket of my ruminations and self-castigations, a thin whimpering voice reached my ear. Another figment? Was I now beset by imaginary voices?

"I had to go along," the whimper asserted. "Think about what they would do if I hadn't. I am not as strong as you are."

Strong as I am? Then I realized the voice was my bunk mate's, little Elschen. I had forgotten about her betrayal. Betrayal of what, of whom? Of me? Absurd. She was after all one of them. She was nothing to me. She was a plain young thing, probably still in school during the war. Besides, what was it to me whether she went along with that silly pact Ilse Kunz made them swear. They all went along as far as I knew. Why try to justify yourself to me? She stuck to me like an irritant burr.

"You must believe me. I was never part of all this," she persisted. Her voice had suddenly taken on a firm, defiant tone. No more sniveling whimper. "But I saw what they did."

"You already told me about that place you call Belsen," I tried to fend off having hear more of her whining.

Unbeckoned, she started talking about her grandmother's farm in the Lüneburger Heide where she and her mother lived during the bombing of Essen. Her mother went back for a brief visit to save some of their belongings from looters. She was killed in an air raid. Her father went missing somewhere on the Eastern front.

Did I want to hear about this? I was too languid to fend her off and so let her prattle on. On the farm, they always had enough to eat, she said. Sometimes one of the foreign farm workers would slaughter a pig for them in return for a share of the meat. Then she suddenly paused and looked at me with squinting her eyes as if something had just occurred to her.

"You never talk about what *you* did during the war," I heard her say

"I was with the BDM work service. Mostly digging potatoes from the ground on a farm in Westphalia with bare hands. Hard on the back, bending over all the time," I spouted out one of the answers I had been told to give should someone ask.

"How come the Brits didn't pick you up and make you do those horrible things?" she asked.

"Luck, I guess."

"You should have seen that place. The stench made us vomit."

"Why do you keep on about this?"

"It's something one never forgets."

I didn't need this little mouse to paint me a picture. I had seen the photographs, the newsreels, had read the newspaper reports when the war was over. General Eisenhower had ordered his troops to document the scenes they came upon when they liberated the camps. We thought we were well informed. But being in close confinement with people who had most likely perpetrated or at least participated and facilitated the murderous crimes was enough to make my skin crawl.

She blew her nose and wiped her tears, shaking herself like a wet poodle. All the while she kept on babbling about the injustice of her situation and how she wished for the good old days.

"You are right not to go along," I heard her say.

"How so?"

"Maybe the Americans will let you off the hook if you are nice to them. Also, that Jew who comes around seems to have taken a liking to you. Could be to your advantage. After all, the Jews are back and in charge now. Who would have thought?"

My heart skipped a beat. He wasn't a figment of my imagination after all! This Kafka was a real person! Others had seen him. A glimmer of hope! Dashed immediately by the realization that I hadn't been around seen him for days, maybe weeks. I had lost count of time.

"You'd better be careful." She patted my hand and gave me a patronizing look assuring me she only had my best interest at heart.

"My grandmother told me the Jews are always out to seduce Christian girls. Once they have their will with them, off they go, never to be seen again. Dropping the poor saps like a used rag. Sometimes leaving them knocked up."

This German grandmother was a veritable fount of wisdom. Just when I wanted to let her know that I'd had my fill of grandma's nuggets, I was spared more of them and other pitiful laments, ironically perhaps, by Ilse Kunz. She popped her pit bull face into our corner and demanded to know what we were talking about.

"None of your business," I shrugged and turned my back on her. It may not have been very prudent, but I had no desire to ingratiate myself with this hag.

"We were just saying how much fun life was in the old days," piped little Elschen.

"Well, it's lights out and silence in this block after ten. I have been put in charge to make sure everybody follows the rules; including you two." Curious. How did she get this position? She gave me a look that boded ill for any kind of peaceful coexistence in this prison block.

Chapter 8

Peace on Earth

Languid in body and soul, I had lost all sense of the passage of time. Dimly aware of the inexorable rhythm of day fading into night, I went about the tasks demanded of me. I spoke with no one and retreated into long periods of sleep in part to shut out the surreal world around me, in part because of fading strength. Lack of appetite and minimal intake of nourishment contributed to the rapidly progressing weakness of my body.

One day, songs proclaiming peace on earth in English penetrated the penumbra of numbness that was swathing my body and soul. The sound of English inspired fresh hope that I would wake from a nightmarish dream. I struggled up from my cot and staggered to the window. Through a lambent veil of snow, a huge fir tree garnished with lights and glittering ornaments became visible. Christmas! Heralding peace and hope. Suddenly, high-pitched female voices chiming in German hymns jolted me from my musings. They could only have come from the detainees.

The Americans cheered the white Christmas with boisterous approval while next to them Ilse Kunz and her cackle of witches trimmed the tree the soldiers had put up, merrily chirping like a bevy of larks the old standbys "*Oh Tannenbaum*!" and "*Oh Du fröhliche, oh Du selige, gnadenbringende Weihnachtszeit*!" (Oh, you merry, oh, you blessed, mercy-spending Christmastide!)

What made me cringe even more was the next one: "*Tochter Zion freue Dich! Jauchze laut Jerusalem*!" ("Rejoice ye daughter of

Zion! Shout out loud Jerusalem!") Were they even aware of the meaning of Handel's hymn they were blurting out so mindlessly as if they were swaying mugs in a beer hall? The words "Zion" and "Jerusalem" flowing from the mouths of those bitches made the acid rise from my stomach.

Any thought I might have had to go along and participate in this Christmas celebration, I now pushed from me. Berlin was far, far away, and out of reach. Let them discover who I am, I told myself. I shall proclaim it proudly: "I am not one of you! I am a Jewess!" If anything, this journey had taught me the impossibility of pretending to be someone one is not. Nothing mattered anymore. My situation was hopeless.

Defiance against acquiescence in my fate mingled in my chest. May the entire world, and especially Major Emil Zweig, the Jewish American officer with the comportment of a Prussian field marshal, may he together with those disgusting women, may they all be damned and go to hell! All I could do was turn my gaze inward, withdraw into myself, into the most intimate chamber of my inner world, and prepare for my impending death. Yes, I was certain then that I would die there and then. But I would go into that night with the *Shema* on my lips. That's what I swore to myself.

In that darkest moment of despair, a miracle occurred. At least it seemed to me like a miracle. I took it as a sign from heaven or from wherever signs emanate. In a state of half-consciousness, I drudged aimlessly through the almost knee-deep snow to get far, far away from that courtyard to where I could no longer hear the cacophony exhorting joy in the birth of a Jewish child in ancient Israel.

I reached the padlocked gate from which extended a barbed wire fence that blocked off the prison grounds from the adjacent DP camp. Seized by a keen awareness of the irony of being separated from my people by a barbed-wire barrier, I lifted my eyes, squinting to make out what was going on over there. The darkness and distance permitted me to see only a few indistinct shadows moving about in what I knew from having been there on work detail was a sort of square bordered by barrack-like lodgings. Clearly visible though, right in the center piercing the surrounding darkness shone nine bright lights of a menorah. The remembrance came to me as of a long-forgotten tale I had heard in another lifetime. Of course, it was Chanukah, the Jewish festival of light and freedom. All the branches were lit, so this was the last of the eight nights.

How long I was rattling at the barb-wired obstacle blocking my way, I don't remember. I awoke in the prison infirmary, both hands wrapped in heavy bandages. One of the medics told me the MPs had to pry me off the fence to which I was obstinately clinging. I resisted their efforts with fierce determination. My hands clawed the barbs until they ran with blood. When someone finally pulled me away, I had lost consciousness.

"You put up quite a struggle, like a lioness fighting for her cubs," he said with an approving smile. These were the first kind words addressed to me in such a long time. I returned his smile to show him I understood what he was saying. There was no longer any point in pretending I didn't understand his language. It was my language. I relished the sound of it. The medic's Appalachian mountain twang was music to my ears.

He was a homesick kid from Tennessee and was eager to talk. He had seen things he would just as soon forget, he told me. Why did he speak to me? Why speak to me, a presumed German and possible Nazi, about what he saw when his unit arrived at a place called Buchenwald in the spring of 1945?

"You are different. I can tell," he said in response.

"How so?"

"You aren't like the others. Whatever they're keeping you here for, I don't believe you did those horrible things. I can see it in your eyes. You didn't do that kind of stuff." He shook his head as if he wanted to exorcize from his memory the kind of stuff his eyes had seen.

"Looks can be deceiving," I said.

He was reluctant to spell out what those horrible things were. I wanted to hear more. Or did I? I wasn't sure I could take any more after what I had heard about Belsen. Now Buchenwald. But I had to. He was a witness to the scenes of horror. He might go home and never speak of it again. To draw him out, I kept the conversation going without seeming too eager.

"I'm a pretty good judge of people," he said with some pride. "I have you know that not all Germans are bad. Look, I have a girlfriend here in town. As soon as we can clear up the paperwork, we'll get married, and then I'll take her home with me."

"You know, terrible things were done to my people too," he said suddenly after a reflective pause. "My mother is Cherokee," he explained in answer to my puzzled look.

I expected a lecture about the injustices the Americans did to the native Indian tribes. No doubt, he grew up with his mother and family telling stories about the Trail of Tears, the uprooting of what the history books call "the civilized tribes of the Cherokee nation" and the tremendous suffering and loss of life it caused.

To my amazement nothing of the sort was forthcoming. Instead, I heard him say: "But believe me nothing like Buchenwald or Dachau or any of the other camps we liberated."

I didn't quite know what to say, so I just said: "You were there?"

"Yeah, as a medic, I had to tend to some of these people. They were more like skeletons; many didn't make it. Died even then before our eyes. Right then and there. Many were too weak to go on. Couldn't digest the food we gave them. Makes me sick to think what they must have gone through. An army chaplain, a rabbi, talked to them in their language. That helped to get some out of their stupor. Our unit had to move on. Most German towns we passed put out a white flag of surrender except for one hold-out not far from here. Even at this late stage of the war, they put up a fight that in the end only destroyed more of their town. Crazy. Go figure what went on in the heads of those Krauts."

"Why are you telling me this?" I prodded. "Don't you think I would know about what happened during the war having lived through it?"

"Not all Germans. When I talk to my girlfriend about all this, she tells me they knew nothing about what the Nazis did to the Jews. People just figured that they had gone away, to some other country."

He looked at me suddenly with a squint as if he saw me for the first time.

"Wait a minute. I thought you didn't know any English. When did you learn to talk so good?"

I debated with myself whether I should let him in on my secret, but then decided it would be too risky. I came up with a rather flimsy explanation with the hope he would accept it.

"I never really said that. I had English in school. But I didn't want the other women to know. You know how they are. They still believe in the Führer and the Fatherland."

"I'm taking German lessons," he went on. "My fiancée has no English. We mostly communicate via dictionary and the language of love," he added with a sweet grin. He didn't seem to give my explanation another thought. I was happy to leave it at that.

A few days later, the bandages were taken off my hands. I was declared fit to go back to the barracks and prison work. My all-too-brief respite was over. I never saw that brave medic again. He was rotated out, they told me.

Chapter 9

Deliverance

There was no rotating out for me. The days and nights rolled into each other like two giant boulders careening down a mountain slope.

Then one day--how much time had elapsed since I had last heard it, I did not remember--the boisterous laughter rang out again. It was audible from far away, gaining in volume until it broke off abruptly at the spot where I was crouched down in the useless task of washing the urine off the cold latrine floor. I had eagerly volunteered for the cleaning detail. Anything to escape the company of those women. My request was denied at first. They feared another break attempt. An assumption not altogether unfounded. Even now the watchful eyes of the MP escorts followed my every move.

"I have a present for you," he said, a big grin lighting his face from ear to ear. He held out a small package wrapped in newspaper.

"Here, open it," he prodded.

Unsure whether he was playing another joke on me, I hesitated. Then again, why shouldn't he? Why wouldn't he take a leaf from the Nazi manual of taunts and tortures now that the tables had been turned?

"Go ahead; open it!" When I hesitated, he grabbed my hand and placed the package in it. It fit right into my palm. It felt very light. Whatever was inside, it had to be something small. When I still hesitated, he took it back and ripped off the wrapping himself. Out came - I didn't trust my eyes— a little brush. Its wooden handle of faded brown; its bristles mere stubbles. He brandished it like a sword or a dagger.

"Do you recognize it?"

I shook my head.

"It's the toothbrush I mentioned. I want you to have it."

"Why? What for?" What did this man want from me? I sent an imploring look toward the MPs who were smoking and laughing in the doorway, paid us no heed on this occasion. Why were they delinquent in their duty the one time when I wished them to order this ghostly visitor to go away?

"This brush, this tiny toothbrush with its tiny bristles, scrubbed the cobblestones of Vienna to a sparkling polish. You should have seen those streets glisten in the sunlight! Pico bello!" He put his thumb and forefinger together and pressed them to his lips with a smack as if tasting a gourmet dish. "Not even the streams of blood saturating the grooves could dull the gloss this little brush put on those stones. Of course, it wasn't just one toothbrush. There were thousands. Imagine, thousands of tiny little toothbrushes like this one scouring away the patina of soot and grime laid down on those streets over the centuries. Even in its time of Habsburg splendor, the streets of Vienna never sparkled as they did back in March of 1938. The Nazis were very much obsessed with cleanliness. Very intolerant of filth."

He looked at me intently. He was waiting to see what effect his harangue would have. I pushed back the tears unable to say anything.

"I want you to have it," he insisted, still holding his little artifact out to me. "Not to use it on these latrine tiles, of course.

That would be blasphemous. No, I want you to keep it as a token, a keepsake. Please safeguard it for me."

I was stupefied, at a loss of how to react. Only slowly did the implication of what I had just heard begin to sink in. Images of what this man and so many had been made to endure unreeled in my head like the dark shadows of a horror film. Even more mortifying was the realization of how chance or luck or my parents' foresight had spared me from the same fate. Tears began to trickle down my cheeks. Maybe this was my punishment for having escaped.

"It won't be long now," he said gently reassuring. "I will come for you soon. Be ready."

My eyes remained pinned on the swaggering figure sallying away in long, measured strides as if he were propelled by a bounding wind in his sails. He tossed off a few joking words in German at the MPs. The Americans laughed good-naturedly, surely without understanding a word. His laughter echoed in the dusky camp yard, fading out as he vanished beyond the alleyways.

Part Two

Wanderings

"Each must feel as if having personally escaped from slavery in Egypt."

Passover Haggadah

Chapter 1

Snowbound

Kafka's sense of direction was unerring. Sure-footed, keen-eyed like a cat on a nocturnal prowl, he cut a trail across wind-swept fields that were blanketed knee-deep with fresh snow and swooping upward from the river valley toward the higher elevation of a dense forest. Me straggling in his shadow. We walked by night and rested by day in whatever abandoned barn or shed we happened to come upon. A grim demeanor overshadowed his laughing disposition since we had left the camp at Steinheim. He spoke little, merely grunting a command now and then. I too kept quiet, too preoccupied with keeping pace with his wide, determined strides. This excursion was not an outing into the blue yonder. Kafka knew where he was going. He had a definite, well-planned goal. I had the distinct feeling that this was not the first time he had been on this route.

He circumvented the villages and towns strung along the river's edge. He also kept away for the most part from the highways and roads congested with heavy foot traffic. The motley groups of people moving like ants hither and thither, pulling pushcarts, handcarts, and wheelbarrows cluttered with goods and belongings, some loaded with children, were periodically herded to the side of the road to make way for the columns of US military vehicles flaunting the might of the victors.

Whether Kafka's itinerary was designed to avoid contact with the local population or if it was the ever-present MPs on patrol in their jeeps, he would rather not run into was all the same to me. I had no desire to renew my acquaintance with either of them, whether German or American. All I wanted was get away, far, far away. And to that end, I had no choice but to hitch my fate to the goodwill of this strange man who called himself Kafka.

By nightfall, we reached the top of a hill capped with a dense forest. Catching my breath from the exertion of the climb, I stood in awe of this cathedral of gently swaying treetops crowned with crystalline kernels of snow suffused with the orange red of the setting sun. A strange sense of deference suddenly overcame me, a reticence to cross the threshold of what seemed holy ground. Kafka had no such qualms. He raised his arm like a sergeant prodding the troops to storm a target.

A canopy of tree branches bent under the powdery weight, trunks spiked with ice daggers, blocked our way. The ground too, overgrown with thick underbrush laden knee-deep with snow, was less than hospitable and amenable to our entering the sylvan sanctuary. Nature seemed intent on thwarting our progress.

As formidable as she may be, she met a match in Kafka. He ramped his broad shoulders against the branches, pushing them aside with grim determination. Stomping vigorously on the ground, he padded down the snow enough to clear a path for me to follow. I too took up battle, treading the ground, breaking off pesky twigs out to scratch my face with pointy little fingers, while pushing ever deeper into the interior.

We finally came to a clearing where we stopped and dropped our packs on the ground. I filled my lungs with clean forest air. Kafka turned toward me a bright smile for the first time since we had left the camp. I hadn't seen his face all day.

My eyes were pinned on his back; he rarely looked behind him, and nary uttered a word.

Again, I wondered about this strange, mysterious man with the darkly gleaming, slightly hooded eyes, a ripping laughter that exuded an insouciant, devil-may-care attitude not altogether fitting in the bleak world of camps ringed by barbed wire, a world where memories of war and death were still festering wounds, a man with whom I now found myself alone in a vast forest. From our first encounter in the latrine—I, kneeling on the cold stone floor, he, lowering his gaze with a patronizing though mocking smile—he had exerted a magnetic attraction over me and my imagination as I had never experienced in the presence of a man before.

At twenty-five, my experience with romantic love was limited to one disastrous brief episode. My celibate condition was not a deliberate choice. The circumstances I had found myself in didn't lend themselves to the pursuit of happiness in that department. Though burnt once, I was still a woman of flesh and blood, not unattractive and generally well-groomed, at least in my New York environment. What my languishing in prison reserved for Nazi criminals might have done to my appearance, I preferred not to contemplate. From the first moment of our encounter, Kafka's presence not only inspired hope of deliverance, but it also made the blood pulse through my veins with a wild desire for being held, and kissed, and made love to. This erotic longing had suffused my dreams and electrified my body sleeping or lying awake on my prison cot.

Now alone with him in the depth of a forest far, far away from a world I had no desire to ever return to, my thoughts about the possibility of a romantic fling returned. Though I had to admit to myself that he had not given any indication of a similar sentiment.

Just then Kafka suddenly turned toward me, put his arm around my waist, lifted me, and whirled around with me in a wild dance. From his chest burst that familiar laughter with the force of a lion's roar, rending the stillness of the forest, a primal scream that flooded my body with ripples of giddiness. I just wanted him to keep on whirling and whirling in a never-ending waltz. But the many romance novels I had devoured in long lonely nights of my youth had probably addled my brain a bit too much.

Still laughing, he set me down on the ground, the ground of reality as it were, with a thump and planted a smacking comradely kiss on my forehead. I am not sure what I expected—a romantic romp in an icy wilderness, teeth chattering and limbs shivering? All I can say is my sense of disappointment almost brought me to the brink of tears like a little child who was denied a piece of cake.

"What was that for?" I asked pouting.

"A celebration of our freedom!" he declared. Then with sober mien, he added: "We have to take shelter for the night."

I looked around. Night was falling. Where would we find shelter from the freezing temperatures that were quickly dropping even lower? He took off his gloves and blew on his hands while rubbing them together. With a reassuring "not to worry," he pulled a piece of paper from his coat pocket and began to study it intently. Next, he pulled out a compass and pointed it around.

"That way!" he said nodding in a certain direction. I saw nothing but impenetrable darkness all around the clearing. He folded the paper which was, from what I could see peeking over his shoulder, some sort of hand-drawn map. He stuffed it back in his coat pocket and pulled his gloves back on. He then shouldered his rucksack and prodded me to do the same. Then we set out to do battle once again with the brush, snow, and ice. Again, I tried to keep up with his determined strides praying he knew where we were going.

He had brought good cheer into my life at the time of greatest distress. He had liberated me from prison as he had promised—though it wasn't clear to me how he had accomplished this feat with such apparent ease. Still, it had been foolish, I said to myself, to indulge in romantic fantasies, even if latching on to such a fantasy world sustained me and prevented me from succumbing to despair altogether and losing my mind in a bleak, hopeless world beset with cruelty and malice. Then again, if he, for his part, wasn't motivated by amorous sentiments, what prompted him to plot an elaborate scheme to spring me from imprisonment and to go me with on the run?

Chapter 2

Freedom Trail

He had been a man of his word. Just twelve hours earlier, he had appeared, as he had promised, in the canteen where I was on kitchen duty, still scrubbing but this time in upright position scouring burned pots rather than urine-stained floors. A few days before he had approached me, as he had done on several occasions before, in the latrine where I had once again engaged in the futile Sisyphean endeavor of shining the worn tiles. When I felt his presence, I rose to my feet. I pulled the little toothbrush from my frock pocket and started moving it ceremoniously like a magic wand over the floor though without touching it.

"I am glad to see you are putting my little treasure to good use." He laughed out loud as usual, but his dark eyes projected a different story.

The little brush had become a bond between us. It affirmed an affinity for our common history, a link in the chain stretching across centuries.

Then, his demeanor changed, and he became all business-like as he laid out his plan. He instructed me to be in the kitchen of the canteen at the DP camp on such and such a day, at such and such a time, early in the morning.

"What if I can't get on the kitchen detail?" It all seemed so fantastic. I had no idea how he could pull off my escape under the watchful eyes of the MPs.

"You must. Find a way! It's our only chance to get away. We can't miss it."

Our chance? *We* can't miss what? He was still an enigma to me.

But what did it matter why he wanted to take me out of that hell? Maybe he had a personal motive. Or he could be acting out of the goodness of his heart, out of pity for a fellow Jew stuck in a mess. He took an interest in me and my plight. Be that as it may. I was getting out of this hell. That was all that counted, and I was grateful to him.

Our rendezvous took place a few days later behind the canteen kitchen. He handed me a package wrapped in brown packing paper tied with jute twine.

"Put this on," he instructed. "And hurry!"

I fiddled nervously with the package he had handed me. When he saw me struggling to untie the string with my stiff, swollen fingers, he took a knife from the kitchen, cut the string, and tore the brown paper.

"Why did you pack it so tight in the first place?" I asked in a surge of rebelliousness over having to take orders and being put to the test all the time.

"It came this way," he said. "I just took it. I hope it contains all you need. Enough of idle talk. Get moving."

Before he threw away the wrapping, I caught a glimpse of a stamp on the paper. It looked to have come from some charitable organization, maybe the Joint. At any rate, it contained used but warm women's clothing. I recognized the American style. The wool sweater felt like a caressing hand on my rough skin. I stepped into a pair of sports trousers with a flannel lining, glad I wouldn't have to go out into the cold in a skirt. There was also a pair of fur-lined boots, too large but the wool socks filled in the space. The coat in the package, though of fine fabric, was better suited for a cool day in Florida than for fending off the harsh elements of a Central European winter. Kafka produced a more suitable specimen. He handed me a silk-lined woman's jacket to wear under a military-style overcoat that was like the one he was wearing. Hefty and a few sizes too big, but it kept me warm. The woman's jacket lay soft against my skin. I didn't have time to ponder its provenance. When I pulled a knit cap from the charity package over my head, Kafka made a tsk-tsk sound and replaced it with a furry Ushanka like the one he wore himself. Outfitted in what one could regard as sensible though hardly fashionable clothing, we started on our path toward freedom. Well, my freedom mostly since Kafka was by no means a prisoner and was free to move about at his leisure.

There was, however, nothing leisurely about the meandering trajectory we took that would take us out of the compound and get us to the open highway and ultimately to this forest. Now we were wedged in the thick of a forest, forbidding and dark. After our brief interlude in the clearing, he once again gripped me by the nape of my neck and steered me deeper into the dense thicket.

"We must seek shelter," he repeated. I couldn't have agreed more. Our coats, though warm, were heavy with dampness. No protection against night dipping temperatures and possible death from frostbite. Where was a sanctuary? Leave it to Kafka!

"It's not far now," he said. "Let's keep going. We'll be there soon."

Be where soon? The answer wasn't long in coming. The place where we would be setting up camp for the night soon came into view. Nestled among the swaying treetops in the pallid light of the moon was a hunter's perch! No human eye ever beheld a more welcome sight.

We scrambled up the rickety wooden ladder, me eagerly taking the lead. Kafka followed close behind, giving my derriere a firm push to keep me from slipping and losing my foothold on the wet, rotting spokes. An ascent into heaven nevertheless! Nor did the wonders cease once we got to the top and inside the crow's nest. Kafka used his big padded gloves to clear the snow that had drifted in. It was a lookout for hunting and not completely enclosed. The spaces between the wooden slats had to be wide enough to point a rifle through as well as affording a good view of the game wandering into the crosshairs. Thus, spoke Kafka, who seemed to be an expert on almost anything.

His clean-up job uncovered a big box, a footlocker in fact, as used by the military. For me, it was a treasure chest from which my companion pulled a trove of canned food items, C-ration type. It must have been the promise of nourishment that made my stomach growl. We hadn't stopped to take a bite all day. Now we sat on the wet floor of this tree house and shoveled whatever was in those cans—a can opener was not lacking, nor were eating utensils, the folding, stuck-together type used for camping or by soldiers in combat. No table, no tablecloth nor napkins, but festive nonetheless, we agreed, giddy with cheer. Neither was there water or wine or any other beverage. The plentiful fresh snow quenched our thirst and helped to wash down the bland fare that was like nectar and ambrosia. We were in full agreement on the deliciousness of the repast even though Kafka preferred less mythological allusions. For him, he said, it evoked the mouth-watering delicacy of a Viennese apple strudel.

Apple strudel? With whipped cream? Oh yes, with lots of whipped cream. Well, *chacun a son goût*! In this case, Viennese taste.

"I didn't say *Kaiserschmarn*!" he said defensively.

"I thought you were from Prague," I teased.

"Same thing when it comes to pastries. Did you ever have Sacher torte?"

"Sure, we have Sacher torte in Berlin."

"I bet it's not the same as the authentic one. The Prussians don't know anything about the fine art of *pâtisseries*."

To counter his assertion, I wrecked my brain for some of the cakes I had in my childhood. From somewhere in the far reaches of my memory emerged the image of a round, doughnut-like pastry topped with lots of powdered sugar or icing.

"I bet you don't have anything like the authentic Berliner *Pfannkuchen*," I ventured.

"Thank goodness, no! Pfui!" he exclaimed, shaking his head as if the mere thought offended his *Feinschmecker* palate.

We were still bantering and laughing when he pulled out another treasure from the magic footlocker: a sleeping bag and a pair of blankets! Could it get any more heavenly? I realized I have been using the word "heaven" and its variants several times in the row now. How could I not? I hope to find forgiveness for this bathetic cliché. But I was truly in heaven. We were still laughing and joking when we crawled, fully dressed, into the sleeping bag.

"Sorry, but we'll have to share this one," he said with a doggish look at what was to be our lumpy bed for the night.

We did not make love that night, not in the common sense of the term. No mingling of bodies in rapturous abandon or anything of that nature. It was a tranquil intimacy, a clinging-together to keep our bodies from freezing. A steady wind blew more snow into the drafty cabin, spreading a white cover over the blankets we had piled on top of the sleeping bag for additional protection against the elements. The thick covering of snow, blankets, wadded sleeping bag, plus several layers of clothing and Kafka's body enclosing mine suffused me with the secure warmth of a mother's womb. Soon enough, his breathing assumed a regular rhythm as he nodded off into a deep, peaceful sleep, his head drooping against my neck and resting there.

The questions I had wanted to ask him earlier dissolved as of themselves. Any traces that may have persisted, I chased away. Unimportant. I put my trust in him, partly out of necessity but mostly because I wanted to. Huddled together in a dark forest, we had never spoken about who I was and why I was on this journey. He seemed to know. There seemed to be no need to dwell on it.

"You are our people, not one of them," he had told me during our first encounter. It would explain why he went to such length to get me out of the company of those Nazi criminals. Back then, I thought it more prudent to maintain my fictive personality, the identity I had tried so hard to assume. As far away and unreachable as Berlin was from this forest somewhere in the middle of Germany, I still shied away from doing or saying anything that might lessen my chance of ever getting there. He never brought up the subject again.

Being a woman, I also liked to flatter myself that he may find me attractive. What woman of flesh and blood wouldn't like to entertain such a fantasy, especially when a handsome man showers her with attention? The weeks—was its months?—in prison with minimal appetite and hard labor had taken its toll. The haggard image that stared back at me from the little mirror in the shack behind the canteen kitchen where I changed into the clothes he handed me was not only unrecognizable, but it was frightful to see the dark shadows around my eyes staring back at me, the hollow cheeks, the unkempt hair grown wild.

In my mind, I went over all the times we had been speaking, but I couldn't point to a single instance when he could be said to "have come on to me" in the blatant sense. When he spoke, his eyes with their dazing, at times dazzling, roguish spark, rested unwaveringly in mine, which effectively made my knees buckle. What to make of his laughter? Before I even saw him, I had heard his laughter, loud and echoing in the yard between the barracks. As infectious as it was, it also induced in me a vague sense of unease. I sensed something darker behind the jollity to put a gloss over a troubled past.

Then I may have been influenced by reports about what the Nazis did to the Jews. I knew nothing about him, nothing about what he may have gone through. The only hint was the gift of that little toothbrush with the wooden handle and worn-down bristles. It had polished the cobblestones of the streets of Vienna, he said when he handed it to me. Not whose hand had guided it. He also told me he was from Prague though he could have been in Vienna at some point.

Maybe the attraction I felt for him came from his name: Kafka. František Kafka, he had introduced himself with a roguish grin, adding: "But you can call me Franz." I wondered if that was his real name and if he was really from Prague.

My thoughts wandered back to the time, so long ago it seemed, at Frau Maibach's pension and my discovery of the writer Franz Kafka. The nights I spent inside his stories and characters, so strange, so different from anything I had come across in my readings, taking me into a universe, seemingly surreal in the telling, yet starkly realistic in holding up a mirror of the human soul.

The Kafka with whom I was sharing a sleeping bag in a dark forest somewhere in Germany, whose bodily warmth kept me from freezing to death, the Kafka who inspired all sorts of fantasies and caused me to ruminate while he was sleeping peacefully, this Kafka was still an enigma to me.

I must have trailed off eventually into a dreamless sleep for I was jolted out of my sleep by a deafening rumble of grunting and snorting sounds. I was tossed about in the violently shaking cabin. Kafka was sitting up straight in a stiff position. Through sleep-veiled eyes, I saw him fiddling with an object in his lap. Holding on for dear life to the wooden slats, I caught sight down below in the graying dawn of not one but two ghastly looking beasts thrusting their tusks against the wooden stilts that held up our lofty refuge. Then the sound of gunfire. Two shots in quick succession, bursting my ears. The beasts gave off a few more grunts and then keeled over. The ensuing silence was even more deafening.

Another surprise! Kafka had a gun. But then, it made sense not to go unarmed into a German forest in times of lurking dangers from man or beast.

"We'd better get away from here before more of their comrades pick up the scent," Kafka said.

"Though they usually roam at night," he assured me.

I was astounded at how much he knew about the habits of wildlife roaming German forests.

"What are they?" I asked, shaking myself with disgust.

"Wild boars. Very common in many parts of Europe. A menace to humans who dare to encroach on their territory," he lectured me without stopping his housekeeping of shaking out the damp bedding, rolling it up, and stashing it back into the footlocker. The gun disappeared in his rucksack which he lifted onto his back with a groan as if heaving a weighty load. I wondered how many weapons he might have. Hopefully, an arsenal was my next thought, that would come in handy to fend off any lurking wild beasts, animal and human.

Chapter 3

A Thieves' Lair

Arsenal wasn't an exaggeration. The half dozen or so firearms Kafka laid out carefully, even lovingly, on the table made my eyes pop. I had never seen so much firepower in one man's possession. I had never met a civilian who was armed to the teeth outside the movies. In fact, I had never ever been near a revolver nor knew anybody who could handle one.

"These are semi-automatic handguns, not revolvers. We are not in the old Wild West," he corrected my misuse of terminology.

As he spoke, he held them up one by one with upturned hands and solemn mien in priestly fashion as if making a gift offering to the gods. I took a few steps backward and surveyed the scene askance.

"You needn't worry. They are not loaded," he said in a surly tone, adding: "Not yet at least. They need cleaning first."

He continued lecturing about the special features and functions and calibers of each item in his precious stash. In a different time and place, I would have thought he was reading off the names of a New York law firm. There was Walther PP, followed by Beretta, Roth-Steyr, Mauser, Luger Parabellum, and Glock. When he came to the last in the bunch, his eyes lit up.

"This is my Polish Tokarev TT-33," he declared with pride. He weighed the weapon pensively in his hands. One might have thought he was speaking of his Polish bride or lover judging from the loving gaze and gentle caress he expended on her forged metal body. Snapping out of what I presumed was a distant memory, he drew my attention to the distinctive design of its frame, the elegant, gleaming carbon steel barrel, the unique lift-out trigger mechanism, and slide catch. All terms that were unfamiliar to me. I learned about her hammer units, locking lug, take-down clip, chamber, maybe not in that order.

He touted the design of the handle, or grip as he called it, gently tracing with his finger the finely carved markings. Maybe he thought I would be more likely impressed by the decorative part. He cradled it in his hand, feeling its weight. In a sudden move, he placed his finger around the trigger and raised the gun and pointed it at the window. Like the gunslingers in Western movies, he squinted above the barrel as if taking aim and readying to fire. Then he put it down and burst out laughing.

"I had you there, didn't I?" he said, relishing my obvious discomfort. He had proven his marksmanship earlier that morning. I needed no persuading that he knew how to use these pieces.

"Are you a gun collector?" I asked meekly.

"I guess you could say that." His great pride, and what I perceived as affection, in his collection lighting up his eyes.

"Isn't it illegal for civilians to carry arms under US military rules?"

"The United States military does not rule Kafka. Kafka lives by Kafka rules alone."

"I shall teach you. You'll see." It irked me to be spoken to as if I was a child. But like his guns, I was in his hands and could not demur. I too had to live by Kafka rules.

Teach me what? See what? I was soon to find out though I had no desire to be instructed in this martial art.

"Now let's make a fire and get something to eat. You must be hungry." He gathered up some pieces from the wood pile in front of the fireplace and stacked it expertly inside the hearth.

"You just sit by the fire and warm up." He refused my help with preparing the meal, such as it was. "Two hands are quite sufficient for opening cans and putting the fare on the plates. It's cold and not very fancy, but we'll cook something tomorrow. I will need your help later with cleaning my babies."

Cleaning guns? Not exactly the romantic evening by the fire this fairytale hostel where we had arrived after we had resumed our trek through the wintry forest early that morning had inspired. We had gotten away, skin barely intact, from our arboreal overnight shelter that had been shaken by the bestial attack. The already rotted stilts holding the cabin aloft began to collapse with us still inside. We scrambled for dear life down the creaking, splintering spokes of the ladder. I gave out a scream when I landed on my bottom right next to the carcasses. Kafka jumped down with the grace of a paratrooper descending from the sky, though without a chute. He landed on his feet just in time before the tower crashed to the ground. I pushed away his extended hand and scrambled onto my feet on my own steam. I still had some measure of dignity left. We skulked around the dreadful beasts lest they rear their dreadful heads, and hurriedly left the scene in a direction Kafka determined with the help of his compass.

The pallid morning sun breaking through the dense canopy of leaves made the forest no more hospitable than it had been the day before. A machete would have been handy in battling the adverse tree branches intent on barring us from penetrating their sylvan realm. Kafka showed me his hunting knife when I inquired. But no, unfortunately, he shrugged with a mien of mock regret, he did not have a machete.

"It wouldn't do here anyway," he added. "This is not a tropical jungle."

The man had answers for everything. What did he know about the tropics? I didn't either. But I had been to the movies where I learned a thing or two. His constant claims to superior knowledge stuck in my craw.

Necessity dictated my getting quickly over my annoyance and follow on closely on his heels. It wasn't so much his heels that drew my attention. My eyes were pinned on his back, his broad, strong shoulders. I marveled at the self-assuredness of his stride, never looking back. I was huffing and puffing enough for him to know I wasn't far behind.

My thoughts wandered back to the previous night in the treehouse, the comfort of his arms, the warmth flowing from his body, the sense of being berthed and secure. What would the night ahead bring? Would we find another shelter? What of the wild beasts roaming this forest? Could he fend them off again? Kafka, the boar slayer!

Several hours into our silent march—it must have been past midday although the time was hard to gauge from the gray sky that was hiding the sun, my energy too was at a nadir, drained from the relentless pace of our foray into the forest—he stopped and consulted his map again.

"Just a little while longer," he said with a reassuring nod. "Hold out. We'll be there soon."

We'll be where? A town, a village? Another hunter's outpost?

My fear of more attacks from a hostile fauna and flora, the lack of shelter and a warm meal were magically lifted when we alighted on another clearing. There, nestled among the trees, was a crooked, charming house overgrown with ivy. It even had a thatched gabled roof. A picture straight out of a fairytale. My delight was immediately dampened by images of witches and big bad wolves. The stories of Hansel and Gretel and Little Red Riding Hood got jumbled up in my head. Of course, I didn't believe in fairytales. I was a little too old for that, but a sense of dread over what we might find inside this gingerbread house took hold of me, nevertheless.

"What if someone lives here?" I whispered in Kafka's ear.

"There isn't anybody," he whispered back with a mock conspiratorial tone.

"How do you know?"

"Trust me." He took my hand and pulled me down the sloping clearing toward the house.

Near the entrance door, for which Kafka produced a key from a birdhouse at the entrance, I noticed a shingle on the ground. The writing was faded, but I made out: *Wirtshaus im Spessart*. The Spessart Inn! Now I knew where we were. The Spessart was a wooded mountain range tucked inside what is called the Main River quadrangle. Though I had never been in this area, the inn was vividly familiar to me from one of my favorite childhood readings, a very popular collection of fairytales by Wilhelm Hauff. One of the stories, "The Spessart Inn," involved a countess, a goldsmith's apprentice, a gang of highway robbers, and an attempted kidnapping for ransom.

The inn served as a thieves' hideout on the run from the law. Ironic that now, after so many years, it should serve us as our hideout as well. Of course, we weren't outlaws, just fugitives from the military authorities. I wondered if Kafka was familiar with this folktale.

For the moment, I was eager to get inside and out of the cold, so I kept this flashback to my childhood to myself.

No predators of any kind, whether human, witch, or wolf, not even a grandmother, greeted or confronted us upon entering the cavernous hall. No sign of any living being except for a passel of mice for whom we were the menace. They scurried across the floor and quickly disappeared in a corner hole in the wall. The robbers of a bygone era were long gone.

I did notice some signs that the place had been visited more recently than the eighteenth century. Neither dust nor cobwebs anywhere. Even the area around the hearth and the narrow bedchamber where I alighted my knapsack onto the quilt-covered bed showed no signs of the gnawing tooth of time. My suspicions about these previous visitors were confirmed when I opened the pantry and found a store of canned foods. Thinking back to the trail we had taken, it all made sense now. Kafka had scouted out this route before taking me on it. The provisions and blankets in the hunter's stand and now this well-stocked hideout all pointed to a specific purpose.

It became clear to me that this inn had been our destination all along. We had eluded the military authorities who were not likely to send out patrols to find us in this wilderness. We had reached a safe haven. The question was for how long we could stay and where we would go from here? Did he have a plan beyond this place?

Kafka didn't give me an opportunity to ask questions. No rest either. We consumed our frugal meal. No time to talk. A better description would be, we devoured the food from the cans he took from the pantry next to the cold kitchen. Whatever was inside those cans, it had no taste but melted like a delicacy on my tongue. With our hunger stilled, he threw more wood on the fire. I drew close to the flames and prepared to hunker down on a frayed little rug in front of the hearth, just short of getting singed. A lulling warmth began to seep into my body, spreading through my limbs like a viscous lava stream running down a mountainside and thawing out their stiffness. Tufts of romantic images began to float through the haze of my drowsy head, images hailing from a previous life in more innocent times, the one I had lived vicariously at the movie theaters in mid-town Manhattan. Ruggedly handsome as he admittedly was, Kafka was no Clark Gable or Cary Grant. I certainly was no Irene Dunn or Myrna Loy either. Our wintry lair somewhere in war-torn Germany resembled but little a luxury ski lodge in the Green or the Rocky Mountains.

I was only vaguely aware of what Kafka was doing while I entertained longings of loving arms and soft lips until I was roused by a rough command: "Time to work."

He had spread out his arsenal on the oaken table. In addition to the handguns, there was a larger object. I had seen plenty of war movies, besides all those Westerns, to be able to identify it as a rifle.

"It's a Karabiner Mauser," Kafka corrected once again my fuzzy proficiency in the firearms department while he attached a telescope—I hoped it was called a telescope—to the top of the barrel. Next, he displayed the cleaning material—Shami cloths, cotton swabs, cans and bottles of fluid solvent and lubricants, pipe cleaners, the lot.

"Let's start with the Roth-Steyr." He tendered a handsome snub-nosed little piece with a mother-of-pearl handle. "This one will be yours."

"Mine?"

"Don't worry. I'll teach you."

"You mean you'll teach me to fire this thing?" My eye must have been bulging while my eyebrows reached my hairline.

"Yes, fire it," he confirmed. "But first it has to be spanking clean."

We spent hours cleaning those damn things. My body longed for rest and love, none of which was granted by this man who doubled as taskmaster and object of my desire. My attention was quickly channeled into the work at hand. As I learned, gun cleaning required considerable skill and concentration. It also required keen eyesight. Mine was dulled by lack of sleep. Yet, I managed to stay alert enough to listen and learn. I even came to enjoy toting the little thing around with my forefinger like a gunslinger. I fancied myself to be Annie Oakley to his Wild Bill Hickok! Yes, he had heard of Buffalo Bill, but not of his partner, the female sharpshooter.

"This is serious business," he reprimanded me. What a spoilsport! I thought. What business? Where had his cheerful disposition gone? The laughter? The spark in his dark eyes? Couldn't a girl have a little fun?

"Too American," he mumbled and reached for the next piece.

It must have been midnight by then. The candles had shrunken to a stump. The logs in the hearth had burnt down to glowing embers. An owl's hooting rent the stillness of the night. I was on the point of collapse. That's what I did the moment I was inside the little chamber that was to be mine. Still fully dressed, my little gun tucked inside my coat next to the little toothbrush I sank onto the bedstead. Now I am in possession of three tokens from Kafka was my last thought before oblivion enveloped me.

Chapter 4

Romantic Interlude

A soft rapping on my chamber door roused me from a deep sleep at the crack of dawn. Kafka stood in the doorway, all smiles. The spark in his dark eyes had returned.

"Come!" he said. He stepped inside and before I knew what was happening, he swept me off my makeshift bed and carried me through the hall toward what used to be a kitchen. I was sleepy-eyed and disheveled and in desperate need of freshening up, as they say in polite society. But this wasn't polite society. Where could we find water? We had tried the faucets the day before to no avail. Not a drop came out of the frozen pipes.

Imagine my surprise! Not to say delight! A fire crackled in the stove. On top was a leaden tub, the kind I remembered from the many cold-water flats my parents and I inhabited on our run across the Continent. Many were only suited for soaking our sore feet. We rarely took a full bath. This one was large enough for a person to fit in. A small person. And, there was water bubbling in it.

"Where did you get the water?" I cried out.

"A well behind the shed outside."

"You pumped water from a well in this weather?" And I had called him a taskmaster and other vile names. I had moped about his lack of attentiveness for my needs when everything he did was for me. Ingrate that I was!

"You must take off these rags if you want to bathe." He lifted the steaming tub off the stove and placed it on the floor. He then turned his attention on the buttons of my overcoat, which was still a damp, stiff shell. It required considerable effort to undo them. The other layers in which I was wrapped like a mummy unraveled with less resistance under his nimble fingers. The tub accommodated my medium frame quite comfortably but was not big enough for two, especially not one of Kafka's size. He had to wait for me to rise, luxuriantly refreshed, like foamy Aphrodite, from the most exquisite bath I ever experienced. He was ready to receive me holding up a large white terry-cloth towel. He draped it around my trembling body and gave it a vigorous rub down.

While I had been soaking, breathing in the soothing fumes from the steaming bathwater that widen my sinuses, he had been rummaging through the inn's closets for something that could serve as a towel. He found several from the time when this place was an inn. The man's resourcefulness, let alone thoughtfulness, never failed to astound. So eager to wash off all the grime that had settled on my body, I hadn't even given a thought to how I would dry myself off.

When he had finished his own ablutions, I was happy to towel him off in return. In the process, our lips and bodies met, and we made love right there in the inn's kitchen.

The ablutions we later applied to the handguns no longer seemed like much of a chore to me. We went merrily to work chatting, mostly silly nonsense. In the afternoon, we went outside. A thin beam of sun cut a bright shaft through the cloud cover. We played in the snow engaging in snowball fights like children. We were all alone in the world. The last two people alive. The echo of his laughter made my heart flutter with giddy joy. For one evening, my romantic fantasy of

the middle of an impenetrable German forest any more real than the wildest cinematic fiction?

The questions and the surprises were never-ending. I had lost the original goal of my journey almost completely from my sight. The woman in Berlin, for whom I had undertaken this journey, had become a minor extra in the drama. The picture I had created of her and carried in my heart and mind, the figure of a lone woman in a chair by a window, her dulled eyes fixed on the outside without comprehension, the envelope in her hand the only lifeline to a former existence, had become blurred, out of focus. Concern for my grandmother had been pushed to the rear of my mind while I was lost in a wintry forest, abandoning my body and soul with here-to-fore unknown passion and desire to a man of whom I knew next to nothing.

The plot was soon to thicken and stick to my feet like hot tar. The knock on the solid oak front door intensified from polite rapping to impatient rapid-fire banging. The pounding of my terrified heart intensified with every knock. What to do? Where was Kafka? I had at least the presence of mind to cover myself. I grabbed the all-too-big military overcoat Kafka had given me from the hook behind the door to our little chamber of love.

Our visitors from what I presumed was the military police had not strayed into this inn by chance. Since hiding would be useless, I decided to face them head-on. Just as I was about to open the door to the vestibule, a booming voice halted my steps, a voice unmistakable and familiar. The Prussian cadence demanding to know if anybody was there made the blood freeze in my veins. Then he said in English: "They must be here. Unless they got lost."

Before I could fathom the meaning of this statement, Kafka came in through the back door with an arm full of firewood. At the sight of the visitors, he dropped the logs on the floor and with a bright smile and both arms extended wide, proclaimed: "It's about time!"

The man was none other than my nemesis I knew as Major Emil Zweig of the United State Army. The elusive Major Zweig, I should say. The man who had thrown me into a pit together with Nazi criminals and left me there to rot. I was not favorably disposed toward this Major Zweig, to put it mildly.

Kafka did not share my misgivings about this Major Zweig. The two men greeted each other with a jovial embrace. Kafka told him about our escape from the camp and the at times arduous foot march through the woods.

"But we made it, we overcame all obstacles," he stated with pride, adding that everything had been found in good order here at the hideout. What did that mean? Zweig warmed his hands over the embers in the fireplace while Kafka threw on a few fresh logs to revive the flames.

The other man who slipped out from under a heavy coat turned out to be, to my delight, the faithful Sergeant Bickers. He seemed a bit at a loss what to do while the conversation was carried on in a language foreign to him. Although he was the one who had taken me to the prison, he had been acting on orders from the Major, and I held no grudge against him. Given the baffling scene that was unfolding before me that morning, the sergeant's presence was a comfort though I knew he would not go against his commanding officer.

"Howdy!" he said to me with a shy crooked grin as I stood suspended in the doorway between the little room and the hall. I took a step back, wishing to quietly disappear. Too late. The merry men at the fireplace turned around just then.

"There she is!" Zweig called out in German.

She? Who was she? No name. I had become a woman without a name. It occurred to me that in all the time we spent together, not even in the most intimate moments, had Kafka called me by my name, not my real name, which I presumed he didn't know, nor that German name I went by. He never called me anything, not even some made-up term of endearment as lovers tend to do.

I took a deep breath, lifted my head, chin up. I would face up to my judge and executioner unbowed. Time to abandon all pretense. He rushed toward me as if he wanted to embrace an old friend. But I kept him at arms' length. As for Kafka, who looked on with an amused smirk as if he were watching a droll theatrical scene, I didn't deign to give him a single look.

"Major Zweig! What a surprise!" I replied in English with all the effluent flair of a salonnière. "Under the circumstances, I cannot say it is a pleasant surprise. I hope you didn't lose your way in the woods in this dreadful climate." The sergeant snickered behind his superior's back. He was on my side.

"My dear Miss Safran let's not be . . ." he began with a hem and a haw.

"Aha! You do know my name!" I called out as if I had caught him in a devious act red-handed. "Let's put an end to masquerades and deceits! Shall we?"

"If I remember correctly, it was you who was doing the masquerading," he replied. "I don't think you are in any position to call the shots."

Luckily for him, I had left my little Roth-Steyr under my pillow, or I would have shot him right then and there with an extra bullet reserved for the traitor Kafka.

"Touché!" I conceded instead. "It may be best for both of us to bury the hatchet for the moment and put our cards on the table."

"Very well, then. But as a courtesy to Herr Kafka, we should conduct this proceeding in German."

"I beg to differ. My preferred language is English. Besides Herr Kafka, if that is his name, is not deserving of any special consideration."

Zweig's eyebrows went up to his hairline. His eyes darted back and forth between my pouting face and Kafka's obliviously amused smug.

"Okay," he concluded. "I can see some clarification is needed here . . . in the interest of all parties."

"Sergeant! Bring in the supplies from the vehicle. And take your time," he ordered in his best Prussian tone. Then switching to German, he asked Kafka if he would give the sergeant a hand.

"Let's sit. We are not in a courtroom, you know." He took the high-back Queen Anne style fauteuil with the worn blue velvet covering. I plunged down into the sinkhole of the saggy sofa.

"Whatever your misgivings about Kafka, he is an essential part of the mission. I am afraid you will have to put up with him a while longer," he began.

What mission?

He would come to that later. For the moment, more immediate matters were begging for an answer.

"You seem to know him well. Is Kafka his real name?"

"Yes, it is. Not uncommon where he comes from."

"And yours is Zweig? How neat!"

"Right again. Not uncommon either, especially among Jews. Sort of like Safran. Or Hauser for that matter. Since I can take credit for that invention, I was naturally delighted that you got the allusion."

"Wait a minute! Wait a minute! You read my notebook! I was wondering what happened to it after you confiscated my belongings and tossed me into a hell with Nazi shrews. If you don't mind, I would like to get my private possessions back, including my notebook."

"In due time, in due time," he waved his hand at me. If it was meant to reassure, it did nothing of the kind.

"It's in safekeeping, and you will get it back, I promise. . . when this is all over. Meanwhile, we wouldn't want it to fall into the wrong hands."

"When what is over? And what do you have to do with the name a man in Amsterdam chose for me?" If I could only lift myself out of the chair and get a hold of my little pistol!

"I understand why you would find all this confusing . . ." he began with an infuriatingly sanctimonious tone.

"Don't patronize me! Bastard!" My shriek spiraled into the upper registers. Never mind the pistol, my bare hands will do just fine for squeezing the daylights out of this scoundrel. Lucky for him the sunken couch held me firmly ensconced.

"Now, now, let's be civil. If you let me speak, all will become clear. You were chosen for a very special mission, a dangerous mission." He paused. His thoughts seemed to float off to somewhere I was not privileged to follow. Chosen for a special mission? Should I be proud? Humbug!

"Stop beating around the bush and get to the point, please."

"Fair enough," he conceded.

I never played chess myself, but I've watched the players in Washington Square Park often enough with fascination to know something about the rules of the game. My opponent in this game wasn't chess mate yet, but I had him cornered and was eager to find out what his next move would be.

He wriggled in his seat and cleared his throat. I didn't need to draw on that superfluous human behavior class I once took to detect his discomfort. He even ran his hand through his thinning, light brown hair!

Regaining his military comportment, he intoned: "Let me start with the mission for which we recruited you . . ."

First it was chosen, now it was recruited. Recruited or chosen for what? I certainly did not volunteer for this mission. Whatever fantastic plot they were hatching here, Kafka was no doubt in cahoots.

At this point, the plot was thickening, even sickening. A cliché? Perhaps, but apt in this case. Clichés give the mind a hook to latch onto when obstreperous puzzle pieces refuse to fit. Still embedded in the valley of the couch and unable to sit up straight, I leaned forward as far as I could. With neck craned, I probed his face, trying to lance his evasive eyes. He grimaced. His head bobbed from side to side. Then he abruptly jumped up from the chair. He stood over me and looked me straight in the eye.

"You will understand once you see the full picture," he said and paused again. This shadow play was more nerve-wracking than our first encounter in Frankfurt.

"I would like nothing better than to understand what the full picture is," I said calmly.

"Please go on," I coaxed in as sweet, conciliatory, non-confrontational, encouraging a tone as my boiling blood would allow.

The "full picture" he finally unveiled was a tableau of a most astounding, harebrained scheme in which I was to play an unwitting lead part.

I should have been flattered, but I was not.

"You knew all along who I was. You knew I understood your conversations with the sergeant. You set me up!"

"You were chosen! Think about it that way!" Zweig tried to assuage my anger.

"Why me? Why would you choose me?" I was close to tears. What irony! I was not only part of the chosen people but chosen from among the chosen.

"Why me?" I insisted over and over. "There must have been others better qualified."

"Don't sell yourself short. Native fluency of language, familiarity with customs and culture were essential."

"I was a child when I left. Any number of people would be more suitable. New York does not lack German émigrés."

"You are also a writer. You have imagination. And, you have shown courage and perseverance during the trial of Viktor Erdos in the murder case of Stella Berger."

"You know about that?"

"Doesn't everybody? It was in all the papers for years. Then there's your book. You are well known. Give yourself some credit."

"Okay, I'll pat myself on the back if you will. I was lured into Germany under false pretenses. Since the country is sealed off under Allied rules, I couldn't just get on a boat and disembark in Hamburg; I had to assume a German identity. I presume the man and his wife in Amsterdam are part of this whole scheme."

"In a way, yes. They are in the people-smuggling business. We were able to win them over for the cause and make good use of their services."

"My compliments! I must hand it to you, Major, a very impressive feat." Winning them over no doubt involved subtle hints their business operation might be in peril.

I finally managed to yank myself out of the sagging couch. I needed to stretch my legs and at the same time clear my head that felt as if heaps of debris had been dumped on it. I paced for a while under the major's watchful eye.

"What about Berlin?" I came to a halt facing him, eye to eye; we were about the same height. "Was that fiction too?"

"That depends on what you would call fiction. . ." "Stop twisting my words. You know what I mean. Was that part of the made-up story, a concoction, a fabrication, a fairy tale to lure little Red Riding Hood into the forest?"

"Yes and no," he hemmed and hawed.

"There is no grandmother, is there? No old woman with amnesia vegetating in a Jewish hospital - if there even is a Jewish hospital in Berlin -- clutching an envelope that bears my New York address in New York. You knew my soft spot. It was a safe guess. Not hard at all. Many grandmothers were left behind and ended up in Theresienstadt. But for you to exploit such a situation, to raise a person's hope that her grandmother might have survived is the epitome of infamy! How cruel can you be?"

"Close but not quite. Cruel times require cruel methods." The sadness with which he said these words made me listen up. I looked at him and saw, for the first time, a man whose face was marked by deep sorrow. Like me, he had been a refugee who was lucky to have made it to America. More I didn't know about him. I could only guess. No doubt, he too had lost members of his family, maybe close family left behind. Even if not, he could not help but be shaken by what had befallen our people. At that moment, my grievances and complaints appeared as petty squabbles. Within the grand scheme, my concerns dissolved as droplets in the vast sea of the tragic events.

"Why all the deception?" I implored him. "Why on earth didn't you or someone come to me directly. You could have won me over in a cinch."

"You had to be put to the test. Tried out in the field. We had to see how you would handle the emotional stress of being in this country, among these people, pretending to be one of them. It would not be a task for the faint-hearted, nor could we risk having a freelancer on our hands. You performed very satisfactorily."

"A trial by fire and water," I demurred. "I don't even want to know by what measures my performance has been assessed, or what criteria were applied. Just tell me, why I had to be thrown into with the dregs of humanity? Which circle of hell did you have in mind?"

"That was the crucible. . ."

"I am glad you have a fancy word for it!" I cried out, unable to again hold back my ire.

"Words, words, words! No word comes even close to describing what I went through in that snake pit! Was it meant to be Purgatory or Inferno? I don't get all the Christian symbolism. I had to descend into hell to be resurrected?"

"My sincerest apologies. Symbolism has nothing to do with it. But the experience with some hard-core Nazi women was an essential step in your training. Kafka was dispatched to help you cope with the rough patches."

"How kindly! Oh yes, he performed very satisfactorily! Outstanding, if you need to know. Like you, he talks a very good game. Two peas of a pod! He's a master of deceit, a virtuoso of the sleight of hand."

"Once you give your bitterness toward him—which by the way I don't understand—a chance to subside, you will come to see him in a different light. Be assured, you will never find a more steadfast friend and protector."

I wondered how well the two men knew each other. Their affectionate embrace on greeting each other, their easy-going camaraderie while chatting in front of the fireplace made me think theirs must be a friendship that went way back, most likely to the time before the war.

My question was blown away by an arctic wind streaming in from outside. The front door flung open with a crash. The crouched figures of Kafka and Bickers exhaling dense plumes of breath hauled in boxes and crates of varying sizes and apparently of considerable weight.

Looks like we're in for a long hibernation, I thought. Although I still questioned the wisdom of the undertaking, I understood, or tried to understand, the two Jewish participants. But why would a country boy from Arkansas like Sergeant Bickers collude in what amounted to an act of treason? Did he put loyalty to his commanding officer above loyalty to his country? Was he mindlessly following orders? In our previous encounter, I had gained the impression of a simple but honest man.

"He's a fine soldier and patriotic American," the Major confirmed. "Like most Americans, he fought in this war for democracy and freedom, or something idealistic like that. The fighting in France was rough going. Once we crossed the Rhine, the German heartland fell into our hands with little resistance. Just one pesky little town near here gave us trouble. They kept us holed up for two weeks in these woods before they finally hoisted the white flag. What they thought to accomplish by taking on the American army was and remains a mystery. Turn the tide of the war?

"But we did get to know this area. We set up quarter in this abandoned inn. Once they finally surrendered, we continued our march south. Our battalion followed the Danube into Austria. It was a beautiful spring day, the sun's glistening rays danced innocently, playfully one might say, on the surface of the rolling waters. The troops were in a cheerful mood; the war was over; everybody felt a sense of relief. The rest would be a piece of cake.

"Then we came upon Mauthausen, a picturesque medieval town nestled on the banks of the Danube. A small town like many others. Abundant Old-World charm! Only this one was metastasized by a cancer. What he saw in the nearby camp shook Bickers to the core. There wasn't a man who wasn't affected by the horrendous scenes. Bickers' face turned from white with horror to red with rage in a second. I had never seen him like this before. He was always an easy-going southern country boy. He swore he would do anything to avenge - he used that word - this horrendous crime against humanity. People react differently and in varying degrees. Most are deeply shocked. They long to forget, go home and get on with their lives. Bickers wanted to do more. For him, the war wasn't over."

"And for you?" My throat was parched.

"How could it be?" he said.

The door was now closed, keeping out the wind though not the cold. I folded my arms around my shivering body. Zweig placed a blanket over my shoulders. We stood in silent accord. I wanted to reach for his hand. Not knowing how he would take such a gesture, I refrained. Instead, we walked together to the entrance of the kitchen. The two men, one from Arkansas, the other from Prague, neither speaking the others' language, worked hand in hand sorting a load of boxes, opening some on the table and leaving others in a corner.

"Shouldn't we give them a hand?" I asked.

"We would only get in the way." Zweig shrugged. "The sergeant and I have to get back to Frankfurt soon. You and Kafka will be here on your own. The operation depends on the participants working together harmoniously. It is important not to let personal rankling get in the way."

The Major and I returned to the fireplace. A long silence ensued between us. We stared into the flames, each lost in thoughts of our own.

Zweig's usually snarky expression had given way to a pensive, even pained mien. He seemed to be straining to retrieve a memory from the distant or even more recent past.

"It was in Mauthausen where we came upon him," he finally began.

"He recognized me right away. He waved and called out my name from behind a barbed-wire fence. Believe me when I say I have never felt such utter shame in my life. Me, the well-fed American officer, the liberator who was riding into camp in a chauffeur-driven jeep yet fully aware that by rights I should have been on the other side of that fence. It was difficult to distinguish between individuals from among the haggard men, their skulls bare, their sunken eyes sunken staring at us. Tt was hard at first to detect the elegant bon-vivant I once knew underneath the shrouded, emaciated body. Then the spark in his eyes and the laughter gave him away."

Chapter 6

A Viennese Bon-Vivant

Hard to picture Kafka as anything but the big strong, self-confident man with the thick, shoulder-length black hair, laced with a filigree of silver threads, a man in the fullness of life. Elegant, effete bon vivant? Possibly. People did have lives before the war, lives that were altered irrevocably. He was considerably older than I, by at least ten years, maybe more. Kafka emaciated and in rags was an image hard for me to conjure up even though it had been less than two years since the liberation of the camps.

I mulled over Zweig's words that by rights he should have been on the other side of the fence. By rights of what? By rights of being a member of a despised tribe? He had a strange way of expressing himself. By that right, we should all have been on the other side of that barbed-wire fence, or dead.

We stood by the fireplace staring into the flames, each trailing off into our world of thoughts. He seemed as much at a loss of what to say as I was. To break the unease of having to move my weight from one foot to the other, I took possession of the high-back winged armchair with the frayed velvet cover.

"You knew him before the war?" I finally broke the silence.

"Yes," he said almost inaudibly, his back toward me. "He was my neighbor in Vienna. He and his wife. We were friends."

Of course, Kafka would have had a wife; maybe children even. Nothing surprising about that. But there surely was more. The far-away look in Zweig's eyes testified to a painful memory of something he had witnessed.

"You have heard of Lenka Ostrova?" he asked. I shook my head.

"Well, no wonder, you were only a child back then," he said as if he had to find an excuse for what would otherwise be an inexcusable gap in my education.

"Lenka Ostrova was one of the greatest operatic sopranos of her time! Perhaps of all time!" he declaimed; his voice rang with unexpected ardor. "Her Traviata, her Carmen, her Tosca brought audiences to their feet all over Europe. But she was equally, perhaps even more, celebrated as a Wagnerian. She was also Kafka's wife."

He gave this information some time to sink in before continuing.

"They met in Prague. He was a medical student; she a budding opera singer. Though she was older than he by several years, he was madly in love with her. When she was called to sing Brünnhilde in Vienna in 1930, Kafka followed her. As far as I know, they got married there. He finished his studies while she appeared at every opera house in Europe. From Berlin to London to Milan, she was celebrated, acclaimed everywhere. Eventually, she settled for a permanent engagement at the Vienna opera, forgoing an offer to appear at the Metropolitan Opera in New York. A fateful decision, perhaps."

Again, he fell into a pensive silence.

"You knew them then?" I prodded him to go on.

"Yes, quite well. I had moved to Vienna in 1936 to finish my studies, which was no longer possible in Germany. Kafka was by then an established physician and my anatomy teacher. We also happened to live next to each other in the First District and so became quite friendly. I was then a great fan of Wagner and opera in general. Kafka often invited me to his box for performances. He was there every night to hear her sing. She sang many different roles from Tosca, Traviata, superb in all of them. But it was Brünnhilde above all. The immolation scene! Nothing more divine on earth!"

"The immolation scene!" he repeated. The glow in his demeanor abruptly turned into a dark shadow. I had no idea what he was talking about.

"That last immolation, unforgettable, yes. You have to picture the scene, the voice, the passion, the intensity, the transfixed audience . . . the awesome figure in a flowing white robe on a horse . . . on that March day . . ." He broke off, seemingly at a loss to put into words what happened.

Opera had never interested me. The few operatic performances my grandparents took me to as a child impressed me as overwrought. I had never listened to this kind of music long enough to appreciate it. A Wagner opera would have been like a forbidden fruit. The name alone, if it were to come up at all, somehow it must have (though I couldn't recall a specific instance), was anathema in the émigré community. A view I would have freely and mindlessly espoused had the subject ever come up. This immolation scene was a place I could not follow.

"They pulled her off the horse," I heard him say in a hollow, far away voice. "Dragged her off the stage. They shouted obscenities at her . . . the usual insults they hurled at Jews. The audience sat transfixed in total silence. It seemed that nobody dared to breathe.

Kafka shot up from his seat, stormed after them. I tried to keep pace. Outside the Ringstraße was blocked by hundreds of kneeling men and women, scrubbing the cobblestones, being taunted and baited by an army of thugs. Her white gown billowed in the harsh March wind. Kafka cut his way through the crowd. He knelt beside her. A thug had put a toothbrush into her hands. She scrubbed furiously at the stones. Hours passed. I spotted the tenor Rudolf Schwamm, Ostrova's singing partner in so many productions, among the local bystanders watching the spectacle of Jews prostrate in the street. Standing next to him, in fact, leaning against him, was another member of the cast, a second-tier soprano, Elfriede Kling. I detected a faint smirk in her face. The diva, who had been worshiped and venerated by the same crowd until just a moment before, had been brought down. Lenka kept on scrubbing and scrubbing furiously. She refused to follow Kafka's entreaties to stop. She was still scrubbing when the sun began to set. Never said a word.

Finally, Kafka pulled her up into his arms and started to walk. The throng of jeering goons parted under Kafka's glowering stare like the waters of the Red Sea. He took her home. The Gestapo came back the next morning. She was still in her white gown, though torn and stained with mud and filth from the street. That was the last time Kafka saw her alive. He tried to find out where they had taken her, where they were keeping her. Her mutilated body, her golden throat cut, was found floating in the Danube canal three weeks later. She did receive a state funeral at the behest of the director of the opera. Probably the last time the music world showed some backbone, the last act of defiance against the propaganda minister.

Wagner's music, defiled by a Jewish coloratura, had been restored to its pristine state, the limping midget declared to the cheering crowd."

"Kafka left Vienna in the summer of 1938. From what I know, he returned to Prague to his mother and sisters and younger brother. I saw him off at the train station, not expecting to ever see him again. There was no laughter; the spark in his eyes had gone out when we said good-bye. His steely gaze and resolute bearing reassured me that come what may, no one and nothing would grind him down. So I tried to reassure myself. When the war was finally over and won, and the stories of the murders and atrocities the Germans had committed came to light, doubts seeped into my mind. Could he have survived? Well, he did. Fate, it couldn't have been mere chance, brought us back together."

"You were always thinking of your friend then?" I said.

"I never forgot him. Always wondered where he was, what might have become of him. I made it to America. I was lucky. My Chicago uncle signed the affidavit. Never got back to medicine. With all the crises, the growing Nazi threat, the disastrous conference in Munich, Chamberlain's surrender of the Sudetenland, then the takeover of the rest of Czechoslovakia, I knew war would come. Even then, I was sure, maybe hoped, the United States would become involved sooner or later. I studied law and joined the US Army. I wanted to be ready for the good fight."

He pulled out a hip bottle together with a pack of Pall Malls. He took a long swig and lit a cigarette. I waved away the offering. The room filled with the smell of strong liquor and smoke. For once, it didn't bother me.

The story he told left me confused and crushed as if a blow from a sledgehammer had numbed my senses and split open my heart. Zweig joined the men in the kitchen. Had he even been aware of my presence while he was reminiscing? I was still grappling with what I had heard when the chatter of an animated exchange reached my ear. Kafka was arguing about something they were doing. Life was going on.

I knew then, I swore then to myself, come what may, I would not let Kafka down. Whatever the task, whatever the mission in which I was to play a part, I would hold up my end.

A sudden deafening noise jolted me out of my ruminations and my seat. Through the din rang out Kafka's laughter and excited shouts of "there it goes! there it goes!" He came running in, seized me by the waist, wrapped one arm tight around me, the other took hold of mine and pulled it high up in the air. Our bodies fused; he bent me over so low I thought my spine would break. Then with a jerking pull, we were again upright, his face close against mine, gliding over the floor, back and forth, in rhythmic harmony to blaring sounds of music.

"What are we doing?" I cried.

"Tango!" he shouted. "Tango, my dear! Let's tango!"

Even though I was not much of a dancer and had never tangoed before, I became a pliable tool in his arms, marveling to myself how easy it was to follow his lead. My last attempt on a dance floor had been strutting the Polka at an Octoberfest in Yorkville on the Upper East Side of Manhattan. But that was under very different circumstances and for a very different purpose. Why would this even cross my mind at this rapturous moment when I was being swayed about, lifted and dipped, by a dream of a man?

But he was no dream. He was very real. He was as adept at practical matters like setting up a gramophone and a radio station, not the least shooting a gun, as at dance moves with the elegance of a Lipizzaner stallion. His more private talents he had demonstrated in the previous night.

The radio was set up in a dank cavern of the cellar with the help of Bickers who was also an army communications specialist. I was struck with amazement to see these two men, the farm boy from Arkansas and the European sophisticate, communicate in the absence of a common language, but both driven by a common purpose.

Chapter 7

The Valkyrie

Our sequestered fairy-tale life, while we were waiting for the thaw of spring, revolved around the gramophone. Before turning in at night, we danced. Kafka's taste ran toward Latin rhythms over Viennese waltzes or polkas. But our life was not all tango. There was a more serious purpose to all this play, as I was to find out much to my chagrin. All this frivolity and swooning in Kafka's arms while soothing my needy soul for closeness aroused in me considerable consternation whenever I took a step back for a broader view of the scene.

The gramophone, as it turned out, had been set up for the benefit of my education, my musical education. I was to be educated, drilled really, not in Latin dance steps, but in the music of Richard Wagner. Six hours a day, from morning to late afternoon, I sat staring mesmerized at this infernal instrument spewing out the screeching sounds from the Twilight of the Gods, recorded on stacks of shellac disks Zweig had scrounged up from somewhere. The pièce de résistance was the much-vaunted immolation scene, Brünnhilde's farewell to the fallen Siegfried, or something of the sort. I listened, over and over, and then once more, never being able to muster Zweig's glowing, almost religious fervor for the bloodcurdling screams of Lenka Ostrova immortalized on those spinning disks.

The voice remained long after the Americans had left. Kafka cranked up the machine, placed the tone arm on the disk, a "black matzah" as a popular song had spoofed the new craze back in the twenties. While it was playing, Kafka went down into the cellar, presumably to listen to the radio leaving me alone with Ostrova's plaintive voice.

Her ululating shrieks seeped into my bloodstream, engulfed my every being, stirred up a witches' brew of emotions. The voice, which reached into staggering registers of lows and highs, the chirping pitch of the music, the absurd words emanating from the well-worn grooves became etched inextricably in my head. My brain itself became a spinning disk with grooves carved ever deeper and deeper. No respite for me from the Valkyrie's anguished vocalizations.

"Stack high the piles of wood at the river's edge!" The screeching sound clouded my brain like smoke billowing from a stake, the preferred method of the Inquisition for punishing heretics and non-believers, even in moments of nocturnal lovemaking.

"What is the matter?" Kafka asked softly. I was sitting upright in bed, my body shaking. He pulled me into his arms, stroked my hair, kissed away my tears.

He could not possibly be oblivious to the effect the presence of another person, another woman, his wife, would have on me. She was there, a ghost, yet very real. Her voice soared over our little fairy-tale abode like lark spreading its wings. She was there on that black disk which he insisted I listen to ad nauseam. Never said a word about her. He had left it to Zweig to relate the story of the life and death of Lenka Ostrova. Was it too painful for him to speak of her, of the events of that spring in 1938? I would understand. But now that I was here, had been drawn into his life, had been wooed and loved, why not speak to me? I had earned the right to know how he felt.

"Talk to me," I begged.

"Talk to you about what?" Could he be that obtuse not to recognize the elephant looming over us?

"About her, about you, about what happened, about what you did before it happened. All that. About why I have to listen to her voice day in day out."

"Zweig told you the story, didn't he?"

The story? Are we talking about some ancient lore?

"Yes, he did tell me a few things about what happened. But from his perspective. I'd like to hear yours."

He mumbled something which vaguely sounded like you must get some sleep. How could he? What was I to him? Just a tool, a diversion, a slave, a means to some crazy end?

The memory of a previous disastrous love affair, better to say entanglement, stoked my anger even more. This situation was different. I wanted this man who could be so kind and gentle, even loving, to talk to me. That's all I wanted. Just to tell me where we were going with this and how the past still informed the present in this godforsaken forest in the middle of post-war, prostrate Germany.

"Can't you understand what effect this presence has on me?"

"What presence?"

"The voice! Her presence!" I screamed. "Your wife's presence. The one whose voice is sucking the life out of me."

"You are speaking of Lenka Ostrova, I presume."

"Yes, who else? I understand if you still love her, that you want to keep her memory alive after all that happened to her.

Nobody has more sympathy. But why are you torturing me? What have I done except love you? I am even willing to be a stand-in for the love you have lost. Only talk to me! This silence, this secrecy is driving me out of my mind!"

"The love I lost?" he repeated. A strange, harsh darkness clouded his demeanor. "Love? Is that what Zweig told you? Don't make me laugh! He was in love with her, with her persona, like everybody else. The siren, the Valkyrie! I hated her! Hated her and that Rudolf Schwamm. But . . ."

Here he used a German play of words for which there is no exact translation. He said laughing: "*Schwamm drüber*!" which means something like let's not talk about it or let's ignore it, basically, enough of this, let bygones be bygones. A nice pun, but rather out of place and not a very satisfying explanation as far as I was concerned. He had just dropped a bomb and then laughed it off. I was in shock.

For a moment, I caught a glimpse of what was behind the mask of the outward bravura. In a way, it was strangely comforting to find he had a vulnerable spot, a Siegfried shoulder, an Achilles heel, or whatever body part was affected.

"Artemisia, my dear, dear Artemisia!" he whispered, gently stroking my head as if to smooth away the pain of an anguished child. My ears went up. For the first time, the very first time, my name, my real name came over his lips.

"When all this is over," he said, still whispering and stroking, a wistful gaze in his eyes, "when what needs to be done is done, then, my darling, we'll go to Palestine, you and I. Life will be good there."

Another war-ravaged country! But, of course, this one would be different. It was the land of the Jews, the ancient homeland of our people. Again, no question whether I want to go there, just the presumption that I would follow. A few days before, I would have declared my readiness to follow him to the ends of the earth, as any love-besotted girl would. But never mind about that just then. I was more interested in probing the first part of what he stated so matter-of-factly.

"When what is all over? What is it that we need to do?" I insisted. "For heaven's sake, stop keeping me in the dark!"

"We shall kill Rudolf Schwamm and his little wife, Elfriede Kling!"

Too many bombshells in one night even for someone like me who had been under bombardment, been battered, crushed and uplifted at the same time during an ill-conceived, ill-fated journey! What could one more blow do to me?

"As soon as the snow melts and spring brings this dormant landscape to life, we shall leave this forest. We are going to Bayreuth!"

One could set this poetic effusion to music and sing a song about it. That is if this were some enchanting fairytale, which it was decidedly not.

Chapter 8

Immolations

"Why?" I asked.

"Why what?"

"Why would you, we, want to kill these people?"

"Artemisia, Artemisia! My dear Artemisia!"

"Stop calling me that!" I screamed. I should have been pleased that he finally called me by my real name. But not like this. "Don't patronize me! I am not a child!"

"Forgive me," he pouted. "I forgot you were sheltered in the émigré haven of New York while here, in Europe, raged an orgy of death."

"This is unfair, so unfair!" was all I managed to gasp. "This is a low blow, the absolute lowest."

The next moment he enfolded me in his arms, begged for forgiveness, he didn't know what had gotten into him, he never wanted to hurt me, and on and on.

I pushed him off and moved away. I had put up with all the volatility, the secretiveness, the unpredictability, mostly because I had no choice, but also because I felt there was a special bond between us from the moment he had told me "You are *unsere Leut*"; a bond that had been sealed by what I thought was love.

"Please, you must forgive me. I don't know what came over me. No excuse. You are right; it is very unfair to you. Not only unfair but outright reprehensible, disgraceful, shameful to say the least."

Piling up self-incriminatory adjectives was not going to assuage my hurt feelings, not then and not so quickly. I pressed for more explanations. I wanted to know more, not only about what he and Zweig called the "mission" but about him, about his wife, about his life.

"Our mission is to avenge the murder of Lenka Ostrova!" he declared sitting up. There was that plural pronoun again. I doubted that he was speaking in the imperial we but meant what he said: he and I were to be partners in crime. Never mind that I hadn't signed up for the part.

"I wouldn't call it a crime. Retribution is a more fitting way of putting it. A Sicilian Vesper! Mine is the vengeance, saith the Lord!"

Now he was waxing operatic and biblical all at once. A small voice in the back of my head sounded an alarm. This Kafka may be a madman; in fact, he may be stark raving mad.

"A moment ago, you told me you hated her. Zweig painted a picture of a devoted couple going through life on wings of love and success—a champagne-and-whipped-cream union." I hated myself for waxing so purple. Damn that Zweig.

"The way he saw it," I added to redeem myself, "the devoted husband practically worshiped the ground under the wife's feet, or something like that."

"Zweig is a romantic fool. He was so besotted with her, a true acolyte. He was the ground kisser. Although I am quite sure, he was probably the one man, maybe the only man, with whom she did not sleep. He's not that kind of a man."

I was too intent on finding out more about Kafka's relationship with the opera singer to care about what kind of man Zweig was. I was determined to gain entrance into the make-believe world of the Kafka/Ostrova operetta garnished with waltzes and whipped cream and all that Viennese schmaltz. It's an age-old piece of wisdom that one never knows what goes on behind the façade married couples put up for public consumption. But I had felt I earned the right to gain a glimpse behind the curtain of this vanished stage.

"If you hated her, why are you so bent on revenging her murder? And wasn't it the Gestapo who killed her? Why these particular people?"

"What I meant to say was I don't love her, not anymore."

"Wait a moment; there is a difference between not loving and hating. You said you hated her."

"An exaggeration." So now it was an exaggeration. A very strange exaggeration considering the passion with which it was uttered.

"Zweig said you stood by her while she was . . . she . . . the incident with the toothbrush . . ."

"Of course, I wouldn't abandon her. How could I? They came the next morning and took her away. By then, there was nothing I could do. I felt helpless. She didn't even ask for my help or beg me to protect her. She knew it would have been no use. I am still amazed at how willingly she went along in accepting her fate. That otherworldly gaze into some distant Valhalla! Even then, under those circumstances, she was still inside the Valkyrie, as if Brünnhilde was a dybbuk come to possess her body. I was her way of dealing with the inevitable. I should have done something. But what?"

He went on about his failure to intervene and prevent her arrest and torturous death. He was still smarting over the fact that he, the strong, powerful Kafka was unable to save her. Then he said something startling, maybe inadvertently, that revealed another angle.

"I should have killed Schwamm long ago," he said. "I had my suspicions that he and his wife were party members even before the Anschluss. They made it big later under the regime. Lenka Ostrova had to be eliminated to make way for them on their path to fame and glory. He knew she was Jewish, even though nobody else did."

"I warned Lenka that he would use it against her one day. She laughed it off. Schwamm, she said, was wax in her hands. Without her, he was nobody. His vocal abilities were minor. He served at the Vienna opera at her pleasure. In other words, she tolerated him at her side on stage as long as he performed satisfactorily in her bed."

A lover betrayed? A cuckolded husband's vendetta? That's what this was all about? A melodrama of betrayal and retribution! How very operatic! Kafka as "Bayazzo" hardly matched the virile picture I had formed of him. For this, I should become complicit in a murder and risk imprisonment or worse. Vigilantism would not find leniency from the Allied Command who had their hands full keeping the lid on seething plots and conspiracies, including acts of revenge and retaliation by unrehabilitated, unrepentant Nazis.

"I did love her once," Kafka took up the thread of his musings in an almost nostalgic tone. "A youthful obsession. The fancy of an eighteen-year-old fed on romantic notions like the Young Werther. One difference, I didn't have to kill myself over unrequited love. When the object of one's veneration requites who can refuse? Later I learned, she had a penchant, better yet, an insatiable appetite for dreamy youths. Why she kept me on beyond my prime has always puzzled me. The other puzzle was how Schwamm fit her predilections."

"She married you, didn't she?"

"No, no. We were never really married. We had a ceremony of sorts, more a big party to which we invited her friends. In the eyes of the public, and indeed in mine, I was her husband. It just suited her to maintain that pretense. There was a husband lost somewhere in the Bohemian woods and unavailable for a divorce. I never found out much about him. Nor did I want to. It suited me to be part of the endless masquerade of pretense."

"Hard to understand."

"You must understand she did not live in the real world. She lived in an opera, a world of intrigue and pretense. She nurtured a perpetual drama in which people pass themselves off as something they are not—a Fledermaus scenario of masked balls, champagne, flirtations, seductions, petty intrigues. Fortunately for me, I also had my real world of medicine. It was a double life, alternating between day and night. I must admit I relished both. I was a sort of Doctor Jekyll and Mister Hyde, in a white coat by day, in an elegant tuxedo at night. Serious by day, frivolous at night. Until the whole artifice came crumbling down."

He shook his head. A wistful look appeared in his eyes.

"Hard to believe now in retrospect that such a world ever existed. Yes, one could say I loved her. A mutually beneficial *liaison dangereuse*. I was her loyal retainer, the one constant pillar in her life, besides her music. Her music was everything.

The ovations were the life's blood she sucked in and lived for like a vampire.

"When they fished her out of the canal, the workers had enough respect to hand her body over for proper burial. Even those—I know their names—who had cut out her tongue and slit her throat, making sure the divine lark would never soar again, appeared at the funeral, heads dolefully lowered, sniffling into their handkerchiefs, hiding the Schadenfreude behind black veils and under broad-brimmed hats.

"The Gestapo collected and destroyed all of her recordings with a bonfire on Saint Stephan's Square, the place of medieval witch burnings. Hordes of Hitler Youths danced around chanting 'The witch is dead! The witch is dead!' All choreographed by the propaganda minister."

"Some of the recordings survived," I stated the obvious to ease the stifling heaviness that had descended around us.

"Yes, they didn't count on our good friend Emil Zweig. He landed in America with a small suitcase and few belongings. But inside that suitcase was a treasure of Lenka Ostrova recordings. As he told me, he further enriched his collection by placing a notice in some German-language newspaper, forgot the
name. . ."

"*Aufbau*," I filled in.

"Something like that. Ironic name. Anyway, he placed an ad that he was looking to purchase any recordings of Lenka Ostrova people might have brought with them and were willing to sell. Several responses from people in need of money yielded a nice cache. And here we are, reaping the benefit of Zweig's youthful obsession."

"You may see it that way. I feel more like being put through the mill of Wagner's grinding tonalities."

"Brava!" Kafka clapped his hands. "Excellent metaphor! I didn't know you had it in you."

"You've been underestimated me all along," I pouted. "You may take me to be some country cousin. I've lived among the finest of Berlin's snobbiety, I would have you know. Coming up with colorful witticism was a popular parlor game in those circles. The more outrageous and far-fetched, the better. I may have been a child, but I had a good ear, I listened and absorbed like a sponge. That's what makes a writer."

"Snobbiety?" he repeated, smacking his lips as if he were tasting the finest caviar. "Hits the nail on the head. Vienna was not so different from Berlin in those days."

"And Prague?" I ventured.

"Prague? Oh no, very different. Very provincial. At least where I came from," he added with a wistful look as if he were reaching deep into a buried chest of memory.

"Where did you come from?" I spoke softly. Was he even real? An avenging angel, fallen from somewhere if not from heaven?

"My cradle stood on the banks of the Moldau, he began. "At the time of my birth, we lived under the Austro-Hungarian Empire, the Danube Monarchy. Our family name was Kaiser. Yes, Kaiser and I was named Franz Josef after our Imperial Father. Then came the war and the cozy Habsburg arrangement of nationalities went to pieces. Kaput! Splintered, gone! The war was lost, the Kaiser was dead. He was around for so long, we thought he was immortal.

"The inhabitants of what were the provinces of Bohemia and Moravia became citizens of the newly formed country of Czechoslovakia. It was quite a shock for us, especially since the Czechs saw us, the Jews, as Germans. We spoke German rather than Czech and they didn't like us for that reason. Probably just one reason among others.

"Some, my father among them, tried to fit in, to transform themselves into Czechoslovaks. Even though most didn't know the language, or had at best a very rudimentary knowledge, the least they could do was change their names to something more Slavic. We became the Kafkas, and I became František. You can still call me Franz."

There was that laughter again. Did this Kafka, as he called himself, take anything seriously? I seemed to have fallen in with a reincarnation of Till Eulenspiegel, the merry prankster.

"What is funny," he continued slapping the eiderdown. "When Lenka was a provincial singer, traveling from town to town in Bohemia and Moravia and other Eastern parts of the 'ka-und-ka' realm, she was Leah Himmelblau. Once she became Lenka Ostrova, her career took a meteoric rise. Of course, she did have the credentials of voice and personality. We were negotiating with the Metropolitan Opera in New York when the Anschluss came. How she would have fared there, in New York, I don't know. I would not have been able to practice medicine in America, at least not right away.

"She was an addict," he explained in response to my questioning look. "As her personal physician, I prescribed dozens of pills for her, painkillers, mood enhancers, stimulants, depressants. Over time she needed more than prescription drugs could provide. To maintain her stamina on stage, she claimed. But it was more than that. She was a very troubled woman, riddled with self-doubts, in need of constant confirmation of her worth. The endless string of young men was no longer enough to satisfy her needs. She clamored for more and more potent substances. She went from morphine to hashish and heroin, the lot. Illegal and accessible only to medical personnel in a hospital.

"Yes. I became a pimp and a thief, and I hated myself for it. I resented her. But I couldn't abandon her. My ministrations were her lifeline. She would have died without me. In a way, I still loved her, if complete devotion to the exclusion of all ethical considerations can be called love. I needed her as much as she needed me. I did not want to give up the kind of life only she could give me. I was content to dwell in her shadow.

"Summers were spent in the Alps, at clinics for treatments. They all promised success. Mostly run by quacks. (He used the word "*Kurpfuscher*"). The withdrawals were murderous, heart-wrenching to watch. She lapsed every time. By the time we got back to Vienna, it started all over again."

"Bon-vivant" was the term Zweig had used to describe his friend. The quintessential Viennese gentleman whose world was his oyster! How little he must have been aware of the hell reigning next door. Or was he and just didn't say?

"Schwamm found out about her vulnerable spot. Why she took up with him, I will never understand. She always favored young, athletic types. Schwamm, the spongy one (schwammig), was rather portly. I suspect he was blackmailing her. This is the only explanation that would make sense. She was so naïve about the real world, trusting in any flatterer. One should think that Verdi, Wagner, or Leoncavallo had taught her something about human duplicity, treachery, perfidy, which is after all the stuff of opera. The emotional power of her Tosca had no equal. Nor did any of the other heroines she portrayed. Every performance was like a ride on the giant Ferris wheel in the Prater. Exhilarating and terrifying, rousing the audience from the lowest depth to the highest heights in a mind-blowing cycle of catharsis. Lenka Ostrova had no equal. What was an Elfriede Kling compared to her?"

"Zweig says he saw this Elfriede and Schwamm watching the scene on the Ringstraße. A second-tier soprano he called her."

"Little Friedl, Schwamm's wife. A minor talent, great aspirations. The pair was in great favor with the propaganda minister. The Third Reich became their heyday. They even performed Tristan and Isolde in Litzmannstadt, as the Germans called the Polish city of Lodz. Their greatest performance, however, specifically hers, was cutting out Ostrova's tongue before they slit her throat.

My eyes began to droop, my body and mind begged to be spared any more bizarre revelations. There is only so much one take at one time. Head swirling, stomach twisted, blood pulsing, I had never been to the Prater, but at this moment I was riding the giant Ferris wheel, confined in a swinging gondola, rising and falling, up and down, to and fro, in a relentless, unending cycle. I prayed to be let off. He was still speaking when sleep finally overcame me at the graying of dawn. Nestled in the arms of my suddenly garrulous lover, I trailed off into the land of dreams only to find it too haunted by ghostly images from the operatic melodrama that was the lost world of Lenka Ostrova.

Chapter 9

Waiting for Zweig

No more immolations! He promised. No more operatic phonations hammering my brain! No more coloratura effusions battering my soul! My education was declared, if not complete, at least sufficient. I had passed the test with a passing grade. The torment had served its end. Which end? I would see.

Waiting for the snow to melt, we tangoed. Kafka preferred tango over a Strauss waltz. It suits his mood, he said. Maybe we'll go to Argentina. Buenos Aires. Not the land of Israel? What about the Palmach? That too. Well, that first. What about the kibbutz and farming the land, our land? That too. I was getting him confused. Then we'll tango on the beach in Tel Aviv. Good.

Meanwhile, we tangoed in an abandoned bandit's hideout deep in the heart of a German forest. Caminito and Carlos Gardel seeped into my bloodstream, took over the grooves in my brain in place of the Wagnerian ululations. Kafka improvised new ways of molding my body to his. The harmonies of love were never more exhilarating. In our spare time, we polished our weapons. In between, I also practiced my marksmanship. My little Roth-Steyr became my trusted friend. In guns we trust! Kafka joked.

The spring rains washed away the snow and ice. We were stuck in the mud. The forest came alive. To the howling of wolves, grunting of boars, and hooting of owls that filled the nights were added the symphonic early morning calls of a variety of chirping birds. The leaves began to sprout on the deciduous trees and underbrush among the evergreens of this mixed forest. Kafka was getting restless.

"Where is Zweig?" he muttered, pacing, stopping at the window, surveying the surroundings, eyeing the road. "He should be here by now."

Something wasn't going according to plan. I kept my head low and polished my little gun. Must have been the best cared-for little revolver in the world.

To make matters worse, our food supplies were running low. Still, no sign of Zweig. We were running the risk of starving. We rationed what was left of the canned food. One morning Kafka appeared in a coat, hat, and boots, his rifle slung over his shoulder. He was going out hunting for something to roast. I stayed behind. Someone should be here when Zweig comes.

I sat by the window, waiting for Zweig. I too felt Kafka's restless, the urge to move on. No paradise lasts forever. How much longer would we be safe in this forest? The awakening of spring would bring people. Germans love their *Waldspaziergang*, going on excursions in the woods on Sunday afternoons. The hordes were sure to come. Time to break camp. Where was Zweig?

Voices outside roused me from my ruminations. Looking out from behind the curtain, I spotted two men, both in dark green suits with green fedora-style hats. They were wading through the mud in knee-high boots, rifles slung over their shoulders.

"Someone lives here, it seems," I heard one of them say.

"Strange," said the other. "This place was abandoned before the war. The Amis were hiding here back in '45 when we drove them out of town."

"Yeah, those were the days," the other reminisced. "Better be careful. There's a lot of riffraff and criminal types on the loose nowadays."

"The Amis are naïve wimps. They don't know how to keep these people under control. They like to be nice. Must say, even in the PW camp, they treated us well. Plenty to eat."

"They caught you?"

"Yeah, at the last moment. Kept me only for a few months when they declared me free of Nazi sympathies and let me go. What about you?"

"No, they never got me. As soon as it was clear the war was over, I went home, took off the uniform and put on my old forester suit. They took me in, asked a few questions, had me fill out their questionnaire. Wasn't stupid enough to tell them anything. I was immediately denazified, as they call it, and issued that ridiculous piece of paper, the Persilschein."

They advanced toward the front door. In no way would I permit them to get inside. I reached for my little gun, made sure it was loaded and cocked. Hiding it behind my back, I stepped outside.

"Look what we have here!" said the older one. "A gypsy, or maybe a Jewess."

"Are there still any of them around?" said the other.

"Oh, yes! They are back and more of them than ever. They must have been breeding wherever they were hiding during the war. You should see how well they are treated by the American military, preferential, like royalty."

I remained silent. Giving them a piercing eye, I guarded the entrance door like a dragon a treasure hoard.

"Do you speak German?" asked the denazified one who had bemoaned the good old days when riff-raff and criminals weren't allowed to roam German streets and woods.

He got no answer. The rain started to come down more heavily. I stayed dry under the overhang to the entrance door. Their green felt suits got drenched with the moisture.

"Come on, you little witch, you can't leave us out here in the rain getting all soaked."

I stood my ground. He used the familiar "Du" to address me. An insult to show contempt and to humiliate.

"Fritz," he turned to his companion, the former prisoner of war who likewise wished for a return of those halcyon times when Hitler saw to law and order and kept the German forests clean of "Gesindel" (riffraff).

"Go around to the back to make sure there's nobody else. I'll teach this stubborn little bitch something about German manhood."

The implication was not lost on me. Pointing his shotgun at me with one hand and unbuckling his belt with the other, he charged up the steps toward where I was standing.

"One more move and you are dead!" The sight of my gun stopped him in his tracks. I relished the look on his face.

"Come on," he tilted his head in disbelief. "Don't make such a fuss. Put the thing away, and let's have some fun."

"One more step and I'll blow your head off!" I said in my best Berlin German.

"Fritz!" he called out; his head bent backward for a look around the corner. "Get back here! We've run into a hitch." No answer from Fritz.

Turning back toward me: "So you do speak German. Then let me lay it out for you. You might as well give up. Consider the odds. As soon as Fritz gets back, it'll be two against one."

I knew Fritz would not come back. In the time of my stay at the hideout, always on the alert for intruders, my ears had been sharpened to a degree that they would prick up at the slightest noise. The faint clicking of a silencer had assured me that Fritz was no longer a threat.

The denazified one made another move toward me. My little Roth-Steyr went off, three times in quick succession.

Kafka's demeanor was calm, even pleased. He nodded his head as if to say: "Well done." We dug a shallow ditch behind the inn near the shed and dumped the bodies. Amazing how we worked together in accord without many words. Kafka lit a fire, taking care to keep it contained within the ditch. When he deemed the bodies sufficiently charred, we filled in the burial ground with dirt and covered it with leaves and brush.

"It won't be long before someone will look for them," I said.

Kafka wiped the sweat off my brow. Our desire and need to get out of this forest had become more urgent now. Still no sign or word from Zweig.

Kafka spent much time in the cellar trying to make radio contact with Zweig or Bickers. No response. Silence on the other end.

We prepared the game he had caught that morning. The enticing smell of roast rabbit and duck did not assuage our concerns. My appetite was gone.

"We walked into this forest, why can't we just walk out of here?" I asked.

"It's not that simple. Germany is under martial law. Without Zweig giving us cover we could be arrested. You are still a fugitive, and I am an accessory."

I didn't quite understand the intricacies of the arrangement he had with Zweig but took his word for it.

Kafka's nervousness infected me as well. I had committed my first murder. In self-defense, I reassured myself to ease any qualms about having taken a human life. The man had threatened me with rape. Then again, I also knew we would have had to kill these men no matter what. We couldn't have run the risk of them alerting the authorities. Gun possession was strictly illegal under US military law, and we had no permits. There were no permits to be had anyway for civilians in occupied Germany.

As I pondered what had happened and considered our options, I realized that I, too, was by then thinking and speaking in the first-person plural. Kafka and I had become "we." His fate and mine had become inextricably intertwined.

Chapter 10

The Old Benz

"We can't wait any longer," Kafka stated the obvious almost ad nauseam.

We started packing. Before stashing it in my coat pocket, I briefly weighed the cool metal of the little gun that had saved my life in the palm of my hand. I gave it a grateful pat with the promise never to separate from it. I put a few toiletries in my rucksack together with the little toothbrush with the wooden handle and the worn bristles Kafka had handed to me back at the camp latrine. He never said so, but I was now sure it was the brush Lenka Ostrova used to polish the cobblestones on the Ringstraße. A token he had kept throughout the war years. Now it was my memento. I swore never to part from it.

I tried stuffing the shellac disks into my sack. They were too bulky and added too much weight though.

"Destroy them!" Kafka commanded. "They are useless now. The weight will only slow us down."

His tone was cold, even harsh. He was making short shrift of something I thought held great sentimental value for him.

"Here," he said when I hesitated. "Let me show you."

He picked up a stack of records and smashed them all on the stone floor. He stamped on the splinters in a wild dance. His head moved from side to side. His long black hair fell over the contorted grimace of his face. He stamped and stamped as in a trance without stopping even when his boots had already ground the shellac into a fine powder.

"Come, my darling! Let's dance on those blasted things!" He beckoned me to join in. His laughter exploded more boisterously than ever, but now there was a manic quality to it. I was sure he had gone mad.

"Zweig won't like this," I ventured meekly.

"To hell with Zweig! Let him go to the devil! That traitor has no right to judge. Where is he? Tell me, where he is? He let us down. He left us stranded in this god-forsaken wilderness. If he thinks we are going to rot here, he hasn't counted on Kafka. We are getting away! Don't worry, this is not the first scrape I've gotten out of! We won't rot here!"

He used the German word "*verrecken*" over and over, which has a stronger meaning than the English "to rot." I was a child then, but I remember the marauding brown shirts marching through the streets of Berlin shouting at the top of their lungs: "*Judah verrecke! Judah verrecke!*" A chilling memory. Why would Kafka associate Zweig with Nazis? Irrational and outright insane! I was in love with a madman. At a loss of what else to do or say, I swept up the pieces and dumped them in the fireplace. Kafka had collapsed in the wing-back chair, his head lowered, his face buried in his hands. I tried to erase all traces of our idyllic stay to expedite our departure.

We carried the gramophone and the radio out to the shed where Kafka had found an ax he now used to hack the US government-issued equipment to pieces. Luckily there was a cesspool nearby, previously covered by ice and snow, but now thawed out. We tossed the pieces into the pit where they sank to the bottom of the muck.

"Not likely to be recovered. Someone would have to dive in," he said, rubbing his hands together. His face was all smeared with mud and oil. So was mine. No time for washing up. Before dawn, we shouldered our packs and climbed up a ravine to gain the road. Where we were going, I didn't know. I doubted Kafka had a plan at that point.

From the top of the hill, I briefly glanced back. Our sojourn in limbo had lasted almost three months. The forest hideout had been our lovers' lair. I had experienced moments of great happiness and, at the same time, had been put through an emotional wringer. In many ways, to my relief this had been my "sentimental education." Now it had ended under a cloud of murder.

Kafka pulled at my sleeve. "Come, we must go," he said softly.

We marched in silence for several hours. Our progress was hampered by a ripping March wind. At noon, we settled down in a ditch running alongside a dirt road. We still had a few K-rations, but soon we would have to find other sources of food. Kafka put his arms around me and pressed me to his chest.

"Something will come up. Something always does," he said with renewed confidence.

Gratified to see that he was his old self again, taking a cool, calculating assessment of the situation, I nestled against him, breathing in deeply the warmth of his presence.

And then, it happened. Something did come up. The sound of a sputtering diesel engine was coming closer. We flung ourselves down and pressed our bodies close to the ground peering at the road through the brush.

The black Mercedes-Benz sedan, obviously not a model of recent vintage, advanced at a slow speed as if whoever was inside was scouring the area. A few paces from where we were holding our breath, the car stopped. There seemed to be a discussion going on inside. Then a few minutes later, a young man got out on the driver's side. He spread a sheet of paper out on the hood and studied it closely while surveying the surrounding.

"It must be near here," he said his head turned toward the interior of the car. "Stay in the car, please. I'll look around." His tone was polite and respectful.

"No, I had better come with you," a woman's voice insisted. "One never knows what lurks behind the trees and bushes."

The moment the young man came into clear view, I knew I had seen him before. Briefly and among a group of other people. Frankfurt! Frau Maibach's Esperanto circle! He stood out because he was the only man, a young man, in a group of elderly women. And sure enough, it was none other than the self-same Frau Maibach who emerged from the car and stepped out onto the sludgy road where the heels of her pumps promptly got stuck.

Major Zweig, or *Herr Mayor Zweig* as she referred to him, had been transferred to the lawyers' trial in Nuremberg, she informed us after a joyful hello and warm embrace. Before leaving for his post at the war crimes trials, he came to her greatly distraught. He had no way of contacting you. Sergeant Bickers' tour of duty had ended, and he was on his way back to the United States.

"So here we are to help as best we can." She spread her arms out wide with a big smile. An angel descended from heaven. She gave me another big hug. Herr Kafka, who it seemed was no stranger to her, got a friendly poke. The young man introduced himself as Peter Waldeck. Ever insistent on formality Frau Maibach corrected him: "Herr Baron von Waldeck." To which the baron rolled his eyes indulgently.

"But let's not stand around here," she waved us on. Kafka took the front passenger seat while I sank into the plush leather in the rear next to my old friend.

"Herr von Waldeck will drive you as far as Würzburg. From there, he and I will take the train back to Frankfurt. He is a medical student, you know, and has to return to his studies."

We thanked Herr von Waldeck, whose relationship with Frau Maibach and involvement in this whole affair was at first unclear. Later we found out that he was her nephew. Not many words were exchanged during the ride beyond chitchat about the weather and how slow spring was in coming that year. Kafka was very quiet, even grumpy.

"You came to our rescue just in time! I cannot thank you enough. We are very grateful to both of you. Don't you agree, Herr Kafka?" I proclaimed loudly, maybe a bit too loudly.

"Not at all. No need to thank us!" Frau Maibach raised her gloved hands. "We all serve the same cause."

Do we? What cause was that? Was she privy to Kafka's masterplan? Hard to imagine this very proper woman would be involved in a conspiracy to commit premeditated murder. But as I had already learned on this journey: *Der Schein trügt*! – Appearances are deceptive!

She unwrapped a variety of provisions, which we wolfed down the sandwiches of German wurst and peasant bread with great relish. She even produced a few bottles of beer. As I had come to know back in Frankfurt, Frau Maibach still had her connections in this time of dearth and shortage. I wondered which one of her prized possessions she bartered off in return for these victuals. Kafka still showed no appreciation for what these good people were doing for us.

We finally reached the end of the forest and gained the open road along the sunbathed river valley. The rolling hills of vineyards and orchards were in full bloom. I shielded my eyes against the unaccustomed brightness.

Emerging into the light from a long dark winter!

Kafka's grim demeanor showed no sentiment of deliverance. He was not taken in by the deceptive peacefulness of the landscape. I knew there was no peace for Kafka. And so there would be none for me.

Frau Maibach chatted on about Major Zweig. He had been posted to the Nazi lawyers' trial at the Nuremberg tribunal. He was very troubled that this assignment prevented him from holding up his end of the bargain he had struck with his old comrade Kafka. This assignment was, of course, a great honor, and he was eager to do his part in bringing the Nazi criminals who perverted the law to justice. Kafka would no doubt understand the significance of this momentous, historical trial.

Watching his reflection in the rear mirror, I gathered Kafka did not understand or didn't want to. He also didn't seem to understand that as a member of the military Zweig was not a free agent. The concept of orders had no meaning to him. Did he even appreciate what his friend had done for him? The risk Zweig had run that could entail a court-martial, imprisonment or dishonorable discharge?

"He also entrusted me with your diary," Frau Maibach said sotto voce close to my ear. "It is safely locked away in a drawer of my bureau." Why this guarded concern over my travel journal? I could only surmise it had to do with fear if found on me by the wrong people—whoever they may be—

the espièglierie would blow up with unforeseen consequences for all participants.

"Oh, just look at what happened to this beautiful, splendid city!" Frau Maibach lamented. We had come to a halt on a promontory overlooking the town of Würzburg. We got out of the motorcar to stretch our legs. Below us the ghostly ruins of the city were sprawled out, aglow in brilliant sunshine.

"Such destruction! Irreplaceable!" Frau Maibach shook her head in dismay.

"Like so many others," shrugged young Waldeck. He was more concerned with the functioning of the automobile. He went around the vehicle with a probing look, kicked the tires, then opened the hood to let out some steam escaping from the engine.

"Peter, you should be more sensitive to what happened to the seat of your ancestors," Frau Maibach scolded. "The von Waldecks are an old Franconian noble family," she explained. Kafka shrugged, still brooding. I tried a polite "I see."

"My Aunt Mathilde is of the old school. She puts too much value on titles and ancestors and stuff like that. Do I like to see cities reduced to rubble? No. Do I like the Nazis? No. Do I like they are gone, defeated? Yes. What we see here and everywhere is the price we had to pay for tyranny."

A remarkable young man, I thought. Refreshing to hear him speak his mind like this.

"You know that I agree with you completely, Peter," Frau Mathilde Maibach, for the first time I heard her first name, replied. "It still breaks your heart, to see so much history gone, reduced to rubble."

I was intrigued, not so much by Frau Maibach's lament about history gone to the shreds, but the Maibach family dynamics. If Peter von Waldeck was her nephew, who were his parents? She meanwhile turned her attention back to Kafka, who was drawing quick, short puffs from a cigarette Waldeck had provided him.

"Herr Kafka, I realize all this must be of little interest to you," she began, her squinting eyes pinned on him. "Who could or even would blame you? But as for Major Zweig, you must know that we are very proud of what he is doing for the cause of justice. We also support what he is doing for you. I think you should know Emil's mother was murdered at Ravensbrück, and we don't even know what happened to all the others. Her sister, my mother, has lost her mind. We have no hope for her recovery. She never got over the death of my sister, Peter's mother. Marrying into an old noble family didn't save her."

Her speech quavered; her breathing became staggered. Her extended arms searched for something to hold onto to keep from falling. Her legs gave way. She collapsed onto the rocky ground beneath her, her hands spread over her heaving chest. In a flash, Kafka was on his knees next to her. He took her hands into his, patting them gently, and instructed her to take slow deep breaths.

Peter and I exchanged a questioning look, our eyebrows raised. We witnessed an almost complete transformation from growling curmudgeon to concerned Samaritan. Was it the automatic response of the physician, or did her story move him? I suspected both, hoped for both. The dull weight of doubt lodged in my stomach since the beginning of the car ride mercifully—or was it magically? —dissolved.

Frau Maibach regained her bearing and with Kafka's help got back on her feet. He led her to the car and made her sit down.

"You are about my father's size." She looked him over from bottom to top with the squinting eyes of a tailor taking measurements. "In the trunk, you'll find a few of his duds. Use them in good health." From the mouth of this very proper, formal lady the use the colloquial "*Klamotten*" for clothing made me smile and brought some comic relief. We all burst out laughing. Kafka's laughter, not heard for so long, gladdened my heart.

The general hilarity increased when she repeated the term to describe a few pieces of clothing she had stashed in the trunk for me and punctuated it with: "A proper young lady doesn't walk around in an ill-fitting, soiled outfit that makes her look as if she had ascended from a manure pit. No criticism intended."

The treasure trunk also contained two canisters of petrol, courtesy of Major Zweig and the United States Army, she emphasized.

Chapter 11

Olga from the Volga

"Well, here we are at what you might call the train station or what's left of it," declared Young Waldeck with mock fanfare. He maneuvered the vehicle through a rubble-strewn square and stopped in front of a structure of twisted, blackened steel and broken glass that could have served as the setting for a surrealistic horror film production in Weimar cinema. Undaunted by the bustling scene of masses of people moving about, I seized the bag of toiletries and clothing Frau Maibach had provided and went inside the hall in search of a public bath I knew was common in such places. At least they used to be as I remembered from my acquaintance with European train stations during my parents' years of wanderings.

Mercifully, the one inside this station had weathered the destruction and was in operation. I was attended by a kindly matron who spoke German with a rolling Slavic accent. She helped me undress and into the tub filled with pleasantly warm water. While she was soaping my back, she chatted on non-stop about the persecution and mistreatment of the Volga Germans during the war by Stalin and the Red Army. I immersed my body in the warm tub, leaned back with eyes closed. A *mechayeh*! The attendant's chatter trickled off my consciousness like the balming oil she poured over my skin.

"Two hundred years," I vaguely heard her lament. "For two hundred years, ever since the great Empress Catherine, a German princess you know, invited hard working Germans to settle in the region. Our home for two hundred years, driven out overnight with nothing but the shirt on our backs. Stalin took everything, everything to the last penny we owned. So many died on the long march to our German *Heimat*." Interesting use of the expression "our homeland" for someone whose ancestors had lived in Russia for centuries, I mused to myself.

Funny my people were driven from their homes and robbed of their possessions and murdered for two thousand years. They had settled in Germany when it was still a Roman back water. When the Romans expelled the Jews from their ancient homeland, they didn't have another "Heimat" where they would find refuge. Even now, the British were preventing them from returning to the land of Israel by barring them from the province they call "Palestine."

A clinking noise roused me from my ruminations. I jumped out of the tub, stark naked and dripping wet, slipping on the damp floor. I barely kept from falling on my face. Olga from the Volga had taken it upon herself to brush the dust off my overcoat. Well-meaning no doubt, but in the process, my little Rohr-Steyr fell onto the floor. She quickly bent down, picked it up and daintily held it up between her thumb and pointer with a questioning look.

"Don't touch that!" I yelled, snatching my cherished piece from her hands. If she hadn't been of sturdy, squad built, my move would have knocked her off her feet. She was visibly taken aback by the vehemence of my reaction, which even startled me. What kind of a savage brute had I become who would assault a woman who had meant me no harm? Forty days in the wilderness with Kafka would do it, I guess.

"A woman needs to protect herself these days," I said in a calmer tone once I had regained my bearings. I patted the mother-of-pearl handle and stuck the gun back into the pocket. She nodded with understanding.

"Tough times, especially for a woman," she said. "I hope you won't run into the Russians. Those barbarians take every female they come across for easy prey. To the victors go the spoils, you could say."

For a moment, I permitted myself to wonder about what this woman of about forty must have gone through. Deprivation and rape were no doubt part of what she endured along the trail of tears toward the land she called "Heimat" even though her ancestors had, as she said, lived on the banks of the Volga for centuries. I quickly shrugged off such thoughts. Yes, they all suffered. Everybody has a grievous tale to tell. Wars do that!

Much more alarming was my sudden realization that this woman had become a liability. She could identify me if questioned by the authorities who, no doubt, were already looking for the people who killed the two foresters.

I managed an ingratiating smile and said something to the effect that we all have our cross to bear. Money being worthless, I put a few trinkets into her hands and rushed outside to find Kafka.

Fortunately, he too had been frequenting the bathing facilities on the men's side and looked very dapper in a suit and tie. He still sported a full beard and shoulder-length hair but now it was washed and neatly combed.

"No place to shave?" I asked.

"It's my disguise so I won't be recognized."

"Well, never mind about that now. Something else has come up. We have to leave here as quickly as possible." I related briefly what happened with the Volga German woman.

"How could you be so careless?" he scolded.

"I was in the bathtub, naked. She just wanted to brush my dirt-encrusted coat. I don't know if we have anything to fear from her. But the possibility exists. And she could identify me if someone came around to ask questions. I imagine a train station would be a logical place to search."

"You presume they found the bodies."

"A reasonable assumption that someone started looking for the missing men."

"We don't know that."

"No, we don't. What's worse, we are completely in the dark. But we have to go on the assumption that they are out there!" The raised pitch of my voice alerted Frau Maibach who approached us with a questioning look.

"Just a lovers' quarrel," said Kafka laughing. I was ready to strangle him.

"I am afraid we have to be on our way," I said to Frau Maibach. "We won't be able to wait for your train back to Frankfurt."

"That's quite all right," she said, ever the gracious lady and willing to be accommodating. "Not to worry. The car is yours. I have Peter to keep me company."

"One small matter," interjected Kafka. "I hope Fräulein Hauser knows how to steer this thing. I don't."

Fräulein Hauser? What are we still playing that game? I was sure at this point Frau Maibach knew my real name, maybe always did and I could drop this odious fake moniker.

"You have to keep it for a while longer. It's also the one in your papers." He lectured me in response to what I hoped were daggers shooting from my eyes at him.

"I have never driven a car," I stated defiantly. "In Manhattan, one doesn't need a car."

"I'd be glad to teach you. It's not that difficult," Young Waldeck offered.

"It's not that easy either," I said. "Thank you, but we don't have the leisure to hang around here and draw attention."

"In that case, it may be best if Peter drove you to your destination. I can manage on the train by myself. He can teach Herr Kafka along the way. Won't you, Peter?"

The person so addressed had no objections to the change of plans. It wouldn't have been of any use anyway. Frau Maibach had made up her mind, and that was it.

"Off you go!" she commanded with a shoveling motion of both hands. M "Take care of yourself and watch out. I shall keep you in my prayers," she whispered in my ear while holding me in a firm embrace of good-bye. "Don't be blinded by love. Come back safely and see me in Frankfurt." Was there a tear in her eyes, a trembling in her voice? If so, it was faint, contained.

"Herr Kafka!" she called out loud. "Don't let any harm come to this beautiful girl!" He nodded but made no promise.

She turned abruptly with determined strides.

Chapter 12

Kafka in the Driver's Seat

Peter rolled back the canvas top of the jalopy. He gunned the engine and off we went in a black puff of exhaust. We soon gained the open road.

"Bamberg 100 km East" read a rusted sign with an arrow pointing toward the road.

Kafka was riding shotgun. I was sprawled out on the backseat, my eyes closed, my face tilted toward the warming rays of the sun and the caressing winds. A picture-perfect blue sky overhead with only a few tufts of white clouds. A lovely spring day for an outing in the countryside. The knot in my stomach almost made me gag.

Since the encounter with the woman at the public bath, my thoughts had been wandering back to the incident in the forest, and the buried bodies we left behind. The image of the man's contorted grimace would not go away. I was justified, I assured myself. It was self-defense, justifiable homicide. Why was I suddenly obsessed with the image of that Nazi storming up the steps toward me? I had given it little thought until the murder weapon fell out of my coat. Remorse? No. I had no remorse. Qualms, yes. Kafka would have little understanding of my qualms. He had a single-minded goal. He would let nothing stand in his way. Not even me. Maybe least of all me. Though the way I assessed the situation, I wasn't entirely dispensable. Not yet, at least.

Banish such thoughts! We had a love, an unusual love, that bound us together. You are still a silly, little girl with romantic dreams, a little voice whispered in my ear. A man like Kafka was hardly the right candidate to fulfill the reveries and longings formed in dark movie theaters. Forget about bourgeois aspirations! Who says I want to marry, have kids and live in a house in the suburbs happily ever after?

My thoughts jumped back to the bodies in the forest. It wasn't remorse that filled me with dread. Fear of detection would be more accurate. I had no doubt someone would soon find the bodies. Could the police—was there even a German police force? — trace us to the Würzburg train station? Should I have killed the bath attendant too? And leave a trail of blood? She did not threaten you, I admonished myself. She had even expressed her understanding that a woman had to defend herself and that carrying a gun was a reasonable precaution in these troubled times.

I realized the fruitlessness of spinning perilous scenarios and forced my thoughts onto a different track toward what lay ahead. Looking forward, however, did little to assuage a sense of ill foreboding. Kafka had already proven to be of no help. So once again, all I could do was ask myself: how on earth did I get entangled in such a mess?

But in a mess I surely was, and up to my neck. And not altogether unwillingly. Inadvertently, perhaps, but not unwillingly once I had dipped my foot, or more precisely my body, into the mire of desire, I was lost.

Suddenly I was jolted not only out of my reveries but was bounced around in the back seat. I had paid no attention to what went on in the front. Kafka was now trying his hand at the wheel after a brief course of instruction from Peter. He revved the engine, and off we went bumpety-bump for the next few kilometers up and down the winding road.

"This is so much fun!" he screamed into the wind with the delight of a child riding downhill in a soapbox derby.

The joyride came to a screeching halt at a military checkpoint just outside the town of Bamberg. The two MPs who flagged us down were forced to jump to the side as Kafka's foot searched for the breaks and hit the gas pedal instead. It was only due to Waldeck's presence of mind—he pulled the hand brake—that vehicular homicide was stopped short at the feet of the soldiers.

"Step outside!" one of the men, a sergeant, bellowed. "Papers!"

Kafka yanked his lanky frame out of the driver's seat and jumped over the closed door. He held his hands high up as in a hold-up and unleashed a squall of profuse apologies in German which he knew the soldiers wouldn't understand. He gave me a side glance with a slight jerk of his head toward the trunk. Though I understood the signal, I had no idea how to keep the Americans from searching the trunk where they were sure to find a rucksack with a stockpile of weapons.

"Papers! Do you understand English?"

I shrugged. The verbal torrent from Kafka's mouth flowed on unabated.

"I know a little English." Peter raised his hand like a good, obedient schoolboy.

"Oh, good! Tell this Kraut to shut his trap," said the sergeant. "His Germanic oompah-pah is enough to drive you nuts. Just tell him to show his ID papers."

"The officer accepts your apology with the request you may kindly show him your papers," Waldeck related the message in German in a politer version. Kafka bowed his head and clicked his heels in good Prussian fashion while forming with his lips the word "*trunk*."

Waldeck, however, was unaware of the delicateness of this situation, for he said: "Well, let's get them then."

Kafka gave off his best rippling laughter: "I wouldn't recommend that," he said, his hypnotic gaze pinned on our companion.

"What's the problem?" the MP asked. "This guy sounds like a nut case."

While this drama was unfolding, my eyes followed the movements of the other MP with growing alarm. His attention was fully absorbed by the car. He circled it several times like a lion closing in on his prey. He bent down to view the undercarriage, kicked the tires, patted the frayed leather interior. He pushed his gum around in his mouth, squinted, weighed his head. An automobile buff, I concluded, though this recognition only heightened my anxiety.

"This is one heck of a Benz! Wonder what year it is." He tapped out a little tune on the lid of the trunk, whistling his appreciation for what to me was a heap of junk.

I shrugged and shook my head.

"*Nix verstehn*, huh! Dumb broad!" I beamed my best dumb broad smile at him. He wouldn't get a rise out of me.

Meanwhile, the situation took on the choreography of a Marx Brothers' comedy. Waldeck, in broken English, trying to explain Kafka's erratic behavior with hints of the war; the Nazis, you know. He also mentioned the word concentration camp. Kafka, though quieter, was still flailing his arms about wildly, even foaming at the mouth, as if he was about to have a seizure.

Realizing that attention had to be diverted at all cost away from the trunk, I tried some quick thinking. Applying feminine wiles was not my style. Had I tried, it would have come off as comical and phony. The jalopy's sex appeal would have much better success. With a squall of meaningless German words, I waved the automobile aficionado to follow me to the front of the vehicle.

"*Schön, ja*?" I pointed at the hood ornament with pretended pride in this symbol of German design and craftsmanship. My MP's eyes lit up. "Sehrrr schohhn!" he agreed, running his fingers caressingly over the silver star.

From the corner of my eyes, I saw Waldeck present his papers, which he carried on his person as the law required. The exasperated sergeant began to inspect them studiously. Kafka took a few steps backward away from the pair toward the rear-end of the car. While one MP had his nose in Waldeck's papers, a way had to be found to get other's nose into something else. The hood ornament would not hold his attention forever. Brainstorm! I needed a brainstorm! Then it hit me. Of even greater fascination than what was on the hood would no doubt be what was under it. I had no idea what exactly was under there, but it had to be the motor that made the thing move. For an automobile enthusiast like this one, a peek at it would no doubt be irresistible.

What treasures his eyes beheld when he lifted the hood, I could only surmise from the glow his face assumed. All I saw was a contraption consisting of a tangle of greasy wires and tubes going in and out of equally greasy metal blocks and other parts I would be hard pressed to name. As for him, his jaw dropped like a child's awestruck by the glittering toy displays of F.A.O. Schwarz at Christmastime. His head remained buried inside this dream world until the sergeant yanked him out from under.

"All's okay, buddy," he informed him. "We'd better let these good people go on their way."

"Good people?" Whatever it was the sergeant gleaned from the papers, no doubt issued and stamped and sealed by Zweig, Kafka handed him, made all the difference in his attitude toward the man he had previously taken to be a raving maniac.

"Take care of yourself, Doc," he said, his tone a mixture of respect and affability. "And," he added with a jerk of his head toward Waldeck and me, "beware of those Germans." Kafka nodded and flashed his most beguiling smile. He didn't understand a word.

My identity papers were found to be in good order as well. In the words of the American, they passed "the smell test." Deadpan. Poker face. No response from me. I was still a German woman named Beate Hauser, though I was writhing like a snake inside that skin eager to shed it. Now there was also the sought-after absolution "Schein" attached, certifying that I, or rather she, had only been a "little" Nazi, a camp follower, a nobody. Not someone of import. A gray-wash, if not a complete whitewash. I swore I would kill that Major Zweig one of these days. For the time being, I had to be grateful to him even if begrudgingly. This all-important *Schein* got me through controls and checkpoints.

How ironic, I thought, considering the double meaning of the word in German. Then again, maybe not so ironic, but strangely fitting. *Der Schein* being any piece of paper that certifies something. It could be just the receipt for a purchase, a doctor's prescription or referral, an enrollment paper, a certificate. The applications are endless. In this case, it was a document about a person's degree of complicity or non-complicity in a national crime.

But *Schein* also has a deeper, more intangible meaning as in *scheinbar*, seemingly. *"Schein und Sein,"* illusion and reality, appearance and actuality—existential concepts philosophers have pondered at length through the ages.

In post-war Germany, the victorious grant certificates of absolution to the defeated based on the answers to the questions in a lengthy questionnaire. An attempt to winnow the wheat from the chaff as in "I will send foreigners to Babylon to winnow her and to devastate her land."

The Americans, incorrigible believers in basic human goodness, do not believe punishment should fall on the just and the unjust alike. The questionnaire, administered with great diligence, was to aid separating the little Nazis from the big Nazis. Another variant of the word Schein comes to mind: *scheinheilig,* pretending to be saintly, German for "hypocritical." How to winnow out the faux saintly when the questionnaire can serve as an instrument through which to shine—voilà another meaning—to shed a good light on oneself? *Der Schein* provides a cover for a multitude of sins, I concluded: masquerade, fakery, sham, dissimulation, feint, hypocrisy, willful misrepresentation, deception, espièglerie.

I too was guilty of at least some of these sins. I too pretended to be someone I was not. Did that make me a hypocrite? More an impersonator, an imposter, I consoled myself. And for a good reason. Even a worthwhile, if dubious, cause. It could hardly be self-serving.

My rambling reflections were once again interrupted by a screeching jolt that flung my upper body over the backrest of the driver's seat. Peter Waldeck had taken over the wheel again after the run-in at the checkpoint outside the town of Bamberg. The decision had been made to take the road leading around the town rather than risk being tripped up by more obstacles. Since the main highway, the more navigable part of the road, ran straight through the center of the city, we ended up on a bumpy field path where we now came to an abrupt halt when Kafka pulled the handbrake. Even for a man as mild-mannered as Peter Waldeck, this was enough to even blow his lid.

"What in god's name are you doing? You could've gotten us killed!" he yelled with a flourish of unmentionables.

"This vehicle is too much of an encumbrance! Too conspicuous," Kafka decreed. "Better take it back with you to Frankfurt. We shall find other means of moving on."

"And please tell your aunt I am most grateful for all she has done," Kafka added as if on second thought that maybe he should show some appreciation.

"What about Herr Waldeck? Doesn't he deserve some of that pretend gratitude of yours?" I cried, no longer able to hold my peace.

"Of course, of course. I thought that was self-understood." Kafka looked to Waldeck for confirmation, but he was about to get back into the vehicle after we had unloaded our baggage from the trunk.

"If it wasn't understood, then I beg your forgiveness, Herr von Waldeck."

"Bon voyage, then! Give my regards to Prague!" Waldeck shouted as he revved up the Benz and took off in a cloud of exhaust, barely giving us enough time to jump out of the way.

Prague? How much did he know about the Zweig/Kafka "mission" we were on?

"That was an abrupt goodbye," Kafka mumbled with a puzzled look.

"Can you blame him?" I said in English too furious to even think in German.

It occurred to me then that Kafka staged this scene to get rid of our companion. The Moor has served his purpose, the Moor can leave, goes an oft-cited quote from Schiller. Waldeck had been made to believe our destination was Kafka's hometown. Another deceptive diversion. Why not just say thank you for all you've done; we'll move on from here? The way normal people in polite society interact. Not Kafka, the dramatist, the master of the sleight of hand. Maybe too much exposure to the grandiose Wagner scenarios had rubbed off on him. I was grasping at straws to explain the inexplicable.

Part Three

Twilight of the Gods

"The Germans have fashioned for themselves
a Wagner they can venerate."

Nietzsche

Chapter 1

Nibelungen Undomiciled

As we were approaching the devastated town of Bayreuth, I was still unsure what role in the looming drama I was to play. The thought briefly crossed my mind what Frau Maibach might say were she to see this medieval pearl on the Red Main River in its present state. Would she bemoan the utter destruction visited upon this stronghold of Nazi ideology with the same pathos she expressed at the sight of the ruined Baroque city of Würzburg? Not that it mattered. Just one of those nuisance thoughts that flit through the mind when one finds oneself at wit's end of how to tackle a situation that blurs the capacity to think.

I found myself alone in the town Richard Wagner had made famous. Kafka was somewhere nearby, he assured me. He thought it best if we weren't seen together. Seen by whom? His facial hair and head hair had grown substantially. With the broad-rimmed Fedora pulled over his eyes, he gave the appearance of a savage creature arisen from *yene welt,* as they say in Yiddish.

We had spent one last night together at a wayside inn we came upon after a long day's walk along the highway populated with hordes of people dispersing to who knows where. As much as I longed to rest in his arms again and to sink into oblivion of this world, the spark that had ignited our lovemaking back in the forest, where the nocturnal stillness surrounding us was pierced only by owls hooting, was hard to rekindle in the raucous atmosphere of this inn. Music blaring, drunkards blurting, women cackling, only served to heighten my ill-foreboding over what lay ahead. Kafka's sullen demeanor, though he tried to be attentive in a mechanical sort of way, didn't help matters and made it very difficult to rev up a romantic mood. The noise outside the door finally died down in the early morning hours, granting us a few hours of much-needed sleep.

Crossing into the town of Bayreuth was like wading into a seething cauldron of teeming masses. One could think of a melting pot; only in this melting pot, the flavors did not mix. There was a veritable Babel of tongues resounding in the narrow streets and alleyways: Ukrainian, Czech, French, Italian, Greek, people who had been dragged into the Reich for slave labor in the war industry. Several DP camps ringed the outskirts of town, set up by the Americans to provide housing for the various nationalities waiting to be repatriated to their homelands or leave for other parts of the world. Most of these "displaced persons" were Polish slave laborers and Jewish death camp survivors.

Volksdeutsche, Sudeten Germans, and ethnic Germans who had been expelled from various Eastern regions in the wake of the collapse of the Reich found accommodations in the town proper in crowded bomb-riddled tenements and other housing. Two years after the end of the war, the scars were still plainly visible everywhere. Finding lodging of any kind was impossible. I slept in the street, huddled in a doorway with one eye open; always on guard for robbers and sexual predators. My body weight was considerably reduced. The emaciated figure looking back at me as I passed store windows was hardly recognizable as me. My biggest comfort was my little Roth-Steyr. I kept it close to my body, hoping, praying, I wouldn't have to use it again, but also determined not to hesitate should the situation warrant.

Kafka stayed at a camp for displaced Jews at the former concentration camp of Flossenbürg. So, he told me. I had no idea where he was keeping himself. He brought me something to eat whenever we were able to arrange a sporadic nocturnal rendezvous. He assured me; he was watching over me. The guardian-angel assurance hardly assuaged my anxieties.

"What are we doing here?" I pleaded.

"Something will come up. Just be on the lookout for any information, any lead."

I scoured the local newspapers for announcements of cultural activities. There were none that summer. The famed Bayreuth Festspielhaus was sitting on a hill unscathed, spared from destruction during the attacks on the city, ghostly presence looming over the town. The lights had gone out. Wagner's music had fallen silent.

Lenka Ostrova once triumphed here, Kafka told me, not without a certain pride ringing in his voice that did not fail to irk me.

Chapter 2

The Wagnerian Shrine

I strolled through the rubble-strewn streets, keeping on the move, trying not to attract attention. My peregrinations took me back again and again to "Wahnfried" Wagner's famed residence. The Italianate villa had sustained minor damage. Now it was guarded by the American military. One of the MP's had already taken note of my daily visits. One morning when I tried to enter the premises for a closer look, he came up to me waving his hands shouting "Verboten!"

I noticed fresh flowers at the entrance gate. The next day I too brought a bouquet, which I had swiped from a windowsill, and placed it at the entrance gate.

"Schrein!" I said to the soldier. Since the word is "shrine" in English as well, I knew he would understand.

"Okay," he nodded. "Wagner fan. Another lady brings flowers too."

I shrugged, feigning regret that I didn't understand. More dissimulation, more subterfuge, more Schein! You are getting very good at this, I told myself. More importantly, I had to find out who this other lady was.

I didn't have to wait long. The next morning, while I was observing the gate to the villa from across the street, I was startled by a bright chirping "Guten Morgen!" behind me. I turned to see who was bidding me a good morning so cheerfully and came face to face with an elderly lady beaming a bright smile at me.

"We seem to have something in common," she said. My demeanor must have gone from startled to puzzled.

"You mustn't be perplexed." she fluted through puckered lips. "I have been watching you for several days now. The American told me what you said about a shrine."

"Oh, that's what you mean! Yes, of course!" I laughed nervously, hoping my dissembling wouldn't be too obvious. "I saw the flowers. So, I thought I'd add some of my own."

I held my breath expecting more questions about where I found them. My offering was a bouquet of wildflowers the person whose windowsill they adorned must have gathered up in a blooming field perhaps on a Sunday walk. I calmed my pangs of conscience with the assurance that the fields were still in bloom; there were other Sundays for the person to gather another bouquet. What had I become? Now I was not only a murderess but also a thief.

To my relief, the chatty lady facing me with a scrutinizing look didn't probe into the provenance of the flowers. She presented a very elegant figure, tall and gaunt, past her prime, but still radiating an aura of dignified charm, very much like the two dogs, one black with white touches and one white with black touches, she held close to her side on a leash.

"That is very nice of you," she said. "Are you an admirer of the master's music."

"Oh yes, very much so!" I feigned enthusiasm.

"Very little is performed now. But his time will come again," she assured me. "Such divinely inspired music cannot be silenced forever. Have no fear, young lady, the Master will rise again."

"I certainly hope so!" I declared emphatically, perhaps a little too emphatically. But my fears were immediately assuaged.

"Wonderful to meet a young person who still appreciates great music. Are you from around here?"

"No, I am on my way home to Berlin. I felt compelled to make a little detour, a pilgrimage. You know, to see how things are after all that happened. . . "

"That is so charming! I am Elisabeth von Bülow." Her gloved hand seized mine and shook it emphatically. There was a certain air of desuetude about her. A relic from a by-gone time.

My training with Kafka, that devil, was bearing unexpected fruit. I am sufficiently acquainted with the sordid life of Wagner and his wife Cosima, in Kafka's version, for my ears to go up at the mention of her name.

"*The* von Bülows?" I cried and reach out for her hand.

"Well yes," she said, pulling her hand back from my firm grip. "My husband, may he rest in peace, was a grandson of Hans von Bülow. My own family is of an older Bavarian noble lineage. You may have heard of the Turn-und-Taxis family."

I hadn't and said so with the excuse that I was from Prussia.

Then, unbeknownst to her, she dropped a bomb for no apparent reason: "One branch of the family, the von Waldecks of Lower Franconia, fell into disgrace during the Reich. The last baron made an unsuitable match."

"He married a Jewess," she said, in response to my questioning look. She kept her eyes firmly fixed on me. She was testing me, feeling my pulse, I could tell. She was challenging me to put my cards on the table. As taken aback as I was by her remark and her way of drawing out the word "Jü-ü-ü-din" dropping her voice at the end of the second syllable, I realized this woman could be very helpful to the cause, Kafka's cause. She might indeed hold a fount of information about the whereabouts of our targets. I lifted my eyes and sank them deep into her piercing grays.

"That's too bad," I shook my head with feigned indignation. A mien of satisfied recognition sealed a silent understanding between like-minded parties.

Mazel tov! You have passed the imposter test! I told myself. You have earned your spurs in the art of dissimulation! If my grandmother could see me now! She most likely would be appalled by such a display of dishonesty. Or would she? Times had changed! My grandmother's world of refinement and gentility was gone, destroyed, futsch. Part of her world was a love of art and music and good manners. I remembered her expressing appreciation of the music of Wagner if not for the composer himself.

I am doing this also for you, my beloved Omi, I prayed silently. These bastards deserve to be deceived and more.

Rather than granting me some respite from her leering gaze, Frau von Bülow now looked me over with even more intense scrutiny and interest.

"Why would a young German woman travel all alone in this dangerous world?" she finally asked.

"I am trying to make my way home with limited means."

"Which is where?"

"As I said, Berlin."

"I see," she said with a pensive mien. She was mulling something over in her head. An explanation of why I was so far away from home was advisable if I wanted to gain her confidence. The war had been over for two years. I had to come up with a plausible account for my whereabouts during that time.

The dogs, two elegantly slender creatures with silky white coats and long pointy noses—borzois or Russian wolfhounds, she told me in answer to my question, one male, one female, Wotan and Fricka by name—had shown admirable docility and patience. Just then they signaled their desire to stretch their long legs. Frau von Bülow invited me to come along on a walk along the banks of the Red Main River. She unleashed the dogs for their morning run. We settled on a park bench nearby while they enjoyed their brief respite of freedom.

We were in a part of town that had preserved its genteel, uncrowded ambiance. Like the Festspielhaus across the river, the area had remained remarkably unscathed from the ravages of war.

We were alone. Somewhere, in the distance, a lone dark, bearded figure hovered in the corner of my eyes.

"So how is it that you are so far from home?" she prodded.

"Work service," I said. "I was drafted for work on a farm in Westphalia back in '44. When the British army came in, I managed to make my way to Frankfurt. I was told it would be easier to get to Berlin from there. No fixed schedule. A lot of waiting. When I finally got on a train, the American controls took me off because I did not have that silly *Persilschein,* as they call it. Since I came from the British zone, I didn't know anything about it. That made me a suspect."

"A suspect for what?" she asked innocently.

With tears in my eyes, I told her about the interrogations I had to endure, the incarceration at a camp for female war criminals, the long, harsh winter, and finally, at long, long last, release and issuance of that coveted piece of paper absolving me from being a criminal. I didn't even have to make this up. My story embellished and exaggerated in my telling though by and large true, enraged Frau von Bülow so much, she did not take note of the deliberately fuzzy chronology.

"With the Russians in control of the East, travel between the zones is very difficult without the right credentials. What they consider the right credentials. I don't even know if anyone in my family is still alive!"

By then the tears rolled freely down my cheeks. It was no longer an act. Recalling my stay at the prison camp for Nazi criminals and the humiliations I suffered there did its part without fail. Even then, the thought crossed my mind that one of these days I would kill that Major Zweig!

"My poor child!" Frau von Bülow patted my hand with sorrowful, empathic mien.

Suddenly she jumped up, with astounding alacrity for her age. I was even more astounded when she placed her thumb and forefinger between her tongue, thus emitting a high-pitched whistling sound. The rallied borzois swiftly crouched panting at her feet.

"I could never do that for some reason," I replied, petting the dogs' long, pointy heads.

"I learned it in my younger days," she laughed. "Maybe I'll teach you."

We had established a certain camaraderie that was quite astounding. Why would this noble lady even deign to shed her lights on a bedraggled vagrant from the street? Perhaps she lost most of her family in the war and was now alone with two dogs. She had to be very lonely and longing for human company, I concluded. Then again, not any kind of human, mind you. She did scrutinize me thoroughly to make sure I was the right kind of human, who would be worthy of an invitation to her home. And for some reason, I passed the litmus test. Should I be proud?

"So, you like Wagner! That's so nice," she said.

I had to make something up to bolster my claim to the status of Wagner aficionado.

"My grandparents once took me to the opera in Berlin to hear Elfriede Kling and Rudolf Schwamm as Tristan and Isolde. I was a teenager then. I was smitten!"

My education in the forest came in handily.

"I can well imagine!" she replied. "Two of our most celebrated Wagnerians!"

"We also had gramophone recordings at home. My grandmother was very fond of a Lenka something, starts with an O I believe. She could never get enough of her Immolation scene in The Valkyrie, which she thought was divine."

"You mean Lenka Ostrova, a Czech Jewess—again she drew out "Jü-ü-ü-din" with puckered lips as if biting on a lemon.

"Well, she could hardly hold a candle to our wonderful Madame Kling. Not a bad voice but lacking that intrinsic German sensitivity it takes to be a great Wagner interpreter. She eventually disappeared from the scene. Rumor had it she was conspiring against the Reich."

She shook her head as if to chase away a distasteful image.

"But let's not talk about unpleasant things. If you love Wagner, you may enjoy a little soirée at my residence. One of our most promising young sopranos will present the Wesendonck Lieder to a select group of devotees. We still try to keep the maestro's music alive, albeit in private, intimate settings for the time being."

I had no idea who "we" might be. Could be the imperial we or maybe she wasn't quite as lacking in companionship as I had at first presumed.

"Can you make it on Friday evening at eight?" Of course, I could make it, but what would I wear?

"I'd be honored and delighted," I said. "Only my wardrobe. . ."

"Not to worry. It's very informal. If you wish, come a little earlier, and we'll find something suitable for you."

"What should I know about the Wesen. . . something Lieder?" I asked Kafka when I told him about my chance encounter with the former president of the women's auxiliary of the Wagner Society, information she proudly managed to weave into our conversation.

"Not much except as a Wagner admirer you should know it's Wesendonck Lieder, a collection of poems by one of Wagner's mistresses he set to music. Not his finest achievement, but pleasant and popular. A good vehicle for a novice soprano."

He kissed me profusely, held me in a long embrace, and kept on assuring me how fabulous I was and how grateful he was. All I wanted was run away, far, far away.

"Let's forget about all this and go to Palestine," I said.

"We shall, we shall," he replied. "Once this is over, we shall go home."

If we live to see that day, I thought. Then the printed images of those bodies naked and dead, which I knew were only a faint reflection of the unimaginable horrors appeared to me, and I knew that my life was inextricably linked to them and Kafka and would be meaningless outside that great chain of being. The opportunity to be a part of such a crusade elevated my spirit.

Chapter 3

Villa Lohengrin

Frau von Bülow's baronial residence was in the genteel part of town within a short stroll from Villa Wahnfried. Most of the villas imitated the Italianate stucco style of the Wagner abode, projecting an aura of Tuscan serenity. Most had been left unscathed by the war. I wondered if this was some deliberate deference toward German culture on the part of the Allied bombers.

Villa Lohengrin, the Bülow residence, by contrast, sat like a grim medieval fortress amid the prevailing southern architectural splendor. The rough-hewn red sandstone exterior, turrets, stained-glass windows and doors framed with gothic arches projected the northern ambiance of a medieval castle. The visitor crossing the threshold into the interior, darkened by polished mahogany wood paneling throughout, was immediately transported into a preserve of nineteenth-century bourgeois opulence. The furnishings and fixtures were not unlike those at my grandparents' villa in Charlottenburg where I grew up or even Frau Maibach's smaller, neatly arranged cozy nest in Frankfurt.

Frau von Bülow occupied a suite in a small, quiet wing of the spacious halls and rooms of what must have been at one time home to a numerous clan. A handful of servants, mostly Sudeten German refugees, were quartered in an adjacent servants' house on the premises. Whether it was a desire for companionship or loneliness, she insisted I stay in what she called the nanny's chamber, a small room with a private bath, down the hall from her lodging. The bed was a narrow cot and the mattress lumpy, but for my bones, rubbed sore from sleeping under bridges and in bombed out buildings, it was a fluffy cloud of comfort.

On the evening of the soirée a new me, freshly bathed and clad in a silky long evening gown of shimmering dark blue from the wardrobe of Frau von Bülow's daughter, whose whereabouts were unclear, made her entry with unstable steps on unaccustomed high-heeled pumps into the drawing room where a small group of dignified-looking visitors was gathered. The glimmer of candlelight shed a festive glow over the room. A set of cushioned chairs was grouped around a Bechstein grand piano at the center.

The hostess herself was decked out in an elegant tight-fitting black gown of belle-époque vintage. She greeted her guests leading a timorous, blond waif-like creature around by the hand. The girl gave the appearance of a typical sixteen-year-old, a socially uncomfortable, pouting adolescent, although, as I learned later, she was of the ripe age of twenty.

On seeing me enter, Frau von Bülow dropped the hand of her protégée and rushed up to receive me with arms wide open as if she wanted to gather me to her gaunt chest.

"You look enchanting! Marvelous!" she cried. I took a step backward in disbelief. Nobody had ever applied such praise on my looks.

"I almost feel I've recaptured a daughter." Frau von Bülow dabbed a few tears from her eyes with a white lace handkerchief. She had mentioned a daughter several times in conversation, but without revealing what happened to her, why she wasn't here, or where she might be.

The last thing I wanted was to act as a stand-in for this lady's lost daughter. She had been kind to me, rescued me literally from the gutter and I should be grateful. Or should I? I reminded myself what she did for me was on the assumption that I was a homeless Aryan girl and that she would, no doubt, be horrified were she to find out who I really was—one of those "Jü-ü-üdinnen" for whom she had expressed such disdain when telling the story about the unsuitable marriage in the Waldeck branch of the Turn-und-Taxis family or referring to Lenka Ostrova. Secretly, I looked forward to the day to seeing her pucker her lips when I would reveal myself to her. But for now, I had to maintain the "Schein und Sein" deception. The shadow of Kafka was hovering somewhere in the wings.

The evening was not without its surprises. The little waif, introduced as Hannelore von Weber, proved to have an expressive, even brilliant soprano voice, astounding in power coming from her frail body. The music itself was rather tedious to my ears. Composition of "Lieder" was not the maestro's forte.

The most jaw-dropping event of the evening was the arrival of the local US Army commander with an entourage of officers decked out in dress uniforms adorned with shiny medals. Colonel Dietrich entered with the confident stride of the victor. He seemed to be on familiar, if polite, terms with the hostess and kissed her tendered gloved hand in the stiff manner of a well-bred European aristocrat. She gushed an effusive welcome in flawless British English.

"The Colonel is a great Wagner admirer," Frau von Bülow informed me in an octave even higher than her usually squeaky voice. "He was billeted here in the villa for a few months at the end of the engagement."

Engagement? It took me a moment to realize she meant the war.

"The Colonel and I formed a close friendship through our common love of art and music," she warbled on. "He is particularly fond of the Ring. There is also his German ancestry which goes back to a young man who served in the army of General von Steuben during the American Revolutionary War of whom he is very proud. A long time ago, but some of that German blood still flows in his descendant's veins. Let me introduce you. I am sure the two of you will get on splendidly."

"Not to worry, he speaks a very refined German," she reassured me when she saw my worried expression.

I suppressed the stirring in my stomach and obediently trotted along to greet the Colonel, who had already taken possession of poor little Hannelore's attention. The ingenue too spoke very refined English.

As for the Colonel's German, it was rather spotty. He had taken the opportunity while stationed as conquering hero in the land of his forebears to improve his high school German and the bits and pieces he had picked up during his childhood from the grandmother on his mother's side who had been a more recent immigrant to America than that legendary ancestor in Washington's army. All this he explained to me in words tiresomely strung together as if he were gleaning the yield of a potato field. I made no move to come to his aid. I rather enjoyed watching his painful struggle of stringing the words together. Serves him right for being a such a toady, I thought. The only encouragement I gave him was a smile and a nod alternatingly expressing agreement and amazement.

"Do I have the honor of speaking with a fellow Wagner admirer?" he asked me. It was clear he had been putting the words together in his head before posing the question in unsure baby steps.

I had just begun to answer his question in deliberately fast-shooting Berliner Deutsch when the hostess announced the beginning of the presentation. We have the good fortune, she said, to hear the extraordinary voice of a young lady, Hannelore von Weber by name, in a selection of the Wesendonck Lieder cycle.

"The full cycle will be kept for another evening," she calmed the demurring of some in the audience who were craving for more. "Fräulein Weber," she continued, "had to interrupt her studies at the Munich conservatory due to the recent turmoil in that city but will soon be able to resume her training right here in Bayreuth with a famous teacher, whose name I am not yet at liberty to reveal."

Remarkable, I thought, how she avoids using the word "war."

"The beauty of her voice and impressive talent will be on full display this evening, as you all will no doubt agree upon hearing her sing."

Frau von Bülow then took command of the piano herself and the young lady, undergoing a miraculous transformation from waif to diva before our very eyes, lunged into the music of the venerated maestro. Not a stir in the rapt audience of mostly elderly widows plus a few professorial types and their wives. Some sat erect, some slumped in their seats; some with eyes closed, some with eyes adoringly pinned on the artist. For me, an hour and a half of excruciating boredom.

I joined in the applause with greater enthusiasm than I felt during the performance, grateful for the relief.

This may have prompted the Colonel to sidle up to me at the buffet—how and where Frau von Bülow had scrounged up such delicacies when most of the country was still struggling to get by on rations was a mystery. The rich still lived high off the hog.

"Bravo, *mein liebes Fräulein*! Here is the answer to my question confirmed. You are a true Wagner devotee," the Colonel stuttered, clapping his hands. When I had become his "dear Fräulein" was a puzzle to me, but I gave it no coin. My mind was still on puzzling over the luscious spread of vittles, the canapés—"*Häppchen*" as the Baroness called them—slices of roast chicken and ham, various cheeses and smoked fish garnished with pieces of fruits and watercress on round cuts of baguette, all laid out on what I presumed was Rosenthal china. Though no expert on fine crockery, I noticed these plates and bowls bore a close resemblance to the dinnerware at my grandmother's Shabbat table.

"You must try these . . . how do you say 'figs' in German?" The Colonel seemed intent on getting a conversation going with me. I shrugged a helplessly. Figs in war-torn Germany? Maybe he was the source of all these goodies. Unless it came from a stockpile in the cellar hoarded in better days of the German Reich.

"Feigen!" Frau von Bülow came to his aid. "Directly from the Holy Land!" Pride of possession fairly made her face radiate. Her voice spiraled into ever higher octaves.

I was about to stop parsing the words in the script of this theater of the absurd when the curtain opened on a final act.

I was beginning to wonder why this professed Wagnerian didn't shower his attention on the true star of the evening. What did he want with me, an inconsequential member of the German *"Lumpenproletariat"* whom Frau von Bülow had scooped up from the gutter out of the goodness of her heart? I had overheard her saying something to this effect, though without the Marxist term, to the Colonel in carefully turned English when she introduced me.

Now she seemed compelled to account for my presence not only at her house but in Bayreuth.

"Fräulein Hauser is on her way to be reunited with her family in Berlin," she explained, not knowing that I understood every word. "But she wanted to stop here in the mecca of the composer she admires above all."

Did I ever say that? Certainly not in her effusive way. She went on to relate how I had been stranded far from home at the end of what she now referred to as "the conflagration." Her English was remarkable.

"Her journey home was impeded by one of the more zealous members of your military who seems intent on catching the bad guys, as you Americans say. Having the right papers has become a matter of life and death for anyone. Unfortunately, the poor girl lacked this famous, or should I say infamous, Persilschein, you Americans insist on, and was escorted off the train to Berlin in Frankfurt." She rolled her eyes and raised her eyebrows in a you-know-what-I-mean kind of manner.

"Oh, dear!" Colonel Dietrich turned again toward me in broken German. "I hope you didn't run afoul of that Major Zweig at the Frankfurt command post."

"The selfsame one," I replied, eager to hear what he had to say about my nemesis. He was equally eager to assure me that not all Americans were like that.

"How do you mean?" I could not restrain myself from inquiring.

"Well, you know. Some of my compatriots lack a certain refinement, a sense of decorum inbred among Europeans."

"The Major spoke German very well, like a native," I interjected.

"Yes, some of those refugees serve in our armed forces. And some of these people tend to be all too eager for revenge."

"You did win the war," I shrugged. "The victors make the rules."

"You are very gracious, dear Fräulein. I can see you come from a home of good breeding."

I swore if he continued to patronize me, I would disabuse him of that notion of good breeding and punch him in the mouth with a few well-placed New York slang words.

"Where I come from the well-bred ones are generally horses and dogs," I replied instead.

He laughed out loud. Then he turned serious. "Nevertheless, I hope you will accept my apologies for the behavior of our American Torquemada, if you know what I mean."

The Baroness gave off a nervous chuckle. Her mouth twitched as if she had bitten on a lemon, a habit she probably acquired during the previous regime when one generally had to presume that the walls had ears.

"We are all of one mind here, Baroness," he tried to assuage her worries of being overheard. "In here *hört der Feind nicht mit*!" he paraphrased a Nazi slogan. Little did he know that the enemy was within earshot.

I was flabbergasted to hear Major Zweig described as a modern-day Torquemada! Every Jewish child with a Hebrew school education, however rudimentary, knew about the Spanish Inquisition, which had ranked among the greatest misfortunes in Jewish history until the Nazis knocked it out of first place. Torquemada's name was inscribed in the annals with that of Pharaoh and Haman, to which more recently was added the cursed name of an Austrian corporal.

That an American officer would decry a fellow officer in such terms by turning the tables was outrageous.

Maybe he wasn't thinking all that far. To him, it was probably a clever joke. Most likely, he wanted to show off his knowledge of European history. I, Nathan Dietrich, proud German American, he seemed to be saying, am not one of those ignorant, uncultured Americans. I found out about his given name later. Not as ironic as I at first deemed it to be. He was a lapsed Mennonite from Pennsylvania and by no means insensitive to the crimes against the Jewish people committed by the Germans. His infatuation with German culture, especially the music, to the point of being besotted, made him play the fool at the musical gathering in the house of a real-life German aristocrat.

My outer shell, Beate Hauser, responded with an uncomprehending, obliging grin, who was too dumb to grasp the meaning of the allusion. Artemisia Safran, stung to the depth of her soul by this carelessly tossed-off remark, clenched her fists, barely able to restrain herself from bursting out of the straight-jacket that held her restrained.

He must have taken my bewildered look for fear of the long arm of the dreaded Major Zweig. In the next sentence, he said: "You are quite safe here in Bayreuth. Besides, let me assure you Major Zweig is an outstanding officer and gentleman. Of German birth, as you no doubt noticed. Tragic family story." He seemed to weigh how much of the Major's background he should reveal. I gathered he was reluctant to discuss the subject of Jews with a German. I was willing to give him the benefit of the doubt, though I thought his toadying most unbecoming as representative of the victorious party.

To my relief, the Colonel finally seemed to tire of me. He turned his attention to Hannelore von Weber whose English was much better than that of Beate Hauser. She had studied the operas of Gilbert and Sullivan during a summer in London before the war, I heard her say.

The name of Major Zweig, however, came up once more before the evening was over. This time in a private *entretien* I overheard between the Colonel and the hostess. She took him aside in a corner. Confident that I didn't understand what they were saying, neither paid much attention to me eavesdropping nearby.

"Is that the same Zweig who is now in Nuremberg?" she whispered with stern mien.

"Yes, his legal training qualified him to be posted with the prosecuting team."

"You promised."

"Yes, yes, of course. I made some inquiries. Unfortunately, my hands are tied. As sympathetic as I am to your concerns, I cannot interfere in the proceedings. The trial is very thoroughgoing. He is among the second tier of the accused. They are mostly out to convict the higher ups. You must be patient."

The company broke early. Most of the guests were of advanced age, elderly couples and widows. The streets were not deemed safe to walk at night with all the riffraff around. Inevitably someone threw in the common phrase "we need to have the old days back again." The old days the speaker was referring to were not the time of Bismarck, as he made clear. His utopia was in the more recent past when law-abiding, well-behaved citizens could walk the streets at all hours without fear.

Every single one of these well-behaved, model citizens shook my hand to say goodbye, assuring me what a pleasure it was and expressing the hope to see me again soon. Inbred, automatic-response politeness. I did not recall having exchanged more than a few words with any of them.

Suddenly I felt as if the wind were being squeezed out of me. I tried, quite unsuccessfully, to wriggle out of the firm embrace of two arms holding me in a vise. But Hannelore von Weber wouldn't let go.

"I must speak to you under four eyes," she whispered, her hot breath burning my ears. The opportunity for the desired private conversation, however, did not present itself for quite some time.

Fräulein von Weber had been crowned the most valued thoroughbred in the von Bülow stable on which the Baroness banked a post-war revival of the Wagner cult. As such the young woman, since her arrival from Munich, had become the apple of her eye she wouldn't let her out of her sight. She too was lodged at the villa though in a room closer to the Baroness.

Starting early in the morning after a carefully planned breakfast and an invigorating walk at dawn around the grounds, the two would sequester themselves in the music room. The Baroness at the piano, putting the hapless young woman through endless hours of vocal exercises.

Scales and more scales, trills and drills, up and down, and sideways. My ears burned, just listening. I fled the scene, the dogs on the leash, roaming the neighborhood hoping to find my shadow. I was never disappointed on that score. Kafka was always somewhere nearby.

Kafka had listened distractedly to my chattering about my encounter with the American colonel at the *soirée musicale*. Strange, I thought, the elderly guests are of greater interest to him than the intrigue between the Colonel and the Baroness and her consternation over the Nazi lawyers' trial in Nuremberg.

"Local Wagner devotees, music lovers," I said in answer to his probing. "And yes, most likely Nazis or sympathizers, big or small. I didn't ask them to show me their *Schein*."

"What about the Wagner clan? Heard anything about them?"

"No one of that ilk was at the recital as far as I could tell. The Colonel would have made a big to-do. The American military are keeping a close eye on villa Wahnfried. I walk by every day with the dogs. No sign of life inside. Not soul coming or going."

Something the Baroness had tossed off about a famous teacher for her young protégée had stuck in my mind. Kafka agreed this might be significant and urged me to find out who this person was.

"Out-of-work opera singers abound in Germany these days. Could be any one of them. Too many questions may elicit questions and arouse suspicion. Someone might begin to wonder why I am still here when I am supposedly eager to get back to Berlin."

"Look, you are still useful to her highness. Who would walk her dogs?" Kafka, the jester, making light of my predicament with his damn laughter. A predicament, by the way, I reminded him, he created for me.

"Jews, as I found out, are not welcome in those circles, not even as dog walkers."

"No one will take you for a Jew. These goyim have neither nose nor ear for it. Only another Jew would be able to divine your Jewish soul."

"Why, thank you. What a relief! That makes me feel so-ooo much better!"

I didn't know if I should slap him or kiss him but did neither.

The dogs were getting restless, yelping and jumping. Maybe they shared Kafka's amusement about my predicament. He helped me rein them in before they could yank my arm from its socket.

"Kafka," I called him back as he was about to move away. "You owe me."

"I know. I'll make it up to you." He touched his lips to my forehead, turned, and was gone.

Chapter 4

Hannah

She stood shivering at the foot of my bed. Her billowing white gossamer nightgown reflected the light of the moon streaming through the open window. A warm May breeze playfully ruffled her undulating blond hair. I rubbed my eyes. An apparition of Isolde of medieval lore as portrayed in myriad artistic representations, most emphatically in Wagner's opera.

I rubbed my eyes again. Was this a dream?

"Fräulein Weber!" I exclaimed. "You startled me."

She placed a finger on her lips. Her eyes darted about the room.

"May I?" she pleaded softly.

I pulled back the covers and waved her in, then folded them back again over her trembling body. For a long time, she lay stiff and motionless, breathing softly, gazing at the ceiling. Not a word. The warmth streaming from her body filled me with pleasant drowsiness. I did not dare move lest she vanish into thin air.

"She's a frightened child" was my last thought before I dozed off. When I woke, she was gone.

At breakfast, my nocturnal visitor kept her eyes lowered on the bowl of farina with raspberry syrup in front of her, stirring it broodingly without tasting. My "good morning" greeting was returned with a mere grunt.

"I'm not hungry," she replied to Frau von Bülow's urging her to eat.

"You need your strength. We have some rigorous vocalizations to go through today," the Baroness admonished. "You want to be in top form for the audition."

"Yes, of course, Frau Baronin," she acquiesced and dutifully filled her mouth with the porridge.

She looked at me askance. At least that's how I interpreted the long look she gave me as she followed her taskmistress to the music room for the grueling exercises that were to test her stamina both physical and vocal.

Why should she be cross with me? What had I done to incur her displeasure? Was she afraid I would say something to the Baroness about her nocturnal visit to my room? Even though I wouldn't have done it, as it turned out, I didn't have to.

The music room faced the path I took every morning to the enclosure where the dogs stayed overnight. All windows were wide open for the German morning routine, amounting to a ritual observed by the German multitude, of "Lüften" - airing.

"I don't want you to disturb my house guests," I heard the Baroness scolding her as I walked by the window of the music room. I halted my steps. What did she mean?

"Don't lie to me. I saw you coming out of Fräulein Hauser's room this morning."

"I had a nightmare" came a lachrymose reply.

"Then you come to me. Next time I expect you to come to me if anything is upsetting you. Is that understood?" I didn't hear Hannelore's reply, but I didn't doubt that she was cowed. Poor thing, I thought.

Something disturbing was going on here. Was the Baroness playing Svengali? She had her hopes pinned on this young woman with the golden voice for a revival of the glory that was Wagner. I didn't know much about what went into the making of a successful singing career, but I did not doubt that strictest discipline was part of the regimen.

This incident made me think back to the moment when the Baroness introduced her protégée to me and later to her guests. Even then, I was struck by a vague sense of something odd, something bothersome in her overbearing behavior toward the ingénue. But I couldn't pinpoint it and told myself I was turning into an intrigue freak.

I had very little interaction with the young woman in the time since that night when she had sought refuge in my bedchamber. I saw her mostly at breakfast. She frequently skipped the other meals. When we accidentally found ourselves in the same company, she said very little. Never looked me in the eyes. Since I wasn't aware of having done anything that might have offended her, I attributed this behavior to an innate shyness or distrust of strangers. I was still an unknown to her. The hours of ceaseless practice likely left her with little time or energy for socializing and small talk.

These were fleeting thoughts I didn't dwell on. My mind was set on what I called "Kafka's mission" but which had by then become mine as well. Nevertheless, during my walks with the dogs along the river that morning, I couldn't get the Baroness' harsh reprimand of her protégée out of my mind. Nothing wrong for a young woman having a nightmare to seek comfort with another woman close to her own age. Why did she have a nightmare? People do have nightmares, I told myself, especially in the nightmarish world we lived in.

Kafka's insinuation that perhaps she doesn't have the stamina for the grueling career of an opera singer ruffled my feathers.

"It takes more than the ability to carry a tune to be a Lenka Ostrova," he said. He raised his eyebrows in the infuriating aficionado snob manner he so often turned up to show his superior wisdom.

"You should hear her. She has an exquisite voice. I think she could be another Ostrova!" I insisted. I had heard both singers, one on recordings, the other in person. To my mind, I had enough of a good enough ear for music to distinguish outstanding from mediocre.

I did grow up surrounded by music of all kinds. I even hailed from musical parentage. My father may be what my grandmother would call a "Musikant," a music maker a grade or two below a true musician. It was when he impressed her with a brilliant rendition of Chopin's Revolutionary Etude that she accepted him as her son-in-law. How often had I heard this story? The point being, I am not as tabula rasa in matters musical as Kafka presumed me to be or as I presumed Kafka to presume me to be. The gap in my musical education had been Wagner, which Kafka had filled to overflowing; more than I ever wanted, but still less than I needed apparently to spout off an expert opinion on the subject.

"The grueling practice sessions may be taking their toll on the girl. The Baroness is merciless in her demands on her. But, there's something else. I sensed a tangible tension between them that may be about something else besides the rehearsal regime. The Baroness is preparing her for an audition with 'a very special person' as she repeatedly warns the poor girl."

"My name is Hannah," she said. "But don't call me that in front of the Baroness." Hannelore, she explained, is more "*treudeutsch*" (true German). She had come into my room again during the night. This time, she didn't have to sneak around. Frau von Bülow was *en voyage*. She had received a telegram message from somewhere which, she told me, required her presence elsewhere in an urgent matter. She did not specify the matter nor the place where she was going, nor when she would return. Meanwhile, she placed her charge or protégée or whatever the young singer was to her, into my care. I promised to do my best to entertain the young lady even though I didn't see why she, who was neither a minor nor an invalid, couldn't manage on her own for a few days.

"Hannelore has a very volatile disposition. It would be best if she did not venture off the premises. And please remind her to adhere to a strict schedule. She can vocalize without accompaniment for a while."

"Didn't she study at the conservatory?"

"Yes, certainly. But she still needs guidance. Discipline, or rather lack thereof, is the rock on which many a talent has faltered."

It turned out, Hannelore von Weber was a very disciplined young woman. Even without admonition and prodding, she faithfully put in her hours of practice. She even accompanied herself on the piano quite competently. She took her métier very seriously even without a martinet beating time. In other ways, rather than being volatile, her disposition was cheerful and pleasant in the absence of her mentoress.

"May I?" She stood at the foot of my bed in her Isolde impersonation with a pleading look. I pulled back the cover as if we had established a routine.

"Come on in! Make yourself comfortable!" I said with a gracious hand movement. We giggled like two teenagers having a slumber party as she wriggled to settle in close to me.

Getting serious, she said: "You know where the Baroness went?" I shook my head.

"Nuremberg. The trial. She worries about her lover."

It hadn't occurred to me that Frau von Bülow might have a lover. When I overheard her conversation with Colonel Dietrich, I thought she might be speaking about a son. On her dresser in her boudoir, I had seen the picture of a man in his thirties, smiling brightly in his SS uniform. The inscription read: "To my inimitable mother, always honor and deference, Her devoted son Odin." Where was he now? The defendants in the current phase of the war crimes trials to which Major Zweig had been posted were the judges and jurists of the regime. Odin von Bülow would have to be a lawyer to be among them.

"Don't be fooled by her noblesse-oblige dignity. It's all façade. She worries herself sick. The evidence against him is unassailable."

"I don't quite follow. How do you know all this? It's hard to imagine she has a lover. And who is he?"

"To that part, I can testify. He's my father. The thing between them has been going on for years."

The plot was surely thickening, prurient-wise.

"He was the presiding judge at the trial of the White Rose. I am sure the Americans are not barbaric enough to hang him on a meat hook."

She had me there. I had no idea what she was talking about.

"Of course, you wouldn't have heard about the White Rose. It was all done in secret. They wouldn't publicize the story of a group of students and one girl who distributed pamphlets at the University of Munich calling attention to the horrors they witnessed at the Eastern Front. The trial was held in secret; if you can call it a trial. The details of the torture leaked out later. How these brave young people suffered before they died!"

She propped herself up on her elbow and gave me a long look with tear-filled eyes.

"Why are you telling me this?" I asked breathlessly.

"Because you are not one of them."

"What do you mean?"

"I mean, you are not who you pretend to be. I don't know who you are and why you are here. But I could tell right away you are not one of them."

Only another Jew can tell! Kafka's words came to my mind. I looked at her, unsure how to respond. She had her glowing blue eyes pinned on my face.

"My name is Hannah, not Hannelore. It says so on my birth certificate." *Geburtsschein*!

"Right after the Nuremberg Blood Laws came out, my father divorced my mother. I was nine years old. He wanted me to stay with him. By the laws' definition, I was a *Halbjüdin*. He thought that with proper guidance and careful grooming, he could foster the Aryan half in me to prevail over the tainted Jewish half. How he underestimated the power of the Jewish blood that is seething in my veins!"

Bettina "Tina" Salomon was a free spirit; a talented artist, dancer, singer, musician, and like many young women of her generation, she poured her soul into things poetic, her daughter related. She was the light and life of Schwabing, the artist quarter of Munich, in the years after the war. She was the only child of Jakob and Amalia Salomon who both came from assimilated families, as it was termed then.

"A Jewish family who, like many, sought to sloughed off all outward signs of Jewishness like a snake sloughs off its skin," Hannah explained. A story not unfamiliar to me.

"They wanted, or hoped, to be like everyone else, blend in with the wider society of the educated, well-to-do bourgeoisie. What they blended in with was a society of other assimilated Jews," Hannah noted.

"What they overlooked, or ignored, or did not take into consideration since they did not think in those terms, was the fact that some of the snake's skin always adheres to its body, and eventually it also grows back and needs sloughing off again." Hannah waxed metaphoric.

"They never denied being Jewish. All they wanted was to be free of the encumbrances of the religion and the restrictions posed on Jews by society. And if one was stung by Jew hatred on occasion, it was the kind one could live with, they rationalized. The hatred was surely only directed against those bearded exotics in strange garb who were flooding in from places in the East."

Amazing words of wisdom from a young woman I had taken for a naïve and an ingénue ignorant of the ways of the world. So much for my insight into the human soul.

Tina's parents, assimilated as they may have been, were nevertheless adamantly opposed to their daughter's marrying a "goy"—though they would never have used that word. She married him anyway, free spirit that she was, and presented them with the fait accompli. Six months later, Hannah was born.

Tina's choice of mate was somewhat odd for an artistic, ambitious, and emancipated young woman from the bohemian precinct of Schwabing. Once they met him, Jakob and Amalia Salomon couldn't find much wrong with their son-in-law except for the flaw that he wasn't a Jew. He was polite, well-mannered and well-dressed, studious with good prospects for a successful legal career. He was, their daughter emphasized, a lapsed Catholic, which stood him in good stead. Putting up a Christmas tree had long been a practice in the Salomon house. They could hardly object to the heathen traditions of that religion if the practice was continued in their daughter's home.

Jakob Salomon was a prominent purveyor of fine leather goods. Through the doors of his establishment on Marienplatz in the center of town passed a prominent, wealthy clientele from all over the country and abroad. Tina had a charmed childhood before the war. She received the finest education. A private tutor filled in for subject matters barred to women. Her doting parents took pride in showing off her precocious musical talent and artistic creations to their extensive circle of relatives and friends. They used their influence to have her paintings showcased at a local gallery. During frequently held musical soirées at their palatial home in Bogenhausen, Tina delighted the guests with Schubert Lieder to which she accompanied herself on the piano.

The outbreak of the war in 1914 put a damper on these activities. Like everyone else, the financial crises of the immediate post-war years brought the Salomon family business to the brink of ruin. Fine leather goods were not much in demand in those days when the currency was worthless. As she later told her daughter, Tina welcomed the financial independence from her parents the company disaster afforded her. She could live freely in a Schwabing garret and support herself, however meagerly, with her art. Her romantic spirit relished the idea of experiencing poverty and to feel for herself the privations and ravages common people had to endure. (Not so different from Weimar Berlin, I thought to myself.)

Like many young people of her generation who came from comfortable upper-class homes, she started reading Marx and the gamut of socialist theorists. She was especially enthralled with Ferdinand Lassalle, the Jewish founder of the socialist movement in Germany, who had later been shunted aside by the Marxists. His romantic life and heroic death in a duel no doubt was enough to catch Tina's fancy more than his political ideas. What kind of socialist would devote twenty years to litigating in the divorce of a German countess and then die in a duel with a Serbian aristocrat over a woman? The stuff to stoke a young girl's fantasies! While all the drama of his life was unfolding, that same Lasalle formulated the theoretical basis of German Social Democracy; ideas for social programs which Bismarck stole from him, and the followers of Marx denounced as counterrevolutionary.

It was, therefore, surprising to everybody who knew her mother that she should have fallen in love with a man of as bland and insipid a character as Adalbert Maria von Weber. He came from a "good" family of a long line of civil servants. His father was a postmaster. His mother was of Alpine peasant stock in an Alpine village. His older brothers, he had three, all of them were "postilions." His sisters, of which he had two, were both married to postal servants. The entire family, mother, father, brothers, sisters, in-laws bloomed as "March flowers"–a Goebbels coinage for the millions of voters who scrambled on board the Nazi bandwagon in March 1933.

At that time, Adalbert, the only one in the family who had gone to university, also added "Maria" and "von" to his name to bolster his bogus claim that he was a descendant of the Romantic composer Carl Maria von Weber. Stability, rigidity, stolidity were characteristics imprinted in his solid square physique. With time his head took on the form of a square block, like a younger version of Hindenburg. By the time the Nuremberg laws were enacted in 1935, he had become a stalwart NS legal apparatchik.

"How can I, a judge of the Reich, be married to a Jewess?" he protested when Tina threw the divorce papers he proffered back in his face. Why she didn't divorce him herself two years before was a question to which Hannah had no answer. He obtained custody for their only child and had her name officially changed to Hannelore.

"Remember you are of Aryan blood," he told his daughter. "You must forget about the woman who gave to birth you."

All his prodding was in vain. Hannah only came out of her room at the lakefront villa in Starnberg when he promised she could go to Munich once a month to see her mother. A promise he frequently broke under all kinds of pretexts.

Hannah lived for the brief visits she was allowed with her mother. A week after Kristallnacht, then twelve years old, she broke out of the prison in Starnberg and moved in with her relatives in the Jewish district on Reichenbachstraße. The devastation she saw there was horrendous. The main synagogue that had rivaled the Frauenkirche in grandeur and splendor had already been torn down several months before on Hitler's direct orders. The writing was clearly on the wall. Jewish lives were no longer safe in the German Reich. Tina made only haphazard attempts to leave.

"How can I live far away from my only child? Not knowing what is happening to her," she despaired. "Though I am sure he would not permit anyone to lay a hand on me."

Could she possibly have thought that? Yes, said her daughter. The capacity for human self-deception can be boundless.

Hannah defied her father and lived with her mother and her grandparents in the ever-tightening living space remaining to them. Beginning in September 1941, the ranks of the remaining Jews in Munich were systematically thinned with deportations to the East. In May 1942, Jakob and Amalia Salomon, now almost eighty, were torn from their beds and put on a transport to a place called Theresienstadt, as Hannah found out later. Her father assured her they would be quite comfortable there; a kind of resort for older people with all their needs cared for by the state. His offer to help Tina cross the Swiss border earned him a glob of spit in the face.

"You and your magnanimity can go to hell!" she screamed at him. "That satisfaction I will never grant you! You made me out to be a Jewess. Well, that's what I am. I will not shy away from sharing the fate you and your cronies have planned for my people. Yes, my people!"

In the time following Kristallnacht November 1938, Hannah had the painful experience of having to witness her mother's gradual descent into a deepening depression and madness. Her best efforts to rouse her from a state of apathy about what was going on around her were as futile as talking to a wall. Hannah wouldn't give up. She couldn't just let her mother be. She couldn't permit her to sit motionless in a dimly lit corner of the room they all shared. One day, Hannah's heart began to fill with hope. Her mother suddenly came out of the catatonic stupor into which she had sunken and asked for books. Jewish books, she specified.

"If I am to be Jewish, I should know something about Jewishness and Judaism. What makes a person a Jew? We surely shouldn't leave it to those criminals and their laws to decide."

Hannah didn't have a good answer. Neither did her grandparents.

"We are Jewish," Tina's father ventured, raising his hands and weighing his head, "because that's what our ancestors were. Your great-grandfather, my grandfather, was a pious man. I still remember him going to synagogue twice a day, in the morning and evening. And the Sabbath was a holy day. All he did was pray. That's all I remember. My father said it was all superstition, outmoded practices unsuited for modern life."

Her father's answer, a meek attempt at an answer, left Tina's newly roused thirst for knowledge deeply unsatisfied. She wanted more. She began to delve into books such as were available. A few times, she even went to the damaged synagogue a few steps down the street where services were still held on occasion. She found the people she met there too preoccupied with their everyday lives and petty concerns, their worries and anxieties about what was happening to them and what suffering lay in the future. She stopped going after a few times and immersed herself instead in her reading material. She would face "whatever may come," she said, "with pride and without moaning and groaning."

"She was not as strong as she thought she was," Hannah said. "Or maybe she was."

Three days after Jakob and Amalia Salomon had been rounded up and taken to a then still unknown place somewhere in the East, Hannah came home from the Catholic girl's school where she was enrolled. On entering the stairwell, her nostrils were stung by the sulfurous odor of rotten eggs. She rushed up the three flights taking several steps at a time to the apartment she and her mother had shared with the grandparents and three other elderly couples all of whom had been taken away as well, so her mother was alone.

Hannah ransacked the empty place room by room only to find her mother lifeless on the kitchen floor. Tina had opened the gas faucet without lighting the flame. On the table was a long handwritten last testament to her daughter. "It is better this way," the letter concluded. She asked her forgiveness and understanding why she had to leave her alone in the world.

"With death, a certainty, it is far better for us to part here peacefully. This way I hope to spare you the sight of your mother being herded onto a train and the agony of an uncertain destination and destiny."

Bettina Salomon was laid to rest with quiet dignity in the Jewish cemetery on Thalkirchnerstraße in Sendling. This much

Adalbert granted her, if for no other reason than to appease his grieving daughter.

Hannah moved from the now empty house on Reichenbachstraße back to the villa in Starnberg. She was placed in the care of one of Adalbert's peasant cousins from his mother's village, her paternal grandparents having passed away a few years before. She received instructions from a private tutor in the subjects of the grade she normally would have attended.

She didn't see much of her father. He was rarely at home. His court duties as the presiding judge over trials and executions of dissidents, required more and more of his time as the war went on. The highlight of his career, for which he was now on trial, though the proceedings were held in secret and Hannah found out about it only later, was his association with the tribunal and torture death of a group of university students who called themselves "White Rose."

It was then that the villa had a frequent visitor from Bayreuth, Baroness Elisabeth von Bülow, the judge's long-time mistress. She soon gave up on her attempts to gain Hannah's confidence and affection. However, at the instigation of the father, who recognized his daughter's talent, she shouldered the task of broadening the obstreperous adolescent's musical education.

In the last year of the war, Hannah traveled several times a week between the villa in Starnberg and the city to study voice at the conservatory. She stayed in a windowless apartment on Königinstraße opposite the English Garden, a once-verdant city park that now resembled a plowed potato field.

"In this Götterdämmerung atmosphere, music making continued in the capital city of the movement as unabated as the Allied bombs raining down from the sky," said Hannah with a wink of sarcasm toward what the Nazis termed the city where their movement originated.

All through the turmoil and upheavals of this apocalyptic atmosphere (*Weltuntergangsstimmung*), the arrest and imprisonment of Adalbert von Weber, the collapse of the currency, shortages of every kind, crowded, dilapidated lodgings, lack of sanitary facilities, Hannah continued her studies at the conservatory. One day the Baroness appeared and urged her to come with her to Bayreuth.

"She found no end in complimenting me on my enormous talent which, with proper guidance, would take me to the pinnacle of success." Hannah was alone in the world. She stayed at the villa in Starnberg for a while after the war had ended. With nothing to do, her heart still with her art, she eventually took up the Baroness's offer.

"She told me she would put me in touch with a famous soprano."

When she mentioned the name Elfriede Kling, I almost jumped out of my skin.

"I don't know if you have heard of her, but she was Hitler's favorite opera singer, a Wagnerian at that. She and her husband Rudolf Schwamm were the darlings of the opera world all through the war years. The Baroness told me they are in hiding somewhere near here. At a mountain retreat. She had no doubt Madam Kling would be delighted to meet me, the daughter of a prominent judge, and take me on as a pupil when things had calmed down more.

"The Baroness asked me to promise not to mention anything about my mother. If they ask, she said, tell them she died in a bombing raid. You are Hannelore von Weber, nobody will question you, she assured me."

"And you are going along with it?" I couldn't help but ask.

"As long as it suits me and furthers my goals, why not?" A grim shadow appeared on her face. "These are hard times. One has to be realistic."

Ever since she was seven years old, Hannah had dreamed of becoming an opera singer. In May 1933, during the Nazi boycott of Jewish businesses, she accompanied her grandparents on a visit to Vienna. Her grandfather wanted to search out opportunities for transferring his business and inventory to the Austrian capital where he had a brother who was in a similar business. While they were there, they took their granddaughter to the Vienna Opera to hear the celebrated soprano Lenka Ostrova sing Tosca.

"She was famed for her Wagner roles, but that time she sang Puccini. I was enthralled. It may sound silly. I was only seven years old, but it was a decisive moment in my life. I vowed to become a singer like Lenka Ostrova. And Tosca would be my debut performance."

Hannah fell into a ponderous silence. I held back my desire to press her against my heart.

"I don't know what became of her," she finally said. "She disappeared right after the Anschluss. My grandmother said she was Jewish and that she heard Goebbels' henchmen in Vienna did away with her."

"I have heard Elfriede Kling sing in various roles. She is not as brilliant as Lenka Ostrova, but she is good enough. If she is willing to teach me, I'll take it. I'll pretend to be Hannelore. Hannah's day will come."

She had been sitting up in bed while she was talking. Now she sank back into the pillows, limp like a wrung-out wet sheet. She snuggled up against me, seeking the comfort of the warmth of our bodies. How much she had gone through in her young life, I thought, enfolding her in my arms and rocking her gently.

"Why are you telling me all this?" I asked her after a while.

"I told you. I know you are not one of them. You are one of us, no matter how much you try to hide it."

"What makes you think so?"

"I can see it in your eyes, everything about you. I lived with my Jewish relatives in the ghetto. I can tell. I have a sixth sense about this. You don't have to explain why you are a guest in this house. I am sure the Baroness has no inkling of who you are. If she found out, she would show you the door. Politely of course, with baronial grace and dignity since the venerated Reich is gone. Kaput! Futsch! You saw how she caters to the Americans whom she despises deep down. Don't be deceived by her fawning licking of the Colonel's boots. The Americans are the conquering heroes now, the current rulers of this land. One bows to circumstance. But nothing has changed in her or anyone else's cast of mind." *Gesinnung* was the word she used.

Chapter 5

Summer Idyll

"Eureka! Eureka!" I called out. The dogs must have felt my excitement. They charged ahead with long gazelle strides, tugging at the leash so hard I could barely keep up and was in danger of losing my balance. When Kafka came into view, they abandoned all restraint. They pulled away from me, leaping up on him, licking his face with eager affection as if they were greeting a long-lost friend.

"These damn dogs," I huffed. "Jumping the gun on me like that. I should be the one leaping up on you."

"You can still do that," Kafka laughed. "What's the excitement?"

"Eureka!" I repeated. Still panting like one of the dogs, I fell around his neck and covered his face with kisses. "We are on the right track!"

Hannah's story intrigued him. But, he advised caution and against taking her into my confidence.

"If she asks questions, you'd better stick to the search for your grandmother in Berlin story." Kafka, the schoolmaster, couldn't help himself. He had to give a lecture on everything.

"This is not what I told the Baroness. Remember, Beate Hauser is on her way to Berlin to rejoin her family there. That's the story I'll stick with," I said scowling.

"Come on, don't be so huffy!" He poked me playfully in the ribs and tried to pull me toward him. As much as I bristled with anger, the man exuded a magnetism I couldn't resist.

Life with Kafka would always be like this. Hard to imagine him as the housefather settled into a routine, reading his newspaper at breakfast, kissing the children goodbye before going off to work. Life with Kafka would never be like that. It would always be a life on the edge. No bourgeois comforts.

"So, what next?" he asked.

"We'll wait and see with what other news heaven will shower us."

I felt back in the saddle, taking charge of immediate strategic planning — the day to day minutiae. I was the one on the frontline and in the best position to decide how to proceed.

"She mentioned a mountain retreat where they are hiding out. But which mountain? That, my dear, is still the question."

"I have full confidence you will find the answer," he said, for once ceding rank to me.

The dogs were getting restless again, and I prepared to leave.

"One more thing," he said pulling me back. "The trial in Nuremberg is over. The prosecution asked for the death penalty in the case of several of the defendants. The judge is likely to get some of his own medicine and will hang. Not good news for the Baroness. But she may take comfort in the fact that meat hooks are out. A sturdy rope will do the job, quick and clean. Then again, he might get only life, I am told."

"Told by whom?"

"Emil Zweig, of course."

When I got back to Villa Lohengrin, Hannah stood sulking at the front door as if she had been lying in wait for me.

"You've been out for a long time," she said. "Where do you go so early in the morning?"

"The Baroness entrusted me with the care of her dogs. Wind hounds need to run, stretch their legs. Can't keep them cooped up all the time. Early morning, before the streets get crowded, is the best time."

"I'd like to go with you sometime. The dogs are not the only ones who feel cooped up and need to stretch their legs."

Poor Hannah! How much I would have liked to free her from the imprisonment she found herself in! But she made a devil's bargain of her own free will with a view toward a higher goal. She was using the Baroness to further her career as much as the Baroness was using her to regain what she hoped was only a temporary setback before the glory days for Wagnerian grandeur would return. Under no circumstances could I permit her to accompany me on my pre-dawn outings, for another obvious reason.

"It's too early in the morning," I said evasively. "You need to be well rested for your daily routine."

"What do you know about that? You don't want me to know where you are going. I bet you are meeting someone. Who are you anyway to make the rules around here?"

"The Baroness asked me to look after you during her absence."

"The Baroness this, the Baroness that! I am sick of having this woman run my life! And you have no right to tell me what to do either."

Had she forgotten what she had told me the night before? She couldn't possibly have made up that story about her family, her mother, her father. What could have been her purpose? I had not taken her into my confidence. I had not admitted she was right about me. Neither had I contradicted her. We had formed a bond, a silent understanding. Should I allow her to go with me to meet Kafka?

"No," replied Kafka. "She has a vested interest and needs Elfriede Kling's coattails, which may still be worth something in some circles. No, no. We cannot trust her, at least not now. But she could bring us closer to our goal."

"I am not comfortable playing a game of pretend friendship with her. Besides, Frau Kling is pretty much washed up. She hardly has any coattails to ride on, except to give private lessons."

"She will be back on stage, mark my word. And so will Rudolf Schwamm. Give it a few years, maybe less, and everything will be forgotten and forgiven. Unless . . . !"

Kafka's determination to hold the two songbirds he held responsible for the murder of Lenka Ostrova to account was unwavering. He had already shown himself to be a cold-blooded assassin as I witnessed and participated in myself. But back then, I acted in self-defense. I told myself when pangs of conscience woke me at night. It was not a planned, calculated killing. Even he acted out of necessity that arose from the circumstances of the moment. In rare moments of contemplation of the consequences, my conscience, in so far as I still had one, recoiled. But I was already too deeply entangled. Even if I wanted to, there was no way I could extricate myself.

Romantic love played a diminished role in my growing commitment to the cause. The bloom of the romance in the forest had lost its luster. It had transmuted into something more solid, a comradeship, a fellowship welded in the cauldron of the experiences of my journey and the broader canvas of a haunting historical nightmare. What goaded me on was grounded in a more compelling sentiment: a firm belief in the justness of Kafka's cause. I do not believe this to have been the result of a Svengali effect. Rather, it was formed by all I had seen and heard and observed on this journey.

The Baroness took to her bed with the vapors immediately upon her return. She had aged considerably in the time of her absence. Her gait was dragging, her shoulders stooped, her mien wearied. Deep furrows I had not observed before carved her brow. Her trembling hand gripped my arm tight as we ascended the stairs, step by step, to her bedchamber.

"You must stay with me a while longer, Fräulein Beate," she implored. "You are the only one I can trust in this terrible time."

I nodded.

"Write to your family. Explain to them the circumstances of an old woman in need of your companionship and care. I am sure they will understand. Promise me, please, you will not abandon me in this my darkest hour."

I almost felt a pinch of pity for her. She had no understanding of the preposterousness of what she was asking, even if it were of a real Beate Hauser.

I promised. I patted her hand reassuringly.

"I still have the means to reward you handsomely," she reassured me with a sly smile.

With the general population of her countrymen living on meager rations, she still had resources and stockpiles of provisions to draw on. By the time we reached the door to her chambers on the upper floor, I had been transformed from casual houseguest and dog walker to handmaiden. Later, private secretary was added to my duties.

"Lend me a hand with my peignoir!" she said, shifting her voice into the slightly higher, more compressed register in which the well-born address their servants.

I helped her disrobe and get into her nightgown. I drew back the bed covers, fluffed the mass of down pillows, and steadied her frail frame as she placed one foot after the other on the little stepping stool to her elevated four-poster mahogany bed. She immediately sank back into the pillows with a deep sigh. She waved her hand at the window, indicating she wished the curtains to be drawn. She was not to be disturbed until the evening meal which she would take in bed, she instructed me. Then I was dismissed with a graceful flutter of her hand.

My new status in the von Bülow household necessitated my move into a room adjacent to that of the Baroness. Since she was in the habit of ringing the bell for assistance at all hours of the day and night, it became difficult for me to tend to the dogs as well.

With the Baroness incapacitated and confined to her bed, it also fell to me to supervise the Sudeten German house personnel.

Hannah raised her eyebrows when I informed her of my new status at Villa Lohengrin.

"Delicious irony," she said. "Whatever your game, it serves her right. I am sure you will rise to the challenge and prove yourself up to the task. I guess congratulations are in order. Or should I say, *mazel tov*?"

I left the answer hanging in the air.

Hannah played her own game brilliantly, growing into the role of prima donna with ease and self-confidence. She ran through a slew of accompanists for her daily, vocal drills chosen from among an army of out-of-work musicians waiting around Bayreuth for better times to come. None of them were entirely up to the task.

"Mazel tov!" said Kafka when I finally had a chance to link up with him for a brief rendezvous one early morning. The dogs were no longer under my care. As much as the Baroness was attached to her canine companions, she thought it unfitting for her "lady-in-waiting" (she used the English term) to be tending dogs. That chore was temporarily passed on to one of the day-laborers until a dog groomer could be found. Was this woman living in the real world? I thought at first, until a real-life "professional" dog groomer, at least one who claimed to be such, came knocking on her door.

His name, he told the Baroness, was Franz Kaiser. He hailed from--would you believe it? --the Sudetenland! Straight from the Bohemian Woods. A dispossessed refugee. His tales of trials and hardship, even imprisonment and an adventurous escape from the vengeful Czechs, conquered the Baroness's heart in a storm.

He didn't have to win over Wotan and Fricka. They recognized him right away and greeted him with lapping affection, convincing their owner that she had found a natural caretaker for her beloved canines.

How this caretaker had found out about the job opening, she forgot to ask. This stranger assuaged her frequently vented misgivings about the riffraff and rabble, the uprooted, homeless, aimless vagrants and drifters, populating the "good German earth" since the war's end to the wind.

"A charming, well-bred compatriot," she told me, "whose presence will not only be good for our dogs but having a man around will be salutary for the security of this mostly female household."

What clinched the pact between them, she confided to me with a sly smile, was the revolver he showed her and his assurance he knew how to use it if need be.

"Are you out of your mind?" I yelled at Kafka when I had an opportunity to stop by the cozy little cottage near the dog enclosure where he had taken up residence.

"Don't you have a saying in America about Smith and Wesson inspiring trust?" He dismissed my concern with a Kafka laugh.

"I wouldn't know anything about that," I shot back.

My annoyance due to fear over what would happen if his stash of firearms were discovered—I kept my trusty little Roth-Steyr always hidden but within easy reach—was quickly superseded by my exhilaration over having him within easy reach. I no longer had to wonder where he was and what he was doing nor worry about his safety. I always had a vague suspicion he may be involved in shady dealings with shady black marketeers that could get him in trouble with US military law.

The benefits of having him on the premises of Villa Lohengrin outweighed any downside. A few times I even took a chance of not being found in my bed should the Baroness call on me during the night for this or that need, as was her wont, and streaked across the grounds for a nocturnal tryst at the dog keeper's cottage. Luckily, the news Colonel Dietrich delivered to her personally one day calmed her spirits, and she slept much more peacefully during the night.

"Good news, my dear Baroness!" the Colonel had declared. "The sentence has been commuted to a prison term. Life, but there's always the possibility of parole." He was in his service uniform for this unannounced afternoon call.

"Well, hope springs eternal as you Americans say," she said with puckered lips in her impeccable British. Together they partook of tea and biscuits from Rosenthal cups and plates. A cozy tête-à-tête in the sunroom of Villa Lohengrin. The sunken world of yesterday still held on to a last breath of life.

"I see Fräulein Hauser is still with you," he noted sending a probing look my way, or so I thought, as he excused himself. His many duties required his attention. But he did not want to be remiss in informing her personally.

"She has agreed to stay on as my companion and private secretary. There are so few people one can trust in these trying times," she sighed pensively.

Then touching her hand to her forehead as if she just remembered something, she added: "You must come to our next *soirée musicale*. A wonderful program of Schubert Lieder in addition to a sampling of Wagner arias."

"I wouldn't miss it for the world."

She accompanied him to the door and waved goodbye from the top of the front steps. He summoned his driver and was about to jump into the jeep when something at the far end of the grounds seemed to catch his eye. He turned to the Baroness.

"You have a new tenant?" he asked. This time I was sure of the probing look in his eyes.

"Oh, yes, a most wonderful gentleman! A refugee from Sudetenland. He takes care of Wotan and Fricka. My beautiful Borzois," she explained when she saw his questioning look.

"Herr Kaiser is very good at handling them," she gushed on. I hadn't seen her in so voluble a mood in a long time. Of course, officially I didn't understand a word of what they were saying. I lingered at some distance, within earshot, always at a ready to fulfill any requests she might have for me.

"He also looks after other matters around the grounds that need doing. It takes a man's hand to keep a place like this in good order. Besides, he is a very well-educated man. But these days one must take on all kinds of chores to get by. I count myself most fortunate to have him in my service."

"Very interesting," muttered the Colonel as he climbed into the waiting jeep. "I look forward to receiving your invitation! Auf Wiedersehen!"

On the way inside, the Baroness hummed a little tune, her gait was light, even bouncy. She waved off my tendered arm on which she had been leaning to steady herself.

"You seem elated," I said. "Did the Colonel bring you good news?"

"Oh yes, he did indeed!" she replied. "Very good news." Nothing more. It irked me somehow that she didn't take me into her confidence. Then again, why should she talk to me about her love affairs? Our relationship was *herzlich*, not intimate. We all had our secrets. It would not have been appropriate for me to press for more. What she didn't know was that I already knew the answer.

She did mention the Colonel's visit and message to Hannah at the dinner table that evening. If she expected an outpouring of gratitude from the girl that her father would not have to face the gallows, she was to be disappointed. Then again, she had no such expectation. She did not pursue the matter further when Hannah, her demeanor more frowning than anything else, just nodded with a shrug and said: "That's nice."

"I hope they'll hang him," I remembered her saying to me.

Later in the evening after I had finished reading to the Baroness a chapter from Stifter's *Bunte Steine*—maybe she liked this author so much because his name was Adalbert—I sought to take Hannah aside for a private talk, but she was evasive.

"Too tired," she said and fled to her room.

Ever since Kafka had moved into the cottage, I felt a cool wind blowing from Hannah toward me. Her most hostile behavior, however, was reserved for Kafka himself whenever he showed up at the main house, which was becoming more frequent at the Baroness' request. Did she see him as an intruder? Into what? He was courteous and very obliging — "Such a well-mannered, polite gentleman!" cooed the Baroness on every occasion that presented itself. Hannah, however, rebuffed his well-mannered, polite compliments about her singing voice with a glaring frown.

He had rarely heard Schubert's "Ständchen," which had been streaming through the house for several days on end, with more empathic sensitivity, he had told her. "What would you know about it?" she huffed.

Herr Kaiser knew quite a bit about Schubert and classical music in general. Moreover, he proved to be quite the connoisseur of the great Wagner. The Baroness was in heaven.

Notwithstanding Hannah's sullenness, our little group, one could almost say family, settled into a pleasant summer at the von Bülow sanctuary, shielded from the unpleasantness of the world outside by a high brick wall and tall bushes. During afternoon breaks in the practice sessions, we gather on the shaded terrace overlooking the well-kept garden. We were comfortably seated in upholstered lounge chairs, fanned by gentle breezes, sipping tea, reading the great German poets out loud to each other (sans Heine of course), or passing the time with a game of backgammon or checkers.

Herr Kaiser became a regular visitor to the terrace. They were flanked by Wotan and Fricka, those perfidious hounds who had shifted their loyalty without a second's thought from me to him. He would then engage with the Baroness in conversations on topics in a language which were both esoteric to me. The philosophy of a man named Schopenhauer (new to me) was weighed against that of Kant (heard the name but knew little). Phrases like "the world is my idea" and "sufficient reason" spouted from Kafka's mouth. I had no idea what in the world that meant. Wagner's innovative harmonies and orchestrations, the poetic genius of his librettos, all were the subjects of lengthy expositions. The word "genius" was dropped frequently and reverentially like a bouncing ball.

Words like "charming" and "delightful" dripped endlessly from the Baroness's mouth when speaking of the newcomer. I didn't keep count. Was it possible? Had the bearded, long-haired stranger, in every way, the antithesis of the blue-eyed, blond Aryan manly ideal in the picture on her dresser, really conquered her heart? Maybe the very prim Baroness had a secret penchant for the exotic, for black hair woven through with silvery filigree, dark shining eyes and a mocking laugh ringing through house and yard. I was reminded of the time when that laughter first rattled my spirit. That was in another yard, one that was dimly lit by craned lamps casting a ghostly shadow on grimy brick buildings.

Sitting next to this pair, bored and left out as I was, I couldn't decide what I admired, and to some degree despised, more about this lover of mine, his great knowledge of so many and varied things that were beyond my ken or his even greater talent for dissembling. Anyone who did not know how much he despised Wagner, his music, and all the Bayreuth ballyhoo, would have thought him to be the most devoted acolyte. That much was clear: the man I loved was a charlatan. But I had known that for some time. And, I had to admit, not without a certain pride, I had proven a talented disciple and would take no back seat when it came to the art of dissimulating.

None of us was what we seemed or pretended to be. Even the Baroness had her secrets, which she guarded behind a grotesque, pasted-on smile. One could call it a comedy of errors or theater of the absurd. In any case, it was Kafka, the Svengali, who dictated the script and pulled the strings.

Chapter 6

A Blood Banquet

My main concern then was Hannah. I never had a close female friend. In my years of growing up, I had always been an appendage to an adult world. I often felt like I was someone who tagged along or had to be dragged along for no other reason than that I existed. Maybe I am doing the people who cared for me and loved me an injustice. After all, they did not create the circumstances, at least not those that befell us all during my growing-up years, "*Backfisch*" years (a peculiar German expression likening a girl to a baking fish) my grandmother would call the period of a girl's coming of age. Mine were not normal.

In my moments of greatest self-pity, I regretted never having known what it was like growing up with girls of my age, having a sister or one special best friend with whom I could share confidences, plotting mischief or whatever it is young girls do.

The secret friendship with Hannah, heartwarming as it was, had come as a surprise to me. Two young women holding on to each other in a world in which both were not at home had not been part of the plan. She had confided in me, invited me into her world, shared the most horrific experiences of her young life, perhaps with the justified expectation of reciprocity. Maybe she felt my silence as a betrayal, which in a certain sense was true. I had let her down by being guarded, not reciprocating her confidences. How could I let her know I was not a free agent?

"I saw you," she hissed more than whispered in my ear one evening. We were all gathered on the terrace for after-dinner tea. Hannah and I were seated on the margin of that stage. At a center table, the Baroness and Kafka were waging war in a card game of Whist—German rules, take no prisoners. Both Hannah and I had declined an invitation to join in a round of the great Bavarian game called "Sheepshead," which requires four players, with the excuse that we didn't know the game. True in my case. As for Hannah, I suspected she didn't want to abandon her vantage point from which to observe the scene.

"I know what is going on," she said under her breath. "This drifter didn't happen to drift in one day by pure chance. I told you I can spot a Jew from far away. Somebody told him about the dogs. The Baroness may be duped. Can't fool me."

"What are you going to do about it?"

"Don't worry. Nothing. Nothing at all. I'll laugh into my little fist and enjoy the show." She gave off a mischievous giggle. Kafka looked up briefly from his cards and shot us a probing glance which I took as a warning to me.

The dogs whose lanky bodies were stretched out next to the card players like elongated foot mats suddenly awoke and rose in unison for no immediately apparent reason other than to indicate it was time to exert those long limbs. The engrossed players readily accepted my offer to take them for a walk.

"I am coming with you," Hannah declared to my surprise.

"I hate card games. Gets boring after a while to sit and watch," she said panting and doubling her step to keep up with me and the hounds who were sprinting forward with vigorous strides as if they had been set free in the wilderness of their native terrain in Siberia. I finally had to let go of the leash to avoid being dragged along on the ground.

Hannah sat next to me on a bench overlooking the river. We were both out of breath. The dogs were celebrating their freedom, leaping and wrestling with each other. I mulled over various ways to draw her into a conversation about what was on both our minds: Kafka. Should I just come right out and confirm what she suspected. Kafka's stern glance during the card game held me back from being completely open as I was wont to be. Hannah had no such reservations.

"How long have you been sleeping with him?" Hannah asked without beating around the bush.

"What do you mean?" was my rather lame response.

"You needn't play coy with me. Even before I saw you traipsing to the cottage in the moonlight, I could tell. People who are intimate often try to hide the fact by pretending just a little too hard to appear distant and indifferent. A discerning observer can sense the aura that swirls around two lovers. I can also see how this Kaiser, if that's his name, has you dancing to his tune with a glance from his demonic eyes."

"You are very perceptive," I said. "But he is not my puppeteer as you seem to think. We are partners. And yes, I won't deny we are lovers. He needed a place to stay. And this arrangement works to everybody's satisfaction. The Baroness appreciates the company."

"But she doesn't know he is a Jew. And a camp survivor at that."

"How would you know that?"

"First, there aren't many Jews around in this post-war world who haven't been in some camp or other. Secondly, I've seen him before."

"Seen him where?"

"He didn't have all that hair, and he was much thinner, haggard like all those who came out of the camps at the end of the war. But even then, there was something about him, his presence, that made him stand out: the self-confidence, the devil-may-care attitude, the undaunted look in his eyes, and, most of all, his laughter.

"He stood out in the line of liberated camp inmates shuffling along the highway near Starnberg. I didn't get his name. It's probably not what he says it is anyway. He is wanted by the American military."

"Wanted for what?" My heart was pounding in my throat.

"Murder. Don't be alarmed." She put her arm around my heaving chest. "It was justifiable, a revenge killing."

"Did you witness the incident?"

"Not with my own eyes. But I observed much of what went on during those days when the war was finally over."

She paused and drew circles on the ground with a twig. With a sudden move, she jumped up and flung it far away. The dogs immediately ran after it. Wotan dutifully retrieved it and placed it at her feet, while Fricka pawed her legs begging for more. This game went on for several rounds until I finally snapped.

"A hen that cackles should lay an egg!" I burst out impatiently.

"Sorry if I left you hanging. I needed a few moments to recall the incident."

"You must have been thinking about it all this time."

"Yes, but I wasn't sure I should tell you. Now that the cat is out of the sack—moving from hen to cat--I should tell you what I witnessed right after the war was finally over.

"In the last days of the war, the situation in the city was so chaotic, it became impossible to study. The conservatory was closed. With nowhere to go, I went back to the villa by the lake in Starnberg to wait out the end of the war. Once Germany had surrendered—the details of the fate of the top echelon of criminals were not immediately clear—my father believed all he had to do was report to the American authorities and put himself at their disposal. He reported to them, and they arrested him. Unbeknownst to him, his name was already on the list of Nazi criminals. They locked him up at Stadelheim, the prison where his victims from the White Rose had been tortured and beheaded. Poetic justice!

"That summer, I found myself alone in the villa by the lake. Information on the extent of the crimes and atrocities was hard to come by. Some of it trickled through. For the most part, there was silence. Silence in the papers and silence among the people who were busy whitewashing themselves. From the window on the top floor of my father's villa, I had a clear view of the highway. Every day, in endless procession, throngs of human skeletons—their wretched condition as enraging as it was heartbreaking—passed from the north, probably from Dachau, to a destination south. Nobody had to tell me that they were Jewish survivors. I went out to meet them. Wanted to talk to them. Silly me! What did I expect? A grateful welcome with open arms? What they saw was a German girl, an enemy.

"I joined a group of Germans who had been part of the Catholic resistance, so they said. They were now setting up tables with refreshments at the curbside for the camp survivors who were passing by in a long procession. They couldn't have done much resisting, I thought. If they had, their bodies would be covered with dirt in a ditch or hanging from a meat hook instead of being here now patting themselves on their backs. 'Inner emigration' they called their way of resisting. All the good that did!

"As matters stood, they were the only Germans I could find who recognized and admitted that crimes had been committed in the name of the German people. Much of what I learned about my father's crimes, I learned from a neighbor, a famous musician and composer. Despite his sympathy for the cause, he had chickened out from involvement with the White Rose. To his everlasting regret, he assured me. Faced with a choice, he did the cowardly thing. It was fame and recognition for his work over speaking out against what he knew was evil. His bargain with the devil paid off quite handsomely. He is now freely enjoying his fame. I won't mention his name. But I digress. This is not what you want me to talk about."

"No, no, it's fascinating. You have a unique perspective on the German psyche. Very interesting to me."

"Good. Now back to . . . let's call it 'the incident'! Most of the hundreds of people on that long march down the highway passed on to some camp the Americans had set up near Weilheim. We served them hot soup and tea. Cold water if preferred. Fresh baked bread and cheese were also on hand. The procession passed by mostly in silence. Very little exchange of words. My attempts to make eye contact met expressionless stares. The exception was a handful of men, as ragged as the rest, who stopped by, cheerfully chattering, even boisterous. Unlike most of the others, they were helping themselves to hefty portions of what we had to offer. Among them, this tall, lanky fellow stood out. His laughter pierced the solemn silence like a high-pitched siren. Our eyes met for a moment when I filled a bowl with a scoop of thick vegetable soup for him. 'Hmm,' he smacked his lips. 'Real vegetables! Tasty. My compliments to the chef. Only next time add some of those liver dumplings you Bavarians are famous for.' I promised to see what I could do.

"That was the extent of our exchange. I presumed he and his comrades would move on to the survivors' camp in the foothills of the Alps. It was quite a surprise when I saw them the next morning swimming in the lake. It was a warm summer day. Nothing unnatural about wanting to take a dip. I gave it no further thought. I had volunteered to spend the day helping in the kitchen at the Catholic church, which served as a center for the food drive.

"That evening a planning committee—yes, believe it or not, there was already a committee—would hold a meeting at the villa of one of the church members. Gatherings of more than six people were prohibited under Allied rules. They made it out to be a small dinner among friends. A member of that group approached me. A wolf in sheep's clothes. Sickening. He expressed his pleasure to see the daughter of Judge von Weber supporting this charitable cause. I couldn't shake a sense of uneasiness about some of the types who were eager to lend a hand to this charitable enterprise.

'You know my mother was Jewish?' I said to the gentleman. No, he had no idea. Who would have thought! 'Well, that makes it all the better,' he said. 'You have probably already been denazified.'

Yes, indeed I was the proud owner of a Persilschein. But why did that make it, whatever *it* was, all the better?

'May we have the pleasure of your presence at our planning meeting and banquet at the villa of Count Hartmut von Graf?' he continued in the most disgustingly oily tone. 'It's a short distance from here. We can send a car around. The fatherland needs people like you in these trying times.'

"The fatherland needs *me?* I had volunteered to aid the victims of that fatherland, but I was in no way inclined to do the fatherland any favors. I declined, politely but firmly. I refused to be used as a fig leaf. These people still lived in plush villas and had private cars? They seem to have convinced the Americans that they were the good Germans, the little Nazis at most. They were all good. I was not so sure of that.

"Then the next morning a shock wave rippled through the town. The news went out that all those present at this charitable banquet had been murdered. A maid found them with their faces in the soup plates still seated around the table. All of them had been shot at close range in the back of the neck. *Genickschuß* –the Nazi's favorite method of execution.

"The tall man with the rippling laughter made no bones about the fact that he had been the executioner. The Americans arrested him and his companions. A few days later, an American attorney arrived from Frankfurt headquarters who interrogated them. Later we heard that his two accomplices were released and sent on to a displaced persons' camp, as they now called these installations. The one identified as the shooter disappeared. Nothing was heard of a trial or punishment. A few days later, he had disappeared. And life went on for the Germans with the business of everyday survival and toadying to their new masters, the US military authorities.

"Rumor had it that all the dead had been high-ranking Gestapo agents. Since the perpetrator was known to be a Jew and camp survivor, one was more than willing, even more than inclined, not to stir the pot. I left Starnberg shortly after that and continued my studies in Munich.

"You must understand how shocked I was, not to say alarmed, to see this man here at Villa Lohengrin, claiming to be a Sudeten German. I am not sure he remembers me. So far, he has given no sign."

I couldn't help but laugh out loud. This was quite a story. And just like Kafka!

"You say an American officer from Frankfurt headquarters bailed him out?"

"How he got away, I don't know. I doubt he was ever charged or tried. I gather he never told you this story."

"I had an inkling of something, but no, I didn't know the details. Thank you for filling me in. Very fascinating!"

"It doesn't upset you? I mean, it doesn't make you uneasy that you are sleeping with a killer?"

No, it didn't upset me nor make me uneasy. When Hannah finished her long narrative, my first thought was: One of these days I'll give this Major Zweig a big kiss!

Chapter 7

Werewolf

Kafka was waiting in the foyer when we came back to the villa.

"You've been out a long time! Madame is waiting. She wishes to retire," he rolled his eyes with a butler's snooty demeanor. I handed him the leash with dogs and turned toward the stairs, stepping lightly as on a cloud. Hannah had made my day.

My duties as lady-in-waiting, or whatever my position was, had me making the bed for the Baroness and helping her with her nightly toilette. I cast a glance backward from the bottom of the stairs. To my relief, Hannah ducked out from under Kafka's mesmerizing gaze by boldly taking a few steps around him toward the stairs where I was standing.

"You must excuse me," she said with stiff grace. "It's late. I have a long day of rehearsal ahead of me. The recital is in two weeks." She quickly went upstairs.

"You frightened the poor girl," I said to Kafka.

"She's not that easily frightened," he said. What he meant by that I would try to find out later. The Baroness was calling from the top of the stairs.

"Of course, I recognized her right away," Kafka said that night in his cottage. "I never forget a face. I was wondering how long it would take her to tell you this story."

"I would have liked to hear it from you," I said. "You never let anything on about it. Why?"

"It wasn't relevant. Not until now."

"Not relevant? How could it not be relevant? How could the episode she described to me not be relevant? What if she had been at that banquet? Would she be dead too?"

"I would have made sure to get her out first. She wasn't on the list."

"What list?"

"The list of murderers and criminals."

"Weren't they part of the Catholic resistance?"

There was that laughter again. Sometimes I loved it, and other times I hated it. This time it annoyed me.

"Let me tell you something," he said in his superior tone that always got my ire up. "As far as this so-called Catholic resistance is concerned, yes, there were a few devout people who were opposed to the regime. Not very effective, mostly splinter groups. When the war was over, these no doubt well-meaning people tried to do something nice for the victims to assuage their bad consciences for having done nothing. I have no quarrel with those. Let them be.

"The people who were executed that night were all part of *Werewolf*, a network of former SS whose aim is to sabotage American military installations. In the Starnberg area, several of them infiltrated the Catholic charity group. They posed as resisters against the regime to elude arrest. The ringleader of this southern Bavarian chapter of Werewolf was an old friend of mine from Vienna, Gestapo chief Hartmut von Graf. He may have thought he was securely ensconced in his villa on the hill overlooking the lake, heavily guarded by his myrmidons. We had it on good intelligence one of their plans was to blow up the refugee camp at Weilheim. Their lust for dead Jews was insatiable. We took them out before they killed more of us. As simple as that."

Kafka poured himself a shot of vodka, a gift, he said, from our benefactress, Frau von Bülow. I waved off his offer to share, too eager to learn more about the Starnberg incident to have my alertness impaired by alcohol. I didn't have to ask for the source for this intelligence.

"Why didn't you leave it up to the Americans to take them out and try them?"

"The Americans? Don't make me laugh. They would have arrested them, put them on trial, eventually, given them jail sentences, and within a few years, they would release them. The Americans are very sparing with death sentences. I wanted Graf to know who his executioner was. Not face him as a witness in some courtroom, out of my reach and shielded from harm by military police. Such niceties would be far too merciful. It was our good luck to track Graf down rather soon. The man didn't even run, so sure was he of his invulnerability. He recognized me right away.

'You have changed, Dr. Kafka,' he laughed into my face. 'The years haven't been kind to you, and yet, I would recognize that arrogant Jewish swagger anywhere.'

"You have to excuse me,' I told him, 'if I don't have time to reminisce.' The punishment for the murderer of Lenka Ostrova was far too quick and painless. He was lucky that sadistic torture isn't my modus operandi. The other committee members were all known Nazi criminals with Jewish blood on their hands. They all had to go."

He tipped down another shot of Vodka. He turned his back toward me and breathed heavily for a few moments.

"Only one more thing to do to even the score," he muttered.

The air in the cottage was so dense it would have required a sharp knife to cut through it. I walked up to him and put my arms around him from behind. I leaned my face against his back. We remained thus embraced for a good many minutes without speaking. That night I loved him more passionately than ever.

Chapter 8

The Recital

A week before the recital another unexpected caller appeared at the doorstep of Villa Lohengrin. It was mid-afternoon. The Baroness was taking her afternoon nap in what used to be the smoking room on the lower floor where a breeze through the wide-open French window brought some relief from the mid-day heat. I answered the door. Much to my surprise, I came face to face with a sweating, somewhat bedraggled-looking Peter von Waldeck.

"I am so glad I finally found you," he proclaimed wiping his brow with a white handkerchief. "I've been scouring the entire town for days."

"Herr Baron!" I called out. "What brings you here?"

"Aunt Mathilde dispatched me. She worried about what had become of you. Every time I see her, she besets me with her worries about you and what that man, as she calls him, is getting you into. As soon as the semester was over, she insisted I come here to find out where you are. And please don't call me Herr Baron. My name is Peter."

"Did you come in your automobile?"

"No, I took the train. Too swanky. Besides, benzene is hard to come by. Had to change trains several times. Schedules are still non-existent."

"I would ask you in, but the Waldecks are not held in good favor in this house. Frau von Bülow referred to your branch of the family as the 'black sheep'. You probably know why."

"All I know is that this Baroness is my grandmother's sister, on my father's side. There was a falling out years ago. When I was growing up, I sometimes caught vague hints from the adults. For the most part, it was left unspoken."

"To her mind, Jews were not to marry into German nobility or rather nobles were not to mingle their blood with that of Jews not even for money."

"Is that what they think? Well, that's just too bad. My mother's family was hardly wealthy, and besides, she was only half-Jewish. Pardon me for saying so."

"She did have a Jewish mother. Enough tainted blood to make your father a renegade in the family. Maybe the Baroness will be happy to meet a long-lost relative now that the bloodline has dwindled. She has mellowed considerably in the wake of what she calls the 'great calamity'.

"Remember my name is Beate Hauser from Berlin and you have never met me. You have also never met a certain Sudeten German named Franz Kaiser, who is the dog- cum-groundskeeper here at Villa Lohengrin. Say a few nice things about Wagner and his operas, and you will have no trouble capturing your aunt's heart."

"The sounds coming from the music room are from Isolde's Liebestod," I explained when I saw his ears go up and his eyes widen. "The singer is the Baroness' protégée and great hope for a Wagner revival."

The Baroness showed herself indeed most gracious toward the last surviving scion of a nearly extinct noble house whom she found waiting in her parlor on a courtesy call.

The young Baron von Waldeck comported himself most baronially. He showed off his good breeding spouting all manner of social niceties. To establish his credentials as a suitable candidate for admittance to the inner sanctum of the grail, he did not fail to allude to the glorious Isolde resonances wafting through the premises.

"The voice you hear is that of Hannelore von Weber. She is our great hope for a Wagner revival. A most charming young woman. An outstanding talent! You are just in time for our recital next Sunday night. The program includes Schubert and Mozart, and Wagner, of course. It showcases our singer's wide-ranging talent. Among our guests are some very illustrious people. Possible mentors."

She added the last words in a hushed tone shielding her mouth as if she were divulging a deep secret.

Their baronial graces spent much time together in the solarium, chatting, catching up on family stories, and getting acquainted. At dinner time, Fräulein von Weber and Herr Kaiser joined us in the dining room. The Baroness made the introduction. Neither one of the men gave any sign of having met before. An awkward moment arose during the table conversation when the subject of the war came up.

"So many had to give their life for the fatherland," the Baroness lamented. She too had lost a son in Poland, she said.

I surmised this was a reference to the model of Aryan manhood in SS uniform in the picture she kept on her dresser. Her daughter too was missing, she said, somewhere in the Russian zone. This was the first time I heard her speak about her children and then only sparingly. Whether it was shame or pride she felt about their involvement in the defunct regime, I could not tell. She had mastered the art of keeping her feelings closely guarded with aristocratic reserve.

"And your parents?" she inquired. "They too fell victim to these terrible times?"

"My parents fell victim to the Gestapo," Peter replied calmly, never deviating from a polite conversational tone.

"How terrible!" she exhaled, turning livid. For a fleeting moment, she allowed us a glimpse behind the mask covering her demeanor. The mention of "Gestapo" evoked terror even among the regime's devotees.

"May I inquire about the circumstances?"

"My father had been an opponent of the Nazi movement from the beginning. He served in the first war, but for this one, he claimed conscientious objector status. The Wehrmacht did not recognize such a status. People who refused to serve ended up in jail or a concentration camp. When he came back from Dachau, he started writing pamphlets about the conditions there. He held secret meetings with like-minded people. The local Gestapo got wind of it—denouncers and informers were everywhere. Well, that was it."

A brooding silence fell over the gathering. The Baroness pulled her shawl tighter around her shoulders as if a sudden chill had come over her despite the evening heat. She tugged on the tassels with a forlorn look.

"Well, the von Waldecks always were nonconformists," she finally broke the silence. "Your father's father, my sister's husband, your grandfather, joined the pacifists as far back as the disarmament conferences at The Hague early in the century. Most unbecoming for a German nobleman. But all this is now in the past. We need to put our minds and efforts toward salvaging our culture for the future. I am very happy that you found your way to my home and that we had the opportunity to mend the rift in the family. Times have changed. We must all hold together for the future of the fatherland."

The Baroness was particularly pleased for they now had a fourth player for the Bavarian card game called "Watten" when Hannah joined them in the waning afternoon sun.

Not being proficient in these indigenous games, I was sidelined to the role of factotum. Among my duties was overseeing and planning preparations for the big day. The Sudeten peasant women did the heavy work of hauling chairs and tables. They also did the cooking for the banquet.

My experience **with** devising elegant menus, choosing wines and hors d'œuvres, and the like was limited. I repeatedly had to turn to Kafka for guidance, which he dispensed generously. The advice from the former habitué of the Viennese beau monde—in the cinematic image I had formed of him back then: bon vivant in the style of the mustachioed Anton Walbrook (formerly Adolph Wohlbrück), coattails, a scarlet silk cummerbund sash, black red-lined velvet cape and black top hat, dancing, champagne glass in hand, to Soupé waltz tunes—proved indispensable for the affair to come off without a hitch.

We had pretty much depleted the hoard from the cellar, but the Baroness still had a king of hearts in her deck. She still had something up her sleeve.

On the day before the banquet, a horse-drawn wooden rack wagon pulled up at the rear gate. The peasant woman who as steering the delivery cart pulled back canvas covering a haul of victuals, which she then carried into the kitchen. Roast pork was to be the pièce de résistance! Succulent pork! A local farmer was fattening a litter of piglets for her, the Baroness explained to me with her hand held over her mouth. At her request, he would slaughter them for special occasions. The farmer also threw in a few chickens and fresh eggs out of gratitude to his patroness who had always been kind, he told me. There was also a large warm round loaf of Bauernbrot (rye bread) exuding a mouth-watering aroma. Villa Lohengrin turned into a veritable *Schlaraffenland*—a land of Cockaigne.

The Baroness expressed her gratitude toward her social inferiors with a patronizing, painted-on smile. The farmer's wife wiped her rough hands on her coarse apron and made a little curtsy. She took hold of the reins, spurred the horse on with a gentle whip, and off she went with the empty cart. No money or goods changed hands. The Baroness kept this card in her deck close to her chest too. Distribution of food was still strictly regulated. News about a horn of plenty at the baronial table could unleashed a storm on the castle by the populace in the streets. But that possibility was of no concern to me then. Preparations for the banquet had to continue apace.

The chickens still had to be plucked clean. I left that task as well as the roasting of the meat and preparation of the other comestible fare to the Sudeten peasants who needed no instruction on how to go about it.

On the afternoon of the big day, a few hours before the guests were to arrive, a crisis arose. Hannah threw a tantrum over the dress the Baroness had selected for her from her own wardrobe.

"It's too tight!" she screamed. "I feel like a strung-up liverwurst! This corsage constricts my diaphragm. I can't breathe let alone sing."

"Please, dear, calm yourself! You must preserve your vocal strength!" The Baroness loosened the sash she had previously knotted around the fledgling prima donna's waist. "But not too much. You want to make a stunning appearance."

"I want to be able to sing not sound like a pig impaled on a spear. I am not modeling clothes."

The garment in question was an old-fashioned gown from the era when the Baroness was the queen of the ball at the turn of the century.

"Antediluvian!" Hannah screamed. "Don't you think so, Beate?"

I merely nodded, thinking it best to stay out of the dispute even though I agreed with Hannah. The gown seemed to have some sentimental value for the Baroness who wore it when she was introduced to Ludwig III, the last king of Bavaria, at his coronation in 1913. This being all well and good, it was inappropriate for this occasion. She finally found another more suitable garment. This one too needed adjustment. Hooks, seams, and tucks had to be loosened to allow the fabric to flow freely around the singer's frame which was of sturdier built than Baroness's willowy physique.

That crisis having been resolved, we moved on to the hair. Hannah wanted her golden locks to cascade freely down her back to project the image of the dying Isolde.

"It's a recital, not a stage performance!" The Baroness was wringing her hands. On this point, Hannah yielded. One of the servants, who had some talent in that area, was drafted for the task. She gathered the voluptuous tresses into two braids and wrapped them around the head in peasant style like a crown and held in place with plenty of hairpins.

"A picture-perfect German Gretchen!" I declared, blinking at Hannah. She blinked her long eyelashes back at me and gave me a playful box in the ribs forceful enough to almost bowl me over.

The finished product was then paraded before the discerning eyes of the gentlemen for inspection and approval. Kafka couldn't let the opportunity pass to show off his superior wisdom even in cosmetics. Maybe the blush on the cheeks could be heightened just a tad more, and a lipstick of a glossier red, he suggested. I informed him that we had only one kind of lipstick and that one would have to do.

At seven o'clock in the evening, the front door to the villa swung open, and the guests decked out in formal attire flooded into the foyer. Many of the faces I recognized from the previous occasion; others were new to me. Colonel Dietrich and his entourage of officers were again in dress uniform. They strutted about like the conquering heroes they were, politely searching out people with whom they could converse in English. The Colonel made his way directly toward me. He was delighted, he said, to find me still with the Baroness. His questions about the well-being of my family in Berlin caused me some uneasiness. Maybe he was making conversation; then again maybe not. An alarm went off in my head when I overheard him questioning the Baroness about the man he had seen when he had stopped by two weeks before.

"You mean Herr Kaiser," said the Baroness. "He turned down my request to join us tonight. He deemed it improper to mingle with society as a man of his station. I told him that such social conventions are now antiquated. For some people it takes time to adjust to more democratic mores."

An awkward moment of silence ensued. The Colonel nodded pensively. Whether he was satisfied with this explanation was hard to tell. The Baroness looked at the clock.

"Time to gather in the music room for the performance!" she declared obviously relieved. Her voice reached an even higher pitch than the one she usually employed when entertaining. She took me by the hand and made me stand next to her as she surveyed the rows of guests filing into the room with a wary eye. Her mystery guest was apparently not among them.

"I hope it hasn't been all for naught," she muttered under her breath.

Just as the room darkened and Hannah had taken a bow and her accompanist, an unemployed local musician, had struck the first chord of Schubert's *Wiegenlied*, a veiled woman entered and quietly took a seat in the back row. Well-positioned for a quick exit. I knew instinctively this woman had to be Elfriede Kling. She had come alone without her husband. I cast a surreptitious look about. Kafka was nowhere in sight, but I had no doubt he was watching everything.

Hannah, Hannelore von Weber as she was billed, performed brilliantly. When the last note of Isolde's Liebestod flew from her lips, there wasn't a dry eye in the room. Almost a minute went by in hushed silence before the storm of applause broke lose. No one present doubted that here was a rising star. My eyes were on the veiled woman in the back row. She rose, clapping her gloved hands together. I was certain I saw an appreciative smile behind that veil.

The Baroness spotted her and walked over.

"So good of you to come," I heard her say to the woman who remained veiled even during the hushed exchange that ensued between them. The chatter of the guests expressing their approval of the performance made it impossible for me to overhear what the exchange between the two women. The Baroness' demeanor reflected glowing satisfaction. I was called away to direct the guests to the dining room for the banquet and oversee the servants. When I caught up with the Baroness again, the woman was gone.

"The lady didn't stay for dinner?" I asked her.

"She had to return to her home, which is at a distance from here. But she was very favorably impressed with our protégée. I am sure an invitation will be forthcoming soon. She requested that I guard her anonymity while she still lives in seclusion."

I was still searching for a diplomatic way to get her to tell me the name of the woman when Colonel Dietrich burst in with florid, effusive praise for the singer.

"What marvelous improvement of voice and comportment even in the short time since the last recital I had the honor to attend," he exuded. What normal, full-blooded American talks like that? I was sure he reserved this stilted language strictly for discourse with the Baroness.

"I would like you to meet a cousin of mine who is currently staying with us." She always used the imperial we when speaking about herself. As Kafka explained to me when I asked him, it was a way of avoiding the vulgar usage of the first person singular.

"See if you can find the Baron," she instructed me.

I knew exactly where to find the young man. All I had to do was locate our singer whom he had been following with puppy eyes since his arrival at the villa.

"Ah, there he is! Colonel, please meet my young cousin, the Baron von Waldeck," the Baroness warbled in the high-pitched octave she employed on social occasions. "He speaks a very refined English," she added in her own refined, British-accented English.

"*Sehr angenehm*," said the Colonel. I couldn't believe he clicked his heels when shaking Peter's hand. "Waldeck, is that correct? Why does the name sound familiar?" They continued to chat for a while in English, but then they were called away by the gong announcing dinner was served.

Was I imagining things again or was the Colonel attaching himself to Peter's heel? Peter, for his part, scrambled to garner a seat next to the apple of his eyes. Although he managed to do so, his attention was drawn away by the Colonel who had planted himself at the table directly across from him.

"Waldeck! Now I remember where I heard the name!" the Colonel proclaimed. "On our way in, in '45, we came across a charming, fairytale castle by that name. Not as large and fanciful as those of mad King Ludwig in the Alps, more *gemütlich*. The owners were gone. We set up quarter in the abandoned place for several days. It was deep in a dense forest. Part of your patrimonial estate, I presume?"

"Yes, I grew up there," Peter replied. "I now live in Frankfurt. I study medicine at university."

Peter's face was glowing red. He tried to get away from the interrogator and turn his attention toward Hannah, who was being courted by one of the younger officers.

"You served in the German army?" the Colonel continued while chewing on a mouthful of the pork roast. "Hmmm, this is delicious. Very rare indeed."

He gave the Baroness an appreciative nod. She smiled back at him and at the same time puckered her lips with obvious disdain for his table manners. He cut up the meat, knife in the right hand and fork in the left. Then he committed the cardinal breach of Knigge rules of etiquette. He put down the knife, switched the fork to his right hand, and stuffed his mouth with a shoveling motion.

"You served in the war?" the Colonel repeated, his mouth still full. "The people in your area gave us a hard time. Even managed to halt our advance for almost two weeks. Were you part of that? Not that I would hold it against you. They drafted teenagers in those last months."

"I wouldn't know," Peter said with a listless look. "My family were conscientious objectors."

"Now that is very interesting. I didn't know you had those in Germany." The Colonel picked up a drumstick and started nibbling on it. "This is a feast the likes of which we don't even have in Scranton," he remarked. "But getting back to that charming little castle, you should look after it. Would be a shame if it fell apart."

The repeated mention of the charming castle triggered an alarm in my head. I was sure the Colonel had more in mind than paying the Baron architectonic compliments and advice. The next sentence confirmed my suspicion.

"Bandits and squatters might damage some of the exquisite furnishings. We were very respectful of your property. Something was recently brought to my attention that shows

Germany is still a lawless place despite the efforts of the American military to establish some semblance of order for the safety of the citizens of your country. They recently discovered near an old abandoned inn, at some distance but not too far from your castle, the shallow grave of two foresters, Germans, shot at point blank. Evidence indicates the murderers had been hiding out there for some time. I mention this because it's practically in your neck of the woods. The German police think they were Poles, former forced laborers. Many have not yet been repatriated to their native country."

"I wouldn't know." Peter held fast under the Colonel's probing gaze. "I hope you are not accusing me of anything. I moved to Frankfurt to stay with my aunt in April 1944 after the Gestapo murdered my parents before my eyes at that castle you find so charming. It has no charm for me. Anyone in need of shelter is welcome to move in!"

"I am very sorry to hear about your family tragedy," said the Colonel momentarily nonplussed.

I was sitting two chairs away from the Colonel between a white-haired former conductor and the widow of a first violinist, as she referred to herself several times. Both were waxing elegiac about Wagner. Thus boxed, my left ear strained to catch what the Colonel was saying with a serious mien, while my right ear was claimed by the white-haired gentleman's reminiscences of dinners past at Villa Wahnfried presided over by the incomparable Cosima Wagner. Since my English was supposedly non-existent, I could not lean over the widow's plate to gain a better listening perch.

However this wasn't the only dilemma facing me. The pork roast on my plate, succulent as it may be, looked back at me with a devilish grin. "Serves you right," it seemed to say. I pushed it around with my knife and fork, trying to figure out how not to eat it without alerting the Baroness. My grandmother's kitchen may not have passed kosher scrutiny by rabbinical standards, but she drew the line at the consumption of swine. Consequently, I found myself physically incapable of partaking of the flesh of this beast whose tastiness was repeatedly praised by the assembled guests. Then something the Colonel said solved the problem for me. Was it deus ex machina or divine retribution? Either way, it was an ironic twist that threw me into a frenzy and my stomach into an upheaval.

"The German authorities may be right that it was Poles who are most likely back in their country by now," the Colonel droned on. Peter still feigned interest although he periodically cast longing glances at the object of his desire next to him. Then came the blow hitting my head like a *coup de foudre*.

"Casting doubt on this theory as well as making it a matter of concern for the American High Command are some of the artifacts discovered at the scene, also carefully buried, though not carefully enough. Empty cans of C-rations and other supplies, a destroyed radio system hint at theft from an American military supply depot. Strangely there was also a stack of destroyed records of Wagner operas by a singer named Lenka Ostrova. I am told she was a famous Wagnerian before the war." Peter's face went livid.

"Very strange, wouldn't you say?" The Colonel's eyes were unflinchingly fixed on the young Baron, who quickly managed to regain his bearings.

"I have heard of her," Peter replied. "She came to a tragic end. She is said had been murdered by the Gestapo at the time of the Anschluss."

My stomach and bowels were churning up bitter bile. I rose abruptly without excuse and headed for the back door. Passing through the open French doors leading to the terrace and the garden, I doubled my pace. I reached the outhouse near Kafka's cottage just as my body convulsed in a violent explosion. Then I passed out in a mire of putrid bodily excretions.

I woke in a familiar bed, shivering in my undergarments, my face and hair damp. My dress was draped over a chair.

"I did some spot cleaning. You can put the dress back on as soon as it has dried." Kafka held my trembling hand, his dark eyes serious and warm.

"Oh Kafka, we are in such deep trouble! Let's get away from here. Let's leave this cursed country tonight. I want to be far, far away; somewhere, just not here." I related to him in so many stammering words what the Colonel told Peter about bodies found buried in the forest near the Waldeck domain.

"The Germans seem to think it was Polish former forced laborers. They point to the name Lenka Ostrova they made out from the smashed records as evidence. They seem to think she was Polish. Maybe they prefer it that way. The Americans are alarmed by the military-issued equipment they found at the scene. Zweig could be in real trouble if they trace it to him."

"I am sure Zweig is already alerted to it. He went back to Frankfurt when the lawyers' trial in Nuremberg was over." Kafka furrowed his brow. "This does complicate matters," he agreed with a pensive nod. He seemed to be talking to himself, oblivious to anguish.

"Let's just get on the next train to somewhere," I pleaded.

"It was she," he heard him say. "I know it was she."

"What are you talking about?" I had forgotten about that veiled woman in the back row. Nothing of what was going on at Villa Lohengrin mattered to me anymore. I wished I had never left New York. Maybe it was all a dream, a nightmare, and I would soon wake up in my bed on Waverley Place. I wished I had never met Kafka, or Zweig, or any of the others, even Hannah. I wished I had never set foot in this cursed country.

"I am talking about Elfriede Kling. She may have been trying to hide behind that veil, but I don't have to see her face to recognize her."

"I don't give a damn about Elfriede Kling!" I yelled, pushing away his hand resting on my thigh.

"Please calm yourself. Someone could hear. I understand your concern," he said as if he had nothing to fear for himself.

"We will leave soon, I promise. I am in touch with Palmach agents at the DP camp. They will get us into Palestine. They need people with my experience."

"What experience is that? Killing people?" I hyperventilated.

"I don't kill people randomly, only those who deserve to die," he grunted. "One more task left to do, then we'll leave all this behind us."

"I know what that task, as you call it, is. But it's yours, not mine. I was dragged into this, tricked. I was dumb enough to fall in love with you. Maybe the lovemaking was part of the trickery too."

"If I told you that this was not so; if I told you that I do too and that appreciate you, it would sound insincere, and you would only accuse me of more lies and deceits. It's better to leave this aspect of the matter aside for now. I still need your help." He realized it would pain him to pronounce the word "love." So, I just let it be.

"You still need an accomplice. That's what you need me for! If you want to play Wild West, be a gunslinger (I used the American idiom which he didn't understand), there is a good war going on in Palestine. Go there! The war here is over. Finished! Over and done with. The enemy is defeated, the country in ruins. Kaput! What more do you want? Killing Rudolf Schwamm and Elfriede Kling won't bring back your Lenka. You had your revenge. The actual murderer is dead, thanks to you. Mazel tov! I applaud your guts. These people were bystanders; their crime is having done nothing. If all tbystanders and camp followers were executed, there wouldn't be anybody left in the greater German Reich, maybe in all of Europe."

I knew my argument was overwrought and absurd, but no more absurd than his mania for vengeance.

"You are wrong. They were more than bystanders. They were beneficiaries. They wanted her out of the way. The Nazis provided them with the opportunity to settle an old score. Both wanted Lenka Ostrova dead. She, the Jewess, had usurped a position that rightfully belonged to a pure-blooded German. She was a Wagnerian soprano and a better one than any of them, especially Elfriede Kling. As for Schwamm, he was a scorned lover, who had been publicly humiliated. Their hands were dipped deep in her blood. They were much more than mere bystanders. They also benefitted royally."

Chapter 9

Lovers in Retreat

The rousing chorus of the Grand March from Tannhäuser jolted me from a fitful sleep. The Baroness had sent Peter to the attic to retrieve an old gramophone and some shellac discs of Wagner recordings stored there.

"What better way to rejoice than to listen to the music of our maestro!" she jubilated.

Looking at me, a heap of misery tottering about like a drunken sailor—I must have looked like death warmed over—she exclaimed: "Oh dear, whatever happened to you last night?"

"Perhaps something I ate that didn't agree with me."

She foisted some of the chamomile tea on me which the servants brewed every morning for her from flowers they gathered in the fields.

"As far as I know nobody else suffered any ill effects from our *repas festif.* I noticed you didn't touch the roast. So, it couldn't have been that."

I tried to hide my face from her stern probing gaze by coughing into the handkerchief she handed me.

"I had some of the chicken," I mumbled. "Maybe it was the vegetables."

"You have been overworked these last few days. You had much riding on your shoulders," she concluded. "A day of rest will do you good. This morning we have wonderful news to share. Hannelore! Where is our singer? Come with me. I want to bring the joyful message to her."

We found our budding diva in the sunroom canoodling with Peter von Waldeck. The two jumped up, faces glowing red.

"Don't be ashamed! I was young once!" Nothing would get in her way of "rejoicing" - the Baroness used the word repeatedly.

"Tell us, what should we rejoice about?" I asked still bleary-eyed and woozy.

"Our Hannelore made a profound impression on Madame Kling," the Baroness chirped the identity of the mystery guest. I couldn't wait to tell Kafka.

A messenger had delivered a hand-written invitation for Fräulein von Weber and Frau Elisabeth Baroness von Bülow to visit Castle Montsalvat as soon as arrangements are made.

"What is Castle Montsalvat?" I asked.

"I am sure you remember Montsalvat, the name of Lohengrin's castle!"

"Oh yes, of course!" I didn't remember since I never knew.

"Our Wagnerians chose this name for their secluded mountain retreat a few hours from here. After last night, Madame Kling will no doubt take Hannelore under her wing. This is such good news for poor Judge von Weber."

The "poor" judge had been transferred to Spandau prison in Berlin, where he was to live out his life in the company of other war criminals. Whether the Baroness's exertions on behalf of her protégée had been out of love for the disgraced judge or love for the, momentarily at least, equally disgraced Wagner or both didn't matter. If they furthered Hannah's career and Kafka's objective, so much the better.

In the days that followed, Villa Lohengrin became a beehive of buzzing activity.

"Ah, Herr Kaiser!" The Baroness's face lit up when Kafka entered the music room where she and Hannah were sorting through a pile of sheet music. "You are a practical man. The automobile in the barn has not been used for some time. Could you check it out to make sure it will be safe to drive? I shall speak to the Colonel about a few canisters of fuel."

"I'll see what I can do," Kafka promised even though his mechanical skills, as we had seen on a previous occasion, were limited, to say the least.

"Maybe I can lend a hand." Peter, who surely remembered the disastrous encounter of Kafka and the driving machine, jumped at the opportunity to get out of the easy chair where he was seated with legs crossed and passing the time flipping through a magazine with bored mien.

I assembled and packed a wardrobe and other personal essentials for the Baroness and Hannah. Some of the items needed cleaning and ironing. I delegated those chores to the Sudeten peasants. My attempts to corner Hannah for a one-on-one talk remained fruitless. During the day, she was rehearsing, and in the evenings, Peter claimed her attention. I also had the feeling she was avoiding me.

By week's end, all was well. The motorcar was humming in the driveway with a full tank, courtesy of the Colonel. All in the interest of furthering Wagner's music. The valises were packed. Peter would drive. Hannah insisted on it, or she wouldn't go. There was no one else anyway. I was to come along as the personal assistant to the Baroness. Kafka declined the invitation. Who would look after the dogs and house?

The night before our departure I was unable to sleep. Dread and anguish over what lay ahead made me break out in a sweat. I didn't believe for one second that Kafka would stay behind. He would find a way to be on our heel.

Come morning, and the god of good luck jumped once again out of the machine, at least for Kafka. A chauffeur arrived from Montsalvat to fetch us in Madame Kling's personal limousine. I had noticed the polished, dark blue Rolls Royce with a light brown leather roof in which she arrived at Villa Lohengrin on the evening of the recital. Wealth and fame, I thought then, does not discriminate against the enemy, in this case, the British, when it comes to luxury and comfort. This same Rolls was to take us to the mountain hideout of Montsalvat. Frau von Bülow's refurbished Benz went back to the shed.

A few kilometers East of Bayreuth the highway started to ascend and then descend again, winding its way through a rolling scenery of forested hills and green dales. Eventually, we entered a dense forest that would accompany us for most of the remainder of the way. The rays of the late summer sun shone through the turning leaves auguring an early autumnal splendor.

For most of the way, the Baroness gazed pensively out the window. Very uncharacteristic for the usually talkative woman. Her frowning forehead and puckered lips as if she had bitten on a lemon made me suspect that she was displeased with the burgeoning romance in clear view on the opposite seat. The lovers showed themselves oblivious to anything that did not concern them. They were holding hands. Hannah's head rested on Peter's shoulder. Her angelically glowing demeanor was in stark contrast to the anguished expression she bore when she had suddenly appeared in my room the night before.

Still anguished by personal matters, I didn't hear the rapping at my door at first. Finally alerted by the hushed entreaty, I went to the door to let her in. Her nocturnal visits when she snuggled up to me and confided her thoughts and feelings—a confidence I had not been at liberty to return—had long been a thing of the past. I noticed a coolness coming from her toward me right after Kafka had moved into the cottage.

So, I was surprised to see her standing there begging to come in. She showed herself very distraught and was at first unable to speak except for some incomprehensible syllables of which I could make no sense. I presumed it had all to do with stage fright about the meeting with the formidable Elfriede Kling. The diva had said some nice things about her talent to the Baroness, but not to Hannah herself. All this secrecy, the veils and the cloaks, was very unnerving. Maybe she was even plagued with self-doubts whether she had what it takes? She quickly dismissed that assumption out of hand.

"No, no! What would make you think so?" she declared sobering up for a moment. "I know my voice is of much greater caliber than Kling's. Everybody who has heard her knows she was second-rate. She rose to fame, thanks to the propaganda minister even though he and the regime are in the past, she is likely to come riding back some day. And, if need be, I will jump on that horse behind her." An awkward metaphor, but I got the meaning.

"I haven't heard her perform, but I'll take your word for it. Others have said the same," I said to say something. She shrugged and made dismissive hand gesture. I sensed that something else was pressing on her mind.

"By others, I guess you mean your Herr Kaiser," she sneered. "I'd rather talk about something else."

"What is it then?"

"It's not easy to say. I need your advice about a matter in which you seem to have some experience."

"What matter?" I had an uneasy inkling where this conversation was going.

"With all the shit that has been going on in my life, I haven't had much time to think about men. Do you know what I mean?"

"Yes, I do," I replied without prodding. Let her come right out and say what's going on.

"I am in love with Peter, and he is in love with me. I want to sleep with him!" She uttered the words quickly in staccato succession as if to assure herself that's what she wanted to do.

"Why ask me? You don't need my permission."

"I was wondering if it could complicate things. I might get. . . you know. . . at this point, it would probably not be good if I got myself pregnant."

"That's always a possibility," I confirmed. "And it may not be very wise at this point."

This conversation made me very uncomfortable, especially since I had been certain for several weeks that I was carrying

Kafka's child. It certainly complicated my situation and added to my anguish. All I could tell Hannah was to be careful and discuss it with her lover before plunging into something they might both come to regret. What hogwash! I told myself. You sound like an old matron.

Kafka and I had never spoken about having a child had not been. We rarely looked to the future. The only future we ever envisioned was going to Palestine where we, or he, were likely to fight another war. As much as I had sometimes secretly wished for a child, this wasn't the right time and place. Maybe not even the right man.

I searched my memory how this could have happened. We had been very good about preventing such an eventuality. Must have been the night when he moved into the cottage at Villa Lohengrin or the night of our conversation about what had happened at the Nazi villa in Starnberg. My first reaction, before reality sunk in, was elation. Since then, I hadn't the courage to broach Kafka with the news. What would he say? How would he react to this collateral consequence? I decided to postpone the revelation for the time being.

A sudden bump in the road jostled us around inside the wagon. The road had entered a steep unpaved path ascending the mountain, the chauffeur explained with a thick Slavic accent. The Baroness's purse had been flung to the floor by the commotion. I bent down to collect the spilled items. Among them was the invitation from Madame Kling. I caught a brief glimpse before the Baroness quickly tore it from my hands. Not quickly enough, though. I clearly made out the handwritten words on the bottom: "Please expect my chauffeur and car to fetch your party."

If she knew a limousine was coming to pick us up, why did she have her Benz taken out of mothball and get benzene from the Colonel? And why would the Colonel accede to her request and steal American military property? Was she colluding with the American in setting a trap for Kafka? I was myself entrapped without any way or means of warning him. He surely would not let the opportunity pass to use the automobile to find his way to Montsalvat, even if he had to drive himself, for the settling of accounts with his enemies. I looked at the pair on the opposite bench, still happily absorbed in each other. A silly, irrational thought of wishful thinking popped into my mind: if only Peter hadn't taught Kafka to drive!

"This is a very well-appointed automobile. The Benz might have broken an axle," I commented.

"You mean British craftsmanship wins out over German quality production?"

She puckered her lips with that lemony grimace.

"It's not what I meant at all!" I protested. "I am sure the German car can maneuver any rough terrain just as well as. Maybe even better. The German car is no doubt sturdier than the British make, which is all glitter but lacks substance."

"The ride may not be so bumpy had we taken the Benz," I added to show my pride in German workmanship. "What a shame that the Colonel's donation for the benefit of German culture will go unused."

My attempt to draw her out had only limited success.

"You mean the benzene the Colonel made available to us? Rest assured, it won't go to waste."

She fell silent once again. Her lips were sewn shut; her eyes fixed on the dense espalier of fir trees fleeting by outside like a squadron of soldiers rushing a hill.

Her attitude toward me had changed. The graciousness and warmth she had shown me had cooled. I suspected it came from something the Colonel told her when she went to see him at the military headquarters a few days before. The invitation was for Hannah and herself. She nevertheless insisted I come along, not as a guest of course, but as her *"Zofe"* –a personal maid. It made perfect sense for a woman of her social position to have a handmaid. Once my suspicions had been aroused, I read portends about something underhanded afoot into her every move. I parsed every word she spoke for veiled meanings. My imagination went into high gear. I envisioned scenarios, dialogues, gestures for the principal characters in the drama I knew was brewing.

A sudden downpour of heavy raindrops pelted the roof of the automobile as it hurtled our motley group of passengers toward the dreaded destination on the mountaintop.

Chapter 10

Castle Montsalvat

Viewed from afar through the gossamer veil of the driving rain, Burg Montsalvat appeared at first as a facsimile of one of King Ludwig's fairy-tale castles in the Bavarian Alps. A multitude of turrets of varying heights, the sylvan setting, the sparkling lake. However, as we came closer, the structure lost its enchanted aspect and came to resemble more a medieval fortress complete with massive sandstone walls, ramparts, a moat, and a drawbridge. A sturdy, square castle-keep complete with battlements cast its menacing stare down on the surrounding countryside. I wondered if there was also a dungeon with torture chambers.

More pressing on my mind was the question: How would Kafka breach this formidable barrier? A small voice inside my head raised the hope he would run afoul of these walls and would turn away. Another voice rooted for him, wanted to see him take the hurdles, if only so this whole affair would finally come to an end, one way or other. I also knew in my heart of hearts, Kafka would not be daunted.

Crossing over the moat and through the heavy wooden portal was like entering a historic preservation site like the town of Carcassonne in southern France. Inside an incongruous surprise awaited us. At the center of an expansive cobblestone courtyard sat a replica of the Italianate Wagner villa Wahnfried. Medievalism was much in vogue in the previous century, a sort of nostalgia for knightly ideals of yore, a hankering for this presumably pristine time as an escape from modernity. Wagner's operas were a musical expression of that yearning for recapturing a bygone romanticized era.

An Italianate villa embedded within a medieval fortress posed a chicken-versus-egg conundrum. Which of the two came first? My guess was, confirmed by Peter, that the massive protective embattlement ringing the compound was of more recent vintage. Possibly erected during the war as a clandestine refuge and hideout should things go sour. Why?

A burly fellow of scowling demeanor came up to the limousine which the chauffeur, who had disappeared by then, had parked and abandoned with us still inside at the far end of the courtyard. He opened the car door for us. No greeting or instruction where we should go. Only a grunt and a hand gesture pointing to the center villa. He led the way across the courtyard. We followed, slipping and sliding on the wet cobblestones. Entering the wide doors, our hair and clothing damp and disorderly, we were transported as through a reverse time tunnel along several centuries from the Dark Ages of northern Europe to sunny Renaissance Italy—though the sunshine was missing from this rain-drenched tableau.

Elfriede Kling descended the curved staircase rising from the center of the marble hall with slow, measured steps giving her ample hips a coquettish swing. She seemed genuinely happy to see Hannah and the Baroness and greeted them with a bright smile of her shiny blue eyes. She was about to edge past her prime, a few years short of fifty, I guessed. Both arms extended, she gathered the Baroness onto her copious bosom that was voluptuously displayed inside the décolletage of a tight-fitting, flowery dirndl dress. Two women of very differing pedigree somehow connected by a common cause. A picture in social contrast: the noble woman's willowy gauntness versus the diva's solid build of Alpine peasant stock.

In the lengthy exchange between hostess and guest, epithets of "my dear Baroness" and "*meine gnädige Frau*" were stacked up like sugar cubes on a silver platter for afternoon tea. Finally turning to Hannah, Madame Kling placed both hands on the protégée's shoulders at arm's length searching her face with squinting eyes for a long moment before gathering her too to her generous bulge. She ignored Peter and me. I didn't mind. I much preferred being a fly on the wall.

Hannah took Peter defiantly by the hand and introduced him as her fiancé. Madame Kling's erstwhile frown changed to a gracious, though bitter smile when the young man's name and title were made known. She was not remiss in addressing him with "Herr Baron" whenever she did acknowledge his presence, which mercifully, so Peter told me later, was rare.

The room assignment caused the first crisis. The Baroness and Hannah were to take up quarter in the guest wing on the ground floor. Peter and I were relegated to servants' quarters under the roof reached via a steep flight of narrow back stairs. This arrangement suited me perfectly. Not so, Hannah. She threw her first fit in her role of budding prima donna. Her fiancé stayed with her or she would leave. Hard to see how she could escape from this bastion. But she had made her point. The Baroness puckered her lips. Madame Kling's raised eyebrows dropped at the sound of a man's voice: "Would you have allowed anyone to banish your lover to the attic when you were young?" The reference to "were young" elicited a huff from the lady of the house, but she conceded the point.

We turned in the direction of the voice coming from the top of the curved staircase. The man made quite an entrance. The built-in lift on which he was seated made a slow descent toward us as in a stage setting. When it reached the bottom, one of the Ukrainians rushed up to meet him. He picked the man up, easy as a loaf of bread, and set him down in a waiting wheelchair. Rudolf Schwamm was a paraplegic.

The only other inhabitant of the attic was a middle-aged woman who spoke no German. My initial hunch that the personnel at this fortress were all Ukrainians was confirmed in due course. From what I was able to learn by using a few broken words and hand gestures, the woman was the only female. She functioned as cook and Madame Kling's personal maid. My only misgiving about this arrangement was the raucous nightly frolicking with the drunken guards who staggered up and down the narrow stairs. Whether it was always the same one or if she was servicing the entire company was no concern of mine. So far, I had counted four goon types around the premises. Would they be willing to die for a pair of Nazi fugitives?

I couldn't help but feel there was something else going on. Something didn't fit together. A rather elaborate structure to hide two people who, though party loyalists, were not directly connected to actual crimes? Their careers benefitted splendidly from their willingness to give the regime a patina of legitimate luster. But that was it.

Kafka's vendetta no doubt stemmed from more personal motives. His desire to get even had most likely to do with something that occurred long before the day Hitler and his brownshirt entourage marched into Vienna.

While I kept a nervous eye out for my demon lover to appear at any moment, I also resolved to do a bit of snooping on my own whenever opportune. Somewhere within these walls was a secret that went deeper than the musical routine into which the inner circle settled the very next day after our arrival.

The acoustics in these "holy halls" were excellent. Hannah's coloratura trills warbled from the music room through the open windows out onto the terrace in the rear of the villa where Waldeck and I listened enthralled. We were both at leisure during the daylight hours, which we spent comfortably seated in cushioned lounge chairs. One could have thought we were enjoying a pleasant summer in the country. Reading was nearly impossible while the practice was going on for hours with the Baroness at the piano interspersed with occasional interruptions and instructions from Madame Kling.

A few times Peter and I ventured forth on a walk in what could be called a stone garden since the compound was strikingly bare of any vegetation. We soon came upon a burly Ukrainian or two—they were all burly—who blocked our way to the perimeter waving the butts of their rifles.

"Seems we are in a prison," I noted.

"Or a concentration camp." Peter gave off a nervous laugh.

"What do you think of this setup here?" I probed cautiously still uncertain whether I should share my suspicions. Not because I didn't trust him but more because I didn't want to look silly by spinning conspiracy theories.

"Elaborate, isn't it? Maybe they are hiding Kaiser Barbarossa somewhere in a dungeon," he chuckled. Every German schoolchild knows the legend of the medieval Kaiser Friedrich I, who died on a crusade to the Holy Land, but who is said to be sleeping in the Kyffhäuser Mountains, further North but not too far away from where we were. Legend had it he would reawaken one day and lead Germany back to its former glory. I was never quite sure which glory that was. Borrowing from this folktale, the Nazis dubbed invasion of Russia in '41 Operation Barbarossa.

Jesting aside, Peter confirmed my suspicions.

"What for?" he noted.

"Exactly my thought."

"The villa is older. By my estimate, last century when Ludwig inspired a building boom in Trianon-style in wooded mountainous settings; not unlike my family's *Schlößchen* in the Spessart forest. Our hosts probably acquired this retreat from a bankrupt aristocrat. Or, ..." he thought for a moment and then raised his finger, "not unlikely, in fact very likely, it is a dispossessed Jewish possession. Could be a gift from the Reich to that pair of warblers. But what about this outer-rim fortification? I have seen and been in plenty of medieval castles and fortifications to tell this one is a replica, a recent faux addition, very recent in fact. For example, did you notice how clean these walls are? No moss, no weathering of the stones by the passage of time. Quite an expenditure too!"

"But why and for what? This compound is in a very reclusive, inaccessible area. If they needed a hiding place, this would be ideal. And from whom are they hiding? The Americans, the Russians, or maybe other Germans?" Peter creased his brow.

"Something is up," he said. "I don't like the smell of it. Hannah has to get away from here."

My sole function as lady-in-waiting was to assist the Baroness with her nighttime toilette and fluff up the pillows of her bed for her night's rest. After combing her silky, blondish graying hair, I massaged her arthritic hands, stiff from hours at the piano, with penaten cream and various salves. Next came her crouched shoulders. I kneaded her sore muscles with such vigor one could have thought my ministrations certified me as an experienced masseuse. Though her eyes were half-closed as she took deep breaths, I had the feeling she was watching me intently. Words had surely been exchanged between her and the hostess concerning the uninvited members of her entourage.

"Madame Kling is concerned about having too many mouths to feed in these dire times," she finally came out with what was on her mind. "This is such a relief. Thank you so very much," she added, opening her eyes with a deep sigh. She held up her hands toward me. Then she let them sink into her lap. She rubbed them together. Slowly. Pensively. I waited for the other shoe. She was biding her time.

"Our hostess suggests having her chauffeur drive you and Peter back to Bayreuth."

Not unexpected. And from the point of view of the hostess, not entirely unreasonable. Deep down I wished nothing more than to hightail it out of this creepy Dracula haunt, the sooner, the better.

But then there was Kafka. Which reminded me, where the devil was that Kafka? He should have appeared already. Let him gun them all down and end this crusading charade. I realized my emotions were once again running away with me. On second, more sobering, thought, it was difficult to see how Kafka could carry out his plan with so many extras around. Hannah and Peter, who had become dear to me, could be harmed in the crossfire. Even the Baroness, though set in her parochial view of the world, I had also come to know as gracious, generous, and benevolent in her own, eccentric way. She certainly didn't deserve to be gunned down. Would Kafka's wrath visit the just as well as the unjust?

"Rest assured. There's nothing to worry about," I heard the Baroness say from far away. She patted my hand reassuringly. "I made it clear to her, not only are you indispensable to me, Hannelore would never hear separating from her lover."

I assisted her in climbing into the cavernous poster bed, almost as high as the one in the story of the princess and the pea, fluffed the pillows and pulled the eiderdown over her skinny body.

"Don't go yet," she beckoned, motioning me to pull up a chair. A melancholic, nostalgic smile appeared on her face.

"Young love!" she cooed. "Romantic and heart-warming! Even Madame Kling is touched. She fears Peter might keep our Hannelore from concentrating on her studies. Now she has come to realize the opposite is, in fact, the case. A headstrong child! A trait she has inherited from her father."

More likely from her mother, from what Hannah told me, I thought.

Suddenly, she gave off one of those nervous chuckles she was prone to and which made her chest heave like a cackling hen's.

"Just imagine," she said. "Madame Kling thinks you might be Jewish. She sensed something not quite kosher about you, as she put it. I told her that it was preposterous. She insisted she had very close contact with Jews back in her day in Vienna and usually could tell. She has a nose for them, she said. I assured her that she was mistaken in your case. I told her that I have gotten to know you very well and have no doubt about the purity of your racial origins. I am sure her suspicions were assuaged. The Viennese are obsessed with ferreting out Jews. A long history, I suppose. But not to worry. Everything will turn out for the best. We must look toward the future when Germany is free again. Meanwhile, preserving the music of our great master for generations to come is our most sacred duty. Hannelore von Weber will be a key player in this future."

My head was spinning. I longed to return to the quiet of my little chamber in the attic. The life that was growing inside of me made itself felt. A new life! A Jewish life! Into what kind of a world would my child be born and condemned to live in? I prayed that my child should be born in America, not on this cursed German soil.

Part Four

Crimes and Punishments

Chapter 1

Odin, God of War

Rudolf Schwamm was not in the habit of taking the evening meals in our company on the ground floor. His wife carried a tray with food up the curved staircase to the private quarters before sitting down with us in the dining room. However, on that evening, he did come down, descending from on high in his lift and was carried by a burly Ukrainian to a chair at the table.

I sat next to the Baroness. Hannah and Peter opposite us. The hosts occupied the ends respectively, separated by the full length of the massive oak table. The Baroness mumbled a few barely audible words of grace. A crackling silence hovered frightfully over the hall like a winged creature.

The first course of soup was served. With necks craned over our bowls, we spooned the broth in silence like members of a religious order engaged in a solemn ritual. From time to time, Elfriede Kling looked up and exchanged long, dark glances with her husband across the expanse of the table. He shrugged his shoulders in return and rolled his eyes upward as if to say, what do you want from me? I caught Hannah's eyes darting back and forth between the two ends of the table with an impish grin. She seemed to be the only one who found this entire scenario amusing. The privilege of youth to be lighthearted. As for me, I could not shake a sense of ominous doom stifling the air. Something drastic was about to happen of which only our hosts were aware but did not speak.

We were getting to work on the pièce de résistance—more pork roast; I made a mental note to put my finger down my throat later—when a commotion in the entrance hall made us all put down our knives and forks and direct our eyes toward the door. My heart beat higher. Had Kafka finally arrived? My hope was immediately dashed.

In blustered an unkempt, wild-eyed creature with a pronounced limp. He brandished a pistol, gesturing wildly and gushing a welter of incomprehensible obscenities. Then, a ghastly, bone-chilling scream rent the air. The outcry coming from the Baroness sounded like "Odin!" Then she fainted and slumped unconscious into my arms.

Odin, it was, indeed. Odin, her long-lost son. However, this hirsute creature, more werewolf than human, bore little resemblance to the dashing officer in uniform with the SS insignia in the photograph on the chiffonier in the Baroness's dressing room at Villa Lohengrin.

"What the hell are these Ukrainians doing here?" he barked at Rudolf Schwamm.

"They are our security guards," Schwamm replied in a sharp-edged tone, his head erect, and chin defiantly upturned.

"Well, they have to go."

"They served the Reich with distinction in a Waffen SS unit on the Western front. They are absolutely trustworthy." At this moment, our chauffeur appeared in the door behind the ranting Baron. He cast a fearful look at Schwamm.

"I don't care. You may trust them. I trust nobody. Especially not some Slavic peasants."

"And where do you propose they go? They couldn't even get out of here, and if they made it back home, Stalin would have them executed."

"Maybe we should spare old Koba the trouble." He pivoted around and fired a volley of shots into the chauffeur's chest. More gunfire echoed in the courtyard outside.

"Does that take care of your problem, Herr Schwamm?" Odin gave off a raucous laugh. "You see how easy it is?"

Two more simians now joined him inside. They pushed their way to the table and fell over the leftovers of our interrupted meal like hungry wolves over their prey.

"The cook can stay!" Odin declared. He wiped his mouth on the sleeve of his greasy jacket. A loud burp issuing from his belly elicited another scream of horror from the Baroness who was regaining consciousness.

"What is my mother doing here?" Odin yelled. "And who are these people?" He pointed at our little group. We had retreated to a corner and were observing the scene with astonishment and dread.

"They are our guests," Madame Kling informed him.

"You are not authorized to entertain outsiders in this place," he shouted.

"This is our house, and we do as we please!" Madame asserted.

"Not anymore. These premises are a designated refuge and storage."

"This may be so. But who put you in charge? We heard they strung you up on the gallows in Poland," Madame sneered disregarding her husband's hushed entreaty not to provoke the beast.

"They failed as you can see. The Poles are not smart enough to subdue an officer of the Reich."

"The American authorities would have a keen interest in that stash in the keep."

"If this is a threat, may I point out that you no longer have a chauffeur to take you away from here. You have nowhere to go. You are all my prisoners until I decide what to do with you. Unfortunately, that includes my mother."

"Odin what are you doing? These people are dedicated to preserving the music of the great Wagner. That's why we have come here. Madame Kling has kindly consented to mentor my protégée so that one day the Festspiele will glitter again as in the old days."

The Baroness had struggled to her feet. She took a few unsteady steps, her arms extended toward her son.

"The old days! Don't make me laugh. My mother, the eternal romantic! Those days are gone. Nobody gives a damn about your Wagner and his music. The new reality is survival. The Poles couldn't hang me; neither will the Americans."

"I don't understand. Why would they do such a thing? You served the fatherland honorably as any good soldier would. I realize we lost the war and the Reich is no more, but German culture and honor are still alive."

"Mother, you are so naïve! What we did in Poland, what we had to do for the glory of the Reich, our enemies would call war crimes. True, we've lost the war on the battlefield. A temporary setback. The old comrades are getting together through clandestine networks of resistance to the occupiers. The means toward that end are right here in this place."

Amazing braggadocio for a man on the lam. He spoke to his mother freely without qualms that others in the room heard what he was saying. Nor did he seem to have any fears of our hosts. Madame Kling's veiled threats about the Americans were more a reaction to his rude behavior than meant in earnest. Whatever conspiracy was being hatched here, I did not doubt that she and her husband were part of it.

I suspected that their plan to use their secluded estate to house some hoard—gold or currency or weapons—and serve as a temporary refuge for fugitive members of the SS should the Reich fall had been concocted long beforehand, maybe as far back as the start of the war. A sort of underground railroad with tentacles spanning the entire old Reich.

He continued his ranting without regard for the presence of Hannah, Peter, and me. Careless one might think to keep witnesses around. For how long? Considering the ease with which the Ukrainians had been killed in cold blood, I wondered when our turn would come. We had no way or means of contacting the outside world. I longed for an entretien with Peter, who was holding Hannah in a tight embrace. We exchanged helpless glances but did not dare to speak for fear of attracting the attention of those miscreant desperados.

My blood began to pulse like a raging torrent when Peter took a step forward during a pause in Odin's rant and confronted him directly. Hannah gave off a muffled scream. I instinctively moved toward her and held her trembling hands in mine.

The Baroness, meanwhile, had calmed down considerably. She sat in an easy chair, her hands folded in her lap, her lips puckered not as if she had bitten on a lemon, but with a faint, somehow self-satisfied smile. Was she proud of her son or just happy to see him alive?

"Don't worry. No harm will come to you," she whispered to us. She had every confidence that inside this monstrous madman was still the good son and gentleman she had raised. How deluded a mother can be was revealed before our very eyes.

"With your permission, I shall gladly chauffeur Madame the Baroness von Bülow and the other women back to Bayreuth." Peter looked the monster straight in the eye. Like a dragon slayer, I thought. And just as audaciously foolhardy.

"Listen to this whippersnapper! Claims he can chauffeur a Rolls!" he rallied his companions with raucous laughter. "On your knees when you speak to your superiors!" he commanded.

Peter stood firm, unwavering even when the butt of the pistol struck him across the face leaving a gashing cheek wound. Hannah shot up like a lioness, ready to jump the assailant.

"You damn swine!" she screamed but was roundly ignored. Odin was more intrigued by the man who would not kneel.

"Who is this knave?" The two men stood eye to eye. "I don't think we have been introduced."

"He is the Baron von Waldeck, your cousin. Distant, but still a cousin," the Baroness interceded. "You shouldn't be so quick to lose your temper, my son."

"Stay out of this, Mother!" Odin shoved her back into her chair with rough push.

"Waldeck! Waldeck, of course!" he mused. "Oh yes, there was a scandal, an impropriety by the lord of that branch. Now I remember, he married a Jewess!"

"Half-Jewess!" the Baroness corrected.

"Doesn't matter. Jewification [*Verjudung*] of the family all the same. I presume this young man here is the offspring of this racial defilement [*Rassenschande*]."

Peter was writhing to loosen the arm lock in which the two goons held him restrained.

No longer restrained was Hannah. She freed herself from my arms holding her and pounced on her lover's tormentor with Valkyrian fury, knocking him to the floor. With a stream of ghastly curses, she pummeled him with a barrage of kicks to the groin. For a moment, he was writhing in pain, but quickly recovered and burst out laughing. He grabbed her foot and pulled her down toward him. He soon gained the upper hand and pinned her down.

"I remember you," he said, holding her down spread eagle. "The judge's daughter!" He turned his head toward his mother. "Very naughty of you, Mother. Fostering a half-breed of the first degree for your Wagner project!"

"She has a beautiful voice and great talent," the Baroness protested. "Nobody needs to know."

"Your infatuation with the judge is clouding your judgment." The mother opened her mouth to object, but her son cut her off with unfilial rudeness. The unexpected presence of his mother at this place was obviously a great irritant to him. Madame Kling's demand for an explanation of what had just been revealed about the protégée was repulsed with equal incivility.

"Never mind now," he bellowed. "We have more important work to do."

He did, however, show some faux gallantry toward the young woman he had just defeated in a wrestling bout and who was still writhing on the floor. He extended his hand with a mock chivalrous bow as if asking her for a dance and raised her to her feet.

"You two stay here," he pointed at the hosts. "Everybody else, out of this hall! You too, Mother!" he hissed.

He handed Schwamm a pistol instructing the crippled tenor to shoot anybody trying something untoward. His myrmidons herded us into the kitchen at gunpoint with shouts of: "*Schnell, schnell*!"

Why the hurry? I thought. There was no train in the station raring to leave. Most likely an old habit acquired during their reign of terror in the East when they were shoving people on a train to the gas chambers.

We found Marina, the cook, in the kitchen. She was barely able to hold herself upright. She was hyperventilating, hands pressed against her chest, her eyes bulging in horror at the dead body at her feet. Since she and I had become kind of friendly in the time we shared the servants' quarters in the attic, I felt compelled to offer her at least a glass of water and a few soothing words which seemed to calm her heaving chest even though she didn't understand the exact words.

While Hannah was dressing the gashes on Peter's cheek and forehead, the Baroness sank onto a footstool. Shaking her head, she mumbled repeatedly: "I don't understand! I just don't understand!" What was it that she couldn't comprehend? Was it that her son was a Nazi war criminal on the run from the gallows in Poland? Or was it that this well-bred offspring of a noble family was capable of such uncivil behavior even toward his mother? Was it that she should have given birth to a devil's spawn, who was now trying to avoid capture and elude being brought to justice?

Considering these revelations, I considered my arrangement with the Baroness null and void. I no longer felt obligated to be at her beck and call. My employment as lady-in-waiting, or whatever function it was I had been fulfilling, was terminated. My mission of tracking down the whereabouts of Rudolf Schwamm and Elfriede Kling also had been fulfilled. Now, where the hell was that elusive Kafka?

The kitchen window faced toward the rear yard. This was no doubt the reason why Odin had us confined in that part of the house rather than in one of the rooms fronting the courtyard from where we would be able to observe what was going on there. We heard shouting and cursing, banging and clanking, and even the roar of motors revving. What our captor in his aristocratic conceit may not have taken into consideration was a servant entrance on the side of the villa. Using this venue, I evaded the guard dogs in the dining hall and sneaked out through the long, vaulted passageway leading to the yard from the kitchen pantry. Hiding in the shadows, I gained a clear view of the courtyard. The two goons who were just then emerging from the keep heaved a wooden crate reinforced with iron bands with obvious effort. Two hulking men, sweating and groaning under the weight of the haul, set down two lockboxes in the middle of the yard with a loud thump next to two similar boxes already there. I turned my attention next to find out where the revving of a motor was coming from. Odin was driving up a canvas-covered truck. Behind him, two huge winged barn-like doors embedded in the massive walls were flung wide open afforded a look into a cavernous space big enough to garage an entire fleet of armored vehicles.

These criminals had come to reap the fruit of a seed planted many moons before. All that boasting about the Reich that would last a thousand years! Not even the SS believed in it. Even the most zealous goose-steppers, rather than putting their blind trust in the Führer and his predictions, had obviously made contingencies to save their own skin for the time should the Reich go up in flames.

The conspirators loaded one truck, then another one. I counted about seven or eight crates. Their weight seemed to vary. Judging from the energy the goons expended in hauling and lifting them, some must have weighed a ton while others required less muscle. What might be the contents? Artwork, jewelry, furs looted and stolen from their victims in the camps and ghettos? Guns and gold bars? My instinct told me it was all of these and more.

But even if they were to succeed in getting the contraband out of this fortress how and where would they be able to liquidate it? There must be a chain of middlemen along a route stretching all the way to North Africa. You've been watching too many movies; I tried to rein in the wilder imaginings stampeding through my brain.

Sometimes life does not only imitate Hollywood fantasies but is stranger than the most fantastic fiction I had just rejoined the group when, in the next film frame, Odin stomped into the kitchen and ordered us out into the courtyard. It looked like we were going on a ride down the mountain. His cronies were already starting up the second truck.

"Madame," Odin said after some consideration to Elfriede Kling, "I am sure you can drive your Rolls. You will take the Baroness back to Villa Lohengrin. The rest of you get in the back of the truck. *Schnell, schnell*!"

Why not shoot us right away? Unless he thought we could be of value as hostages.

"What about my husband?" Madame Kling lamented. "He is in no condition to travel."

"That can easily be fixed." Odin trained his pistol at the man in the wheelchair and fired several shots. Rudolf Schwamm slumped over with a groan. Elfriede Kling rushed to her husband's side with a horrified scream. "You damn cur!" she screamed.

"Get my mother out of here!" Odin commanded her and turning to us: "I told you to get on the truck."

One of the trucks had already left the courtyard. As it passed through the gate heading toward the lowered drawbridge gunfire erupted.

Kafka had finally arrived!

He made a grand entrance, armed to the teeth with an array of the finest weapons we had polished together back in our forest idyll. That was so long ago. He was clean-shaven. His long hair trimmed, still black but woven through with more grayish filigree. In the corner of his mouth, a cigar, unlit. He always had a flair for the dramatic.

And there was the laughter, mocking and clear like a bubbling brook, bouncing off the massive enclosure with a ricocheting echo.

"Kafka!?!" Elfriede Kling called out aghast as if she was seeing a ghost.

"Herr Kaiser! I am so glad to see you!" the Baroness proclaimed.

"It's Kafka. František Kafka!" He performed a gallant bow before the Baroness. "I have come to bring your misbegotten son to justice for crimes against humanity."

"The cargo of these trucks is herewith confiscated and declared the property of the Jewish fighting forces in Palestine!" he proclaimed.

"Rudolf is badly wounded!" Elfriede whined, in total disregard of the momentousness of Kafka's declaration. "That miscreant shot him in the chest. He's still breathing. You must do something, Franz!"

"What would you have me do, Madame? And, pray tell, why should I do anything?"

"Because you are a doctor and you have a sworn duty to tend to the sick and wounded."

"Is that so? I haven't practiced that métier in many years. As Madame is surely aware, my career was interrupted by superior forces. Not so your own career and that of your pathetic spouse. In fact, the same forces who impeded mine fostered yours."

He pointed a disdaining finger at the slumped figure in the wheelchair. "But I shall see what I can do. I don't want him dead, not yet. Before I dispatch him to the fires of hell, we have some accounting to do."

He had not come alone. He was flanked by two men, who had their guns trained on Odin. Behind them, in the shadows, I made out about half a dozen more men in khaki uniforms. The other two Nazis were, no doubt, already dead.

Kafka turned the men in khaki. They spoke in a language strange to my ears at first, but then I recognized the Hebrew cadence. I remembered him mentioning something about a connection with the Palmach, but it wasn't clear then that they had operatives outside of Palestine.

One of the men handed Kafka a medical emergency kit. He went to work on his enemy. Only the patient's groaning and occasional subdued whimpering from the Baroness broke the silence. We were holding our breath, while Kafka performed a makeshift operation to keep alive the man he had gone to great length to find and planned to kill.

Hannah, Peter, and I arranged a few chairs in a row as a perch from which we watched the scene as if it was a performance at a theater. The Baroness had collapsed onto another chair next to Madame Kling at a distinct distance from us. The lines had been drawn. Missing was Marina, the Ukrainian cook, who had disappeared. I never found out what became of her, poor soul.

Kafka's companions guarded Odin in a more distant corner of the room. His face was still snide and contorted with disdain. The grim demeanor of the two men holding him captive though did not bode well for his fate though.

"I recognize those two men," Hannah whispered in my ear. "They were with Kafka in Starnberg."

His medical intervention complete, Kafka washed up in the kitchen. He looked drawn as if he hadn't slept in days. In the courtyard outside, the trucks were still raring and ready to go. Kafka went outside. Eager to have a moment alone to find out what was going, I followed him. I regretted not being able to understand his animated conversation with the men who were sorting through the cargo. There was a lot of nodding and waving of arms and hands, some laughter, good cheer, congratulatory back-slapping. The one phrase I did catch was the Hebrew for "Next year in Jerusalem!" On that note, they got into the trucks and were off in a cloud of suffocating exhaust.

"Just as I suspected," Kafka said with a satisfied mien, rubbing his hands together. He spoke more to himself than to me who was standing next to him. I wasn't sure he was even aware of my presence.

"Suspected what?" I said emphatically to draw attention to myself.

"Gold and weapons. Much needed. A boon for our fight against our oppressors."

"How do they expect to get the loot through the American occupied zone without being intercepted by military patrols? Colonel Dietrich is no doubt on his way here right now. There's only one road down this mountain."

"I am sure he is and so is half the 89th Infantry. But our men are not driving West. There is another road down the other side of the mountain which leads East. We are very close to the Czech border. On the other side of that border, planes are ready to take the goods to Palestine. Odin von Bülow's gamble went up in flames. Little did he know his shenanigans would benefit the Jewish army of Palestine. Poetic justice, wouldn't you say? And now, Odin will stand trial for his crimes against humanity."

Chapter 2

The Travel Companion

The trains leaving Vienna for Prague in the summer of 1938 were packed to capacity. The mass exodus of Jews from the Austrian capital began right after the *Anschluss* of Austria to the German Reich. Czech citizens received preference at the border crossing. Thousands who found themselves stateless also were granted refuge by the Beneš government.

Citizen Kafka returned home after years of absence. The Austrian capital had become an odious place to him as it had for all Jews. The abhorrent murder of his wife was a discomfiting memory. His eyes fixed on the gleaming green and yellow summer landscape fleeting by once the train gained momentum in the open countryside, his mind embraced the future. He had snagged a window seat in a first-class coupé and arranged himself as comfortably as possible. Class separations on trains had become effaced. The jostling, prattling masses spilled over once strictly enforced class lines. Baggage with salvaged belongings filled overhead racks, trunks and suitcases blocked passage in the corridors; for many of the passengers, they served as seating available.

Kafka traveled light. Only a few personal items. One small leather satchel, plus, a physician's bag. All appurtenances and trappings of his former life of luxury, he had left behind without regret. He never looked back.

"We should be on a train going to Istanbul."

Kafka turned his face unwillingly away from the window toward where the voice was coming from. Seated across from him was an elderly gentleman who flashed a benevolent, though somewhat condescending smile. He raised his markedly bushy eyebrows that were matched by an equally bushy, drooping mustache trimmed in Alpine peasant style. His garb, too, was Austrian traditional: a gray knit waistcoat under a greenish loden frock and knickerbockers with knit socks and hiking boots. The clean-shaven Kafka in a custom-tailored striped gray double-breasted gabardine suit, white starched shirt with golden cufflinks and a crimson necktie presented a stark contrast. Although both men wore fedora headgear, the man's hat was moss- green felt trimmed with a twirled rope and a coquettish little yellow feather; Kafka's was a gray broad-rimmed Bailey fedora with a wide black band, the preferred headgear of theater impresarios.

The provincial and the man-about-town. How appearances can deceive! In due course, the man revealed himself to be much worldlier than his appearance suggested.

Kafka's surly questioning look bounced off the man's bright demeanor to no effect.

"We should all get on the Orient Express, going East to Palestine," the man stated.

"It only goes as far as Istanbul," Kafka muttered crankily and turned his attention back to the fleeting scenery outside.

"Herzl had it right," the man continued unperturbed. "We need a state of our own. It's the only way we can find peace."

The man's use of the first-person plural as if it were only natural that he and Kafka should belong to the same species aroused Kafka's ire.

"What makes you think I am the least bit interested in what you have to say? And stop inferring that I am part of a 'we'."

"You are Doctor Kafka, aren't you? Am I wrong to presume you are leaving Vienna to get away from the Nazis? We are all in the same boat, you know."

"Yes, I am Doctor Kafka. But I don't see what concern it is of yours where I am going and why."

The man laughed out loud as if he had heard the drollest story.

"I am Doctor Rosenfeld," he extended his hand, which Kafka took after some hesitation. "Oskar Rosenfeld, I am a journalist and a writer. Not a famous medical doctor like you. Several years ago, I had the honor of being invited to your home in the First District - I wouldn't expect you to remember - to interview Madame Ostrova."

"I do remember," Kafka replied in a mollified tone. "You published a very flattering piece about my wife in that Zionist journal. . ."

"*Die Neue Welt*, now defunct, of course. We, the entire Jewish community that is, were shocked, profoundly shaken by Madame's tragic end."

"It was murder! Heinous murder!" Kafka shouted at the poor man whose face expressed sincere sorrow. "She was murdered. There was nothing tragic about it. Tragic would imply a sacrifice for a higher cause. The Gestapo tortured her, then butchered in the most sadistic, degrading manner. You should write about that for the world to know!"

"I shall, I assure you. Let this be my promise to you and all those who are made to suffer."

"The world must know about this crime and all other crimes against the Jews that took place when Hitler and his hordes invaded the Austrian capital. The *Jewish Chronicle* in London has offered me a position as a staff writer. I am on my way to England. My wife and daughter are already there."

"Then why on earth are you going to Prague if you have a visa for England?"

"To take care of some personal, family matters. It is also easier to make travel arrangements from that point of departure."

The two men whiled away the remaining time on the train with an intense discussion of the situation. Will Hitler dare fish in the troubled waters stirred up by the Sudeten Germans' clamoring for autonomy? What are England and France likely to do? What would be the best course for the Jews to take? Will there be war?

Kafka still doubted the truth of Rosenfeld's assertion that the Nazi regime had further expansionist designs beyond the Anschluss. Austria was, after all, a historically German land, he argued. The two parts had only been separated by Bismarck's schemes to establish Prussian hegemony. So are at least parts of what now constitutes Czechoslovakia, Rosenberg droned on citing historical facts Kafka was fully aware of as well. He wouldn't put it past the Führer to lay claim to those lands as well. And get away with it, he added ominously.

"But you are still here on this abysmal continent," Kafka noted not without a hint of skepticism when Rosenfeld concluded a long harangue about Herzl's philosophy and his efforts on behalf of the establishment of a Jewish state in Palestine with the words: "I had the good fortune to meet the great visionary in person shortly before his untimely death."

The travel companion proved to be a visionary himself. Later, when the Nazi war machine dismantled his homeland piece by piece, Rosenfeld's prophetic words were brought home to him daily with a vengeance. Within months after he had settled into a comfortable bourgeois life in his native city of Prague, had established a medical practice, had even married and for the first time in his life was expecting to be a father, Citizen Kafka found himself the resident of a fictitious entity called the Protectorate of Bohemia and Moravia. That was March 1939, and life went on with quotidian routine.

Chapter 3

A World of Illusion

In the decade of his absence, Kafka had visited Prague only once briefly in 1935 to attend his father's funeral. Contact with his mother and other family members had been sporadic. Even exchanges of Christmas/Chanukah greeting cards, at first faithfully adhered to, had petered out over the years. Adding to the estrangement was his mother's disapproval of his relationship with Lenka Ostrova, whom she regarded as having a centrifugal effect on her son's loyalty to the family. No one from his side made the journey to Vienna for the lavish civil ceremony.

Now the native son had returned. He was gathered back into the bosom of the close-knit inner family circle. Lenka Ostrova's ghost was present in the Kafkas' parlor like Krylov's elephant at the museum, but her name was left unmentioned. No one inquired about the circumstances of her death. Nor did anybody extend condolences to the bereaved husband.

An obituary in a local Jewish newspaper which Kafka was sure everybody had read did not mention her celebrated Wagner performances. The note recalled her humble origins in a small Bohemian town near the Polish border and listed some of the high points of her operatic career among them an acclaimed Schubert Lieder recital with Richard Tauber on the centenary of the composer's death. Also mentioned was a landmark production of Korngold's opera "Die tote Stadt" in which she partnered with Joseph Schmidt. The cause of the diva's demise was described as "mysterious circumstances." The fact that the Gestapo had murdered her—travelers from

Vienna surely spoke about it to illustrate the horrors of the Nazi regime—was glossed over in embarrassed silence.

Kafka, for his part, was quite content to pass over the story of the deceased and his years in Vienna in silence as well. He had closed this chapter of his life. All he wanted then was turn a new page, build a new life. It was his longing for tranquility, away from the turbulent roller-coaster Vienna years, that made him amenable to his mother's urging to marry a young woman she had in her employ.

A severe case of gout, arthritis, and diabetes confined Hedwig Kafka, née Lustiger, permanently to her bed. Even in her bedridden state, the matriarch ruled over her children and the family fabric and millinery business from inside her "mattress crypt"—she adopted this phrase from her favorite poet Harry Heine (she called him by his given name), who suffered from a similarly debilitating condition—in her bedchamber. Neither pain nor stiffness in her gnarled, swan's neck fingers could prompt her to relinquish the task of making the entries in the business ledgers herself.

When Kafka arrived home, his mother was in the care of a docile nurse, who tended to her needs with grateful devotion in return for the special kindness her patroness had extended to her when no one else would. Madame Kafka had taken the young woman into the family when her own family and friends had shunned her, due to an indiscretion the girl had committed several years. She was still young and pretty, though faint signs of fading youthful bloom were beginning to be noticeable around her eyes and mouth. This was the woman Kafka's mother urged him to marry.

"Society has not shown her any mercy for a youthful misstep. Society has branded her, unkindly and unjustly, as damaged goods. Remember how this kind of philistine attitude destroyed Anna Karenina? Well, I couldn't permit this to happen to a kind-hearted young woman like our Maya," she said to stir her son's compassion for this "unfortunate soul."

"And since I am as good as damaged goods as well, you think we would make a perfect pair," Kafka sneered.

"Don't be snide, Franz! It would do you good to have a good wife," his mother protested.

"You know that Anna Karenina is a fictional character."

"Of course, I do. But the story is so true to life. Tolstoy was the absolute master. He painted with great perspicacity the effects of societal norms and prejudices, the iniquities and injustices a woman who strays from the path is made to suffer! Let those who are free of guilt toss the first stone!"

"I believe that's a Christian concept," Kafka interposed.

"Where do you think, they took it from? You are still the contrary child, Franz."

Maya Levy was the daughter of a Chassidic rabbi in a small, secluded town in the mountainous hinterland. He enjoyed something of a reputation as Talmudic sage and healer. People came from surrounding villages to his court for advice and special prayers. After a certain incident involving the miraculous recovery of a young girl suffering from hysteria became known, multitudes of the infirm in body and spirit were brought to him for the laying on of his healing hands.

"In other words, he's a charlatan like the man whom you just quoted," Kafka noted as he rolled up the several layers of sleeves of the gown and robe that covered his mother's arm so he could take her blood pressure.

"It's no use talking to you. You have been exposed for far too long to the worldly cynicism of Viennese coffeehouses, my wayward son."

"No, please. I want to hear the story of this young woman you seem to have taken to your bosom. I sense she has been the victim of religious bigotry," Kafka insisted.

"You won't get an accurate reading if you keep on nettling me. Not only the religious kind but the bigotry of the wider society, of educated, worldly people who go about flaunting their open-mindedness that was her undoing. The cause of it all was, of course, the treachery of a male of the species."

Against the will of her parents and in violation of tradition that prescribes a domestic role for women, Maya had followed her calling to become a healer of the sick herself. Only she chose the established medical path rather than mystical mutterings. She left her hometown for the capital and enrolled in a nursing program at a hospital operated under the auspices of a Catholic women's religious order. She excelled through dedication and quickness of mind. She often told her benefactress, Frau Kafka, the story of the nuns prodding her to get baptized. She resisted no matter how enticing the benefits, both worldly and otherworldly, that the Sisters dangled before her. She steadfastly held to the faith of her forebears.

Not so steadfast was she in resisting the advances of a certain staff physician with a reputation for getting young girls into trouble.

"A notorious predator," Frau Kafka punctuated her remarks with disdain for the roué.

The resulting pregnancy was blamed entirely on the girl. The fetus was aborted eventually in the second trimester with the connivance of the seducer's wife, though not before the details of the affair had become known and were circulated in ever more embellished, if that is the right word, versions.

The nuns who had been so eager to gain a convert banished her as if she were afflicted with leprosy. When word about the disgrace reached the Chassidic court in the girl's hometown, her father said Kaddish for his daughter, pronouncing her dead.

"Schnitzler couldn't have made up a more sordid tale," noted Frau Kafka.

"One day she came into the store asking for work. She was hungry and looked to be in poor health. She would do anything for little pay and a corner cot to rest her head, she said. I knew right away who she was, not that this town is lacking in young girls who have fallen victim to predators and subsequently end in the gutter; even the flesh trade. Not this girl if I could help it. She has been a joy and comfort to me as a companion and caretaker in my declining years. I want to be sure she is well cared for after I am gone. It is my dying request to you to make her your wife."

"My mother, the drama queen! You are not dying, at least not yet," Kafka protested maybe a little too emphatically for he knew she was right. Her days were indeed numbered. It was only a matter of time.

In the months that followed, his mother's body slowly succumbed to the various ailments that ravaged her body if not her spirit. Maya gained Kafka's respect and admiration not only for the devotion she showed her benefactress but for her skills and medical knowledge in providing the dying woman with the needed comfort to spare her much pain and agony.

Two weeks before the old lady breathed her last, she saw her most ardent wish fulfilled. Kafka and Maya tied the knot in a Jewish ceremony followed by a traditionally raucous celebration. The entire Kafka clan joined in the dancing and feasting. No one from the Levy side made the journey to attend.

The wedding was a dance on a volcano. If such a thought crossed anyone's mind, as might very well have been the case, the celebrants and guests kept it to themselves, unwilling to permit a sense of impending doom permeating the air to spoil the merriment. It was March 1939.

The chilly day on which Hedwig Kafka, née Lustiger, was laid to rest in the Jewish cemetery of Prague coincided with the demise of the Czechoslovak state. Henceforth the living found themselves in a German-created entity called the Reich Protectorate of Bohemia and Moravia. Mercifully for her, Frau Kafka was not conscious when Hitler came to Prague one day before she departed this earthly realm.

These were Kafka's words. I had joined him during the night of the vigil at the bedside of the delirious Rudolf Schwamm. The months we had spent together had been a prelude toward the day of reckoning with the perfidious couple whom he accused of complicity in the murder of Lenka Ostrova. He would find them, with my help, confront them, and take his revenge. That was the plan. Pure and simple.

Only nothing in life is ever pure and simple. Not even the great Kafka was able to control all angles and unforeseen circumstances. Instead of putting a bullet into Schwamm's head, Kafka extracted several slugs from his enemy's chest and stomach. Instead of dispatching the despised rival to hell, he spent the night hoping he would stay alive. It seemed he had been cheated out of his grand accounting by an enemy of greater evil than the miserable, little cog in the wheel.

Elfriede Kling sat at some distance on the other side of her husband's bed. Her head was sunken on her chest. It was hard to tell whether she was listening to Kafka's tale. For whose benefit was he telling this story? At first, I had flattered myself that he was talking to me, but the intensity with which he spoke made me think he was talking primarily to Schwamm even though his eyes, those dark mesmerizing eyes, were pinned on me all the while he spoke. Then, as his story unraveled further, another suspicion took hold of me. Schwamm and Kling may not have been his primary target at all. He may have known all along what and whom he would find once he tracked them down.

Chapter 4

A Tale of Two Ghettos

Prague

"It's a paradox," Kafka took up the thread again, giving off a staggered laugh. Not his rippling, loud laughter, more a 'you may find this hard to believe' kind of laugh. "It may seem paradoxical to say that the following two years were the happiest time of my life. But so it was."

Paradoxical it would truly seem to be given the events that were drawing an ever more encroaching circle around the existence of the Jews of Prague. Did he deny reality? Doesn't sound like the Kafka I know, I thought. But by the time we met, he had been to hell and back several times. Considering his later progress from the first hell he had glimpsed in Vienna toward the crucible he was made to wade through shoulder-deep, the brief Prague interlude when he was blessed with marriage and fatherhood, the practice of his profession, and the respect and admiration he gained from the community must have been like paradise or at least a welcome respite in limbo.

What gave him succor and strength was Maya, the helpmate at his side. The life and family they built together, on sand to be sure, was an illusion. Both were aware of its fragility. For the time being, they made it what they wanted it to be.

One month after the war broke out, the German invasion of Poland which at last prompted the Allies, who had balked at defending their homeland and looked on as it was dismembered and preyed upon, to declare war against the German Reich, Maya gave birth to their son. They called him Chaim, life--for the life Maya had lost and for the life Kafka had gained and the life they would build together. An illusion, yes. But an illusion willingly entertained.

The child became the center of Kafka's existence. From time to time, he thought of the man he had met on the train. He recalled what he had told him about the vision of a Jewish homeland, not just another place of refuge, but a state, a country where Jews lived and governed themselves. He began to read what he could find about Zionism and Palestine. He came across a copy of Herzl's book *The Jewish State*. Other writings and pamphlets impressed him deeply about what had already been achieved by those who had returned and were rebuilding the ancient Jewish homeland. It was in this place where he wanted his son to live and to grow.

Meanwhile, an endless stream of laws and injunctions concerning the lives and livelihoods of the Jews of Prague gushed forth from the German rulers of the Protectorate. Jews were forced out of their places of residence and herded together into a Jewish district that quickly became overcrowded due to the influx of people from the countryside. Following the model in force in Germany and Austria, Jewish property and businesses were confiscated and "Aryanized."

The Kafka department store was put into the hands of a non-Jewish "trustee"--another euphemism of which the regime was so fond. Jews were expelled from their positions at universities, the civil service, and the professions. The fact that he could treat only Jews in his medical practice didn't bother Kafka very much. He had plenty to do. It was the "senseless chicaneries" he had already experienced in Vienna, the *Verbot* for Jews to sit on park benches, attend the theater, use public swimming pools, stay at hotels, drive cars that alarmed him. Not because of any inconvenience to himself but because he sensed in them a harbinger of worse to come.

Neither he nor Maya harbored any illusions about the German's true intent. They arranged their life in one small room looking out on a drab rear yard at the end of the corridor of a five-room apartment they shared with four other families. Kafka couldn't have been happier. An immense, indescribable feeling of love and bliss filled his wings and made him soar above the miseries, the cruelties, the injustices.

Kafka wandering around the ghetto streets making house calls, Maya at his side and little Chaim in a basket on his back, became a familiar sight. A ministering angel they hailed him when they saw him coming. Sometimes outcries for a golem, a savior, could be heard. In many parts, Jews would pray for the coming of the Messiah. In Prague, the desire for redemption got mixed up with an expressed longing for a golem who would save the Jews.

Kafka had grown up with the legend of the Golem. His father, though not religious, loved to tell and retell stories of Jewish folklore. The story he told his children most often was that of a medieval rabbi who breathed life into an inanimate figure he had fashioned whose magic would prevent the Jews of Prague from being expelled from the city. As a very young boy, Kafka was fascinated by the idea that a human could fashion a figure and not only bring it to life but make it do his will. Precocious and inquisitive as he was, the four-year-old set about to figure out how to make a creature that would be at his beck and call. He whiled away many hours of his childhood forming figures of clay, some even of lead like the soldiers he played with, before eventually conceding defeat. He was unable to endow his creations with a soul, he said.

What he meant was he couldn't make a clay doll speak. There were other aspects about the lifeless, insentient thing, but what bothered him most was his inability to get any words out of it.

For a while, he tried alchemy bent on turning base metals into gold. That too ended in defeat. His dabbling in Kabbalistic endeavors came to an end when he turned six and started school. His inquisitive mind then took up more promising experiments. He always had a project of some kind or other to occupy his mind. Most involved scientific principles of chemistry and physics.

It was a long time before he would create a sentient being of his own. No golem this time, but a human being of flesh and blood and with a soul. In time the boy started to walk on his own and, to the delight of his father, expressed his will in spoken words. But even before he learned to walk and talk, Kafka carried him to the old medieval Jewish cemetery and sat with him at the resting place of the Maharal, the purported creator of the Golem of ancient lore where he told him the story his own father had told many times.

"It's a nice story," said Kafka to the people gathered that night at Castle Montsalvat. "Alas, no such savior appeared. No golem to thwart the schemes of the evil-doers."

"That's it for now," he concluded. He rose and stretched his long legs. He breathed in deeply doing some callisthenic movements with his arms. "You should all get some sleep. The trial will take place in the morning."

I fell asleep for I don't know how long in a chair next to Kafka who would not abandon his vigil at his patient's side. Neither did Elfriede Kling.

Kafka's companions kept Odin von Bülow in irons under guard in the tower keep overnight. In the morning, they hauled him back into the dining hall. They placed him in a chair in the middle of the room. Kafka stood a few feet away, staring him down. Odin did not flinch. He held his opponents gaze with defiant steadfastness.

"Let us begin then with the trial of Obersturmbannführer Odin von Bülow," Kafka declared ceremoniously.

At this point, the Baroness asked to be excused. She would rather not be present when her son was pilloried with outrageous accusations, she said.

"Herr Kaiser, I am very disappointed in you," she added. She still addressed him in the fictitious name, ignoring Kafka's correction. Her lips pursed as if she had bitten on a bitter lemon, she went off into the room she had been occupying since our arrival at the castle. Kafka did not hold her back.

"How about something to eat and drink?" Odin's voice had lost nothing of its Herrenvolk cadence though his eyes bespoke some quiet desperation as he cast a longing look at the leftovers from the breakfast food Hannah and I had scrounged up earlier in the morning. Kafka ignored his request.

Hannah, Peter, and I comprised the audience. I looked around for Elfriede Kling. She was still near her groaning husband. I had no doubt she was listening attentively.

"Hunger," Kafka began, then paused, permitting the word to hover in the air over the room for a while and sink in. "Hunger is no doubt a sensation new to the Baron. Hunger, the constant gnawing feeling in the stomach, the inability to fulfill the body's craving for nourishment. Hunger makes people do irrational things. It can drive them insane. And, of course, if unsated, it kills. Even worse, its companion: thirst. The lack of water. The parched throat. The cleaving tongue. The dried lips. Hunger and thirst lead to an all-consuming desire for relief, to the exclusion of all else. To satisfy this need, to still the pangs of hunger and quench the thirst brings out the animal instinct in humans.

"We, however, are not barbarians. We take no pleasure in watching our fellow human beings grovel for a crumb and a drop. It is our custom to share our bounty, to feed the hungry. 'Let all those who are hungry, let them enter and eat'! We say on Passover. It's a beautiful notion and custom."

Kafka lunged into a clinical lecture about the body's need for nourishment to sustain itself, of how it absorbs the nutrients thereof in the cycle of metabolism, and even how it eliminates waste material once processed. Odin's bulging eyes threatened to pop out of their socket. Hearing it thus described by Kafka in graphic detail, we all began to feel some of the effects of hunger edema in our own bodies.

When he finally finished his long harangue, Kafka turned to me with the request: "Please be so kind, Artemisia, and hand the Baron a glass of water and a crust of the bread."

Odin stuffed the hardened bread crust into his mouth and washed it down with the water blowing up his cheek while chewing. His mother, had she witnessed the scene would have been appalled by his ill manners. Maybe she also would have seen the monster inside the skin of the mannerly gentleman she thought she had raised.

Kafka remained standing, towering, moving about, waving his arms to emphasize a point. He was in full command of the stage and the dramatic presentation under his choreography. I suspected he was still mostly playing to his adversaries Schwamm and Kling. Odin didn't need to be read the litany of SS crimes. He knew it very well. He was a brutal thug not worth anybody's breath. Here he was the strawman. The rest of us were fringe characters; essential to the overall scene but not a driving force. The two people who had sold their souls to the devil and in turn had reaped applause and had basked in veneration, adulation from millions of Wagner idolaters, who had benefitted copiously in material rewards, were the true target of Kafka's *J'accuse*. The Christian parable of the thirty shekels in return for betrayal would be a fallacious comparison for two reasons: thirty shekels is a paltry sum compared to the riches these Wagnerians amassed; the recipient in the ancient story, as it is told, was so plagued by remorse, he hung himself. None of this applied to Kafka's former friends.

Ghetto Litzmannstadt

The order came in October of 1941. Kafka found the letter which had been pushed under the door during the night as he was leaving to make his rounds in the morning. He was instructed to report with his family to the *Messepalast* on such and such a date. He went on his daily rounds of visiting the sick. The decree from the Reichsprotector Neurath had been posted all over the ghetto of Prague. It proclaimed the formation of five "transports" of one thousand persons each. They would depart the city on designated dates. The uncertainty of a destination caused much speculation and debate as well as anxiety. Doctor Kafka's consultation room was filled to overflowing more than ever with people seeking advice and spiritual comfort. He may have been familiar with the theories and treatment methods of Sigmund Freud, whom he had known personally in Vienna, but he was not a trained soul healer. He did his best to dispense reassurances even though he felt like a charlatan not knowing himself the answer. However, his instinct told him that the removal of the Jews from the city was only the first leg of a journey toward a sinister end.

In the early light of dawn of the day he was ordered to report to the Messepalast, he led his wife and child through the narrow, crooked alleyways of the Jewish district. Public transportation was no longer available. Jews were forbidden to use of taxicabs. They undertook the long demarche to the outlying, now empty, hall where seasonal fairs and commercial exhibitions were held on foot. So as not to be overburdened with possessions that would prove useless, Kafka and Maya packed lightly. He carried a rucksack with provisions on his back and held the child tight in his arms against his chest. Maya juggled two pieces of hand luggage with only bare necessities, a few toiletries and warm clothing in anticipation of winter, which was already heralding its imminent approach. Anxious not to get separated from him in the jostle, she took quick little steps in double time to keep pace with his long, firm strides.

A sea of yellow blinded their eyes as they entered the hall. Yellow, because everyone inside wore a patch of yellow on their clothing in the shape of what was called a *Judenstern.* Wearing this patch on the chest of their clothing had been made obligatory a month before, on September 18, by orders issued from Berlin.

An unintended irony was that these felt patches, a revival of medieval decrees marking Jews as Jews in public places, sprouted like wildflowers daubing the dreary Jewish district with a festive tinge of spring. Many residents displayed what was meant to be a mark of shame with an attitude of *davka,* defiant pride. They remembered an article by the Prague native Robert Weltsch in a Berlin publication back in April 1933 with the headline: "Wear it with Pride, the Yellow Patch!" in which the writer exhorted the Jews not to be cowed by the new regime.

Kafka's name was on the list of the transport for doctors, lawyers, and other professionals such as university professors, writers, and journalists. Separating doctors was understandable to some extent since medical care would be needed. Why the other professionals? Kafka thought of the reports that had reached Prague in the autumn of 1939, shortly after the war began and Soviet Russia invaded Eastern Poland. Thousands of Polish intellectuals were reported to have been massacred by Stalin's forces in the Katin Forest near Smolensk. A Nazi scheme to wipe out Jewish intellectuals to staunch any protests and resistance on the same scale was quite possible.

As Kafka looked around for a quiet corner, he could lay claim to for his wife and child amidst the swarming, ear-shattering chaos, he felt a tap on his shoulder.

"Doctor Kafka," said a not unfamiliar voice, "how terrible to see you again under such dreadful circumstances."

Kafka turned and came face to face with his erstwhile travel companion.

"Doctor Rosenfeld! I should have thought you were in London by now. It is indeed most regrettable to find you still here. What happened? You had a visa."

"The war. The outbreak of the war. The Reich Protector Heidrich first wanted to get rid of as many of us as possible, then they blocked all exits, especially for those of us who had very sparse means to sign over to their coffers. In my case, a journalist with a visa attached to a work contract with a Jewish publication in London might sully their reputation abroad. Ever so shy of negative publicity, those Nazis!"

"Now we are going on another train ride together. This time: destination unknown."

"I see you have a child. Yours, I presume."

"Yes, I've become a family man." Kafka beamed proudly showing off his offspring.

Oskar Rosenfeld exchanged smiles with the boy who was peeking out at him with a bright-eyed curious look, his face half buried inside his father's coat.

"He has your eyes," Rosenfeld noted. "What is his name?"

The man nodded pensively when he heard it. Then he took a few sudden steps forward. He placed his hand on the boy's head. "Little Chaim," he murmured. "May the Lord keep you and bless you, may he shine his light upon and bring peace." An ominous silence ensued between the two men amidst the deafening noise around them. Then the boy started to fret and reach his arms out to his mother. After a polite introduction, the stranger walked away with a heavy gait, his figure soon lost in the crowd. It was much later, on yet another train platform, that Kafka saw him again.

The train filled with human cargo huffed along a circuitous route difficult to gauge with any degree of certainty where it was headed. There was only one stop in the middle of the night. The steam rising from the hissing engine blurred Kafka's view from behind the mud-splattered window on the surroundings. As they pulled out of the station in the graying of dawn, he faintly made out a sign saying "Breslau," which was Northeast of Prague. Out in the open countryside, the train's trajectory changed directions in an erratic zigzag pattern, eventually settling on a course Kafka determined was due East. The train frequently came to a screeching halt in the middle of nowhere. The passengers were left stranded without food or water for hours.

The sun had come up and set again three times when the phantom train pulled into a railway yard in the dark of night. The place was clearly marked. A large sign proclaimed in big red Germanic-type letters:

"Welcome to Ghetto Litzmannstadt!"

There was no station or platform, merely a twisted tangle of tracks stacked with equipment. Commanded to disembark by the shouts from hoarse anonymous throats, the passengers spilled from the train, said Kafka, into a slippery snake pit of iron rails and wires. They swarmed about blindly stumbling, groping, toppling over each other, reaching out for someone or something to hold on to so as not to fall and be trampled underfoot. Much of the meager baggage they carried still carried got lost in the scramble. When they finally managed to clamber onto solid ground, the Polish-speaking guards herded them into an abandoned school building, inadequate to hold them all. And yet, it did. Another scramble ensued in the hallways and in what was formerly an auditorium to secure a spot where they could rest their weary bones.

Then the wait began. Long hours spent in idling, uncertainty. Then came the hunger. No provisions to feed a thousand newcomers. What little food they had brought with them was quickly consumed. Sporadically some people showed signs of going mad.

Sanitary conditions were stinking to the high heavens, Kafka added. (Is there some irony that our first encounters took place in a latrine? I too had been thrown into the pit of a crucible. Though, as I was told, not to demoralize me but to test my mettle.)

Kafka perceived a deliberate plan, engineered by faceless puppeteers, calculated to demoralize the victims to drive them mad and set them against each other. An artificially engineered Darwinian struggle for survival. Artificially engineered famine! A famine not by crop failure, flood, or other natural disaster. No, starvation of human design. If the captors intended to mount a gladiator spectacle, a dog-eat-dog drama, of people fighting each other to the death over a crumb of bread, they surely must have been disappointed. (He used the German word "inszenieren," a theater term like *mise-en-scène*, several times.) Most of these languishing humans were far too drained of energy in body and soul to turn against each other. At the end of the first week, members of the Jewish ghetto police finally brought in a vat of watery soup once a day. One ladle per person in a tin cup. A loaf of stale, hard bread had to last a week.

Kafka had staked out a space for himself and his wife in the corner of what was once an indoor tennis court. He never let his child leave his arms, except to have Maya hold him whenever he needed to have his hands free. With the boy on his shoulders, he and Maya walked about looking after the sick and dying —without medical supplies and medications, there was not much they could do beyond dispensing encouraging words neither he nor Maya believed.

Two weeks went by. Why this long, endless, wait? A demoralizing stay in limbo before the final descent into hell was Kafka's assessment. The conditions in the cramped space at the schoolhouse became increasingly intolerable. The rattling, drafty windows and doors did little to protect the masses of people huddled together against artic-like winds that chilled them to the bone. Their ranks thinned quickly. The dead were left to rot outside in the courtyard, without prospect for proper burial. The stench burnt the nostrils and eyes of the living.

The nightmare finally came to an end with roll call. Kafka noted that the arrivals' names and other statistical information about them had been carefully recorded. A strutting guard read them out loud from a prepared list. Many of the names called went unanswered. Those who were still alive and even those who could stand upright were ordered to line up in military formation. Kafka noticed that the strident voices giving the orders came from Jewish policemen who seemed to have adopted the manners of their German masters.

A man who introduced himself as Chaim Mordechai Rumkowski, head of the Elders of the Jews in the ghetto, addressed the assembled. He assured the bedraggled lot facing him with weary eyes all would be well if followed all orders without demur.

"This is a work camp," he declared in a high-pitched voice. "For as long as we are indispensable to them, for as long as we produce what they need, we will be safe."

The punchline, which he repeated several times during his longwinded, rambling harangue, was the promise: "Those who work will eat!"

Kafka sneered as he recalled the scene. He was to hear this line of reasoning a hundred times from the mouth of this deluded man, who thought he had found a formula that would throw a wrench into the Nazi killing machine and keep at least a select few alive.

The transport from Prague, as the human cargo was collectively referred to, was assigned living spaces in the apartment buildings from which the Polish residents had been evicted. As a physician, Kafka was quartered with his wife and child in a small apartment facing a dingy courtyard in the rear of a make-shift clinical facility. As medical workers, he and Maya received a slightly larger bread ration. Not as much though as that self-appointed king of the ghetto and his passel of Jewish policemen who were riding around the ghetto streets in patrol cars keeping the masses in check with orders blaring from loudspeakers.

Kafka and Maya set up consulting hours at this clinic for the mornings. In the afternoons and evenings, they made the rounds of the lodgings, looking after the bed-ridden and the dying. Kafka with the boy on his shoulders became a familiar sight in the ghetto as he had been in Prague. When the boy became too big to ride on his father's shoulders, he tagged along in his father's shadow. Kafka never permitted his son to leave his side or get out of his sight. Then one day Maya was drafted for work in one of the garment factories from five in the morning to seven at night. Father and son became an even more close-knit pair.

Medical supplies and equipment were always scarce. Tending to the many ailments of the disease-ridden ghetto residents was a nearly futile task.

It was a struggle between Sisyphus and Thanatos, said Kafka about his labors in the ghetto. Thanatos representing the forces of death. Unlike Sisyphus in the story, who held back Thanatos at least for a while, Kafka's efforts to shackle the evildoers and halt their progress was a fight with windmills, Kafka explained, mixing metaphors and literary allusions to abandon.

Chapter 5

A Paragon of the Master Race

He had seen him strutting and swaggering about the ghetto in shiny, black riding boots, perfectly creased uniform, the empty eyes of the Totenkopf grinning from his lapels. A paragon of the *Herrenvolk*! Odin von Bülow was the all-around prototype of the master race. The poster image of Aryan virility. Tall, slender, athletic, blond, steely blue eyes, a strong chin, self-assured, nothing was missing from this perfect specimen. Unlike most of the SS men who remained in their enclave on the edge of the ghetto area from which they pulled strings governing people's lives and letting the Jewish elders and police do their bidding and dirty work, Odin von Bülow was highly visible. His chauffeured Benz convertible streaked through the ghetto streets parting the crowds like Moses parting the sea. In kingly manner, he waved to his subjects flashing a gracious smirk. The cigarette in a holder permanently stuck in the corner of his mouth was a trademark he seemed to have copied from the American president.

One morning in late spring, the waiting room of the clinic was filled with the infirm and ailing, this prime specimen of Aryan pride came limping into Kafka's clinic. Dragging one leg, he burst into the consulting room and demanded the doctor's immediate attention.

Kafka removed the blood-soaked shirt that was tied around his leg and examined the wound. A small caliber slug was lodged in the thigh. But why come to him? The German doctor at headquarters surely was better equipped to operate. The condition was not severe. With the proper instruments and sedation, it could easily be fixed — none of which Kafka had.

Obersturmbannführer von Bülow, he introduced himself, as if he needed introduction. Kafka noted the twisted expression in his face. The man was obviously in pain.

"Herr Doktor Kafka, I presume that's your name," he said through clenched teeth, "I have a confession to make. I am in a bind and need your help. No one must know about this visit."

Sapperlot! Kafka thought to himself. Wow, this was a twist: the SS Obersturmbannführer and a Jewish father confessor! He suppressed an urge to laugh. He may be bound by a code of patient-doctor confidentiality, but trust was another matter.

"It was a hunting accident," Odin said with a still subdued voice. "We are not allowed to hunt around here in the countryside while the war goes on."

The Obersturmbannführer had gone hunting in violation of orders!

"I cannot extract it with my bare hands," Kafka stated the obvious, searching for an excuse not to get entangled in this officer's affairs. No good would come of this, he was sure.

"We don't have the necessary equipment nor medication here. There's also the danger of infection during recovery and the potential for gangrene if not properly treated."

"I will get you what you need. Meanwhile, can you stave off the bleeding with a fresh bandage, can't you?"

"We are very short on supplies." Kafka's effort to protect the small, dwindling stash he had was quickly pooh-poohed by Odin's patting of the whip attached to his belt. Suddenly the German was not so docile anymore, confirming Kafka's instinct not to trust this man.

He came back the next morning with all sorts of medical supplies from a list which Kafka had provided. The operation went without a hitch. The wound healed without complications. Only a limp remained. Odin von Bülow was profuse in expressions of gratitude.

"My father used to say: 'Jewish doctors are the best'!" he proclaimed laughing. "I have to give it to him."

During the last follow-up visit, Kafka noticed the Baron's eyes pinned on him more piercingly. Had he now become expendable? Eliminating an accomplice, the only one with knowledge of a crime, was the criminal's way to cover his tracks.

"I have been thinking and thinking where we met before," Odin began in a chatty tone. "It just came to me. Vienna! You may not remember me, I was a boy, and you were the husband of a famous opera star."

"That is true," Kafka admitted with unease.

"My parents were great patrons of opera. Our home in Bayreuth was a temple of Wagner worship. I never quite could match their enthusiasm for the Maestro as my mother referred to him. Her mouth and heart were overflowing. That's all I heard my entire childhood long. For my tenth birthday, they took me to Vienna to expose me to one of the greatest Wagner singers, they said. We had plenty of those in Bayreuth, but my mother insisted none could hold a candle to Lenka Ostrova. She puts them all in the shade, my mother said. We met this divine singer at a glittering reception after the performance.

She was very kind and kissed me on the forehead. You stood right next to her like a bodyguard.

"We knew that you, her husband, was a Jew. In those days, one didn't fuss much over such things. But she was billed as a Czech soprano. Can you imagine how crestfallen my mother was when she heard this revered diva was a Jewess? The greatest Brünnhilde of all time a Jewess?! We heard she came to a tragic end."

Odin went on unperturbed, lacing his chatter with girlish chuckles as if spouting off some amusing anecdote at a cocktail party, oblivious or just callously disregarding who it was to whom he was speaking.

"She was murdered. The Gestapo murdered her at the time of the Anschluss," Kafka informed him dispassionately.

"Ah, yes! Most unfortunate!" Odin gave off a nervous laugh. "Then again, maybe it was for her best. Otherwise, she would be here with you in this misbegotten ghetto, wouldn't she? Most unbecoming for a Wagnerian diva."

Misbegotten indeed. The image of a misbegotten, callous man sat right there in front of him.

Without showing an inkling of awareness of how tasteless his remarks were, Odin suddenly became aware of another presence in the room.

"Is this your son?" He pointed at the little boy on the floor in a corner. He was quietly playing with a set of lead soldiers a patient had given him who had found them in one of the abandoned apartments. While the consultation was going on, the boy didn't make a sound. Life in the ghetto had taught him at an early age how to be unobtrusive, to look down, to listen, and not to speak in the presence of the German soldiers.

Odin limped over to the boy. He bent down and patted him on the head. "You are a good boy," he said. "Here is a reward for you." He reached inside the pocket of his jacket and produced a bar of Swiss chocolate. The boy gave his father a questioning look. Kafka nodded imperceptibly.

"Here take it," Odin prodded. The gift earned him a serious "Danke schön, Herr Obersturmbannführer" but no smile.

"What else can I do for you, Herr Doktor?" he addressed Kafka. "Extra rations, maybe some meat, chicken? More chocolate?"

"You can see what our needs are here in the clinic and at the infirmary. Medical supplies, medicines, bedding. I can make a list."

"Very crafty that Kafka!" Odin waved his finger at Kafka like a schoolmaster. "You shall have your wish. I already have your list. That should suffice."

A few days later two Jewish policemen made a special delivery of medical and other supplies. The items were very useful, though hardly enough and were quickly depleted.

The ghetto population too was constantly depleted through attrition and then replenished with new arrivals. Transports from Germany and other points West filled the vacated spaces in a continuous cycle of coming and going. In the streets, people stumbled over the dead and dying who had become a common site. For each transport out of the ghetto, the Jewish police were charged with rounding up a specified number of people. They took the sick and old from their deathbeds to meet the fixed quotas stipulated by the SS leadership. Rumkowski, the Elder of the Jews, addressed the masses through a bullhorn from a platform set up in the central square pleading for cooperation. His trumpet calls of pleas "to help him save lives" resounded through the streets and alleyways like marching music. Those unfit for work had to sacrificed to save the able-bodied doing slave labor in the factories and workshops.

The factories produced supplies for the German army, Kafka explained. Uniforms, boots, coats, gloves, hats, and the like. Even some weaponry and munitions. Maya worked in a shop that milled out women's garments, like dresses and coats, for the consumer market inside the Reich. A major beneficiary of these wares produced with slave labor was the German department store Neckermann.

The Polish province of Lodzie had been annexed to the Grossdeutsche Reich (Greater German Reich) and renamed Wartheland. Within its borders was the city of Lodz, which was renamed Litzmannstadt.

The Elder's dream, pipedream indeed, was a model workforce, efficient and disciplined, whose output would indispensable for the German war effort. Toward this purpose, unproductive elements had to be winnowed out. The wheat had to be separated from the chaff or maybe vice versa. Put another way, those who didn't work didn't eat.

Into the category of useless, unproductive mouths fell the children who were too small to be put to work. Children under the age of ten.

Kafka paused in his narration. He took several menacing strides toward Odin. His tall, slender frame, taut and erect betrayed no emotion. His eyes squinted, pinned on the man tied to a chair. Not a single facial muscle moved. His favorite Glock was boring into the miscreant's forehead. Minutes ticked away. One could cut the air with a knife. We held our breath. Then a blood-curdling scream tore the air from the other side of the hall. The Baroness came running out of the room where she had been hiding.

"What are you going to do to my son? Please, Herr Keiser or Herr Kafka, whoever you are, hear a mother's plea!"

Kafka lowered the gun. The muscles in his face sagged.

"Never fear, dear lady," he said gently as if speaking to a hurt child. "We don't murder children in front of their mother's eyes; neither do we murder mothers before their children's eyes. But we do bring murderers to justice."

She covered her face and sank sobbing and shaking onto an empty chair.

Kafka asked for someone to bring her a glass of water. I rushed into the kitchen. When I came back into the hall with the requested drink, I heard him say to her: "You may want to stay and hear the rest of this story. I must warn you though; this tale is not for the faint-hearted. What I have to relate is no fairy-tale."

It was not his story, but this story, the story, this tale. His own story was not one of individual suffering. He wasn't merely relating a personal episode. He embedded his story within the overall fate of his people. His experience, as he presented it, was emblematic of that of all tormented Jews.

"Artemisia!" His commanding voice startled me out of my thoughts. I looked up at him. Our eyes met in mutual understanding. It had been so long since we were alone together, since we had kissed and embraced each other

"Artemisia!" he repeated. His tone sounded officious like an executive's who is calling on his secretary to take dictation. "Take heed of what you hear! You may want to write this story down someday. As you should. It's the stuff of a novel. Only this isn't fiction."

The life inside of me, of which he was still unaware, unleashed a barrage of vigorous kicks as if to register its approval and stir me out of my stupor.

Chapter 6

Kinder Aktion

"*Leute höret die Geschichte*! [People listen to the story!]", began Kafka imitating the rallying call of the medieval *Bänkelsänger,* wandering minstrels, of familiar German folklore. "*Die Moritat des Odin von Bülow*! [Ballad of the murderous deeds of Odin von Bülow!]" –an allusion to the Ballad of Mack Messer of Three Penny Opera fame.

A gasp rose from the Baroness's chest. This time Kafka paid no heed to her anguish. Having elicited a chuckle for this ironic allusion from Hannah and Peter, he went on.

In September 1942, the Nazi Moloch issued a demand for twenty thousand living bodies to be delivered within a week. The monster had consumed most of the disabled and the old. Now it lusted after the children, children too young to be productive in the slave labor factories. Useless mouths, life unworthy of living, they called them. The spaces on the transports had to be filled. The trains could not run empty. Efficiency was of prime importance.

Efficiency was also the theme Rumkowski, the Elder of the Jews, emphasized in his address to the mass of ghetto residents assembled in the central square on that rain-drenched day.

"Give me your children!" he implored the ghetto dwellers. "There is no way around it," he wailed into his bullhorn. They had to comply, had to meet the quota, or the Germans would carry out the *Aktion* themselves. The sacrifice of twenty thousand children will save the lives of two hundred thousand able-bodied workers! The ghetto will become an efficient production machine turning out the material and goods needed to conduct the war. He had worked hard, he said, to set up a mutually beneficial symbiosis. He went on and on with assurances that he tried everything to avert this catastrophe. He had tried reasoning, he said. He had presented alternatives. All to no avail. He didn't specify the alternatives he had proposed.

None of these hollow assurances appeased the people, standing in the rain, soaked to the skin. People who had already lost everything were now asked to sacrifice their most precious possession in exchange for a life that had become indeed no longer worth living.

Jewish policemen conducted the hunt. They stormed through the habitations, tore down walls, ripped open suspected hiding places, knocked down parents blocking their way. The kicking and screaming victims were thrown out of windows from several stories high onto the back of trucks waiting in the street, their motors revving and roaring like unleashed monsters clamoring their fodder.

Kafka did not let his son out of sight. Everybody knew the father-son pair. The Jewish policemen and even the German guards patrolling the ghetto streets would call out to them and wave. To the residents, they were a comforting sight, a symbol of life and maybe even hope.

While the razzia was underway, Kafka barred the consultation room and kept the boy's right hand tied to his with a string. Maya was at the factory. Then a call came from the infirmary. A seriously ill patient required urgent medical attention. No other doctor was available. Kafka didn't think it wise or safe to take the boy outside with him. He decided to lock him inside the crawl space behind the consultation room with strict instructions not to make a sound. He would be back as soon as he could.

He returned within the hour. As he approached the clinic, he noticed a commotion. He rushed in. In the corridor, he collided with Odin von Bülow, who was limping along, the boy slung over his shoulder. A posse of armed SS men had taken over from the Jewish police.

"Get the doctor out of the way!" Odin shouted as he headed for the exit. The miscreants pushed Kafka to the ground. Outside a flat-bed truck was waiting with the motor running. Kafka quickly regained his bearings from the blows to his head and rushed after them. He met his son's imploring eyes amid a mass of squirming, crying children that had been tossed onto the truck like so much rubbish. Odin stood next to the truck, a self-satisfied smirk on his glowing red face. SS goons held Kafka back at gunpoint, preventing from getting closer. Then an anguished scream rent the air. Maya was pushing her way through the crowd. Somehow, she reached the truck and flung herself on top of the heap of children searching for her child.

Odin yelled at her to get down. He ordered her to stop making a disturbance. She paid him no heed. She kept on calling out for her child. Odin pulled out his gun and unloaded it into the back of her head point blank. The truck took off with her body sprawled out over the children.

Odin von Bülow had deliberately come after Kafka's boy. He saw the father leave the infirmary without the child. He knew the boy had to be somewhere inside.

When Kafka returned to the ransacked consultation room, he was struck with evidence of the vilest rampage. Walls had been ripped apart; cabinets had been pried open, their contents, medicines, bottles, flasks, instruments, bandages, strewn about and trampled on; floorboards had been pulled up; the little door to the crawl space hang limply unhinged. The brute had left nothing unturned to find the child.

"I didn't know she was your wife," Odin crowed.

"Gag him!" Kafka ordered his companions.

The Baroness's wailing intensified. Elfriede Kling had a fit of hysterics. Rudolf Schwamm was still in the twilight. It was unclear how much he had heard or understood. Hannah and Peter held each other trembling in a tight embrace. I just sat there with numbness in my heart. Even the life inside of me was still as if it understood the solemnity of the moment.

"Why such bestial ferocity?" said Kafka after some pondering. "There is no answer. Never will be."

He finally stopped pacing and sat down in a chair near me. He looked at me with sad eyes and nodded. Our eyes remained locked in silence for a long time. Should I let him know that he had fathered another child? Would it be a consolation? No, the time was not right just then. It had to wait for another day, maybe a brighter day. Right then it would be like an intrusion. I knew my child could never be a replacement, a stand-in for the one he had lost. Nor would I want it to be.

"We knew nothing about this, Franz," Elfriede Kling whined. "You must believe me. If we only had known anything of this."

"Just go to your pathetic husband!" he snarled.

We finally had some time alone while everybody in the room was trying to come to grips with what they had heard. We went out into the stone yard behind the villa. We embraced. Words failed me. "What happened then?" I finally asked.

"Life in the ghetto went on, if one can call it that," he began with a wistful look over my shoulder. "I never saw Odin again. He must have been transferred out to other death mills in Poland. The ghetto machinery kept running for two more years. I had my profession to keep me busy. The ghetto was liquidated, as they called it, in August 1944. The remaining inhabitants, the surviving remnant from among thousands, were ordered to report to the *Umschlagsplatz,* the station platform from where normally merchandise was shipped.

"As I stood among the waves of people crashing against me, trying to assess the situation—I knew this could only mean the end no matter how much they spoke of resettlement—a hand on my shoulder made me turn around. There he was again: Doctor Rosenfeld. Our third encounter. He always seemed to appear at critical moments like a messenger sent from somewhere. I like to think from heaven

'Doctor Kafka,' he said. 'Do not go on that train. You must avoid getting on this train at all cost. This train leads to certain death. You must get away from here. Go to Palestine! Tell the people there, tell the world what you have seen and experienced. I wanted to write a book about life in the ghetto, but I am afraid it is too late for me.'

"We argued back and forth for a while. How was I to accomplish this with the SS and their dogs all around? 'You must find a way; you are a clever man.' Cleverness alone would hardly be enough. A hefty dose of incredible luck to pull off a game of deception was indispensable.

"We did it. The two fellows who are here with me and I managed to exploit a weakness we found in the perfect design to slip away like Job by the skin of our teeth. We were in hiding and on the run for many months. We joined partisan groups for a while, but our goal was always Eretz Israel. In January of '45, we reached Palestine. We immediately joined the Palmach and after extensive training parachuted into Hungary on a special mission. We were caught and ended up in Mauthausen. You know the rest."

"I know what you are thinking," he said as if reading my mind. "One day I will tell you the whole story, but everything you now know is true. Unfortunately, the matter at hand requires attention before we can find a moment of peace."

He took me into his arms and kissed me. He pressed my body tight against his. Could he feel the life stirring inside me? He gave no sign of recognition. Should I tell him? Better wait for that moment of peace. We went back inside where everybody still sat in stunned silence.

He turned to his companions who were waiting with the accused between them.

"What say you members of the jury?" Kafka asked them.

"Guilty as charge! The sentence is death by hanging!" they replied.

"Before you take him outside to carry out the sentence take the gag out of his mouth. Does the accused have anything to say in his defense?"

"You made me a cripple!" Odin shouted.

"Get this piece of shit out of here!" Kafka shouted back.

Piercing laughter, more high-pitched than ever, issued from Kafka's throat. He and his companions took the convicted man out into the yard.

A heavy silence still hung over the hall. Both the Baroness and Elfriede Kling stopped moaning. The two lovers were in a world of their own. I was alone suspended somewhere in the middle as we waited for the sound of shots to go off. An eternity seemed to pass.

"Fräulein Hauser," the Baroness whimpered meekly. "Can you tell me who you are? You gave me so much hope for the future. Now, all this. It's terribly confusing. Nobody seems to be who they said they were."

I didn't inquire about what she meant by hope for the future. What future? Whose future? Germany's? The future of Wagner operas? Why me? Or better that simple young woman called Beate Hauser who never really existed? The world of Elisabeth von Bülow too was merely an idea, an illusion. I had nothing to do with it. I just said: "My name is Artemisia Safran. I was born in Berlin. There is no family, not anymore. No one is left. Those who got away in time live dispersed over the globe. Those who didn't make it are dead, murdered."

"Were you in the camps?" she sniffled.

"No, I wasn't," I said. I wanted to add, not in body, only in spirit. I left it at that. She wouldn't understand. Her world and mine were two ships passing each other in the dark of night without mutual recognition. She had been kind and generous to me. But that kindness and generosity were meant for Beate Hauser. Would she have done the same for Artemisia Safran?

Not likely. She also had created a monster for whom she was now praying. Any gratitude I might have owed her was canceled out. Nothing more needed to be said or done where she was concerned. I had no greater desire than to be relieved of having to share the same room, the same country with her. A forceful kick in my womb signaled that it was high time to leave this place.

Chapter 7

Here Comes the Cavalry!

We were still listening for the sound of gunfire that would signal Odin von Bülow had been dispatched to the fires of hell when an ear-splitting ruckus jolted us from a state of almost unbearable suspense. Motors were howling and revving. Men shouting. In English! The door flung open. Kafka and Odin, the latter shackled, were shepherded back into the hall at gunpoint by Colonel Dietrich. And at his side, none other than my old nemesis, Major Zweig. Behind them glittered white and silver MP helmets, and further back olive drab field uniforms of more US soldiers.

"Ladies and gentlemen, the party is over!" the Colonel announced. "The execution will not take place. Not here and not now."

The Baroness' face brightened when she recognized her old friend, the Wagner devotee. She rushed up to him with open arms. "You are a blessing sent from heaven, Colonel! You have come just in time to prevent a terrible injustice! I cannot tell you how grateful I am to you for saving my son's life. I always knew the Americans are a fair people."

"My dear Baroness!" the Colonel began and then broke off. He weighed his head from side to side, visibly discomfited. He stopped and started several times before finally coming out directly with the bitter truth. "I am afraid you are not aware of the full extent of the situation. Your son has been tried and convicted of war crimes in a Polish court by the laws of that country. He escaped captivity before the sentence was carried out. We have no choice but to return him to Polish jurisdiction."

"But he was only serving his fatherland! You cannot possibly put his life into the hands of vengeful people like the Poles!"

His eyes bespoke profound pity for the Baroness. His mouth said, "Sorry, that's how it is." He shrugged. "I too am serving my country. We fought this war to restore the rule of law and to bring criminals like your son to justice."

While the Baroness was coming apart at the seams, the American military police took Odin von Bülow into custody. No mother/son embrace and tearful goodbye.

The only words he had for her as they took him away were: "Your fawning, Mother, disgusts me. It is despicable and unbecoming a German woman of your standing. Odin shall enter Valhalla with his pride and dignity intact." To the very last, haughty, remorseless, no sense of wrongdoing. His mother had aptly named him after the most violent of the Nordic gods.

Looking around the scene where the drama had unfolded, I spotted Major Zweig and Kafka conferring with each other in a corner. The tall, willowy Kafka leaned over his shorter, stockier friend like a tree spreading its branches over a low-growing brush. From their rapid hand movements, one could have thought they had a heated argument. I walked over curious to find out what was going on. Mostly I wondered where we would be going from here. Zweig's mien was serious, his voice animated. A sinking feeling gripped my stomach with intimations of impending doom and gloom.

"They have the evidence, and they can trace it," I heard Zweig say. The conference between the friends was just then interrupted by the Colonel.

"Where the hell did all these dead bodies come from?"

"Our bodyguards. Ukrainians. Murdered by Bülow and his gang," Madame Kling ventured to explain forcing a wry smile onto her face.

"Thank you, Madam, much obliged. We'll get them to the morgue for identification. An ambulance is also on the way to take you and your husband to a hospital."

Colonel Dietrich was in the unenviable position of a traffic cop in a busy intersection with vehicles approaching at top speed from all sides. Dead bodies were strewn all over, a man with bullet wounds clinging to life, and then there was the search for weapons.

The army had it on good intelligence that the SS housed an arsenal of weaponry in this place as well as a hoard of gold and American currency, that was most likely counterfeit. So far, the search had turned up none of it. In his frustration, Dietrich turned to Kafka.

"Herr Kafka, would you have any information about the whereabouts of the SS treasure?"

Kafka shrugged and shook his head to indicate he didn't understand.

"Doctor Kafka speaks many languages fluently," Zweig chimed in. "German, Czech, Hungarian, Polish, Russian, Yiddish, Hebrew, even some Italian, unfortunately English is not one of them."

"Zweig! Cut the crap! The official language around here is English, good old American English. If he doesn't understand it, you will have to translate for him."

"Since I was present at the time, I can fill you in," I said in my perfect, good old American English.

"Oh yes, Fräulein Hauser, or whatever your name is, suddenly she is fluent in the English tongue."

"The weapons were here. And the gold. All confiscated by agents of the Jewish fighting forces of Palestine. They are on their way to the Middle East right now," I explained, feeling quite proud of my part in this operation.

"Major Zweig!" Colonel Dietrich exploded. "Do you know anything about this?"

"No, Sir. This is the first I've heard." He didn't blink an eye. What a liar! I was now sure he was behind the whole operation. A sneaking suspicion took hold of me. Maybe Schwamm and Kling had been only marginal characters. It now seemed that Kafka and Zweig had been after the SS treasure and Odin von Bülow all along. It was quite in the realm of possibility, considering his position, Zweig had heard about the prison break in Poland. It was generally known or at least presumed that the SS had contingency plans in the event the Reich should go down in defeat. When Bülow's escape became known, it was an easy guess that he would attempt to retrieve the cache of arms and gold and other valuables that had previously hidden somewhere. It would also be reasonable to presume that such a hiding place would be somewhere near Bayreuth, Odin's hometown. They also apparently knew of Schwamm's and Kling's collusion. Only the exact location was unknown.

Enter a fake German woman playing the role of scout. Once she had found out the location, they could move in with a contingent of Palmach operatives, secure the SS arms and gold and transfer the cache to Palestine. As a bonus, Kafka could have his revenge against Odin von Bülow at the same time. Talk about killing two birds with one stone. Only a fool would believe that those planes sitting ready on a Czech airfield close to the German border just happened to be there.

At first, as so often on this journey, two souls fought within my chest. Resentment of having been made a tool battled with pride in having contributed my share to a cause I wholeheartedly approved. I consoled myself with the thought that my bruised ego mattered little within the universal order of things. *Sub species aeternitatis*! A cog in the wheel, but an essential one, nonetheless. Not so bad. I was pleased with what I had done.

Chapter 8

Incarceration

Fortress Plassenburg, Germany

Artemisia Safran's prison journal

5th of October 1947

A brisk wind chills the autumn air. I pull the coat Kafka gave me during the previous winter to keep me warm tight around my shivering body. I finally had time to take a closer look at the label sewn to the inside: "Neckermann." of a well-known German department store. If I had ever wondered why he would have carried a woman's coat with him, I soon forgot about it. Now the significance becomes clear. The coat was manufactured in the ghetto of Lodz. A tremor seized my entire body. Not only made in the ghetto but most likely made by the hands of Kafka's wife, Maya. As he mentioned, she had been drafted for slave labor in the garment factory producing women's clothing for distribution in the Reich.

As I pull it even more tightly around me, I breathe in the musty smell that clings to the rough, stained camel-hair fabric. How did he come by it? Did he steal it from the workshop where she was doing slave labor? Did she wear it? A token? A small woman's size, even a bit tight on me. He had carried it with him until he gave it to me to keep me warm. I wonder what this coat had seen, what it had been through, in the time between the ghetto, on the trek from Eastern Europe to Palestine and then to Mauthausen. An incredible journey!

My thoughts turn to the remarkable friendship of Kafka and Zweig. After all this time and what we had been through together, it still puzzles me. Maybe it's not such a puzzle at all. Some friendships, I guess especially between men, are built on a foundation so solid nothing can shake them. The plan the two had hatched worked out rather well. Odin is back in Poland where he will get his just deserts. The weapons cache is in the hands of the Palmach. Rudolf Schwamm and Elfriede Kling had their day in court. Whether their eyes were opened to the crimes by the regime to which they gave their support and benefitted from, even if indirectly, is unclear. I wouldn't bet on it. But it is no longer important.

Then there are the other players in the drama. The Baroness Elisabeth von Bülow is back in her villa in Bayreuth, no doubt telling anybody who will listen she did not know about the crimes her beloved son was accused of by that perfidious Jew who had stolen his way into her home. The word "crimes" would never come over her lips, I am sure. She will dedicate her remaining years to the revival of the Wagner Festspiele.

Peter Waldeck is back in Frankfurt completing his medical studies. Hannah followed him there and is staying at Pension Maibach. Her last letter informed me that she enrolled at the local conservatory and is studying mostly a whole range of operatic repertoire. Sans Wagner. She will soon appear in the title role of a student production of Carmen. She hopes, she wrote, to see me at the premiere. I don't want to make promises I am unlikely able to keep.

The great master plan did work out. The conspirators could be satisfied with what they achieved were it not for one slight glitch. Kafka and I had shrugged off the incident as a mishap, an unforeseen irritant. Turns out not to be so slight after all.

When all the ugly business at Castle Montsalvat was over, the extras had cleared out, and the soldiers had secured the perimeter, the remaining characters—Kafka, Zweig, Dietrich, and I—settled down for coffee and stale leftover cake I scrounged up from the larder off the kitchen.

Dietrich swung his legs up on the table, sipping his coffee and munching on the stale cake with relish. Then he fished a pack of Luckies from the chest pocket of his field uniform without offering one to us. Just as well. None of us were smokers. Zweig shot up with a lighter he seemed to have at the ready to flick for his superior officer. We then settled down watching him leisurely inhaling several deep puffs and exhale them in a stream of swirling rings.

"Miss Safran!" he abruptly turned to me. He threw the stub of his cigarette on the stone floor and stumped it under his boot. "Do I have this right? Your family name is Safran, right?"

"Yes, Artemisia Safran."

"Beautiful name. More colorful than the other one. Well, we'll have to get to this matter of your illegal entry into a restricted zone under US military control later. First, please kindly inform your friend here, Herr Kafka—that's his name, isn't it—that he is under arrest for the murder of one Fritz Hilbert and one Heinz Sauer, or maybe the other way around. Doesn't matter."

Who? was my first reaction. Then it began to sink in. I never knew their full names, but it was clear he was referring to the two men and the unfortunate incident at our hideout in the Spessart forest.

I looked at Zweig. He was gazing at the sliver of sky peeking through the window. What is the matter with him? I thought. Why doesn't he say something? And why is the Colonel asking me to translate? Disregarding the Major's precarious position as an officer of the US Army and a friend of the accused, I was fit to be tied over what I regarded then as his treasonous behavior. One of these days I would kill this Major Zweig. I swore, I would.

Kafka gave a calm nod when I related the Colonel's message to him. He had already caught on. I remembered the snippet of the conversation he had with Zweig earlier.

"Tell the Colonel," he instructed me, "I am at his disposal."

"Very sensible of him to cooperate," said the Colonel. He rose and gave the order to handcuff the suspect. As the MPs tied Kafka's hands behind his back, the full extent of the situation hit me like a flash of lightning.

"Wait a moment!" I called out. "I am as guilty as he is!"

"Nobody is guilty until proven to be so in a court of law," the Colonel retorted. "But do explain what you mean."

"I mean to say it was I who fired the shot at the older man. In self-defense, of course. He was coming at me with the clear intent of assaulting me."

"Did he do that?"

"I didn't give him a chance. He was dead before he could carry it out."

"And how did you know that was his intent?"

"Because he said so. Something about showing me his German manhood."

"Why wouldn't Herr Kafka protect you?"

"I was alone at the time. Kafka had gone out hunting."

"Another illegal action! Anyway, it will be up to a military judge to get at the truth. MPs!"

I stretched out my hands to receive the cuffs.

While this exchange with the Colonel took place, I noticed Kafka from the corner of my eyes vigorously shaking his head. Zweig stood close to him, his mouth by his ear, saying something to him sotto voce.

"With the Colonel's permission," Zweig gave the military salute, "I would like to confer with my clients in private."

"I am not sure who appointed you counsel of non-military suspects. But okay! Permission granted. Just make it quick."

The three of us huddled in a corner under the watchful eyes of the MPs. Kafka's and my hands were still manacled. The Colonel meanwhile strutted about seemingly admiring the architecture of the place. He lit another cigarette, breathing the smoke in and out with an air of satisfaction.

"The American military has to go through this formality to appease the Germans," Zweig explained, still sotto voce, a conspiratorial expression on his face. "We could have kept you out of this," he said to me, "you should have kept quiet. This complicates things."

"Things are always complicated," I said, unable to suppress a rising truculence. "What I said is the truth of how it happened. I am sure the investigators found two different types of bullets."

"The little woman has become a sophisticated forensics expert!" Zweig sneered. "Good work, Kafka!"

I no longer had my little Roth-Steyr, or I would have made good on my promise and killed Major Zweig right then. And where was my knight in shining armor to defend his lady's honor? He was standing there, a forlorn look on his face, his thoughts a million miles away, so it seemed.

When he finally returned to our earthly sphere, a frown wrinkled his forehead. Turning to Zweig, he growled: "Show some respect, Emil. She deserves our appreciation for all she has done and been through." His tone was flat more irritated by the distraction than outraged by the scorn heaped on his woman. Not exactly what I hoped to hear, but we had more pressing matters to consider.

Squabbles and insults aside, Zweig assured us again it was a formality, a chunk of meat to satisfy the barking dogs. Who was to be the chunk of meat? The trial would take place before a closed military tribunal. He would conduct the defense. It would all be over very quickly.

"Even if you are found guilty," he chuckled, "in the worst scenario you will both be expelled from German soil.

"Kafka go back to Palestine and Miss Safran to New York," he proclaimed with a roguish chuckle. "What more desirable punishment can you wish for? It will all be over in no time."

Zweig joviality struck me as out of place. I looked askance at Kafka. His pensive, grim demeanor indicated he was not pleased with his friend's making light of the situation. Zweig's optimism was anything but reassuring.

"Major Zweig!" Colonel Dietrich's booming military voice cut into our deliberations. "Time to pull out of this joint! My troops have been idling far too long."

Flanked by two MPs, Kafka made a move toward me with a sad look of his even darker eyes.

"I am so very sorry for all of this," he said softly, almost inaudibly. "I hope you can forgive me for causing you so much pain and trouble."

I didn't know what to say. The tears welling up choked the words I wanted to say. Kafka took one more step toward me. Our hands were tied behind our backs. We faced each other like two wingless penguins longing for an impossible last embrace.

"Our time together will be eternally sacred to me," he said. What? Are we in a Lehar operetta? Was that all he could come up with? An affair dipped in Viennese schmaltz? Before I could answer, they had taken him away.

Chapter 9

A Count of Monte Christo

Fortress Plassenburg, Germany

Artemisia Safran's prison journal

25th of October 1947

The few short weeks Zweig predicted have now stretched into a long month. The trial seems far off. The military tribunal that is to hear our case has not yet convened. I am still thinking of one case. Kafka and I are linked inextricably together in my mind. He is in some other part of this vast, labyrinthine medieval fortress, a real medieval fortress as I have been able to determine during the days of enforced leisure. Kafka is close by but unreachable to me. My imagination is running amok during those long night hours along. Ominous scenarios batter my brain and make sleep impossible. I see Kafka in a dungeon, manacled to a wall oozing saltpeter.

My lodgings are not altogether unpleasant. The door to the small, windowless barrack-like room opens to an enclosed inner courtyard, probably a former military proving ground. I walk around the perimeter of the yard, breathe in the crisp air and soak up the few rays of the sun that manage to peek through the dense clouds that hover like iron fists overhead.

I read whatever material I can find. While rearranging the furniture, if you can call the iron bedstead with a lumpy, stained mattress, a small worm-eaten writing table and stool, all of it might well date from the Thirty Years' War, furniture. I moved the bed around, away from the wall into the middle of the room. And what do I find in the corner? A German translation of the Count of Monte Cristo! This novel had been one of my treasured readings during years of wandering across the Continent with my parents now a lifetime ago. Back then, I worked my way through it in the original French. Now I delve right into it. The irony of finding this book here in this fortress strikes me as uncanny.

Who was the reader of this hefty, mouse-nibbled tome? A prisoner languishing within these walls like Edmond Dantès in the fortress of Château d'If perhaps. What became of him? Maybe it was a woman. Though it wouldn't have been the fifteenth-century noblewoman Barbara of Brandenburg, whose father confined her in this castle for eighteen years for refusing to be made a pawn in a dynastic marriage arrangement and insisting on divorce from an unconsummated marriage to the king of Hungary so she could follow her heart. The stuff of historical romance novels. The paramour, a lowly knight, eventually chickened out and she was left in the lurch. Most unlikely though that she occupied a dingy cave. Her abode, I imagine, was more one of the royal apartments upstairs with a huge comfortable poster bed where she could sink into a mountain of fluffy pillows and down comforters, attended by a passel of servants while smarting for her lover. Compared to these shenanigans, what are our troubles?

The days are getting shorter and colder. My enceinte is beginning to show. The fetus is making its presence felt with increasing vigor.

Zweig drops by from time to time with updates on the proceedings. His assurances are always the same. Soon. Soon it will be all over. And then nothing happens. We chat. He is beginning to show impatience with the delays. It's the system, the bureaucratic maze, the military's hurry-up-and-wait watchword. Not much comfort to be gained from that.

The Major has taken a special interest in my condition. Makes sure I get what I need for comfort. He comes by every day now. Badgers me with questions. Does Kafka know? No, I reply. Better not. I'd rather wait for quieter times to tell him, I say. Maybe it's just as well that he doesn't see me now. I long for a peaceful reunion with the father of my child. Incurable romantic that I am. Then again, I despair it will ever happen.

Sometimes I think I am in love with a man sprung from the figment of my imagination, a man of my own creation. The Kafka enigma! Does he even exist? The kick in my stomach reminds me he does indeed exist. My child was not sired by a demon lover or an incubus, even if it sometimes seems to me that way.

"Something I still can't get quite through my head," I told Zweig the other day. We had fallen into the habit of speaking English, which allowed for a more casual, informal discourse. "Something you said to Kafka. You told him the trial was just a formality to appease the Germans. And blah, blah, blah. Then you added, even if found guilty he would at most be banished. I remember you made a joke of it. Banished from Germany! What a punishment that would be! Irony of ironies!

"Why do you think they would let him get away with murder?" I asked.

"Kafka is a Palmach operative. You didn't know?

"Palmach operates in many of the DP camps in Germany. They provide humanitarian and educational services and look for recruits. The Americans know they are there but prefer to turn a blind eye. Sometimes they even facilitate their activities. It is not in the Americans' interest to make this known and broadcast in the press."

"Amazing how he made it from Poland to Palestine," he changed the subject. "Someday, I hope he'll tell the story. Though I wouldn't bet that we'll ever get to hear all of it.

"It was never quite clear to me how they ended up in Mauthausen. Whether the Gestapo caught them or, judging from some comments he made, he and his comrades entered the camp voluntarily in the confusion of the flight of the SS guards and mingled with the survivors. With Kafka, one never knows which version reflects reality. Dissimulating seems to be a habit going back to his Vienna years. Maybe it is the key to his survival."

Zweig's insightful comment has giving me much to reflect on this character called Kafka. It fits the psychological profile I have formed of my lover during the whirlwind rollercoaster ride of our year together. A man of conflicting traits who does not behave as one would expect. What Americans call a maverick. A man who follows a different drummer, dances to a beat only he can hear.

If the story of his turbulent relationship with Lenka Ostrova shows anything, he is a man of unfaltering loyalty. So does his relationship with his second wife, Maya, and his actions in the ghetto. Loyal, steadfast, tough, a profound sense of justice. That he should have returned into the inferno of the still-raging war after escaping from it is typical. It shows his willingness to put his life on the line for a higher cause. But is he capable of love? The kind of love I always dreamed about? My sense tells me the child he lost, the murdered boy, may have been the only thing he ever truly loved.

Chapter 10

Kafka on Trial

Frankfurt/Main, Germany

Artemisia Safran's Journal

19th of November 1947

I haven't seen Kafka until now, the day of the trial. And then only across the courtroom from the witness stand. Zweig worked out a deal, so he told me. No charges against me. I would be called to testify for the defense. Kafka acted to fend off a sexual assault against me, he would argue. My testimony was to support this contention. It would all be over in a day, at most two.

But we all know about the best-laid plans and deals. Before I took the stand, a snag arose. The prosecution had a witness too. Not an eyewitness, but a man connected to the dead foresters and the recovery of the bodies.

His name was Wilhelm Dietz, chief forester in the area where the incident took place. He did not speak or understand English. The search for a "reliable" interpreter caused another delay in the proceedings. The American military was not lacking in personnel fluent in German. But the presiding judge ruled out all former refugees. A question of impartiality may arise. A "good" American whose ancestors had come to America several generations ago was finally recruited for the job. The man's knowledge of German was hardly up to speed, but this could be to our advantage, so noted Zweig.

The prosecution called Forester Dietz. I was not in the courtroom and so did not hear his testimony directly. I was out in the hallway. The pins and needles under my seat got pricklier by the hour. What could take so long? Then I remembered that there was a lot of back and forth. From the protocol, I read later plus Zweig's running commentary, I got a good picture of what went on inside the courtroom.

The German's testimony was read into the record in English translation. Zweig's cross-examination too was conducted in English. The answers were then translated for the record by the flawed translator. I can well imagine the high-strung Zweig's frustration with having to hold back his easily ignited fuse and badger witness and translator in blunt German. The hapless translator, a kid from Wisconsin, came out of the courtroom looking like a dowsed poodle flattened by a train.

The forester's testimony, after a lengthy, stuttering account of his job as caretaker of the forest, boiled down to a fawning plea to American fairness and justice. Reading his words about a heinous crime that had disturbed the peaceful German woods made me wonder if he had spent the last two decades in a cave deep in the backwoods, like the Giant Rübezahl.

Back in the spring of '47, he related, he sent out two of his deputies to investigate shots they heard coming from inside the woodlands. They presumed poachers were out hunting in disregard of the American authorities' anti-firearms ordinance for German civilians. He made an unctuous, deferential bow toward the representatives of that authority.

"There are always some people who will defy the law, who will ignore the rules and find ways to get around them. And law-abiding citizens like us are left to bear the brunt," the chief forester philosophized in his garbled account.

He started to worry when the men hadn't returned at the end of the day. He got even more worried when several days went by without a sign of his deputies. A search party of concerned citizens, no less, from villages in the area, who had reported strange goings-on in the forest earlier during the winter, was organized.

"Why didn't you alert the proper authorities when you became aware of strange goings-on?" the prosecuting attorney asked.

"We didn't know who the proper authorities were anymore. We didn't want to get the Americans involved since we considered it an internal Reich matter. I have been chief forester since long before the war. I continued in my job after I was cleared by the occupiers, I mean, the Allied command."

"Go on. But get to the point and leave out the irrelevancies," the prosecutor snarled.

"The search party found the bodies, thanks to our well-trained tracking dogs. German shepherds are the best suited for the task. They found them buried near the old, abandoned inn. Once upon a time, this inn had been . . ."

Was he that dense to evoke the tracking skills of German shepherd hounds?

"Never mind about that," the prosecuting attorney put a sharp halt to what boded to turn into a retelling of local folklore and legends.

"The bodies bore the marks of point-blank execution," the chided witness sulked. "Heinz with a Russian semi-automatic handgun; and Otto with a small-caliber Roth-Steyr, the kind ladies carry in their reticules. Both shot multiple times. You can read it in the coroner's report. Eyewitnesses saw a man and a woman coming out of the woods. They were dragging heavy bags along the road that had just thawed out. Then, out of nowhere a black Mercedes pulled up - people knew it was a Mercedes from the tock-tock sound of the Diesel motor—the man and the woman got in, and the car sped off. We then had to involve the Americans since the fugitives had to be foreigners, Poles or Ukrainians, probably former workers recruited by the Reich. There are still a lot of those transients around since the war." He used the word *Gesindel*, meaning riffraff, which the translator rendered as transients.

"Very good. No more questions." The prosecution rested.

"The witness is dismissed and may leave," said the judge.

"Your honor!" Major Zweig couldn't let the opportunity of doing a bit of grandstanding slip through his fingers. "The defense wishes to cross-examine."

The judge told Zweig to approach the bench.

"Are you out of your mind, Major?" the judge growled in an undertone. "Just call your witness and let's be done with this."

"We wouldn't want to give the appearance of a kangaroo court, would we?" Zweig flouted likewise in an undertone.

"No, we wouldn't. But we also don't want to drag this out. Save your oratorical brilliance for more important cases."

Zweig's eagerness to take a stab at the credibility of the witness by exposing him as an unrepentant Nazi was thus thwarted. He had to be content with calling me to the stand. He still used the fake name he had cooked up for me. To add to the confusion, the prosecuting attorney addressed me by my real name.

Seated on the witness stand, a few feet across from Kafka, my right hand on a Bible, I muttered the words I was asked to repeat without fully comprehending. I hadn't seen the father of my child for many weeks. Now he appeared to my blurred vision as through a fractured looking glass. His face seemed drawn, hard, the body I had come to know so well, taut and erect. I wasn't sure this was the same man with whom I had shared all those many adventures and nights of grand passion. An imperceptible nod from his blinking dark eyes, those dark, mesmerizing eyes, once again scattered my doubts like dandelion seeds blown into the air.

Zweig's steadying hand guided me over the rock-strewn path of half-truths I was navigating with a fluttering heart. It was all over very soon. I was as concise as possible. No extraneous descriptions, no mention of the weather, most of all no explanation what we were doing at the forest inn.

The men came to the door. I was alone. Kafka was out hunting. They taunted me. The bigger, older one came on to me. Said he would teach me something about German manhood. He started toward me with his gun pointing, clearly intent on carrying out his threat. Just then Kafka returned and saved me from a fate worse than death. We dug a ditch, dumped the bodies in and covered them with dirt. Then we left the scene.

"Dumped the bodies and left the scene!" the prosecuting attorney repeated leading into his cross-examination. "Why didn't you report the incident to the authorities?"

Zweig objected.

"We didn't know who the authorities were in this lawless land," I replied, ironically echoing the German's statement.

"This is what the American military is for, to prevent vigilantism."

The judge ordered me to answer the question before the two attorneys were to get into an altercation.

"My illegal status in this country made this, at the time at least, seem unwise."

"Your illegal status . . ."

Another objection from Zweig: "Irrelevant to the case."

The judge admitted the objection with the adviso to the prosecutor to stick to the point, no harangues, so they could all go home for dinner.

The prosecutor threw up his hands and sank into his chair. "No more question! The prosecution rests."

"The witness can go!" declared the judge. "I shall deliberate and return with the verdict."

Mercifully, the judge returned with his verdict long before dinnertime. I sat in the back of the room; the chief forester sat on a bench in the front. The verdict was in English. There was no translator, the previous one having fled in horror of Zweig's chicaneries. The chief forester didn't understand a word of what the judge said, but seeing Kafka led away in handcuffs, he left the courtroom with a smirk, satisfied that the German side won out and the Jew received his just desserts.

The judge's verdict was justifiable manslaughter on two counts. The convict would stay in custody until arrangements were made to return him to Palestine. He was also banned from German soil indefinitely.

My impulse to run up to him, throw my arms around was thwarted by the MPs who ushered him out of the courtroom without delay. He looked back at me with a nod as if to say: "Chazak! (be strong)"

It was the last time I saw Kafka. The image of his dark, glowing charcoal eyes was forever burned into the depth of my soul.

Coda 1

A Return Home

"It was the month of November somber,
The days grew bleak and bleaker,
The trees were swept bare by the blowing wind,
That's when I left the land of the Germans behind."
(A not very masterful paraphrase of Heine's poem.)

"I have returned home," begins the sketch "Heimkehr" by the writer Franz Kafka. Standing in front of his parents' house, the narrator is filled with dread and anxiety how his family would greet him after a long absence. He thinks back to the home he had left and wonders what he would find. He imagines what goes on inside, in the kitchen, the hearth in the house of his childhood. Despite the warmth of the smoking chimney, the smell of coffee brewing, he does not go in. He turns away. Impossible to go home; impossible to resume a life interrupted. My homecoming was mercifully less Kafkaesque.

My heart too was filled with trepidation. How would my parents receive their long-lost daughter? The biting wind sweeping through the ghostly, abandoned streets of lower Manhattan chilled me in body and soul on the long walk from the docks on the Hudson River to my parents' place in the Village, The Dovecote, a recreation of the cabaret they once owned in Berlin. I pulled the threadbare little coat with the Neckermann label tighter around me. I put my hands in the coat pockets. I felt a small, hard object inside. I pulled it out.

The toothbrush with the brown wooden handle and the worn-down bristles, Kafka's first gift to me. I had had it with me all this time.

I halted my steps in front of my parent's establishment, unsure of what to do next. The familiar sound of a piano touched my heart. Musical phrases repeated over and over. My father, always composing new songs to add to my mother's repertoire. My hands and feet were frozen stiff. The wind burned my face. I entered through the unlocked side door.

My parents had been without news from me for a year. Only when I had set foot on American soil again, did it occur to me what it must have been like for them not knowing anything about the fate of their only child who had traveled to the country from which they had fled for their lives a decade before. No doubt they were plagued with uncertainty and worries.

Their happiness over my safe return soon overcame any misgivings they might have had. I was welcomed back with a big hello, hugs and emphatic gestures and assurances of not to worry. Maybe if the narrator in the Kafka story had overcome his trepidations and entered his parents' house instead of turning away and resuming his wayward path out in a cold world, he would have found what I did when I went inside. But in the end, mine was not a Kafka story.

"Schwamm drüber!" said my father without realizing the irony of this common German expression meaning "let bygones be bygones."

When my condition became apparent, my parents luxuriated in anticipated grandparenthood. They wouldn't be my parents were they not to respond with grandiose, effusive outpourings. Word of the errant daughter's return quickly got around. The Dovecot regulars, most of them former émigrés who chattered in their preferred language, English with heavy German accents, gathered the following night to celebrate my homecoming as well as my impending motherhood. My father even whipped up a song or two for the occasion. If they had questions about the provenance of the child, they didn't ask. They were bohemians and didn't stand on such ceremonies; which was just as well.

Kafka's daughter was born on the 16th of April 1948 at Saint Vincent's hospital on West 12th Street in New York City. I named her Maya. Besides wanting to honor his heroic late wife, I liked the name for its various meanings: "deception or illusion" in Sanskrit as in the veil of the Maya; in Hebrew, it was derived from the word "mayim" for water, which is the staff of life.

Whether Kafka would like my choice, I didn't know. I had no way of finding out whether he would be pleased that I wanted to honor the memory of the woman who had thrown herself on an open-bed truck loaded with children to rescue his son. I did not much care at that moment what he thought. Whether he would consider it an intrusion into his private sphere, or whether he would consider it a usurpation on my part into a painful phase of his life, all this was immaterial to me. He had fathered a child, my child. To my mind, Maya was emblematic of all the mothers whose children had been torn from them and murdered before their eyes.

"Maybe you should add Lenka to the name," Emil Zweig suggested. "Maya Lenka."

My nemesis, the Major, had appeared out of the blue and was sitting, his legs crossed, at my bedside, chatting away about this and that. He was in town to organize a shipment of guns and sundry supplies for the Jewish fighting forces in Palestine. He had retired from the US Army and would be on his way to the Middle East as soon as "everything" was cleared.

"I don't think that would have the same meaning," I replied to his suggestion to insert the name of the woman of his youthful infatuation.

"She too was a victim. If you want to memorialize victims," he said with blasé mien. More than ever, I felt like killing this Major Zweig.

I wasn't inclined to explain what the difference was for me. Not that the story of Lenka Ostrova's murder didn't touch me, but my purpose in naming my child was a very different one.

My mother was standing at the head of my bed, her eyes fairly popping out in wonder at this man with the stiff spine and commanding voice of a Prussian Junker.

"*Wer ist der Yecke*?" she whispered into my ear, using a common nickname for German Jews, even though he spoke in perfectly constructed American English idioms. Perhaps a bit too perfect like so much about this Major Zweig.

"*Ist er der. . .?*" my mother kept on whispering.

"No, he isn't the one!" I replied emphatically in English.

"Okay, no need to belabor the point," Zweig went on.

"On a different matter, I propose we get married before I ship out."

"Are you out of your mind?" I screamed when the meaning of his words had sunk in. "To hell with you!

"I was merely suggesting making an honest woman out of you and give the child a name."

"My child has a name, and I resent that honest woman bit!"

"The man's suggestion is not all that unreasonable," my mother interjected. "A child out of wedlock in our society . . ."

"Stay out of this, Mother!" I growled. "You don't know what you are talking about or what is going on here. And please, spare me a lecture about that bourgeois crap. It doesn't suit you. And now, please leave, both of you! I want to be alone."

After I had finished feeding Maya and she was back in the nursery for the night, I finally had some quiet time to clear my mind and gather my thoughts. The most puzzling question was why Zweig would want to marry me? I was certain he would never betray his friend and try to take advantage of his absence. Their friendship was solid as a rock. No woman could ever come between them. He had never shown the slightest interest in me as a woman or any woman for that matter. Zweig's infatuation with Lenka Ostrova was that of an admirer of the diva's art. Kafka had told me how Zweig adamantly fended off the advances she made toward his friend on several occasions.

There could be only one reason for his preposterous proposition: Kafka was dead. Zweig wanted to be sure the child had a father! That's what it must be. The thought bored into my brain and wouldn't let go.

Why hadn't I heard from Kafka? My heart beat in my throat. Kafka was dead! What other explanation could there be? During the remaining hours of the night, my mind was spooked with various scenarios of how Kafka's death may have occurred. One more fantastic than the next. But when it came to Kafka, fantastic was the norm.

One such version went: The Americans never returned him to Palestine but shot him along the way and disposed of his body in a German forest. If not the Americans, then the maybe British did him in. They had a more pressing reason to be rid of the irksome Palmach operative. They intercepted the transport ship on which he was sailing to Palestine, executed him and tossed his body overboard.

Another, even more fantastic, scenario spinning in my head was Odin and his death-head gang escaped again from Polish custody—I didn't trust the Poles to finally dispatch that monster to the —and came back to take revenge for the trick Kafka had played on them stealing their weapons cache and hoard of gold from under their eyes. That being unlikely, he could also have been captured, tortured, and beheaded by Arab marauders. His mutilated body thrown to crows in the desert. Were there crows in the desert? I had no idea. No matter, whichever the birds of prey were who made their home there, I saw them feasting on the body of my beloved and the father of my child.

A bit overwrought, but possible. One read stories like that in the papers. There were many factions and people who could have it in for Kafka. Luck may have run out for the man who had escaped from a train to Auschwitz and had made his way through hundreds of miles in a war zone to Palestine, only to come back to the Continent as the avenging angel in the guise of a Palmach operative. My imagination remained in high gear, jumping from one frenetic scenario to the next. I was finally returned to the ground of reality in the early morning hours when the nurses brought in my newborn child for the morning feeding.

I had barely caught a few hours of sleep when a knock on the door to my hospital room roused me again. I opened my bleary eyes to perceive the blurred outline of my nemesis filling the doorway.

"Kafka is dead!" I cried out at Zweig who held a big bouquet of yellow roses in one arm and a load of several packages in the other.

"Peace!" he proclaimed. But I was not appeased.

Behind him, my mother shuffled in with my father in tow.

I was not inclined to exchange familial niceties. Instead, I battered Zweig with accusations, mostly irrational.

"Kafka is dead! Isn't he?" I repeated, my voice breaking into hysterics.

"He is not dead!" he replied. He handed the roses to my mother and dropped the packages on my bed. His hands freed, he seized mine and shook me until I finally simmered down if only to ease the pain of his grip.

"What makes you think he is dead?"

"Where is he then? And why would you make that preposterous proposal if he were alive?"

"My apologies," he said. "Not a well-considered move on my part. I should have anticipated your impetuous reaction. I only meant to be a stand-in. Give the child a name. I wasn't angling for spousal privileges."

"Was that Kafka's idea?" A suspicion arose in my mind that he may want to shirk responsibility for his child and put the burden of responsibility on his loyal sidekick.

"Last I heard he was in Cyprus. The Brits set up detention camps there to house what they consider illegal immigrants to Palestine. He's probably involved in people smuggling. You know him. He's a fighter. Wherever there's a war going on against our people, Kafka is there."

I nodded. Too true. And I was proud of him and loved him even more for it.

My mother put the flowers in a vase she got from a nurse. My father stood by with a befuddled look.

"Can someone tell me who this Kafka is?" he said.

"He's the father of your grandchild," I said.

"We thought you went to Germany to look for your grandmother. What happened to that?"

"Life sometimes leads you along strange and unforeseen paths. Isn't that so, Major?" I replied. "I never made it to Berlin thanks to the Major here."

"I wish you would call me Emil," he fretted.

"That would take some getting used to."

"I made some inquiries." Zweig turned to my mother. He pulled out a document, written in German, that confirmed the death ("*Ableben*") of Clara Wertheim, née Liebermann, shortly after her arrival in Theresienstadt in October 1942. The cause of death was noted as unknown.

"My profound condolences. This must be very painful but also a relief to know," he said with a dour expression.

"Thank you. It was to be expected," my mother replied sniffling.

"You knew this all along!" I burst into this exchange.

"I only received this document a few days ago," he said defensively. "I began an inquiry into your grandmother's fate after I returned stateside. I thought I owed you this much."

"This and more, much, much more," I sulked.

My mother sank into a chair next to my bed and began to cry softly into her handkerchief. I wanted to put my arms around her, but I held back in Zweig's presence.

"And what about that woman in Berlin? The one you used as bait! Was she real?"

"There was such a woman. I visited the hospice looking for relatives who might have survived. This woman was sitting by a window in a stupor. She vaguely reminded me of an aunt. When I walked up to her to see her face, I noticed she was clutching an envelope to her chest. I pried it from her hand. It bore your name and address. I recognized your name as the author of a popular book about the trial of the murder of Stella Berger. In this book, you had written affectionately about your grandmother. How this woman had come by this envelope is not clear. Maybe your grandmother gave to her, or the woman took it from her. We'll never know." He paused a moment as if wrestling how to put what he had to say diplomatically without once again getting my ire up.

"However, it gave me an idea," he continued. "You seemed the ideal person for our mission. And I was right as it turned out. You were the ideal person."

"Yeah, your ideal patsy! Don't try flattery with me. By 'our' I presume you mean you and Kafka."

"Yes, and the Jewish people who wish to return to Palestine."

In my heart, I couldn't have been prouder and more pleased to have been part of the Zweig/Kafka conspiracy. My contribution to its success gave me a great sense of gratification and accomplishment. I had played a key role in an extraordinary coup while experiencing a kind of love unlike any a girl could imagine in her wildest dreams.

"Can anybody explain what is going on here?" my father finally broke the silence that had descended in the room.

"Oh, Papa," I said. "That is such a wide field!"

"Don't feed us the old Fontane line," said my mother. Before this conservation escalated into further recriminations, Zweig diverted attention to the packages he had brought. He didn't wait for me to open them. He ripped off the wrapping of the first and presented its contents with a beaming smile.

"From Tante Mathilde!" he said, holding up a knit baby outfit and booties. "She's been knitting ever since you left Frankfurt. Be prepared to be showered with more to come."

I buried my face in the soft wooly weave of the gift from the wonderful Frau Maibach who had been like a mother to me. A soothing warmth suffused my soul.

"And Hannah and Peter?" I asked.

"Busy with their studies, both! Hannah will soon make her debut at the Frankfurt Opera as Mimi in La Bohème. She now goes by the name of Hannah Salomon, which will appear in bright lights."

"No Wagner, I suppose."

"She's done with Wagner, Tante Mathilde tells me. At least for the time being. She may come back to it. I hope. At this stage of her life and career, it's better that way. Too much Brünnhilde too soon can ruin a voice." Wisdom from the mouth of Zweig, the opera buff!

"It can ruin anybody's hearing. I certainly hope never to hear another note from the Maestro! No more endless immolations for me!"

"You have to separate the music from the man," he lectured, his finger extended upward. "The man and many of his admirers may be despicable, but the music, ah, the music, that's still divine!" He touched his fingers to his lip as if savoring the foods of the gods.

"Your opinion. For me, it chars the hearing and grinds on the nerves. By now, it also has too many unpleasant associations."

"Well, the Baroness has launched an energetic drive to get the Festspiele back off the ground. At her side is Elfriede Kling, though she won't appear on stage anymore. Schwamm is still in a semi-comatose state. Her most indefatigable sponsor is Colonel Dietrich. He is retired from active duty and is currently, even as we speak, on a fundraising tour of the United States for the good cause. The love of music brings even enemies together. *Seid umschlungen Millionen. . . ,*" he hummed the chorale from Beethoven's Ninth weighing his head with a dubious chuckle.

"Oh, spare me that sentimental Schiller claptrap! People will never live in harmony. Beethoven, on the other hand, now that's divine!" I laughed.

We were both seized by side-splitting laughter, further befuddling my parents over this sudden gush of merriment.

"What's in this package?" I pointed at a flat, brown somewhat frayed envelope on my bedcover, while still wiping the tears from my eyes.

"Go ahead! Open it!" he prodded.

I weighed the envelope in my open palms. Slowly, with bated breath, as if expecting to be struck by lightning for opening a secret, forbidden text, I fiddled with the seal.

"Go ahead! It won't bite. You'll see."

With a determined move, I ripped the paper off, et voilà! there it was like a treasure before my eyes: my notebook. The gray, cardboard cover was inscribed in my hand: Artemisia Safran's travel journal, started on the 11th of November 1946 on a train somewhere in Germany.

After Major Zweig had confiscated it from me during the interrogation in Frankfurt, he gave it to his aunt, Frau Maibach, for safekeeping. She had told me so. My abrupt, forced deportation from Germany in November 1947, under military escort, had left no time for a visit with her at the pension where I had found shelter and kindness to say goodbye and retrieve my cherished notes about my first impressions of a journey into, what I termed, the heart of darkness.

The day after Kafka's trial ended and he was taken away in handcuffs by the American military police, I too was ordered to appear before a military tribunal. The charge was illegal entry into a country that had been declared off-limits to civilians of any nationality. The verdict, quickly pronounced: immediate deportation and repatriation to the United States. Imagine this, I was deported, expelled, from Germany to the freedom of my adopted country! A nice twist of irony considering that I could have gotten time, maybe several years, in some godforsaken jail. But I was small, if irksome, fry and the military authorities had me just as well out of their hair.

This was Zweig's explanation though I suspected that he had something to do with this mild punishment for what was a major offense under martial law prevailing in the defeated nation. Had I been put on trial and spilled the beans, as they say so nicely in gangster movies, under the pressure of cross examination, Zweig himself could be court-martialed and sentenced to a long stay in the stockade.

I was whisked away on a military convoy going North to Bremerhaven, the entry port for US military personnel and supplies. We traveled in the dead of night in a canvassed truck. I was too drained physically and emotionally for a revisit in my mind of the train ride that took me into the heart of the country of my birth that had by then reduced to ashes and rubble. I closed my eyes, shutting out the surroundings. As I paid heed to the gentle tapping of the life inside of me, a great sense of peace and gratification came over me. My child, Kafka's child, would be born in the land of freedom, far, far away from this dark place.

Before boarding the military freighter that was to return me to America, or stateside in Zweig's military jargon, out of the blue the little, speckled suitcase with my clothing and personal effects, plus my American passport, I had left behind in Amsterdam, was handed to me by one of the sergeants. Courtesy of Major Zweig, he said. Though the Major was trying to make it up to me, I was not yet appeased and still hoped for a chance to pick a bone with him.

While I was eager to get away from this continent a second time, a dim sense of regret filled my heart for not being able to say goodbye to the pious couple in Amsterdam. As was clear now, they too were part of Zweig's network of conspirators, yet I felt I owed them a thank you for their hospitality on a memorable Shabbat. I promised myself I would write.

I met many kind people along this weird, often arduous trajectory my journey took. Most of all there was Frau Maibach. Her pension provided a warm refuge after a chilling train ride that felt like a passage into the heart of darkness. She too would have to wait for an epistolary thank you note since the military judge did not permit me to spend another day on German soil. Hannah and Peter as well would have to be content with an exchange of letters. I am still awaiting the day when Hannah will make her New York debut which, I am sure, is not too far off.

A sense of regret overcame me when I thought back on my time as the personal assistant to the Baroness von Bülow. Regret because I found myself unable to gather up more sympathy for her and her plight. She was not an evil person. That much I can say. But maybe that is the problem. She lived, and no doubt still lives, in a world of delusions—*Luftschlösser* in German. She wouldn't see evil if it stared her in the face. She would always come up with some extenuation. She had been kind to me, opened her home, took me in from the gutter, and to some extent into her heart. As she did with Kafka when he appeared at her door as a certain Herr Kaiser. But I could not forget that she extended this kindness and her hand to people who did not exist. Had she known who I was, had she known who Kafka was, the door to her mansion would have remained shut. As a "Jü-ü-üdin" I could not forget those puckered lips when she pronounced that word as if she had bitten on a lemon.

The Atlantic crossing put my stomach through a wringer. I am just not made for rocking sea voyages. When I wasn't on deck with my head leaning over the side of the ship, I remained curled up for most of the seven days and nights on the bunk in my tiny cabin. Even the most attentively prepared dishes from the ship's cook wouldn't stay down the hatch. My state of misery didn't ease even when we reached the American coastal waters.

As a result, I missed the ship's grand entry into New York harbor. Only when I had disembarked and staggered with uncertain steps down the gangplank to finally stand weak-kneed on firm ground did I wave a wistful "hello" from the dock to the lady in the harbor, the torch of freedom raised high in her hand—not a sword as Franz Kafka, the writer, and my lover's namesake, had presumed it to be.

Coda 2

Rebirth

New York City

Artemisia Safran's journal

15th of May 1948

The Dovecote was packed last night with regulars and not so regulars. There was much merrymaking, dancing and singing, cheering and drinking, of course. Champagne corks popped at the news on the radio: The State of Israel was reborn.

"The Phoenix has risen from the ashes!" proclaimed my mother. My father immediately started to compose a song for the occasion. The entire assembly chanted "Hatikvah!", the anthem of hope.

I stayed on the sideline of the festivities. The child on my knees gave me a broad toothless smile. As much as I would have liked to share in the euphoria, a sense of dread held me back. Intimations of ill-foreboding gripped my heart. My friend Viktor Erdos, the wistful violin player, sidled up to me. He has been like a grandfather to my child. Every evening before bedtime, he comes over to my studio apartment on Waverley Place with his violin. He plays a soothing lullaby or a Kreisler melody while the child trails off into a dreamland suffused with sweet melodies.

That evening at The Dovecote, amid the boisterous celebration, Viktor alone knew what was in my heart. He gave me a nod with a serious glance from his wistful blue eyes. He understood. No need for words between friends.

The following morning, it was a Shabbat, we heard the other news. The armies of five Arab countries have streamed over the porous borders of the fledgling Jewish state. "Bombs Falling on Tel Aviv!" screamed the headlines, prematurely as it turns out.

Kafka has another war to fight. No telling how long it will take. No one knows what the future holds for the world or for Kafka and me. I have his child, a little coat, and a wooden toothbrush with worn bristles to keep me company. I have a story to write while I bide my time—the story of an extraordinary journey into the twilight of a land immolated in an epic conflagration of self-destruction.

CPSIA information can be obtained
at www.ICGtesting.com
Printed in the USA
FFHW021128110719
53567159-59228FF

9 781644 387696